OUT OF MY DEPTH

Also by Emily Barr

Backpack
Baggage
Cuban Heels
Atlantic Shift
Plan B

Emily Barr

OUT OF MY
DEPTH

headline
review

First published in 2006
by HEADLINE REVIEW

An imprint of Headline Book Publishing

1

Cataloguing in Publication Data is available from the British Library

Hardback (ISBN 10) 0 7553 2543 5
Hardback (ISBN 13) 978 0 7553 2543 5
Trade paperback (ISBN 10) 0 7553 2544 3
Trade paperback (ISBN 13) 978 0 7553 2544 3

Typeset in by Garamond Light by Palimpsest Book Production Limited,
Polmont, Stirlingshire

Printed and bound in Great Britain by
Mackays of Chatham plc, Chatham, Kent

Headline's policy is to use papers that are natural, renewable and
recyclable products and made from wood grown in sustainable forests.
The logging and manufacturing processes are expected to conform to
the environmental regulations of the country of origin.

HEADLINE BOOK PUBLISHING
A division of Hodder Headline
338 Euston Road
London NW1 3BH

www.reviewbooks.co.uk
www.hodderheadline.com

For James, Gabe and Seb

Thanks to Lisa McLean, Georgie Morgan, Bridget Guzek, Maria Gentile, Kate Ireland, Michelle Arscott, Jane English, Gail Haddock, Chris Harbach, Jan Kofi-Tsekpo, Peter Webb, Jonny Geller, Jane Morpeth, Rebecca Purtell and everyone at Headline. And thank you as ever to my boys, James, Gabriel and Sebastien.

chapter one

Susie

Les Landes, France

January

It was cold, in the south of France, in January. In winter, nobody wanted to visit me. The last visit was always in October; the first was at the end of March. Even though everybody said, on the phone and in emails, throughout the winter, 'I bet the weather's better where you are!' they must have known, really. Otherwise they would have come.

This particular afternoon, the winter was as bad as it got. I would rather have been in Wales. The wind was howling outside my painting shed. The sky was low and grey, and the rain was imminent. Worst of all, it was cold, and my shed had wooden walls and nothing remotely resembling insulation. I was painting an urgent commission, with two electric heaters beside me. I was wearing a tweed dress, thick woollen tights, two sweaters, a scarf, a pair of beaded slippers and a woolly hat. Yet I could still feel the cold of the tiled floor on the soles of my feet, even when I was standing on a rug, and I still shivered as I worked.

It was ridiculous. I was going to move my studio indoors. The shed was romantic and shambolic and sweet, but it was not practical, not today. I remembered a builder, a couple of summers ago, suggesting that he might line the walls of this old chicken shed with insulating plasterboard to keep me warm while I worked.

1

I remembered myself refusing, telling him that I wanted it to be like a beach shack. I vaguely recalled the look he had exchanged with a colleague. He had been right. I was wrong.

I smiled at myself. We had a whole house, absurdly large for the two of us, and yet I spent my days shivering outside, and Roman spent his time in the attic, or out. The house stood as empty as a holiday home, until we convened in the kitchen for meals.

My mind wandered, aimlessly, mulling over the cold and the likelihood of rain, and the commission I was painting, until it stumbled upon the plan. While I thought, I applied myself to the canvas, which had to be finished by Friday afternoon at the very, very latest. One moment I was trying out the colour for an electric-blue sky. Then, suddenly, I was planning. It was as if the idea had always been there, had probably been there for years and years, but I had never before managed to face it.

On the surface, it was trivial. Everyone had school reunions, from time to time. Catching up with old friends was the least remarkable of impulses. Yet this was a dark idea, with the potential to change everything. It had the potential to ruin my life, or to make it better. It was an open-ended thing.

I heard Tamsin's voice in my head, years ago, in a pub far away. 'Why don't we meet up,' she had said, 'when we're really old? When we're, I don't know, thirty-two.' I heard the echoes of our laughter as we had imagine ourselves at such a grand age. I pictured Tamsin, clearly, with her long unbrushed hair and her idealistic pale face. I hadn't thought about Tamsin for years. At the same time, awareness of Tamsin had shaped my life.

I hugged myself, and turned both heaters up to their highest settings.

'It's mainly about showing off,' I told Roman, over lunch. 'You know. This place is finally looking good. I'm sure my schoolfriends will want to see it.'

I smiled around the dining room. There was a fireplace, with a fire made up for the evening. The high ceiling was supported by original oak beams. The walls were rough, whitewashed. Everything about our house was a cliché incarnate. We even had garlic hanging on the kitchen walls. It was good to show off. People liked staying with us.

Roman smiled, his teeth even and white. My smile widened. Roman and I had been together for four years, and, to my slight surprise, we didn't seem to be getting tired of each other. I loved the fact that it was just the two of us for half the year. I loved the fact that we both worked at home. Roman was half French. I would not have been here without him. He took care of all the social niceties for me, because my mastery of the language was rubbish, and I was secretly shy.

'Sure,' he said. 'Schedule them in. Who are they? Have I heard of them?' He frowned. 'Met them?'

I shook my head. 'Life moved on pretty soon after we left school.' I said it as lightly as I could, trying to make it all sound normal. 'We were close at school, the four of us. Amanda was my best mate, my partner in crime. She was tall and blonde and skinny.' I smiled at a memory of the lengths Amanda had gone to to keep herself unhealthily thin. 'Isabelle was beautiful. She had amazing long auburn hair. She was the prettiest girl in the school, and the most stylish, too. Jackie used to have a crush on her.'

Roman laughed. 'Your sister had a crush on a girl? Remind me to take the piss next time she rings.'

'Oh, I'm sure you'll remember. Everyone had a crush on Izzy. And then there was Tamsin. She was . . .' I swallowed, and made myself carry on. 'Into politics. She was funny. She was living in Australia, last I heard.' Again, I pictured Tamsin. I pictured her, almost the last time I had seen her, looking awkward in a black dress that didn't suit her, wearing some garish make-up, with her hair in a bun.

'And you expect her to fly over from Australia? For a weekend?' Roman raised his eyebrows.

I shrugged. I fully expected her not to. That was my get-out clause. If Amanda and Isabelle came to stay, we would be able to

3

have a lovely weekend together. We would know that I had invited Tamsin, that I had done my best to make amends.

'Well,' I said, 'I'll ask. You never know.'

Roman nodded, and finished his soup. He looked perfect here. His mother was French, his father English. He looked French. His dark hair was longer than usual, at the moment, and I liked the shaggy look. He needed to shave. He was wearing a red jumper, which suited his dark colouring. As usual, I couldn't believe how lucky I had been to find him. I had kissed a lot of frogs along the way.

I was glad that Roman didn't have a job. It meant I got to have him near me all the time, to eat lunch with him every day. He was happy dabbling in whatever caught his fancy. He was devoted to snowboarding, and surfing and climbing, as well as to eating well, drinking good wine, and relaxing. He was good for me.

'Not Alissa?' he asked, pleased with himself for remembering someone's name. 'Isn't she your schoolfriend?'

I shook my head. 'We got closer after school. These are a different crowd.'

Roman was bored by now. 'Can I go boarding in the morning?'

'You don't have to ask!' I told him, tying my thick hair into a knot. It was black and shiny, and people sometimes told me I looked like Catherine Zeta Jones. I loved it when that happened, although I always brushed the compliments away. 'Of course you can. Do what you like.' I stood up and took his bowl.

'You could come. Conditions look perfect. Waist-high powder.'

'Can't. Deadline.'

'Deadline, plus too cold and too wet?'

'You know I like my exercise safe and warm.' I sighed. 'Warm. Remember that?'

'But it's romantic to be on a mountainside in virgin snow with the man you love.'

'It's not romantic when your bum's so covered in bruises you can't sit down. Thanks all the same, though.' I thought about it. 'I'll come next time. Sometimes it's worth it just because I appreciate it so much when it's over.'

*   *   *

I took a cup of strong white coffee back out to the shed, to warm me. The wind whipped my cheeks as I crossed the corner of the lawn to get there. There were no birds. Even the grass looked cold. The garden here was too big for us, really. This was the only corner I used, in the winter. The rest of it was wasted for half the year. I stopped, nipped by the freezing wind, and stared down at the back of the garden, trying to make out whether the digger was moving. Supposedly, there was a pool under construction, back there beyond the trees. As long as it was ready when spring arrived, I didn't care whether the workers were knocking off at lunchtime, particularly not on days like this.

The clouds were blacker than they had been earlier. It was definitely about to rain.

The wind slammed the door with a loud bang behind me, and even though I knew it was about to happen, it made me jump and spill a few drops of coffee on my dress. Paintbrushes clattered in their jar, and the easel rocked slightly. I straightened it with a hand and stared at the painting as I exchanged furry boots for slippers, and pulled my hat down over my ears.

I got back down to work, and tried not to think about my friends. My job, today, involved copying a postcard onto a canvas. This might not have constituted art in its purest form, but it worked for me, for the moment. What I did was, increasingly, a craft, or even a trade, although I would not have admitted that to anyone except for Roman. This particular masterpiece was going to need a huge investment of time and effort if I was going to finish it by Friday. The client was sending a courier on Friday morning, and he needed to present the painting to his wife on their wedding anniversary on Sunday. The pressure was on.

I picked up the postcard. There was a blue sky, a stone village clinging prettily to some hilltop, and the odd splash of green grass. I would add some bright flowers to the grass and make the track slightly less dusty and more verdant. I looked at the back of it, to remind myself of where it was that I was painting. Gordes, in Provence. The other side of southern France from here.

I sat on my chaise longue, which was below the window, and

winced at the draught. This was my favourite item of furniture. It was more of a day bed than a true chaise longue. It was high off the ground, and piled up with pale green cushions, and it was made from walnut wood, with elegant curves at each end. I was always careful with my coffee when I sat on it, and today I wiped the drips from the cup with tissue paper, just in case. My pinboard was on the white wall opposite me, and I stared at the photo of the woman, and then at my canvas, and then at the postcard in my hand. I tried to work out exactly where I would place her.

The woman was to go somewhere in the foreground, at my discretion. This was her reward for staying married to my patron, Neil, for ten years. Her photograph had been on my pinboard for weeks. I fetched it from my board, and hopped back onto the bed. She was thin and blonde, aged about forty. I generally painted brightly coloured landscapes with blue skies and green grass and red and purple flowers. If there were people involved, they were languid, elegant women, ripped off shamelessly from Modigliani (although mine were clothed). This woman, I decided, could easily be transformed into one of my trademark ladies.

I would sit her on a wall. I got up, carefully put my half-drunk coffee on the table, and started sketching her in. There was a low wall in the foreground. She could perch on it, knees up by her chin, or legs crossed, and gaze wistfully out of the frame. I would let some of her hair curl around her face. Her eyes would be almond shaped, her head tilted slightly to one side. It was working. I knew I had to concentrate on this, and not allow myself to drift off into memories of my Cardiff schooldays.

I would write to Amanda at the most recent address I had for her, in south London. I could get my parents to find out where Izzy lived, from her parents, who still lived in Dinas Powys. I was fairly sure Izzy was still in London, because she worked in publishing and publishing was probably all in London. As for Tamsin, I would send her letter to Penarth, to her father's address, and write a note on the envelope asking him to forward it.

There. It was settled. I turned my attentions back to the woman. I wondered whether she would be surprised to receive an oil painting of herself on holiday for her wedding anniversary. I wondered why Neil hadn't wanted himself in it too. He could have had his arm draped over her shoulders. That would have been a more romantic anniversary present. Would anyone really want a portrait of themselves, painted by someone they had never met?

And would Roman ever go to lengths like this on my behalf?

chapter two

Amanda

Clapham, London

February

The school run was bugging Amanda. It was really, seriously bugging her. If the roads weren't so full of bloody mothers, each carrying one tiny child in an enormous SUV, then she might actually be able to get Jake and Freya to school without having to allow forty-five minutes to drive less than two bloody miles. She let out a small scream of frustration and knocked her head against the steering wheel.

'Are you all right, Mummy?' Freya sounded nervous. Amanda raised her head and shook it.

'Fine,' she said sharply.

'Mum,' said Jake. 'We could get out here and walk. It'll probably be quicker.'

Amanda looked at the road ahead of her. The traffic was inching along. It was moving quite quickly in the other direction. She could see those drivers laughing at her. She knew they were enjoying her misfortune. She did her best to glare at them all, as they sailed by in their Mitsubish Shoguns and their jeeps but she kept missing eye contact.

'Of course you can't walk,' she snapped. 'It looks like rain, and besides that, anything could happen to you.'

'We'd be fine,' Freya said. She sounded almost wistful. 'We could actually walk all the way. Every day. You could walk with us. It would be . . .' She tailed off as Amanda turned in her seat and silenced her with a look.

'. . . quicker,' finished Jake, bravely.

'Fun,' added Freya, almost in a whisper.

The two blond children looked at each other, counting down the seconds. On cue, Amanda exploded.

'Do you think I do this for *fun?*' she demanded. 'Do you? Do you think I sit here in this bloody car, eating up our money on petrol, polluting the planet, sitting in this bloody traffic, twice a day, crawling through bloody south London, *for fun?* No, children, you cannot walk to school. The streets are full of all sorts of perverts and drunks. Freya, you are seven years old. Jake, you are eight. In the car you're safe. My job is to keep you safe. I am your mother and I am in charge, and please, both of you, stop showering me with bloody stupid ungrateful suggestions and *sit there quietly*. You must have some homework to be getting on with or something.'

'Sorry, Mum,' said Freya.

'Sorry, Mum,' said Jake. Neither of them responded to the part about the homework, because they knew, from experience, that it was a trick.

Luckily, the boys' school and the girls' school were within two blocks of each other. First Jake was out, swinging his bag onto his shoulder with a cheery, 'Bye, Mum! Bye, Frey!' Then Amanda double-parked in a side street and took Freya to the school door, to be sure she was not abducted or otherwise interfered with during her twenty-second walk. She kissed her, and raced a traffic warden back to the Range Rover. As Amanda clicked the doors open with her key, the warden looked at her and raised his finger above his electronic keypad. She forced herself to smile. He moved to where he could see her number plate. She ran over to him. He stroked his digital camera.

'Sorry,' she said, brightly. 'Just taking my daughter to the class-room. You can't be too careful, can you, these days?'

'Double-parked, madam,' he said, avoiding eye contact. 'Oh, just bugger off and I'll turn a blind eye.'

'Thanks,' she said, tersely. She pulled up the collar of her pale pink fleece, and drove off. *This bloody city*, she thought, as she drove home in a quarter of the time it had taken her to get there. *Every single day. There is no let-up.*

And there wasn't. Every weekday morning she drove the children to school. Every afternoon she went through the same purgatory to pick them up, but in the afternoons it was generally worse because, depending on the day, there was ballet, orchestra, judo, or drama to accommodate. On Thursdays they both had after-school activities and she was able to pick them up, in one go, at five. That was her best day. On Monday she had to take Freya to ballet straight after school, drive back to Jake's school, wait in the car for half an hour, pick him up from his trombone lesson, drive back as fast as she could, which was not as fast as she would have liked, to fetch Freya from ballet, and then drop Jake at judo on the way home, except that it wasn't on the way at all, take Freya home and make her do her piano practice and homework, then take her back out in the car to collect Jake at half six. That was her worst day. It was Monday today. Weekends were just as bad, because Patrick was home, the children still had activities, and there were a thousand other things to factor in.

When she got in, Amanda punched the code into the burglar alarm and paused for a moment, as the nasty beeping stopped, to savour the silence. There was always something special about her first minute home alone. She picked up the post from the doormat and unlaced her trainers. She kicked them off and skidded along the parquet floor to the kitchen in her socked feet. She caught herself looking critically at the kitchen again. She had redone it last year but now she was beginning to hate it. What had seemed like a perfect, subtle, dusty pink now looked, frankly, peach. Every time she thought about this, she became furious. She should have gone for the wood and chrome. Patrick had been no bloody use. He had made it plain that nothing could have interested him less.

'You choose,' he had said, ruffling her hair. 'It's the kind of thing you do best. Not me.' He still managed to forget that he was not allowed to ruffle her hair, that every strand was where it was for a reason. It drove her insane.

The kitchen was big and it had French windows leading out to the back garden. It was quite a triumph to own a back garden in this part of London but she didn't care any more. All it meant was a hefty monthly cheque to some boy of a gardener who wasn't even nice to look at. The kitchen, including brand-new French windows, had cost Patrick a fortune. It had cost her several weeks of five o'clock starts, when she woke up tossing, turning and stressing about everything. When this happened, Amanda had learned, she was not going back to sleep. She needed to get up, have a shower in the downstairs bathroom to avoid waking Patrick, and make herself a cup of tea. She needed to take a marker pen and Freya's whiteboard, and she needed to write it all down. Sometimes when she saw her problems in front of her, they melted away. At other times, her subconscious ambushed her, and she was horrified at what came out. She would scrub the board clean again and again, paranoid that Freya would decipher what had been there.

She put the kettle on and thought about biscuits. She made her tea and thought about biscuits. She opened her Visa bill, and a bill from the gardening service, and three Caribbean holiday brochures, and decided that she was allowed one biscuit. She sat on a high bar stool with her tea and ate a chocolate digestive. She opened the hand-written letter from France, which she had been saving for last, and read it in astonishment.

Dear Amanda,
An invitation!
Remember how we always said we'd have a reunion when we were 32? Well, that day has arrived, as you know. And I am taking the liberty of changing the venue.
You, Isabelle and Tamsin, plus husbands, partners and children, are invited for a long weekend, and a huge amount of catching up. I can offer food, wine, champagne (even Southern Comfort if that's still your tipple of

choice!), plus a big garden, and a swimming pool. I'm suggesting the first weekend in August, maybe making it Friday till Monday, but if anyone can't make it then we can rearrange.

I look forward to hearing from you!

Masses of love,

Susie

Amanda found herself smiling, which was a rare event these days. The four of them had been inseparable at school, a tight-knit clique which had disintegrated abruptly before they left. She had never imagined rekindling those friendships. Too much had happened.

She ate two more digestives as she thought about Susie's offer. She had missed Susie and Isabelle, and she knew she would go. She would take Patrick and the kids. It would be a family mini break and it would do them all good. She would be able to show off her model family.

She crammed another biscuit into her mouth and wondered what Susie was like these days. Rich, obviously, and keen to show it off. Horribly successful with her cute little pictures.

Susie and Amanda had once made a formidable pairing. Suzii (as she had then styled herself) had been small, dark and curvaceous. She looked Italian though she was a Londoner by birth and lived in Wales. Amanda had always been tall and blonde, and they had both been paranoid about their weight, their hips, their thighs. They had encouraged each other in crash diets. They had competed to see who could eat the least for the longest, and then, together, they would slip out of school in the afternoon, buy a carrier bag full of chocolate, and sit on a bench in Roath Park and eat it methodically. Amanda was sure Suzii had made herself sick afterwards. She knew that she had, without fail.

She remembered a couple of times when the school had ill-advisedly encouraged pupils to do a sponsored famine for Oxfam. They were all supposed to fast for twenty-four hours and to collect sponsor money for doing it. Amanda remembered how they had laughed and called it sponsored anorexia; remembered that they could not believe their luck.

She tried to convince herself that her attitude to food was healthier now than it had been then. She pictured Suzii, in the sixth form, when they had no uniform. Her black hair was always spiked up on top, and longer at the back, touching her shoulders. She usually wore skin-tight jeans to school, with a paisley shirt which signified non-conformism. Amanda had stuck to Benetton. She used to like big blocks of navy, yellow, pink. Occasionally she would wear jeans and a rugby shirt. Back then, her blonde hair had been much longer, and she had forced a side parting as close to her ear as possible, so she could flick her hair across her face, and brush it back with her fingers.

Lodwell's was a private girls' school. To an outsider, it seemed like a 'nice' place to get a privileged education. Parents looked around and agreed that it would be a lovely environment for their daughters. The headmistress, Miss Higgins, had lived within the school building, with her dog Amber, and had (wilfully, Amanda assumed) overlooked the ferocious reality of her empire in favour of pretending to live in a fifties girls' school. The parameters that defined 'a nice school for girls' were all there. There was a morning assembly (in Welsh on Fridays), which was called 'Prayers'. Hymns were sung, prayers were said (the Lord's prayer, the Blessing, even the School Prayer). Notices were read about sports matches and drama clubs. Each morning a prefect prepared the assembly hall by opening the high windows, checking that the flowers on the desk were fresh, and pouring Miss Higgins a glass of water. The girls would troop in, in alphabetical order within their forms, and would stand in neat rows, the younger ones in pleated grey tunics and green and white striped shirts. In summer they had actually been forced to wear boaters.

Amanda could scarcely believe it, looking back. She tried to imagine Freya's reaction if she were told she was going to have to wear a boater to school. She smiled.

Lodwell's had provided school plays, two orchestras, hockey

teams, an annual prize-giving. It ticked all the boxes. There was even a dreary school song which, Amanda was pleased to discover, she had forgotten. And the prim and proper façade had masked what really went on. Lodwell's School had been a hotbed of underage smoking, drinking and sex. Amanda could think of six girls in their year who had had abortions, and that was just the ones she knew about. Fiona Bignold – Fiona Bignose – had had a nose job, and the school happily accepted the note, allegedly from her mother, which explained that she had fallen downstairs and suffered some bruising. Everybody smoked. Fag ends floated in the sixth-form loos. Girls went to lessons reeking of stale smoke, filling classrooms with the stench, and their teachers pretended not to notice. Peer pressure had forced Amanda to start smoking at the age of fifteen, and it had been a bugger to give up when she got pregnant with Jakey.

She, Amanda Castleton, as she had then been, had had her first sexual experience with a builder who had been working on the new junior block. It had involved lager, crisps, a van, and a level of passion and abandon, undiminished eighteen months later, that she had never experienced since, and would never know again.

She smiled and reached for the biscuits. She had never shared that story with Patrick, and she never planned to. As far as he knew, he was her first, her last, her only.

Tough little Suzii had been a godsend in that harsh environment. She was streetwise, probably because of growing up in London, and she had taken no crap from anybody. She had not let Amanda or Izzy be picked on, either (Tamsin was able to look after herself).

Isabelle had always been the glamorous one among the four of them. She was a Pre-Raphaelite painting brought to life. She drifted around in long skirts and flowery blouses, teamed with Doc Marten boots. Her hair was long and auburn, and her skin was clear and creamy. She was always on her way to orchestra practice, with her clarinet, trailing a crowd of hangers-on from the music department in her wake.

Izzy was far too sensible to diet. She had never understood

Amanda and Suzii's shared obsession with junk food. She would stop eating when she felt full, and she would usually turn down chocolate on the grounds that she 'didn't really like it'. She was always being asked out, and she had an impressive, but not sluttish, turnover of boyfriends. She had conducted a leisurely search for her Prince Charming, and, as Amanda recalled, had enjoyed herself immensely along the way. Looking back, Amanda wondered why she had never hated Izzy. It had never occurred to her, before.

Izzy was a dreamer. Amanda was forever laughing at her for doodling wedding dresses in her notebooks, usually accompanied by a hypothetical married name. 'Isabelle James,' she would write. 'Isabelle Williams. Isabelle Jenkins.' She would scribble them, sometimes. 'I'm practising signing cheques,' she explained.

Amanda tried to imagine Izzy now. She was married, of course. That had been a foregone conclusion. Amanda and Patrick had been to her wedding to Martin, a tall and handsome charmer quite a bit older than Izzy. Izzy had been breathtaking in her wedding dress. Amanda tried to imagine them now, a devoted married couple. She hoped the institution of marriage was more fulfilling for Isabelle than it currently was for her. Isabelle was bound to have some children by now. She pictured a brace of mini Isabelles, with flowing hair and Monsoon dresses. Izzy would have given them romantic names. Raffaella and India. Something along those lines.

She looked at the invitation again. It was going to be interesting to catch up.

The name 'Tamsin' ambushed her, circumventing her attempts to ignore it. Tamsin lived on the other side of the world. She wouldn't come. Susie was only inviting her for show.

Tamsin had been thin, angular, and opinionated. Amanda had liked her, but had always been wary of her, even back then. She knew that she and Tamsin were at opposite ends of the group of friends. Amanda was close to Suzii, who was friends with Izzy, who was best mates with Tamsin. Amanda and Tamsin had never been as close as all the rest of them. Sometimes she would try to persuade Tamsin to dye her mousy hair, or to have it cut into some sort of style, but Tamsin just laughed. Tamsin had always been different and Amanda, who had never been interested in politics, and who could never make herself care as much as she should have about apartheid and starving babies, tended to edge away from her.

That was then. Now she had the urge not to edge away so much as to run as fast as she could in the opposite direction. But Tamsin was as far away as could be, and that was as it should be.

Amanda allowed herself to remember Mrs Grey, Tamsin's mother, for an instant. Mrs Grey had been as easygoing as her daughter was difficult. She had always worn an amused little half smile. She had been most people's favourite teacher. Tamsin had never known whether she was more mortified that her mother was the careers adviser and French teacher, or because her mother had better social skills than she did.

Amanda knew that she had been wildly jealous of Tamsin, and that nothing would ever have made her say so. Tamsin had been blessed with the gift of not caring in the least what anyone thought of her. She was unashamedly aloof from the rest of the girls at school, engaging them only to argue about politics. She used to dress in embroidered skirts with little mirrors on them, and grey men's macs she picked up at the indoor market. She and Izzy would laugh as they hypothesised about the guy who had died in the mac, the pervert who stood on street corners feeling his balls through his pocket.

Of course Tamsin would decline Susie's invitation. Amanda decided she might as well finish the biscuits before going to the gym.

chapter three

Susie

Paris

March

I loved to get a fix of shops and cars and apartment blocks and people from time to time. As soon as I set foot in Paris or London, I sparked up. I felt parts of me coming to life, parts that I had not realised were dormant. Country life was good. It was what I needed, to get my work done. But the city made me feel whole.

It was, I decided, as I took the steps up from the Metro at rue du Bac, because I had grown up in London. Until I was fourteen, when my father's job whisked us to Cardiff, I had never contemplated anywhere but London. It had never occurred to me that anybody might want to live anywhere else. And even now, there was something about the city – any city, the bigger the better – that made me feel I had come home. In fact, I had never said it to anyone, but I was often happiest when I was in my little flat in London. There, I could wander from bedroom to tiny kitchen to minuscule bathroom to sitting room, without feeling guilty about dusty neglected rooms waiting to be inhabited. I was glad we were in the countryside, but as the months and years went by, I felt more and more certain that we were not there for ever.

Paris in the spring was a cliché, but it had become one for a reason. The spring air smelt of bread and exhaust and budding leaves. The people were as good-looking and well-dressed as anybody would expect. There was a warm breeze. I took off my cardigan and slung it over my handbag. I was here for a few days, shopping for art supplies at Sennelier's, going to a few meetings at the gallery, and hoping to carve out an hour or two somewhere to start assembling my summer wardrobe. The summer visitor season was about to start, back at home. We were booked up with guests for most of the summer, and I was itching to socialise. Roman managed our winter social life, and he enjoyed it a lot more than I did. I could never find the confidence to say what I wanted to say, in French. It was a huge failing on my part. I was forever catching up with conversations just as they moved on.

The reunion was working out exactly as I had hoped. Izzy and Amanda had replied to my invitation straightaway, enthusiastically. I was itching to see them both again, to catch up. There had been nothing from Tamsin. I knew it would take a while for the letter to reach Australia, but it had been two months now, and I could safely assume she wasn't coming. Nobody in their right mind would fly round the world for two nights. I felt hugely relieved. It would be odd to see my friends. We had not so much drifted apart as agreed, without ever talking about it, to drop each other. It had seemed the only thing to do, but now we were thirty-two, and it was time.

Three hours before my train home to Dax, I rushed into the gallery and flung my things down.

'Hi,' I said, speaking English and, for once, not caring.

'Susanna,' said Marc, with a sunny smile. He went into French. 'You look tired. Sit down. Coffee?'

I nodded. 'Mmm, coffee. Yes please.'

'Everything's great, as ever,' he said. 'Selling faster than you can supply them. And there's a couple more commissions. Remember a guy you did a painting for in January? With a woman in it?' I nodded. It had been a rush to finish that one in time. 'Well, he liked it so much that he wants you to do something else for him. With his wife in it, again.'

'Great. When and what?'

'He'll call you himself, if that's OK. He's got your studio number from last time. That all right?'

'Of course. His wife liked the present, then?'

'I guess.' Marc disappeared to find the coffee, and I leaned back in my designer chair, which was less than comfortable, and looked at the walls. They were not, naturally, my exclusive domain, but I was happy to see a lot of my work up there. They displayed them perfectly here. The walls were almost aggressively white, and they set off my blue skies and turquoise seas to perfection.

My mobile rang. I looked around, but Marc was still off making coffee, and the place was deserted. I answered the phone, turning towards the wall, and speaking quietly. I hated ostentatious mobile use.

'Hello?' I said.

There was a crackle. Then the line calmed down. 'Hello?' It was a woman. I recognised her voice instantly, but I pretended not to, because I didn't want it to be her. 'Hello?' she said, again. 'Is that Susie?'

'Yes it is,' I answered crisply.

'Hi! Susie, it's Tamsin. Calling from Australia!'

'Tamsin!' I said, hoping I sounded suitably enthused. This was ridiculous. I had got in touch with her, not the other way round. 'Tamsin, wow. It's amazing to hear your voice.' I remembered the last time I had heard her voice, how distant she had sounded, even though she had been right in front of me. 'How are you?'

'I'm good,' she said. She had picked up a slight Australian accent. 'Susie, I've just received your letter. I was in New Zealand for a while. It's so great to hear from you. Is it too late to say yes?'

'Of course it isn't,' I told her firmly. 'Are you serious? You're coming all that way?' I thought about it. 'Would you like to stay longer?' I asked politely.

Tamsin laughed. 'It works out perfectly.' I still couldn't believe that this was actually Tamsin, that she still existed, and that I had the gall to speak to her. 'You know, my dad's getting remarried? At last. To a lady called Val? She's a lovely lady. I mean, I've only met her a couple of times. But he's happy. It feels a bit . . .' She pulled herself together, audibly. 'So the thing is, I'm coming over anyway this summer. I'll fiddle the flights around a little bit. No problem. Are the others coming?' She laughed. 'This is going to be so weird.'

'Mmm. Yes, they are. The four of us will be reunited. How's Australia, anyway? What do you do?'

'I run a bar. It's a bar at night, a café in the day. By the beach? How about you, Susie? What do you do, out there in France?'

Marc appeared, with my coffee. I waved at him, trying to indicate that I would only be a second. He smiled, put my coffee down on the arm of my chair, and wandered away.

'Erm.' I had, vainly, assumed that everybody knew I was a painter. I was the most commercial type of painter in the world. I was always finding my stuff on greetings cards. 'I paint. Pictures. Actually, Tamsin, I'm going to have to go. I'm just at an appointment right now.'

It was getting dark by the time I reached the Gare d'Austerlitz. I pulled my long coat tightly around myself and sought out the platform I needed. I had three bags full of art materials, a few clothes, some shoes, and a good haul of new make-up. The bags were pulling on my shoulders, but I could not find the energy to find a trolley and a euro. I lugged it all to my train, and stowed everything away, and sat by the window to read.

I couldn't concentrate. There was something magical about sitting on a sparsely populated train, in a Parisian station, waiting to be whisked south to arrive home in the early hours of the morning. Outside the window, the station's lights were bright, and they made the darkening sky look black by contrast. Paris was sitting out there, under the fat moon. Most of France was about to flash past the window.

I decided to cancel the reunion. It would be rude, but that didn't matter, because Amanda and Isabelle and Tamsin were no longer a part of my life. If I offended them, it would not change anything.

We had diverged. Isabelle had written an enthusiastic letter in response to my invitation. She lived in Cardiff again now, in Pontcanna, and she was separated from her husband, which was surprising. Now, she was a single mother of a little boy. She had raved about how wonderful it would be to come to France. She said her son had never been on an aeroplane, and that they were both excited. It made me feel uncomfortable, as if Izzy and I had accidentally swapped lives. If, back in our day, the American custom of voting pupils 'most likely to' do anything had caught on, Izzy would have been most likely to live in the south of France and be skinny and successful with excellent clothes. I would have been most likely to get knocked up and abandoned and to become wildly excited about the idea of going on an aeroplane.

Amanda had rung me a week or so later, and as soon as I heard her voice, I knew that, like me, she was in two minds. Of course, she couldn't say anything, but she picked delicately around my motives.

'Is Tamsin coming?' she'd asked.

'I haven't heard back from her yet.'

'She's still in Australia. Mum ran into her dad a while ago and he said she's still in Sydney.'

'Yes. I invited her but I don't expect she'll make it.'

At that, Amanda's voice lightened audibly. She began to sound like a forceful London mother.

'Well,' she said. 'We would love to come, Patrick and the children and me. Can't wait, in fact. Can't wait to see what kind of a place you've got for yourself out there. Anyway, Susie, how are you doing? Is there a Mr Susie?'

I laughed. 'Not tied to me in wedlock. And I'm not sure he'd appreciate the name, but yes, there's a Mr Susie. He's half French, half English. His name's Roman.'

'Oh, my. How glamorous. Roman.' Amanda had tried the name out in a French accent. '*Roman*. Nice.'

'He is,' I told her, and I couldn't wait to have Amanda back in my life.

Now, two months after I decided that Tamsin could not possibly be coming to visit, everything had changed. As the train pulled out of the station, a chill passed through me, and I noticed, in a distracted way, that my fingers were trembling as I opened my newspaper. Because I knew that I couldn't cancel. I was going to have to go through with it.

21

chapter four

Lodwell's, 1987

Suzanne Chapman was fourteen, and she was moving schools. She was furious and terrified. Nobody wanted to move house and leave their friends behind. Her parents didn't understand that at all. Her little sister Jacqueline didn't get it either, because she was too babyish. She was only eleven and she thought it was exciting. She was pathetic.

Nobody had a clue what Suzanne was going through. She sat in the front seat of the car, fiddling with her brand new uniform. Her breath was coming quickly, though she was pretending, for her dad's benefit, to be cool. Too cool for school, she thought. If only. Her old school, in London, had a navy blue uniform, and one, Suzanne now realised, that was halfway decent. It was a normal, knee-length skirt, and a white blouse, and a blue blazer. There had been nothing stupid about it, nothing that marked you out as particularly different or posh. Now she felt ridiculous in a grey pinafore with pleats that made her bum look gigantic, and a green and white striped blouse underneath it with a strange little round collar. On top of this awful combination, she wore a dark green blazer, and, worst of all, she was holding on her lap a shocking object: the school hat. This was a green felt monstrosity, which perched on the top of the wearer's head like an old-fashioned air hostess's hat. Apparently you were supposed to keep it in place with hair grips. It made Suzanne sick. She had begged to be allowed to go to the comprehensive, but her parents wouldn't let her. They thought she needed the discipline of a private school.

She had spiked her short hair up, defiantly. Neither parent had said anything. They had exchanged looks over her head. Nothing was going to make her flatten her dark hair down. She knew she looked stupid with flat hair.

Far too soon, Dad stopped the car. The squeak of the hand-brake going on made Suzanne's stomach turn over. She swallowed. She wasn't going to know anybody. She was the new girl. She was going to hate every moment of every day. She would spend break times writing letters to her friends in London, plotting to run away from home. She would catch a train back to London and live with, say, Kathy's family until she was sixteen and could do whatever she liked.

Jackie jumped out of the back door as soon as the engine was off.

'Wow,' she said, staring up at the dull grey of the gothic building.

It was the oddest looking school Suzanne had ever seen. It looked half like a church, half like a haunted house. It should be full of bats and ghosts and chains. Those, Suzanne thought, would be better than teachers and blackboards and strangers.

'Come on then!' Jackie said, standing by the passenger door. 'Bye, Dad! See you later.'

Suzanne knew that her father was looking at her. He was off to work now, at the hospital. It was all his fault that they had moved. He had got some stupid new job. As if there could possibly be a job in Cardiff that was better than a job in London. It made no sense, and at first she had thought they were joking, but Mum and Dad had insisted. She avoided his eyes.

'Bye, Sue,' he said, trying to lean over and kiss her. She didn't reply, and didn't look at him. She just slammed the car door and stalked off. She didn't look back, although she knew that Jackie was leaning into the car for her goodbye kiss. Jackie was tiny, like a fairy child. She was skinny and cheerful, and Suzanne hated her.

She knew that, next to Jackie, she was a fat, ugly, spiky-haired toad. So she quickened her pace and made it to the door before her sister caught up.

There were hundreds of girls milling around on the first day of term. Not many of them looked lost. Suzanne hastily picked one who looked about her own age and decided to follow her, ignoring everyone around her. She could not, however, help feeling like a lost outsider when she heard them greeting each other. That accent! It was the strangest way to talk.

'All right?' girls shouted. They ran up and hugged each other. 'What you been up to, then? How's it going?' They formed tight little clusters, surging eagerly into the school buildings, on their way to new classrooms.

Inside, it smelt of polish and officialdom. The girl Suzanne was following had long blonde hair and she was quite tall, so it was easy to keep her in sight. The corridors were long and unfamiliar, and she felt sick with longing for the old, comfortable school, where she had known everybody since she was seven, and everybody knew her. She looked at the cracked cream paint on the walls. She reached out and pulled a bit off, just for the hell of it. The plaster work behind it was crumbling. Crumbs of plaster fell onto the tiled floor. Suzanne walked away quickly. She had lost the blonde girl. She felt tears in her eyes, and she blinked them back furiously, stopping for a moment and breathing hard in an attempt to get rid of them before she embarrassed herself.

A teacher walked by, and Suzanne tried to walk alongside her. The lady was about her height, and she looked weird. She was almost spherical and there was a big wart on her chin. Suzanne managed to say, 'Excuse me,' but at the same time a much bigger girl walked up to the teacher, and said, 'Hello, Mrs Spencer. Good holidays?'

Suzanne dropped back, disheartened. She was going to have to try harder to ask for help. She stopped walking, and a girl walked heavily into her back, pushing her forward and making her stumble.

'Hey!' said the girl, who was broad and dark with thick eyebrows.

'Watch where you're going, will you?'

'You watch where *you're* going,' Suzanne muttered, wishing she had some gum to pop at this horrible girl. People swept past her. She was not going to cry. She was not.

The woman put her hand on Suzanne's shoulder before Suzanne noticed her.

'Hello,' she said, in a kind voice, smiling. 'You look lost. Are you new?'

It was a teacher. She was skinny, with brown hair in a bun, and a flowery blouse with a funny brooch on it. She had a friendly face and she was the first person in this awful school who had shown any concern for Suzanne at all.

'Yes,' Suzanne said in a small, grateful voice. 'I'm in the fourth form. I don't know where to go.'

The woman smiled again. 'Don't worry. We'll soon have you in the right place. Do you know who your teacher is?'

Suzanne shook her head.

'Well, we'll find out. I'm Mrs Grey. I teach French and I'm the careers adviser too. I'm sure we'll be coming across each other. I'll be looking out for your spiky hair. My daughter's in the fourth form. Tamsin. What's your name?'

Suzanne had loved Mrs Grey for that, and by the time she found herself in a big, airy classroom, she had recovered some of her bravado. Her form mistress was a wiry little PE teacher called Mrs Davis, who welcomed her in quite a friendly way and picked on someone called Amanda to look after her. Amanda, Suzanne discovered, was the blonde girl she had followed. That almost made her smile: if she had carried on trailing her, she would actually have brought her to the right place. She wasn't sure that she liked Amanda, who seemed a bit snooty and was always twirling her long hair around her fingers, but she supposed she had no choice. She had to hang out with her for a while.

The fat rude girl with big eyebrows was in the room too. She was called Janie, and she glared at Suzanne, who decided to stick with Amanda. Janie whispered to her friends, and the other girls turned to stare at her. Suzanne thought they were laughing at her

Emily Barr

hair. She was the only new girl in the year. She thought about her real friends, in London, and made pacts with God. If He would perform some miracle to transport her back there, she would literally go to church every single day for the rest of her life. She would become a nun. A missionary in India. He wasn't listening. Either that or He didn't believe her.

At break, Suzanne followed Amanda out into the playground, and two other girls soon joined them. One of them was skinny, with greasy brown hair. The other was someone Suzanne had noticed across the classroom, because she was the only really striking member of the form. She was a glamorous girl with very long, slightly curly hair which was reddish brown. Her complexion, Suzanne noticed enviously, was flawless and creamy, and her face was perfect. Suzanne wanted to be this girl. This girl was prettier than anyone she had ever met, and she was slim as well.

'This is Suzanne,' Amanda said, bored. 'This is Tamsin, and this is Isabelle.' She turned her back on Suzanne, and the three girls swapped stories about their summer holidays.

Amanda had been to Majorca, and was pleased with herself. She recounted several stories about boys at the hotel asking for her phone number, and then told them about one occasion when she had pretended to be sixteen and gone on a date with a waiter.

'Except bloody Mummy saw me leaving,' she said, flicking her hair back. 'I mean, Mummy! She never notices anything, but for some reason this time she did. And she sent Daddy to find out where I was going because she didn't believe me that I was going to meet this girl. So he finds us in the bar, me with a bottle of lager in front of me, and he marches me straight back upstairs. I was *so* mad. But they were even madder with me, and then – it was *so* embarrassing – Daddy went to the hotel manager and said the waiter was buying drinks for underage girls, and poor old Pedro was sacked on the spot! So that was the end of my holiday romance.' She shook her yellow curtain of hair down over her face, and tossed it back again.

26

The others made sympathetic noises and agreed that it was both embarrassing and unfair.

'We went to France,' offered the beautiful Isabelle, 'and I didn't even have *any* amount of holiday romance. We were staying in a gîte with my cousins. All I did was lie around and read magazines and stuff. But it was nice. Hot, though, and I knew I was going to burn, because I always burn with my skin. Or get freckles, which is worse. So I had to keep in the shade.'

Suzanne stared again at Isabelle's alabaster skin, and made herself look away.

They looked at skinny Tamsin. 'Went to London,' she said. 'On my own. Well, I stayed with my penfriend but her parents were working so we just did what we wanted. It was cool. We walked around loads and saw the Houses of Parliament and Tower of London and all that, but the best bit was, Ellie knew all the pubs where we'd get served, so we got to spend most afternoons sitting at tables on the pavement, getting slowly pissed.' She smiled. 'Or quickly pissed. My best holiday ever, actually.'

Suzanne felt small. She wanted to talk to Tamsin about London, but they all seemed to have forgotten she was there. Eventually, Isabelle turned to her.

'What about you, Suzanne?' she said, speaking as if to a four-year-old child. 'Did you do anything fun?'

Suzanne forced a brave smile. 'Moved to Cardiff. That was the main thing. We moved from London. I've always lived in London, until now. So that was a bit weird.'

Tamsin was pleased. 'You're from London? That's cool. Someone to talk to about it! I'm in love with London now. We could go back up there together at half-term.'

Suzanne was delighted. 'Well, I'm definitely going at half-term. I've got all my friends there. In Hammersmith. You could come with me, no problem.'

Tamsin nodded. 'So why on earth would you move from the world's coolest city to this shithole?'

Amanda looked affronted. 'Cardiff's wicked! There's nothing wrong with it, if you know where to go.'

'Oh, God, Amanda,' said skinny Tamsin. 'You have no idea.'

Suzanne swallowed. 'My dad's job,' she said. 'At the hospital. I didn't have a choice.'

'That's a bit rough,' Isabelle sympathised. 'I mean, Lodwell's isn't a bad school, I don't think, but I'd hate to leave all my friends and start again somewhere fresh, however good it was there.'

Amanda looked at her watch. 'Hey, guys. Let's get chocolate. Only five minutes left.'

Isabelle shook her head. 'Yeuch. I'm hardly awake. Count me out.'

Tamsin shook her head. 'Not hungry.'

Suzanne touched Amanda's arm. 'I would *love* to,' she said. She felt that chocolate and a fizzy drink might well get her through the rest of the morning. 'Where do we get it?'

Amanda looked surprised. 'Really? Excellent! A snacking buddy. The fourth form sell it in the corner of the hall. I could murder a Mars Bar and a Diet Coke. How about you?'

'Mmm. Twix. And Diet Coke.'

And they walked off, arm in arm. Suzanne was pleased to have a tall, blonde friend who liked chocolate, and she made a point of blanking Jackie, who was skipping around with two other girls, trying to catch her sister's eye.

chapter five

Susie

Les Landes, France

August 2005

We were sitting outside, on a warm evening. I could barely remember the winter. It seemed to have been hot for ever.

There was a bowl of cheesy vegetable pasta in front of me. This was my favourite dish from Roman's repertoire, and I was relishing the prospect of eating it. I speared a pasta butterfly. Inside the house, the phone rang.

I looked at Roman pleadingly.

He shook his head. 'It's for you,' he said, in the drawling public school English that he had learned from his father. 'You know it.'

I sighed and scraped my chair back. During the summer, we entertained so often that when we had a few days without any guests, I liked to savour the peace. In winter, I would rush for the phone. Now I resented it. I was precariously balanced between terror and excitement about the upcoming weekend. I didn't need anything to disturb my equilibrium.

I decided to answer it in the office. I hoped it was neither Jackie nor Amanda. Amanda had called four times over three days, wanting to know about the night-time temperatures, the necessity of jackets, whether I wanted her to bring me some Marmite, and whether I had a cat. One of the children was 'sensitive' to cats. Luckily we ran a cat-free household.

Amanda had always been demanding. I couldn't wait to see her, but speaking to her all the time without having caught up properly was weird. As for my sister, she had been trying very hard to muscle in on my reunion. We had completely fallen out over my refusal to allow her to join us.

'*Âllo?*' I said in my best French voice, hoping to confuse whichever of them was disturbing my evening.

'Hello,' said a woman. She sounded unsure of herself, which ruled out both Amanda and Jackie. 'Erm, is that Susanna Chapman?'

I sensed a work call, so I put on my polite voice.

'Yes it is!' I said. I sat down at the trestle table where our finances were supposed to be managed by whoever could be bothered to do it, which was generally me. 'How can I help you?' I picked up a pen and doodled a flower and a bumble bee on a post-it note.

'Um. This is going to sound odd.' Her voice was crisp. 'We haven't met, but I believe you have painted some portraits of me. Which is weird, isn't it? My name is Sarah Saunders. There's one picture where you painted me lying by a swimming pool. One where I'm sitting on a wall by a village on a hill. And one where I'm reading a book outside a cottage in Greece or somewhere. They all have your signature on the bottom corner. It's taken me a while to track you down.'

I smiled. This sounded like another commission, and although I was already busy, you could never be too popular. I forgave her for coming between me and my dinner.

'Oh!' I said. 'Hello! Of course I know you. You're Neil Barron's wife. You're lovely to paint.' I swivelled in my chair, trying to see whether Roman was eating my food.

'I'm Neil Barron's wife?' she echoed.

'Aren't you? He commissioned them for you.'

'Neil Barron?' She sounded lost.

I frowned. 'Yes.'

'You see, I'm not married. And I don't know any Neil Barron.'

I stopped drawing. 'Seriously?'

30

'Absolutely seriously.'

'So who is he? I mean, he must be your husband. He sends me photos of you. He sends me postcards of places he's been with you. If he's not your husband, then who could he possibly be?'

'This is what I was hoping we might be able to work out.'

Ten minutes later, I went back out and started picking at the cold pasta.

'Want me to stick that in the microwave?' Roman asked.

I looked at the cheesy pasta and thought about my thighs and waistline. Then I remembered my eight kilometre run that morning, and vowed to do another the next day.

'Go on, then,' I said. 'Why not?'

He disappeared. I watched the sun becoming huge and holding itself above the horizon, bleeding into the field of maize. It had been a hot, dry summer with ferocious water restrictions, and even though the farmers irrigated anyway, the crops were clearly unhappy. Even in this light, I could see the brown tips on the leaves.

When Roman came back with a plate that was too hot to touch, the sun had almost disappeared.

'That was someone called Sarah Saunders,' I told him. 'She's that woman I keep having to paint into postcard scenes.' I looked to him for recognition.

He nodded. 'The blonde. With the husband.'

'Mmm. And yet, not-mmm. She's the blonde. But she says she hasn't got a husband.' I burnt the inside of my mouth, and gulped champagne to cool it. 'Ouch,' I added. 'She says this guy leaves my paintings in her porch as strange little presents.'

'Like something the cat dragged in?'

I looked at him. 'That's my art you're talking about. But yes. Exactly.'

Roman smiled, and dimples appeared in his cheeks. 'So you've got to dig out everything you've ever had from him and hand it over to the police? Can I help? Can I be like Rebus?'

I shook my head, my mouth full. 'Nope,' I said, probably indistinctly. 'She hasn't told the police. She reckons it must be someone she knows.'

'So sharp she'll cut herself. I stand corrected. I'm not Rebus. She's Miss Bloody Marple. Quite the little detective.'

I ignored that. 'The sum total of everything I've ever had from him has been three photos, three postcards, and probably a couple of answerphone messages that have long since been recorded over. All the paperwork's with the gallery.'

'Tell me she's talked to the gallery, at least.'

I shook my head. 'Just to get our number off them. On the grounds that they'd already given it to her supposed husband.' I paused, thinking. 'Which means she must have pretended to be his actual wife. Which is weird. She doesn't speak French so she wants me to explain it to Marc in the morning.'

Roman leaned back in his chair and smiled. 'Just what you need!' He was sarcastic. 'You're already having kittens because your long-lost best friends in all the world – people you've never mentioned once in the past four years – are coming to stay the day after tomorrow. And now you have to get involved in a Kay Scarpetta operation at the same time. Brilliant.'

'Yeah.' I slumped back and pushed my plate away. 'No, though. Kay Scarpetta cuts bodies open with a saw. I hope it won't come to that. But that bloke. He was so jolly on the phone. I never for a moment thought he might be a weirdo.' I stopped myself. 'I haven't even got time to think about him very much,' I said firmly. 'There's so much to do before the girls get here.'

The evening was perfectly still, and the light was rapidly fading. I tried to tell myself that everything was under control. I took a deep breath. We had entertained visitors throughout the summer, and I was sure that most of them had been more demanding than my three schoolfriends. I was an expert hostess. There was nothing to worry about. Neil Barron should have been my only concern. Yet I was petrified. I felt constantly nauseous at the knowledge that Tamsin was about to come to my house.

Roman put a hand on my shoulder. 'You're not stressing about the girls, are you?' he asked, his confusion showing in his voice.

'No,' I lied. 'Just tired. That phone call's freaking me out. And it's been nonstop visitors this summer, hasn't it?'

'And I've never seen you fret about any of them. You do it so well. You're relaxed and welcoming and happy, and everyone has a superb time from the moment they step in through the door. As for the stalker – if he *is* a stalker – you're not his target so you don't need to worry.' He looked into my eyes. 'Susie, it has nothing to do with you.'

'You're right.'

Roman refilled my glass and I sipped the champagne gratefully.

It was nine o'clock. There were still a couple of tiny, rosy clouds by the horizon. It was comfortably cool. I looked past the lawn, past my studio, and through the cluster of trees. The swimming pool had been finished two months ago, and it glinted temptingly, still golden with the memory of the setting sun.

'Hey,' I said, nodding my head towards it. 'Swim?'

Roman grinned and downed the last of his champagne. 'Skinny dip?'

'Always.'

We stood up and raced down the garden. Roman was faster than me. He was fitter than me, bigger than me, stronger than me. I didn't mind that at all. I was fit. I ran every day, so I was not exactly lumbering fatly after him. In fact I was close behind when he reached the pool.

I stopped and looked at it. This was my swimming pool; my favourite thing in the world. I never tired of gazing upon it. Perhaps I was vain and superficial, but the pool made me prouder of myself than almost anything else in my life. It represented everything. Without my niche art market, there would be no pool. If my cards weren't stocked by Ikea and W. H. Smith and WalMart, there would be no pool. If I didn't have a huge garden, there would be no pool. If the house were not renovated and thoroughly, delightfully, quirkily habitable, there would be no pool. The swimming pool was a luxury during a drought. A mass of water in the garden. It was elemental, indulgent.

I pulled my cotton wrap dress open and let it fall to the ground. I shrugged out of my pink underwear, ran through the open gate, and dived in at the deep end. The water felt like velvet. It caressed me.

I came up to the surface, giggling and rubbing my eyes, and trod water and looked at Roman. He was swimming underwater, and he surfaced, as ever, right next to me. He grabbed me around the waist and pulled me to the side of the pool. There was always the frisson of danger with skinny dipping: the next door farmhouse, where a gruff farmer called Pierre lived with his silent wife, overlooked us. At least, the far end of their vegetable garden overlooked our pool from a considerable height. There was always a remote possibility that one of them could be standing there, peering down, possibly with binoculars, watching us.

I looked up the hill, and couldn't see anything.

'It's nearly dark,' Roman pointed out, following my gaze. 'He would have to really, really want to catch a glimpse of your treasures to be out there spying now.'

'Well, maybe he does really, really want to catch a glimpse of my treasures.'

'Of course he does.' Roman grinned. 'Tell you what, let's make it easier for him.' He pulled himself out of the pool and ran naked to the pool house, where he flicked a switch. The pool lit up, bright turquoise, easily visible to anyone in Pierre's garden. I squirmed and shrieked, but the exhibitionist in me liked the danger.

'He never speaks to me apart from *bonjour*,' I said, with a laugh. I flipped onto my back and looked up at the starry sky.

'Because he's paralysed with lust,' Roman said, diving back in.

I waited for him to surface. 'And she *never* speaks to me if she can help it.'

'Paralysed with lust too. It would make a great lesbian porn flick, actually. Bernadette the farmer's wife runs, in slow motion, through her fields to join the beautiful foreign artist, naked in her outdoor pool.' He nodded appreciatively. 'Mmmmmm. Would work, you know.'

'Great,' I told him, suddenly annoyed. I kicked myself upright in the water. 'Well, you pop up there and ask when would be convenient to film it, then.' His hands were suddenly on my waist. I shook them off and started swimming away. Insects were flying kamikaze missions into the pool, drawn in by the light. There were going to be dead moths all over the surface in the morning. 'Have you checked the pH lately?' I asked, sharply.

I heard Roman sigh. He was swimming up behind me. 'Yes,' he said, in a bored voice. 'And I'll do it again before Friday. And I'll clean the filters again, and the pump, and I'll wash out the baskets and check the temperature and the water level. It will sparkle and shine as if it were wired to the electricity. Every molecule will be clean and clear.'

'Thank you.' I turned and kissed him.

'Oh, she likes me again now.'

'I always like you.'

'Prove it.'

So I did. Swimming-pool sex was one of our favourite activities that summer.

Later, we lay on the prickly grass, and looked for shooting stars. My hair was wet, and my legs were sticking to each other, awkwardly unmoisturised. The moon was nearly full. The trees cast shadows.

'It must be weird to have a stalker,' I said, staring at the white smear of the Milky Way.

'Don't think about it,' Roman instructed. 'Just send her the stuff he sent you and let her sort it out. It's not your responsibility.'

'Oh, very caring.'

'Hey, there's no point losing sleep over it,' he pointed out. 'Worry about your visitors, if you must. Not about this strange lady.' He paused. 'Do the stars make you feel insignificant?' he added.

I giggled. 'Not really. You?'

'It takes more than an infinite and unknowable universe to dwarf Roman Jackson.'

35

'I wish I could stare at the sky and stop fretting over the weekend,' I said. 'But all I can think about is stuff like, I'll do a big supermarket shop tomorrow. I've got a list written but I'll rack my brains for things to add to it in the morning. In fact I'm going to sleep with a pen and paper on the bedside table for all the things I remember in the middle of the night.'

'Mmm,' grunted Roman.

'Breakfast cereal. All the fresh milk Intermarché have got, which won't be much. Why don't they do fresh milk in France?'

'Because they do UHT milk instead. I don't know. That's just the way it is.'

'It's weird.'

'Yes. I know. To put so much effort into cheese, and then barely to bother with fresh milk at all is, indeed, weird.'

'So I'll buy all the fresh milk there is, and then I'll get long life. What do children eat? Fish fingers? Ice cream? Biscuits?'

'Yep, yep and yep. Are you going to make them eat like little English kids, at quarter to five or some ludicrous hour?'

I smiled in the dark. 'Yes, of course I am. I want them packed off to bed before dinner, thank you very much. That's what the English do and I am thoroughly in favour.'

'Well, of course, from our point of view. But it's still a fucked-up way to raise a family. I mean, my mother would not have *dreamed* of giving me my own little tea at *goûter* time and then sending me off to bed. It's bizarre. Don't these people *like* their children?' He propped himself up on his elbows and looked at me, earnestly. 'And if the parents work, what on earth possesses them to pick them up from crèche or whatever at half six, and then pack them off to bed an hour later? Do you know, there are kids who get picked up from nurseries in Britain in their pyjamas? Jackie told me. Are these parents insane? Do they not want to see their offspring *at all?*'

I giggled. 'Maybe they don't. I don't know. But that's just the way it's done in the UK, and that's that. And British parents would think you were mighty weird if you said any of that to them, because for them it's completely normal. They would be horrified at the idea that toddlers could stay up until ten.'

'Yeah, because then they couldn't spend their evenings watching hardcore porn.'

'Well, we're doing it the British way this weekend, even if it does mean cooking two dinners.'

Roman reached out in the dark and stroked my cheek. 'That's one of the best things about you, you know, Suze. The fact that you don't want kids. Most women of your age would be washing contraception down the sink by this stage of a relationship, and secretly buying soft little baby clothes and stashing them in drawers. But you're rational about it, and I love you for that.'

I reached up and stroked his hand. 'We're too selfish to have children,' I said. It was almost mechanical. I had said it so many times that by now it had to be true. And it worked both ways: one of the things I liked best about Roman was the fact that he hated babies. If he didn't want to have them, it meant I couldn't. It meant I was safe. 'So,' I continued brightly, 'I'll get in lots of children's food. Pasta twirls and chocolate biscuits in animal shapes. On Friday we can go to market in the morning and stock up on fruit and veg, before I go to the airport. There's a market somewhere on Friday, isn't there?'

'Sure to be. You just want to tell them everything's fresh.'

'Of course I do. People love that. Can you run over to Pierre's tomorrow and pick up some eggs?'

'Eggs from those chickens over there?' He pointed to the hillside next door. The chickens had long since gone in to roost. 'Yes, I can see that would work. Scrambled eggs for breakfast? They're from, oh actually, you can see the chickens! As if you've just remembered.' He was silent for a moment. In the moonlight, I could see him frowning at me. 'Susie?'

'Mmm?'

'These people are your friends.'

'My oldest friends.'

'So why does everything need to be perfect? It's not a hotel and nobody expects it to be one. Let them muck in and help cook. They're hardly going to mind.'

'*Because* they're my friends. I want it all to go smoothly, for them and for us.'

'I know you like to take care of the details but when, say, Dylan and Esme were here, two weeks ago, you weren't like this.'

I shook my head. It was hard to explain. 'You don't understand. Dylan and Esme are our friends. They're from our world.'

'They're more high-powered than your lot. They have serious jobs and responsibilities. Your schoolfriends have crappy jobs to pay their mortgages, like most people. But you were relaxed with Esme and Dylan. And now you're having kittens over a bunch of miserable housewives. *Pourquoi?*'

I sighed. It was impossible to explain it. 'Because I know where I stand with our friends. I'm successful in my own right, too. And you are.' I looked at him, nervously. He didn't contradict me. 'Esme and Dylan have a house in Umbria. They know the score. There's nothing at stake with them. But I have no idea what Amanda and Izzy and Tamsin are like any more. I'm . . .' I stared at the sky, at the millions and billions of stars above us. My stomach was in knots. 'I just want to be the best.' I said suddenly, briskly. This was something Roman would understand and accept. 'I'm really proud of this house and our life here, and I'm happier than I ever thought I could be, and I suppose I want them to see what I've done. I want them to think I've done well. I want them to be jealous. At school I was the new girl. I was always catching up. I was the one who got Bs for everything. I was good but never *very* good. Not even at art. Now I'm *very* good. I'm very good at what I do, and selling pictures faster than I can make them. I have the best house, the best partner, the best life. I suppose I think I can cement that this weekend.' I forced a smile. 'Not very nice, maybe, but there's your answer. I'm also three stone lighter now than I was at school, and that has to be worth displaying.'

Roman reached out and found my hand. 'You're not being nasty,' he said, sounding relieved. I knew it was because he understood me again. Roman could not bear neurotic women. 'You're sharing your good fortune. That's all it is. The girls are going to be blown away.'

chapter six

Amanda

London

Amanda was packing. The big suitcase was open on the king-sized bed, and clothes were piled neatly beside it. Deciding what to take was driving her demented, and she didn't mind admitting it. She couldn't trust the kids to pack their own bags. They'd only take useless junk. Books, magazines, biscuits, and ancient, random toys. They would forget toothbrushes and underwear and swimming things. Patrick was just as bad. Left to his own devices he would go on holiday with a spare pair of pants, a packet of crisps and a Terry Pratchett novel, and he would probably be happy enough. Nobody was going to thank her for folding casual clothes, smart clothes, pool clothes and pyjamas, and packing them neatly into their two matching cases. Nobody would notice that she'd done it. They would not hesitate, however, to come running complaining if she left anything out. It was a mother's lot to be unappreciated. She was coming to see that it was a wife's lot, too. Patrick sat around having his convenient headaches, while she did everything.

She wondered about jackets and sweaters. On impulse, she picked up the phone and dialled. Susie answered, slightly breathless.

'*Âllo?*' she said, sounding quite French. It threw Amanda off her stride.

'Yes. Right. Susie?' she asked.

'Amanda! How are you doing?'

This was the fifth time they had spoken since the invitation arrived, but they had always kept their chat to a minimum, saving the proper catching up for the weekend. Susie always sounded friendly. Amanda thought she'd sound friendly too if she had a farmhouse and a French boyfriend. If she got paid a fortune for painting pretty pictures.

'Fine, thanks,' Amanda said, rather more curtly than she had intended.

'You're not pulling out on me?'

Amanda looked at the lilac walls, and the matching floral bedlinen. It was time to get their bedroom redone. It looked terribly Laura Ashley; the lilac had somehow mutated to pale mauve when she hadn't been looking. Why did that always happen?

'Oh, God, no,' she said, vehemently. 'I can't wait. And the kids are manic with excitement.' This was a lie. Jake and Freya were rarely manic with excitement about anything their parents arranged for them, but Susie didn't know that. 'Just packing, and wondering about the weather.' Amanda looked out of the window. It was drizzling gently, and the sky was thick with cloud upon cloud upon cloud. The windowpane was smeared with the tiniest of raindrops. 'I'm sorry to keep asking. You see, it's disgusting here,' she explained. 'Not at all August-like. November has come early. You're well out of it.'

'Oh, you don't have to tell me. It's sweltering. Really, truly hot, sweetie. Bring the flimsiest things you can. It doesn't even cool down at night. I know it's hard to imagine, probably, if it's grim in London, but I promise you, I haven't worn a cardigan for months. Trust me.'

'Fabulous. Thanks, Susie.'

'See you at Pau.'

Amanda smiled as she put the phone back on its charger. Her jealousy under control. She was pleased with herself. Susie had been her best friend, her tuck shop buddy, and she was glad she had done well. They had *both* done well. That was what made it bearable. They had both done well, in different ways.

She packed for herself and Patrick. Her clothes took up three-quarters of the suitcase. He only needed a few pairs of shorts, some trousers, a couple of T-shirts and a shirt. She, on the other hand, needed dresses and accessories, hats, jewellery, skirts, sarongs and God only knew what else. She undressed quickly, avoiding the sight of her naked body in the mirror, and tried on her white and gold bikini. It felt all right, and she turned quickly to try to catch her reflection in the mirror while she was still slightly off guard.

Jesus. What a pig.

Amanda despaired of her body. She was grossly overweight and there was no way she could be seen dead in this bikini, even if it was Versace. Her stomach lolled over the top of it, saggy and disgusting. Her thighs were pasty and white and thunderous. They were riven with cellulite. Every part of her was descending. Her tits needed far more support, these days, than a little bikini like this could possibly give them. Her upper arms were a disaster. This bikini did not work miracles, so it was no good. She took it off quickly, and changed into her pink one-piece, throwing the bikini into the bag anyway, in case she had a moment alone to soak up some rays.

The one-piece was much better. It was a fat lady's swimsuit; fifties-style, with a wide bottom and a halter neck that, somehow, flattered her sturdy shoulders.

Amanda pulled out the scales. She lied to everyone and told them that she had no idea how much she weighed. But she knew precisely, and she weighed herself at the same time every day. She stood on the scales while the machinery considered her bulk, and waited for the number to flash up. Thirteen stone thirteen: unlucky indeed. A pound more than yesterday. The number was mounting and mounting at the moment. She was a whale.

Thirteen stone thirteen was probably what she had weighed at Izzy's wedding, the last time she had seen Izzy and Susie. She'd had an excuse, then. Jake had been six weeks old. Amanda had fought her way to the wedding through a haze of undiagnosed post-natal depression. She could, unfortunately, recapture precisely the way she had felt that day. The six-month-pregnant stomach that did not respond when she tried to pull it in. The uneasiness she felt at being dependent on a pink Ghost dress. She had invested everything in the hope that the dress was transforming her battered body, and secretly she had known that no piece of cloth was that capable. There were the slipping breast pads that she kept yanking back into place, terrified of leaking milk everywhere. Her confusion that the breast milk was just coming and coming, even though she was bottle feeding. She had had her hair done, applied a full face of make-up, and wrapped Jake in angelic white. Patrick was supporting her as best he could. Still, Jake did three huge poos during the church service, and her dress had ended up stained with yellow. Her left breast managed to ooze a small patch of milk around the pad and onto her dress, where Patrick assured her it was not visible (she chose to believe him, and avoided mirrors). She had battled constantly with the feeling that this was not how her life was supposed to be, that there had been an enormous mistake, that she was only twenty-four and it wasn't fair.

And then, at the reception, when she felt done in and desperate to go home, some middle-aged woman made a bitchy comment, and finished her off.

It was ludicrous, she thought, that she could transport herself back across eight years so easily. The woman, Martin's aunt, had said, loudly, to the man she was with, 'There's so much public education out there now about breast being best. But some people just don't seem to *want* to give their children the best start!'

It had destroyed Amanda. She had tried to breast-feed, and now, eight years later, she could privately admit that she gave up too soon. But it had been agony! The baby had been crying from hunger, and she had been crying with pain and frustration, and both of them had breathed an enormous sigh of relief when she offered him the bottle. Besides, it meant she could share night duties with Patrick.

She had never expected her personal decision to be a matter of public comment. Hearing the woman's snide remark shattered her, instantly. Patrick led her, sobbing, out of the room, and made her tell him what had happened. She wanted him to go and confront the woman, but he gently declined.

'This is Izzy and Martin's day,' he said, in his spineless, conciliatory voice. 'We can't pick a fight with one of their guests. Don't give her the satisfaction of knowing she's got to you. The only thing to do with people like that is to ignore them.'

She had acceded to his platitudes, but she was, to this day, furious that he hadn't stood up for her. Izzy had sorted it out, after Amanda cried all over her, and left mascara on her wedding dress. The woman had conveyed an apology via the bride, and the incident had been forgotten. Except that it hadn't. Amanda had left Izzy's wedding reception, clutching her baby, forlorn with the realisation that her joint second-best schoolfriend was a better friend to her than her own husband would ever be.

Izzy had been beautiful that day. She'd worn an ivory silk dress, with a very simple cut, with roses in her hair and curls all the way down her back. There were photos, somewhere. Izzy had always been the pretty one (Tamsin had been the brainy one, Susie the character, and herself the blonde one).

Susie, she recalled, had been quite skinny at Izzy's wedding, and slightly nervy. She had already been selling paintings. She and Patrick had probably patronised her about it. If so, then the joke was on them. Amanda wondered whether she ought to commission Susie to do a portrait of Jake and Frey. She probably should.

The doorbell rang. Amanda realised that she was still wearing her swimsuit, and tried to peer out of her bay window to check on her caller without being seen. Whoever it was was standing right on the doorstep, so she couldn't see them. She threw on her white fluffy dressing gown, and tied it tightly at the waist. She couldn't be bothered to fling her clothes back on. It was certain to be one of the local mums, and they would all think she was having an affair if she answered the door in her dressing gown. Well, let them talk.

In fact, it was only the postman.

'Sorry to disturb,' he said, looking her up and down with a smile. 'Bathtime?'

'Mmm.' She refused eye contact. 'Do you need a signature, then?'

'Right here, if you wouldn't mind.' She signed. 'Cheers. Enjoy your bath.'

'Fuck off,' she said, but only after firmly shutting the door. She looked at the letter in her hand. It was boring. It was for Patrick, from the BUPA hospital. Typical of him to have made sure his health stuff came registered. She tossed it onto the hall table, and went back upstairs. Later, she would open it to check he wasn't hiding the clap from her.

Halfway up, she changed her mind and went back into the kitchen and poured herself a glass of ice-cold Sauvignon. She needed some benign fortification.

chapter seven

Lodwell's, 1989

On the first day of the sixth form, Isabelle strode into school, with her head down, feeling ashamed of herself. She twisted her hair around and pulled it over her shoulder. She frowned. She had always sworn she would leave Lodwell's as soon as she could. All the way through school, she had quietly chafed against it. She hated being different from her neighbours, disliked the way that, the moment she first balanced that ridiculous hat on her pony-tail, at the age of eight, she was ostracised. Her former friends had spent years whispering that she thought she was better than them. She didn't; not at all. They said she was posh. They excluded her. In her turn, she had quickly grown used to going to school in an entirely privileged, female environment, and this made her nervous around what she came to think of as *normal* people. She had soon come to feel that she lacked the resources to deal with them, even though Lodwell's demanded coping strategies and a thick skin, and a very specific method of dealing with feminine sniping.

She marched through the front gate, and paused to look up at the grey towers of the school building. It always reminded her of gothic horror, which was apt. She should have left, and here she was. She had let herself down. The first-day-of-term atmosphere was overwhelming, and when she looked at the smaller girls in uniform, she already felt nostalgic.

By now, she, Tamsin, Amanda and Suzii had formed an inseparable group. Izzy was comfortable with them. She knew she was too comfortable. She should branch out, meet some other people. Over the past few years, her life had completely diverged from the lives of many of her former friends. She was getting closer to some of them now, as they could find common ground over a pint in the pub. Others, though, were living lives that she knew she would never understand. Several of her childhood friends were mothers, and that chasm, Izzy felt, was unbridgeable. She ought to have left after GCSEs. But she hadn't. She should have done her A levels in Dinas Powys or Penarth. She knew a few people at Stanwell, which was a good comprehensive. If any of her friends had been planning to leave, she would have joined them like a shot. To her surprise, however, Suzii, Tamsin and Amanda had all decided to stay put. She could not find the impetus to strike out on her own, which she knew said bad things about her character.

She pulled her bag up on her shoulder. There were kids in uniform everywhere, and she was pleased that, at least, she didn't have to wear that any more. She had wanted to burn her old uniform, but her mum had rescued it and sold it second-hand. Her parents were pleased when she caved in and agreed to come back here. She told herself, weakly, that the sixth form might be better. At least, with no uniform, she wouldn't have to walk self-consciously around town with her hat stuffed into her bag, a big coat over her blazer, and that green stripey shirt half hidden by a scarf. At least she would be able to look like herself.

She knew she was making excuses. For years she had railed against private education, and particularly against her own participation in the divisive and unjust system. And here she was, like a white South African enjoying the privileges afforded by apartheid. She was going to have to live with herself for two more years.

It felt funny to be at school wearing a dress of her choice. She almost felt like a teacher. She had kept her burgundy summer dress hanging in her wardrobe, spotless and ironed, for the past fortnight. It had small white flowers dotted over it, with green stems snaking between them. She had tied a burgundy silk scarf around her head so it trailed down her back, under her hair and then beyond it, down to her waist. Her shoes were classic black Mary Janes. The whole outfit was from Miss Selfridge, but she hoped it looked a bit classier than that implied.

She looked closely at her fellow sixth formers as they arrived. Most of them had opted for jeans and cotton shirts. In fact, the more classmates she saw, the more it looked like a new uniform. Some jeans were tight and stonewashed, while others were wide and indigo, but almost everyone was wearing them. They were walking differently; showing off to the younger girls while slouching in what was meant to be an adult kind of a way.

She noticed younger girls looking at her and she smiled. Suzii's little sister Jackie was waving from across the drive, and she waved back. Jackie adored Izzy, to the point where Izzy would walk the other way if she saw her coming. Now, she quickened her step towards the sixth-form block.

It was nice to be senior. But, as she smiled, she remembered that she was nearly seventeen, and that she didn't need to be in school at all. She could be married. She could be working full time, paying tax, and living in her own flat. Her primary school friend, Andrea, was living with her boyfriend and expecting her first baby before Christmas. It had, apparently, been a planned conception. Andrea, Izzy was sure, would end up as a single mother. Izzy was equally sure that *she* would never meet such a fate.

She walked in through the sixth-form door, a sacred privilege which didn't feel quite as grand as she had always supposed it must. It was a pathetic offering really: she was still at school, still confined within the institution that had held her since she was eight, but now that she was nearly an adult, she was able to use the side door. Peeved, she set off up the sixth-form stairs. This felt equally bathetic.

She had chosen English, French and music for her A levels. At least it would be pleasant to be studying subjects she enjoyed. There would be no more multiplication of negative numbers, no more bunsen burners, no sedimentary rocks. There would, however, still be compulsory morning assembly, compulsory praying to a God in whom she did not believe, and compulsory PE. Being seventeen should involve more freedom than this. She had let herself down, and she knew it.

Suzii caught her up at the top of the stairs.

'Hiya!' she exclaimed, with a grin. She was slightly breathless. 'I've been shouting but you were in a world of your own. You looked a bit glum.'

Izzy hugged her friend. 'Just wondering how come I'm still here. How are you?' She looked at Suzii. She was dressed in tight pale jeans and a man's shirt with swirly patterns on it, which was tucked into her waistband and pulled partly out again, and she had had the spiky tips of her hair bleached. 'You look great,' she said. 'Very unschooly.'

'Thanks. So do you. Well, you look lovely, as usual.'

'Where do we find out whose form we're in?' asked Izzy.

'I think there's a list. Look, Amanda. Hey! Amanda!'

Amanda was in dark blue jeans and a pink rugby shirt. They all hugged again. Izzy noticed that Amanda smelt of soap and moisturiser and CK One. There was something very wholesome about Amanda. Her hair was newly bleached, so she had no roots at all, and she had managed to fix it so half her face was obscured under the blonde thatch. She was wearing pink lipstick, and her fingernails had been French manicured. They had seen each other several times a week through the holidays, so it was not a real reunion. Amanda and Suzii seemed genuinely excited to be in the sixth form. Izzy was fighting a growing nausea at the enormity of her mistake.

It got worse. Mrs Spencer was Izzy's worst teacher by a million miles; the only one she actively hated. And, of course, her and Tamsin's names were both down on Mrs Spencer's list. That, Izzy knew, was karma. Suzii and Amanda were with Mrs Grey and Isabelle longed to swap with one of them. Tamsin, of course, couldn't be in her own mother's form, but Izzy could have been.

Everyone congregated in Mrs Grey's classroom, because it consisted of two large tables in the glorified corridor which led to the common room and the other tiny classrooms. The upper sixth – the year above – bustled around importantly, making a show of looking down on the upstarts.

Tamsin was morose. 'My bloody mother!' she said, sitting on the edge of a table and pulling her thin, jeans-clad legs up so her knees touched her chin. 'I mean, I like her as a mother. But why does she have to be a teacher? Why? And why does she have to be in charge of the best classroom so I have to see her all the time?' She turned to Izzy. 'Why didn't we leave?'

'I wanted to!' said Izzy, appalled. 'I thought you didn't.'

'I was too lazy. I couldn't be arsed to find somewhere to go. You should have made me.'

'I wish you'd said that. We could be at Stanwell. Atlantic College, even better.'

'God. Shall we wear black every day for the next two years? To mourn lost opportunities?'

Izzy shook her head. 'Let's leave that to them.' She indicated the Goths with her head. These were two extremely polite and rather shy girls, called Beth and Bobs. They were celebrating their first day of freedom from a dress code by wearing floor-length black skirts, long black cotton tops with wide sleeves, black Doc Marten's, and striking white face paint with black eye make-up. Their lips were purple, matching their fingernails. Izzy had a sudden urge to find a red pen and draw some blood dripping down their faces. She was sure they would have appreciated it.

'Hey, Beth!' Tamsin called across the room. Beth looked at her with a friendly smile. 'Do you reckon you'll get away with it?'

They both giggled. 'Only one way to find out,' said Bobs, in her quiet voice.

'No chance!' Suzii informed them. 'It says on the sixth-form rules that "a little subtle make-up" is permitted. There's no way in the world they'll let you walk round school like that.' She thought for a moment. 'Good luck, though,' she added.

'Thanks,' they chorused, sweetly.

Izzy sat on a table and tried to blank out most people. She saw a few new girls looking lost, and she felt sorry for them. She wondered why they were there. Not one of the new girls was wearing jeans. They were dressed safely, in sensible skirts, blouses and cardigans, with their hair neatly tied back. She imagined mothers insisting, 'I know there's no uniform but you have to look smart.' She wondered how long it would take them to change into jeans. A day, probably. She could not bring herself to get up and walk over to them and say friendly things. She would make a point of being friendly to any who were in her classes, and that was all. There were plenty of busybodies around who were going to be only too happy to take them under their wings.

Izzy ignored most of her schoolmates. She didn't feel she had anything to say to the likes of Alissa McCall, who was nearby, chatting excitedly to her friends about the half marathon they had done, for God only knew what reason, during the holidays. Instead, she looked around for her music friends. She had no idea why the girls who studied music were nerds, but there was no doubt about it, they were. She saw them arriving: Mary-Jane – MJ – who had the social graces of a lonely baboon. Jennifer, small and blonde and so shy that, when she did manage to force a word out, it came in a whisper. Felicity, who was so caught up in practising her cello that she barely noticed anything that happened around her, and who was roundly ignored by everybody. Izzy smiled at them all, the outcasts of the school year. These girls only came into their own in the music block. Most sixth formers would be hard pushed to put a name to any of them.

Mary-Jane saw Izzy looking, and ambled over. 'All right, then?' she said. She was tall and broad and carried herself awkwardly. 'Had good hols, have you? Have you practised lots? We've got an orchestral recital coming up before half-term.'

Izzy couldn't help laughing a little. 'It's hardly a recital. We're playing in assembly!'

'And we hardly want to be a laughing stock!'

50

'Mary, no one in this school could give a flying fuck if the orchestra's crap.'

MJ looked around. 'I don't care what these ignoramuses think. It's about perfectionism, Isabelle, you should know that. I'm concerned about starting A level, too. We've got to do harmony, you know. It's going to be quite a jump from GCSE standard, because let's face it, a trained *monkey* could do GCSE music! How did your results go, by the way?'

'Fine, thanks.'

'Me too. I assume you had an A for music?'

'Yes.'

'Me too.'

'What other subjects did you go for in the end?'

'History and geography. You?'

'English and French.'

'Oooh, you're mad! All those books to read. And *French*? Couldn't you just stick to Debussy?'

Mrs Grey's entrance sent Tamsin and Izzy scurrying to their own classroom. Mrs Spencer! Hairy Mary! Izzy still couldn't believe her misfortune.

Tamsin looked at her and grimaced. 'I don't know how you deal with those misfits,' she remarked, as they sat down together at the furthest table from Mrs Spencer's desk.

'Oh, MJ's all right,' Izzy said, mildly. 'You just have to get used to her. She's led a sheltered life and she doesn't know how to talk to people.' She thought about Mary-Jane in the wider world. 'She's probably a bit autistic or something.'

'Your music lessons are going to be a laugh a minute.'

Izzy's heart sank still further. 'I know.' She looked at Tamsin. 'We still could leave, you know. It's not too late. We haven't started anything yet.'

'Yeah. We could, but we won't. We'll stay here and hate it and get some A levels, and then we'll run away from Cardiff and never look back.'

Mrs Spencer strode into the classroom. Tamsin and Izzy looked at one another. Mrs Spencer was the very queen of the misfits.

She was as broad as she was tall, just about, and in years to come Izzy would be unable to differentiate her, mentally, from Anne Widdecombe. There was, however, something more sinister about her than about the future prisons minister. At least, later on, once Ms Widdecombe went blonde, Izzy came to regard her as a benign form of Mrs Spencer. Mrs Spencer had platinum blonde hair, which she wore in a Beatles cut. She wore two-piece suits with buttons that stretched over her saggy front, where breasts and stomach merged into one amorphous bulge. Her shoes bulged out, the leather taking the shapes of individual toes. None of this mattered, of course. Izzy would not have dreamed of thinking less of someone because they looked weird. It was just convenient that Mrs Spencer's appearance provided a focus point for the girls' hostility; because Mrs Spencer was malign and mean and unfair, and drunk on her own power. Isabelle had long loathed her. She started hating her one day in the fourth form, when she had taken her grade five clarinet exam. The exams were held in school, and girls missed lessons to go to them. Everyone knew that. Her exam happened to fall in a biology lesson. It went well, she was relieved, and when she slipped into the lesson, to catch the last fifteen minutes, she was smiling because it was over.

Mrs Spencer was in the middle of explaining osmosis, with the aid of a complex diagram on the blackboard. She broke off, mid-sentence, when she saw Izzy, and stared at her thunderously, sucking her breath in ominously past her teeth.

'Sorry I'm late,' Izzy said, walking to her desk and sitting next to Suzii. 'I had my clarinet exam.'

All eyes were on Mrs Spencer. Several of the girls had music exams that week, and Izzy's behaviour was entirely normal and sanctioned. Yet Mrs Spencer had the evil glint in her eye.

'You had a clarinet exam?' she shrieked, suddenly and furiously. 'Well, I HAD A BIOLOGY LESSON!'

'Sorry,' said Izzy, confused, and she started taking her books out of her bag.

'DON'T YOU LOOK AWAY WHEN I'M TALKING TO YOU, YOU IMPERTINENT GIRL! STAND UP!'

Izzy stood up and, for five minutes, Mrs Spencer yelled at her. A stream of unfocused rage ended with the demand to know, 'WHY DID YOU NOT TELL ME YOU WERE GOING TO BE LATE?'

Izzy tried to stand up for herself. 'Because you don't have to with music exams. They're part of school. Mrs Twiss specifically said we didn't need to excuse ourselves from lessons because all teachers knew there were music—'

'YOU ARE EXTRAORDINARILY RUDE! I HAVE OFTEN NOTICED THAT GIRLS WHO DO MUSIC ARE RUDER THAN GIRLS WHO DO NOT. STAND OUTSIDE THE DOOR AND COME AND APOL-OGISE TO ME AT THE END OF THE LESSON.'

Oh, piss off, you sad, power-crazed bitch. Izzy didn't say it. She took herself out into the corridor, tears pricking her eyes. There were still ten minutes of the lesson left. She stood outside the door for a while, then sat down and took some homework out of her bag. She couldn't focus on it. She had never been sent out of a lesson before and Mrs Spencer's fury seemed so random and yet so personal that she was stunned. Izzy avoided trouble. She had never been someone who could laugh off verbal assaults. She hated the woman, hated her. She comforted herself with the rumours. Mrs Spencer was said never to have been married, but to have changed her *Miss* into a *Mrs* to quell suspicion. She was said to be living in a flat in the Cathedral Road with a sixth former from a couple of years ago; a girl Izzy vividly remembered as the only 'out' lesbian the school had contained within anyone's memory. They had all been fascinated by Heather, with her short hair and her manly clothes. She would turn up in a man's suit, right down to the waistcoat and tie. It was, Izzy admitted, highly unlikely that she was actually living in domestic bliss with Mrs Spencer, but it was an excellent rumour. 'It's true!' Janie had said the other day. 'My sister's friend saw them buying a bed in Habitat!'

And, Izzy told herself, biting back her pain, *and* she is a sad woman who counts for nothing in the real world. She just gets a kick out of humiliating people, and probably most of all out of humiliating people like me who aren't used to trouble.

As she heard the chairs scraping back, she jumped to her feet and prepared her apology. It stuck in her throat, but Mrs Spencer hardly seemed to care. She gave her a detention, almost as an afterthought. When Izzy complained to Mrs Twiss in the music school, the head of music said nothing. She just rolled her eyes and gave Izzy a conspiratorial glance, accompanied by an expressive shrug. Tamsin, Suzii and Amanda all agreed that Mrs S must fancy Izzy. The thought made her gag.

Now Izzy sat as far away from the woman as she could, and she avoided looking at her. The vivid recognition that *that's not fair* was still burning in her, two years after the humiliation. She had kept quiet in biology classes for the rest of the GCSE course, had flinched if the woman so much as looked at her, and had put her head down and done the work as averagely as she could, so she wouldn't stand out. One of her chief joys on the completion of GCSEs had been the knowledge that she would never again have to sit in the same classroom as that bitch. And now, here she was, on her very first day in the sixth form, fiddling with her pens and notebooks and, once again, trying to be invisible.

Mrs Spencer sat on a table, her feet on two different chairs, and none of her charges dared to giggle. She looked around with her funny pointed smile, and said, 'Hi there! Welcome to the sixth form, ladies.'

'Hi!' said a couple of the more conformist members of the form.

'Right, well, first of all, things are going to be very different now from the way they were for you all last year. Bobs, nice try, but no chance.' She inclined her head and Bobs meekly headed out of the room to wash off her make-up. 'Oh, and welcome to the new girls.' She bestowed a malevolent grimace on two girls who were sitting at the front. They both looked nonplussed.

'Hello,' they said, in unison, uncertainly.

'Which of you is . . .' she consulted a list. 'Which of you is Joy Wong?'

'I am,' said one girl.

Tamsin giggled. 'No shit,' she whispered.

'So you,' said Mrs Spencer, 'must be Rose.'

'Yes,' said the other new girl. 'I'm normally called Rosie, though.'

'Rosie it is! Everyone got that? Joy and Rosie, our new girls. I'm sure your time with us will be a *joy* and the future will be extremely *rosy*.' There was a wave of dutiful laughter.

Izzy found the whole thing excruciating. Worse still was the way Mrs S sauntered over to her and Tamsin afterwards and perched on the edge of their table.

'Always pay close attention to the girls at the back,' she said, with a cackle. 'That's what every teacher learns over the years. How are you two?'

'Fine,' Izzy muttered.

'Not bad, thanks, Mrs S,' Tamsin said, brightly. 'How are you?'

'Very well, thank you, Tamsin. Thank you for asking. Now, let's all get off to assembly, shall we?'

Izzy knew it was her punishment for abandoning her principles. In a way, it was funny.

chapter eight

Susie

Les Landes, France

August 2005, Friday

As I was walking out of the door, the phone started to ring. Our telephone had a habit of ringing at the least convenient moment, so this was, in many ways, entirely expected.

'Roman!' I yelled. I yelled it even though I knew he wasn't there. I knew he wasn't there because I had sent him out myself, fuelled by paranoia and anxiety, to buy toys for the children. He had laughed, had told me that, firstly, children came with their own toys and, secondly, they ought to be able to improvise, considering that we had a large garden with climbable trees and a swimming pool. He had humoured me and gone anyway, and now I wished he hadn't. I was leaving for the airport, and the phone was ringing.

I wanted to let the answerphone get it, but I couldn't stop myself. I ran back into the house, and snatched it up. I even forgot to answer it in my French voice.

It was a man. 'Susanna,' he said. I couldn't place him. Very few people called me Susanna, least of all because it wasn't actually my name, but an upmarket variation of my name that I had assumed for work purposes.

'Yes?' I said, cautiously.

'Neil Barron.'

'Oh,' I said. I sat down. 'Hello.'

'You sound nervous,' he said.

'Not nervous,' I said, hoping my voice was steady. I kicked off my beaded flip-flops and rested the soles of my feet on the cool tiles. 'Actually, I was just walking out of the door. I've got some friends I haven't seen for years coming for the weekend.' I pulled the strap of my dress up. My dress was white and pale green, calf-length and clingy, and I hoped it looked as good as it felt.

'Apologies,' he said. 'I won't keep you.' He was waiting for me to say something.

'I've got ten minutes.' I had an hour, but not for him.

'Then I'll spare you the formalities. You've spoken to my wife.'

I was hesitant. 'I've spoken to Sarah Saunders. Who says she isn't your wife, in fact.'

He laughed, too loudly. 'It's too embarrassing for words, isn't it? I mean, ludicrous. He says. She says.'

'Yes, it is. Confusing. And I don't think it's something I need to be involved in, if that's all right with you.' I shook my head. Had I really just said 'If that's all right with you'? I was glad Roman hadn't heard that.

'I quite agree. For what it's worth, my wife – Sarah Barron, née Saunders – has been suffering with something akin to a nervous breakdown. And she's extremely angry with me. She had a right to be cross, but not to drag you into it, and I can only apologise again.'

He was too glib. 'Can I speak to her?'

'She's not here. She doesn't know I'm calling you. It's a little, well, delicate.'

'So you're telling me to forget all about it?'

'I'm suggesting you should.'

I sighed. 'I wish I could. But I need to speak to her first. Can she call me tomorrow or something? You do understand?'

'What, that for all you know, I might be the murderous art commissioner?' He chuckled. 'Yes, quite. Speak to her in the morning.

'And then I'll be done with it.'

'Which is for the best. For all of us.'

*   *   *

I was uneasy as I started the car. I wanted to believe him. She hadn't sounded mad. Both of them were plausible. He was charming, as he had been when I'd spoken to him previously. I pulled my little Mercedes out of the drive, and turned left at the end of the road, taking the cross-country route towards Pau. It was hard to appreciate that one of them was a liar, and that the liar was telling outrageous lies to my face, or at least to my ear. I desperately hoped it was her.

My old friends were arriving. I was worn out with preparations and tired of stressing about children's bedlinen and every other mundane detail imaginable. Buying the food and planning menus had been the easy part. Getting the house ready for four adults and three children had been more complicated than I had expected. Normally, with guests, I just made up the spare bed and put some towels out. This time I had bought three sets of garish duvet covers, featuring Barbie, Action Man and the Teletubbies respectively, and I had brought in two metal bedsteads from a shed (left behind by the previous owner with specific kind instructions that we must use them when we had our own children). Izzy's boy was having to sleep on my chaise longue, because I had been too proud to accept Izzy's offer to bring a 'sleepover bed' which was apparently inflatable and bore a picture of Spiderman. There had been a rickety old wooden bed left behind in the shed, and I had earmarked this for Sam. Roman, however, had other ideas.

'He's not sleeping on this piece of shit,' he announced, when we went to fetch it.

I laughed. 'Roman! He's three years old! He doesn't care if it's a bit manky.'

'Obviously,' he said, rolling his eyes at me, 'I don't give a fuck what the child makes of it. If he's happy to sleep in the shed then he's most welcome. I'm talking about this woodworm. What have we spent on termite treatments?'

I nodded. 'Ten thousand euros.' There were multiple certificates to prove it. I had put up with four young men clumping round my house for a fortnight, injecting every piece of wood with foul smelling chemicals and stubbing their cigarettes out in my basins.

Reluctantly, we took the chaise longue apart, and reassembled it upstairs. My beautiful day bed, my most prized piece of furniture, looked so ludicrous dressed up in Teletubbies bedlinen that I caressed it apologetically. I couldn't even sit on it, because the plastic under-sheet was crinkly. Neither of us had a clue whether three-year-olds wore nappies at night, but if the boy wet the bed he would ruin it and I knew I would find it hard to keep my temper if that happened.

After this visit, we were going to be left with all sorts of rubbish we would never use again.

Maybe we would though, I mused, as I sped through villages. Perhaps, in some unimaginable way, the friendships would be rekindled, and the visits would become regular. If not, I would use the duvet covers as novelty dust sheets.

I parked as close to the airport building as I could, and looked around the interior of the car, putting off stepping into the heat. According to my dashboard, it was forty degrees outside. The car was spotless. I had vacuumed it, and cleared out all rubbish and sundry items. All I had in the car now were three small bottles of mineral water, inside the passenger door, for my guests. There was a little booster on the back seat, which was an unfamiliar addition to my life. I glanced down at myself. This was it. I hoped I looked good enough, because my surface was all I had.

Pau airport was tiny. It looked like a stylish shed in a field. Its roof curved, and its windows were wide and surrounded by wood. I strode in, running through my mental checklist. Menus were planned. Most of the meals were prepared. The drinks cabinet was so full that the door was not shutting properly. Each bedroom, except for the children's room, had vases of flowers that were just about to open. I had ironed the towels, with lavender ironing water. The cleaner had been. Everything was ready.

The only international flight from Pau was this one to Stansted, so almost everybody in the building was British. You only had to take one look at them to see that.

I pulled my hair over my shoulder and tried to look French. I had never, so far, been identified as English before I opened my mouth, because I didn't let myself burn in the sun and because my hair was black, rather than any shade of mouse or ginger. I tried to strut, like a French woman, and I gazed disdainfully at the people around me to get into character.

In fact, though, these travellers were positively endearing. They were a benign subset of the British Abroad, far removed from their distant cousins in Falariki. I followed a couple with my eyes as they walked, hand in hand, across the shiny atrium. They were in their fifties, and in spite of myself, I envied them. They looked so happy together. They were lugging rucksacks on their backs, and looked windswept, so I guessed that they had been walking in the Pyrenees. The woman's hair was naturally grey – I shuddered, as I had no idea what salt-and-pepper would currently be plaguing my head if I let it – and she wore it in a wiry ponytail at the nape of her neck. The man was half bald, and had grown the rest of his hair long in compensation. He looked like a professor of Ancient Greek, and she looked as if she taught evening classes in pottery. Her cotton trousers were slightly too short, and the neckline of her blue T-shirt was too tight. The man's baggy shorts – or perhaps the knobbly legs that stuck out from them – made me laugh. I was jealous of their closeness. I was jealous of this woman, of the fact that she could look like herself, and that even on a bad day this man would still adore her.

Suddenly, I wondered whether my old friends were going to like me. I had lived my life for years on the assumption that I was, in every way, better now than I used to be. I had gone upmarket: from Suzanne to Susanna; from Suzii to Susie. At school I was bossy and headstrong. As an adult, I had learned to cloak all that in feminine sweetness. I had been masculine, as a teenager. I had not known how to make the most of myself.

Roman had remarked to me, earlier, 'You must have been jail-bait when you were at school.' He went a bit quiet. 'I can see you in a uniform. Taunting men with those eyes of yours. You must have been quite the Lolita. Fuck.' He had a faraway look in his eyes.

I had laughed nervously as I shook my head. 'You didn't see my spiky hair,' I told him, suddenly afraid that someone might bring photos. 'Or my stonewashed jeans. Or my ginormous arse.' I had no photographs. There had been a ceremonial burning, years ago, attended by nobody but me.

He snorted and ran a hand over my silky hair. 'Guess what? I don't believe you.' He pulled me in close and kissed me.

I knew that my friends were going to see through me. They had known me as I really was. They would discard the surface with one glance, and see everything.

chapter nine

At the airport, Amanda tried to pretend she was on her own. She was never bloody on her own any more – not out of the daily domestic drudge, anyway. She never got to go to airports or on planes by herself. Taking the children to Stansted to board a cheap flight was not a relaxing start to the holiday. They had parked in long-term thanks to Patrick's tight-fistedness, and then waited for ever for a shuttle bus which took about an hour to get them to the terminal. Then there was the check-in queue.

She was playing truant from the check-in queue now; grabbing a quick, yet large, coffee, by herself. She had asked for an extra shot. Jake and Freya were engrossed in their Nintendos, and Patrick didn't mind standing in line behind a family of noisy Spaniards. Amanda looked with distaste at the people around her. There were too many of them, and they were too common. They were, she thought, self-consciously using a word she had never used before, chavs. Nobody with any taste would fly from Stansted. It epitomised everything that was wrong with travel at the moment. Travel should be exclusive. Not the preserve of these people. She stared hard at a group of young men, sitting in a bar with pints of lager in front of them. They must be a stag party, she thought. They are binge drinking at nine in the morning. They have no idea of what is classy. She shuddered. One of them saw her.

'You wish, darling!' he shouted. She looked furiously away as the boy's friends all looked up at her, and started jeering.

'Who ate all the pies?' chanted one, and his friends joined in. Their chant followed her as she stalked away, as she tried to pretend that she was not the object of their derision. When the child ran into her legs, she was ready to snap, and the poor kid, who was only knee-high, copped Amanda at her worst.

'You little bastard!' she shouted at him. He looked up at her, confused. 'Piss off! Where are your bloody parents?'

He pointed, but she was not interested. She got back to the check-in queue to find Patrick two from the front. She knew that her cheeks were pink, and she knew that she was on a knife edge, and she did her best to overcome her rage and act normal.

At the gate, she stared sharply at all the passengers, searching for Isabelle and Tamsin. They both had to be here. She was sure she would recognise them. She was relieved to see that, so far, the abusive young men were not on her flight; with all the cheap and beery destinations available, she would be surprised if they were spending the weekend in Pau. In fact, the people here looked fairly civilised.

Jakey and Freya sat a few seats away from their parents, with their heads still buried in their Gameboys. Amanda disapproved of this in other people's children, but in her own she positively encouraged it. There must be some positive effect on hand-eye co-ordination and speedy reactions. There was an indisputable positive effect on her own state of mind. The children were occupied, and Patrick was reading the *FT*, and so, cradling a double mochaccino with extra shot, she was free to stare around, trying to corral all the women's features into those of her old friends. Across the waiting area, a woman was holding up a copy of the *Guardian*, hiding behind it. Amanda could just see her long fingers with clear nail varnish on them. Her nails were well tended, though shorter than Amanda liked to wear hers. The woman's black skirt, or dress, ended at her knees, and her legs were bare and thin and brown, one crossed elegantly over the other. She had black sequinned flip-flops on her feet. She was lazily flipping one of them back and forth with the toes of her left foot. She was, Amanda decided, a likely candidate for Izzy; and with the paper held up like that, providing a barrier all around her, Izzy was certainly hiding. Hiding from Amanda. She pictured Isabelle behind the paper: her auburn hair loose down her back, yet styled artfully around her face. The black dress would be beautiful and cool, perhaps worn with a teeny cardigan. She couldn't wait to see Izzy again.

She was considering walking over and peering over the top of the paper. She was putting down her cup, preparing to do it, when she heard someone calling her name.

When she looked up, a fat woman was standing a couple of metres away. Amanda frowned. Then the brat she had sworn at looked out from behind the woman's knees.

'Oh, Jesus,' she said. She was probably going to have to apologise, and she hated that.

'Amanda?' the woman asked again.

Amanda was confused. 'Mmm?'

'Amanda!' said the woman, with a sincere and slightly familiar smile. 'I recognised you straightaway. How are you?' There was a short pause. 'Izzy,' the woman added.

'Izzy!' Amanda exclaimed. This woman had short, greying hair and fat calves. She was dressed in stretchy High Street clothes, and that white top did nothing for her stomach. This woman could be forty-five, not thirty-two. This could not possibly be Izzy. If this had happened to Izzy, then anything could happen to anybody.

And the brat was staring at her. He reached for Isabelle's hand. 'Mummy,' he said, in a loud whisper. 'That's the *mean* lady!'

'Oh, Sam,' Izzy said to him. 'You ran into her, didn't you? Sorry, Amanda. It's lovely to see you again. You haven't changed a bit.'

Amanda searched for something to say. She was about to point out the *Guardian* reader and tell Izzy about the mistake she had been about to make, but she suddenly felt it would be too cruel. Instead, she turned to Sam.

'Hello, Sam,' she said, in a baby voice. 'Don't worry about before. I'm sorry I told you off. How old are you?'

He glared at her and pushed his lips tightly together. He looked like an angel, but Amanda knew trouble when she saw it.

'Sam? Tell Amanda how old you are,' said Izzy. He shook his head, still scowling. 'He's three and a half,' she said.

'Well, Sam,' said Amanda, testily. 'I've got some children too. That's them over there. They're bigger than three and a half, though. Jake and Freya. Ask them to show you their Gameboys.' She raised her voice. 'Jake! This is Sam. Be nice to him.'

Jake rolled his eyes but nodded, and Sam trotted off to annoy him. Amanda turned back to Izzy, who had sat down beside her. She had no idea what she ought to say. 'I didn't know you had a son,' she said. 'Susie never mentioned it. How's Martin? Is he here?'

Izzy shook her head, and smiled a tight little smile. 'No. Martin's not with me. Not in any sense. I'm expecting the decree absolute any day.'

'Oh, I'm sorry. Sorry we've lost touch, too.'

'I know. Me too.'

Amanda waved a hand. 'You remember Patrick?' It was Izzy's turn to look surprised, and Amanda smiled as she realised that last time Izzy had seen Patrick, he must have had a full head of hair. He, too, had aged dramatically between mid-twenties and early thirties. He worked too hard. That was what had happened to Patrick. He worked hard to keep away from her, and to provide for the family, and now he was getting his boring, persistent headaches as a result, and the doctors were encouraging his hypochondria by inviting him for a scan.

Patrick and Izzy exchanged pleasantries, and Amanda tried to keep on top of her feelings, to hope that her mixture of triumph and dismay did not show on her face. The fact that Izzy had recognised her at once must mean that she looked better than Isabelle did. Isabelle had been ravishing, with her auburn hair and her swishing skirts and her black lace-up boots. She had become anybody, nobody. If this was what divorce did to you, Amanda decided she had better not take Patrick too much for granted.

*   *   *

She sat by the window. The children were still obsessed with their stupid games, and Patrick was not remotely interested in views. Apparently they were going to be seeing the Pyrenees at the end of the journey. She was the only one likely to notice. They were sitting miles away from Isabelle and her boy. Amanda had contrived that by, for once, not taking up the offer of early boarding with young children. Jake and Freya were too old for that really.

There was plenty of time for catching up, later. She'd like to talk to Izzy, to try to fathom out exactly what had happened to her (motherhood alone could do that to some people, she supposed), but since her own kids were big enough to amuse themselves, she balked at the idea of sharing plane space with a three-year-old. Particularly with an unruly and sulky one.

'Want me and Jakey to swap with Isabelle and the boy?' Patrick asked casually. He wanted to, she knew it. He wanted to kick back and pretend he was single. Jakey would obligingly ignore his father for the whole journey. Patrick would call a hostess over and make her bring him a whisky. Then he would make Amanda drive the hire car.

'No,' she said sharply.

'Go on. You haven't seen her for years. Of course you'd like to chat.'

'I said no, and I meant no. Feel free to swap with Izzy, but you can keep Sam with you. Entertain him. Take him to the loo. Give him sweets and colouring books. Does that appeal?'

Patrick slunk down in his seat. 'Say no more.'

Amanda ignored her family and stared out of the window. She would not admit it to anyone, but she was almost paralysed with nerves. She swallowed hard and clutched the armrest during take-off. She had no idea whether Tamsin was on the plane. She had to be; and that meant she was almost certainly the woman hiding behind that newspaper. She had scrutinised the crowd, and there were no other candidates, unless Tamsin had become as unrecognisable as Izzy.

The trolley came round, and Jake and Freya suddenly came to life. Amanda realised they shouldn't have let them have the two aisle seats.

'Dad,' said Freya, who was sitting next to Patrick. 'Can I have a Coke? Please, Dad, I'm sooo thirsty. And I'm starving! How about . . .' She consulted the card in front of her. 'Pringles?'

Jake said nothing. He knew that whatever Freya obtained, he would get the same. Coke and Pringles sounded fine.

'Please, Dad?' Freya reiterated.

Patrick laughed and nodded to the stewardess. 'Two Cokes, please, and – what flavour Pringles?'

'Salt and vinegar,' said Freya, promptly.

'Cream and chives,' said Jake.

'OK. And I'll have a beer.'

Amanda leaned over. She couldn't help herself. 'Gin and tonic, thanks. And a large Galaxy muffin.'

She refused to catch Patrick's eye. He squeezed her thigh.

'It's going to be fine,' he whispered, as he solicitously placed her drink and her cake on her tray. Patrick knew too well when Amanda was self-medicating.

Half an hour before landing, she moved everyone out of her way and went to the loo. She scanned the fellow passengers as she edged down the aeroplane. Izzy and Sam had chosen, for some reason, to sit right at the back. She looked at them. It surprised her again. Izzy looked as if she had ambled in from a Weightwatchers meeting in a village hall. She had squandered the beauty she was born with. She was just like anybody else, now: a single mother, on the heavy side of normal, with a masculine haircut and cheap clothes.

Then she saw that Izzy was laughing. Sam was on her lap, and they were both smiling at the woman next to them. The woman was laughing too. She had jaw-length hair now, cut stylishly and blacker than it had naturally been, and she no longer wore glasses, but Amanda would have recognised Tamsin anywhere. Her eyes were big and dark without the old specs to obscure them. She was wearing a black dress that suited her slender figure perfectly. Amanda recognised her fingernails. The *Guardian* was on her lap. She had probably seen Amanda and hidden from her, but when Isabelle appeared she'd come out of hiding to share a joke and to talk about old times. It was a dagger through her heart. Izzy and Tamsin were laughing, without her. They were laughing *about* her. She was instantly madly jealous. She and Izzy had chatted politely about each other's lives and children. They had not laughed.

'Well, well,' she said, stopping right next to Tamsin and glaring daggers at her. She was trembling at the sight of her. 'Tamsin Grey,' she said, swallowing all her complex feelings and focusing instead on the fact that she had been slighted. 'How the devil are you?'

chapter ten

Lodwell's, 1989

It was a vicious grey day before Christmas, and Tamsin seethed by her mother's car. She waved a terse goodbye to Amanda and Suzii, who were heading off to town together. Isabelle had slipped out earlier, illegally, and Tamsin envied her. She hated standing by her mum's car. All the juniors, in their stupid uniform, kept walking past and staring at her. Some of them thought she was a teacher.

She felt sorry for the fourth and fifth formers whose breasts bulged around the bibs of their tunics. At least this was the season for blazers and for gabardine macs, which hid the worst of that. But she hated going to a school that had such a stupid uniform. She hated lots of things, at the moment.

She hated Lodwell's and the stupid girls who went there. She hated the fake freedoms of the sixth form: hated the rank instant coffee that the girls made for each other in the common room, handing it out grandly in brown-ringed mugs as if it were a badge of adulthood rather than a nasty drink. She hated the fact that, at the age of seventeen, she was compelled to keep the same school hours as the seven-year-olds in the junior school. She hated the consensus, amongst her year group, that a lack of uniform and the occasional free period added up to some sort of genuine

the rules. Some of her classmates even seemed
.ey were, she supposed, institutionalised. And right-
. stupid. She replayed the argument she had had that
,n, with Janie, in her head.
.sin shifted from foot to foot. She was ready to leave this
dun,p and never look back. She leaned on the car, which was a
battered red Astra. Mrs Davis reversed out of the next space in a
cream Skoda, and gave Tamsin a little wave, which she returned
with the smallest hand movement she could manage.

She hated the fact that most of her contemporaries stank of
smoke and spent much of their time climbing over the back fence.
That should not have to happen. She would have the vote in less
than a year. If, as Mrs Spencer insisted constantly, they needed to
learn to organise their time like adults, then surely they should
be allowed the adult privilege of nipping to a shop if they needed
something, or researching an essay in the city library, or simply
writing it at home. Why did this institution have a right to compel
her to partake in 'Prayers' every morning? She thought there must
be a law against that, but when she asked Mrs Spencer to excuse
her on the grounds of atheism, Mrs S laughed and patted her
bottom.

The best thing about school was the work. Now, there was
something she could never say out loud. There was a sentiment
to cause raucous laughter in the sixth-form common room, where
banal conversations revolved around boys and 'going out' and
Simple Minds and boys and boys and sex and blow jobs and boys.
Many of her contemporaries were alarmingly experienced. In fact,
she thought there were probably about thirty virgins, in a year
group of ninety. The only ones she could be sure of were herself
and Isabelle, and she was fairly sure that Suzii and Amanda would
have told all if they had *gone all the way*.

The boys she met did not particularly interest Tamsin.
Sometimes, at the Square Club, she would get off with somebody,
but she had yet to meet any boy she could talk to without the
conversation seeming to be at cross purposes. From time to time
she wondered whether she might be a lesbian. Was it a coinci-

dence that she – a girl whose own mother soothed her with the promise that 'you'll grow into your looks' – was best friends with the most beautiful girl in the school? Everyone was spellbound by Izzy. The music nerds couldn't believe their luck to have someone so enchanted walking among them. Tamsin sometimes examined her feelings for her friend, but she never found anything sexual in them. No, she was certainly heterosexual. She just had a feeling she was going to have to go a fair distance from Cardiff to meet the man of her dreams.

So while the others talked about boys, Tamsin felt like a member of a different species. She threw herself into economic theories and calculus and *Othello*, where she came up against sexual passion at a certain remove. Studying was the best way of shutting out the sex talk. It was also her passport out of South Wales. She was taking maths, economics and English. She had put down English because she hadn't known what else to do, but after less than a term it had become her favourite subject. Now, she thought she might apply to universities for English, rather than for economics. She was beginning to wish she had taken art instead of maths but she thought it was too late to change.

'Hi,' she said to her mother, who half jogged up to the car, carrying her huge bag in both arms like a misshapen baby.

'Sorry, darling,' said Mrs Grey, who was slim and smart, with her hair in a bun. She was completely different at weekends, and Tamsin still found her teacherish uniform odd. 'Got caught up with some in-fighting in the staffroom.'

'Who?'

'Can't tell, I'm afraid.' She unlocked the driver's door, and the central locking clunked open.

Tamsin climbed in gratefully and set the heating to come on as high as possible when the engine started. As they pulled carefully out of the drive, her mother anxious not to mow down eleven-year-olds, Tamsin said, 'Would they let me swap maths for art?'

Her mother laughed. 'No. *They* wouldn't and I wouldn't. You know what I think of Ros Powell.'

'I know she's scatty.'

'She's worse than scatty. She's bollocks. Don't repeat it, but honestly.' She turned to Tamsin and frowned. 'I mean, I'm not a philistine. You know I'm not, don't you? I like a Rothko as much as anyone does. But the woman has no idea. To be a credible abstract artist, you need to be able to be figurative first. Otherwise it's just Emperor's New Clothes. No fourteen-year-old has earned the right to be abstract. So what's she doing papering the corridor outside the art room with pretentious sub-sub-sub-Pollock drips, produced by the fourth form? No wonder they love her. They can get away with anything.'

'Suzii's enjoying it.'

'Tell Suzii to watch out. It's all very well putting a leaf in a matchbox and calling it "found art", but it won't wash with the examining board. That's why Ros's results are always so lame.'

'Yeah, but Suzii can draw. She quite likes it that she doesn't have to, though. I'll tell her to keep practising.'

'Do.'

They sat in silence for a while. Tamsin fiddled with the radio, eventually fixing on Red Dragon FM. Her mother left it for a couple of minutes before switching to Radio Four. Mrs Grey indicated right and pulled out onto the dual carriageway that would take them home to Penarth. She looked at Tamsin, and Tamsin smiled back.

'You hate school, don't you?'

'Can you tell?'

'You never smile until we reach this part. The fast road home.'

'Of course I hate it. I despise everything about it. It's a shithole.'

Mrs Grey laughed. 'That's my office you're talking about.'

'I don't know how you stick it.'

'They pay me. And I can see precisely why you hate it, but I'm glad you decided to stick with it. You'll get good grades there, and that's all you need. Just hold on to that. And whatever you do, don't change to art. I will personally tell Mary Spencer not to allow it. In fact I'm going to tell her pre-emptively.'

'Don't! She'll only squeeze my bum again.'

'So I'll tell her to squeeze your bum if you so much as mention the word "art".'

'Point taken. You win.' She looked at her mother. 'I had a huge fight with Janie.'

'So I heard.'

'Fat racist bitch from hell.'

'And you already knew that, so it might have been a little ill-advised to pick a fight about apartheid with her.'

'But I can't, Mum.' She looked at her mother. 'I just can't let her say that stuff without charging over. You do understand, don't you? Did you hear what she said to start it? I was sitting with Izzy in the common room, and she said loudly, looking at me out of the corner of her eyes, something like: "They need the whites, you see, because it's us that keep the peace. Otherwise they'd just be having tribal wars." And then she waited for me to pick her up on it. So I had to.'

'And it descended into quite a brawl, if my class were correct in their reporting of it.'

'Of course it did. I told her she was racist, she said her uncle lived in South Africa so she has a first-hand account of the situation, unlike me who just believes whatever I read in the *Guardian* – and she spat out "Guardian" as if I was reading Trotsky.'

'So *you* said?'

Tamsin remembered the conversation.

'You might not like it,' Janie had added, 'but it's a fact. It may not fit in with your world view. That coloureds are downtrodden and repressed and we're mean and oppressive. But did you ever think about this? That whites are far more advanced than the coloured races for a reason? That we have an innate superiority?'

Tamsin snorted. 'Have you ever heard of a man called Hitler?'

'This has nothing to do with him. His issue was with the Jews. Although my uncle says the Holocaust has been exaggerated. But that's a different issue. The fact is, you don't know what really goes on in South Africa.'

'Whereas your Uncle Adolf is thoroughly *au fait* with the politics of the townships?'

'He has servants from places like that, yes. Which amounts to a lot more experience than you have, Tamsin Grey.'

'Lucky servants. Those lazy Africans need British men like him.'

Janie, who had a particularly fine zit between her overgrown eyebrows, raised her voice at this.

'No!' she said. 'No, my uncle *is* African. That's something that *really* bugs him, the fact that he's supposedly never going to be a "real" African because he's white. If that's not racism, I don't know what is!'

Tamsin had been incredulous. 'Um,' she said. 'I think I know what is. Racial segregation of beaches and parks? Mixed marriages and interracial sex being illegal. The Black Homeland Citizenship Act – you know what that means? That black people were told they weren't even citizens of South Africa. The Sharpeville massacre, that was pretty racist. Having to be white to be allowed to vote? Racist. And locking up Nelson Mandela. He should be President, not your racist Mr de Klerk.'

Janie looked at the crowd, which was now considerable. More of them were sympathetic to her than to Tamsin.

'Did you hear that?' she asked, laughing. 'Nelson Mandela for President? If he's ever President of South Africa, I will dance naked down Queen's Street. The man is nothing but a black terrorist, and you are nothing but a *red Communist*!' She looked at the audience. 'De Klerk's almost as bad, mind. But, Nelson Mandela? Tamsin, you make it too easy. He'll die in prison. And you can go back to Peking with your Communist friends!'

Most people laughed.

In the car, Tamsin looked at her mother. 'You teach Janie,' she said. 'How can you? Why don't you get a job at a proper school, where there wouldn't be so many fascists? Whatever the issues might be, at least normal schools don't accept fascism. Doesn't it depress you?'

Her mother fiddled with a strand of greying hair. 'Don't misuse "fascism", Tamsin. It devalues it. I teach her French. That's all I do. If I taught politics, or religion, or even history or geography, I can see that I'd find it harder. As it is, we just talk about hobbies and transport systems, and *Le Grand Meaulnes*. And when there are subtexts, Janie doesn't get them. And you know what, Tam? You make me feel bad. You're so passionate about things that I believe in too that I feel slightly ashamed of myself because I never bother to pick anyone up on anything any more. I ought to stand up for my principles, like you do. And maybe I should leave Lodwell's one day and go and teach at a comprehensive. I've always said to your dad that when you and Billy leave home, we should go abroad. I'd like to do VSO or something, teach in Africa or India.'

'Good plan.'

'I'm sorry you hate school.'

'Not your fault.'

'Why don't you start planning a gap year? Sign up for a programme somewhere. Get out there and make a difference, and meet some like-minded people? Put a big distance between yourself and the Janies of this world.'

Tamsin thought about it. She had never seriously considered a gap year. That must mean she was institutionalised, too.

'I'll think about it,' she conceded.

Meanwhile, she was counting off the days. She had made herself a neat calendar, each month on its own sheet of A4, which she stuck across the wall above her bed. Every single afternoon, she would cross a day off the list as soon as she got home from school. She already felt as if she had been in the sixth form for ever, but the calendar revealed otherwise. It was not quite Christmas. She was almost one-sixth of her way through, which was demoralising.

She threw herself on her bed and thought about homework. There was nothing she had to do for tomorrow, because she had started her English essay in the library earlier. She looked around. Her bedroom was her little domain, and she vowed to get a Nelson Mandela poster for the wall, to go next to her *Cry Freedom* one. She had the Cure up there, and the Smiths, and U2, although she was considering taking that one down. She was particularly proud of her Ladysmith Black Mambazo picture.

Her clothes were all over the floor, and there were books piled up on every surface. Many of them were overdue library books. Some of them had coffee rings on them, and on the window sill there was a cup she kept forgetting to take downstairs. The small amount of coffee in the bottom of it had first grown a soft skin, and then green mould had started to climb up the sides. It was delicate and rather beautiful, and she kept putting off the day when she would wash it all down the sink.

She had bought a purple Indian bedspread at a junk shop a while ago, although she always forgot to pull it over her bed, so it was usually, as today, crumpled on the floor. In fact, her room was a complete mess. She had only one solution: to go downstairs for some toast. And then she would think about a gap year.

Izzy came by later, on her bike. She was fearless at negotiating the busy road between Dinas and Penarth, and she made no concessions to practicality in her outfits. She turned up in a thick grey skirt that reached her ankles, and a pair of high-heeled black boots. Her helmet was still swinging from her handlebars, where it had encumbered her progress for the three-mile journey. She stood on the doorstep, rosy-cheeked and happy.

'Railway?' she asked Tamsin, who picked up her coat and called to her mother.

'Off to the Railway!'

'Be home by eleven!' her father called, from somewhere in the depths of the house.

'Quick!' Tamsin shut the door behind her and set off as briskly as she could up the garden path. It was starting to rain, but she didn't care, partly because the pub was less than five minutes' walk from her house, and partly because she didn't look any worse with wet hair than she did with dry. They had almost reached the corner, with Izzy pushing her bike, when Tamsin heard fast footsteps behind them.

Billy was out of breath. He caught up, and Tamsin turned and looked daggers at him.

'Can I come?' he asked hopefully. He took something from his pocket. 'Look!' he said, straightening a ten-pound note and showing it to the girls. 'It's my round!'

Tamsin looked at her brother. He was fifteen and annoying. She did not want to be seen in the pub with him, and normally he wouldn't be seen in her company, either. He was, however, infatuated with Izzy, which meant that whenever Isabelle was nearby, hostilities were suspended. Billy had a babyish face, with clear skin that his sister envied, and wide, lazy eyes. His looks held together in a way that Tamsin felt her own pointy countenance did not, and she was certain that in a few years he would have girls falling at his feet. Nothing would have induced her to tell him that.

She looked questioningly at Izzy.

'Sure,' said Isabelle. 'The others'll be there and I think Jackie's going to come along with Suzii.'

'Urgh,' said Billy, smiling at Izzy. 'That Jackie is a pest.'

'Really? I'd have thought you'd have liked her. She's very pretty.'

'Nah. Not my type.' His gaze did not deviate from the object of his adoration. In fact, the sole thing he and Jackie had in common was their shared love of Isabelle.

'Jesus, Billy,' said Tamsin, disgusted. 'You're like a lovesick puppy. Leave Izzy alone. You're embarrassing her.'

They found Amanda and Suzii occupying a booth, which was modelled on some sort of old-fashioned train compartment. It was a prized place to sit. Both of them were drinking Southern Comfort and lemonade. Although it was a Thursday, the pub was packed with their contemporaries, with people they had known for years and years. Tamsin was finding it easier to chat to normal people these days, and she was happy to be friendly to people who had previously given her the wide berth that was merited by someone who wore a green felt hat to school.

She and Izzy squeezed in. Tamsin turned to Billy.

'Go on then,' she ordered. 'Buy us a drink. Let's see you getting served.'

Billy rose to the challenge, taking his ID reverently from his pocket, straightening it out, and clasping it between finger and thumb as he elbowed his way to the bar. It was a bad double photocopy of his birth certificate, with the date of birth ineptly Tippexed out and inked in with a biro. Since he went to the local comprehensive, Billy was on easy terms with everybody in the room, and Tamsin envied him that as well. She watched him smiling, waving, slapping shoulders as he worked his way through the room. Then his back was absorbed into the throng, clad in a shabby, baggy charcoal jumper. Twenty minutes later he reappeared, and triumphantly placed five glasses on the table.

'Southern Comfort and lemonade all round!' he announced.

'They served you?'

'Looks like. Budge up.'

'Did they look at your ID?'

'Nope. Not even.'

Tamsin shook her head. 'This place is long overdue a raid.'

'You do realise,' said Amanda, 'that we won't be able to come here any more when we're eighteen. It'll be too annoying for us, seeing everyone else drinking underage.'

'I know,' Suzii agreed. 'We won't even need ID any more.'

'We might,' Izzy pointed out, 'but we can use real ID. Too easy.'

They all nodded, frustrated at the distance that still lay between themselves and real adulthood. Tamsin imagined going out for what her parents liked to call 'a *civilised* drink', by which they meant a nice pub or bar, somewhere that was not crammed with vomiting teenagers. She pictured herself at university, perhaps in Cambridge, sitting in a beautiful old pub filled with dark wood and leaflets for Bach recitals, sipping a glass of cold white wine. Izzy could be with her.

She glanced at Amanda, who was currently throwing herself wholeheartedly into a Sloaney aesthetic. Amanda was wearing a navy blue rugby shirt with its collar turned up around a string of fake pearls, and a pair of tight cords, and she had already gulped down her Southern Comfort. She wore frosted pink lipstick and pale blue eyeshadow, and Tamsin was unable, for now, to place her in the Cambridge pub. The same applied to Suzii, who was laughing raucously with a tall, spotty boy who was standing next to their table. He was looking down at Suzii, whose hair was shorter and spikier than ever, with a glint in his eye. Suzii did that to men. They took one look at her, and decided that she was sure to be up for it.

'Amanda,' Tamsin said, suddenly wondering why they hadn't been having this conversation incessantly.

'Mmm?'

'Where do you want to go to uni?' None of them had really bothered deciding yet, although many other girls in their year were frantically obsessing over courses.

'Oh, shit, I don't know,' Amanda said, leaning across the table and shouting over the din of U2. 'Bristol, maybe? Exeter? Durham? Not really thought about it. Might do history. You? After today's little fight you must be doing politics, yeah?'

'Maybe English. Not sure. But I was thinking of applying for Cambridge.'

Amanda laughed. 'Yeah? That would be cool. We could all come and visit you, go punting and shit. English at Cambridge. Very un-Tamsin.'

Izzy butted in. 'I'm going to apply to music colleges as well as for English. See if anybody wants me for either. But I think it's more interesting to think about what we'd like to do afterwards. I mean, where do we see ourselves in, say, ten years' time?' They all laughed at the very idea of being twenty-seven. 'OK,' Izzy continued, still obliged to shout. 'I'll start. I'd like to be married to someone wonderful. With a job in an orchestra or maybe working for a publisher. Have my first child on the way, a girl who I will call Poppy. Living in a big house in London, but going to the seaside for weekends. We'll have a gorgeous little cottage right on the beach, somewhere like Suffolk.' She smiled. 'Amanda?'

'Oh, shit. Me. Um, married too, and not having to worry about cash. I'd like to work in PR, running my own incredibly successful company. My husband would need to be filthy rich, too, probably one of those city guys. So we'd be in London as well as we'd have dinner parties with Izzy and her man. Holiday home in the Caribbean, and a cleaner, and designer clothes made specially for me by the designers who are so grateful for the amazing PR I do for them. Child some time after I'm thirty, but only one because I wouldn't want it to get in the way of my career or my flat stomach.' She smiled, pleased with her vision. 'That's me. Suzii?'

Suzii was still trading banter with the young man, so Tamsin stepped in instead.

'I want to do something that matters,' she said, suddenly fired up. 'I want to make a difference to someone. In ten years, I'd like to be living in South Africa, running an orphanage or something. Working with children in the townships. I could have a boyfriend, but I'll be married to my work, and my children will be the kids I look after, because there'll be no point me bringing another child into the world when there are so many who have nothing. I'll live on a pittance but it won't matter because I'll still be rich compared to everyone else.'

'Oh, Tamsin!' Amanda complained. 'Now you've made me and Izzy look really grasping and uncaring.' She tugged Suzii's arm, and forced her into the conversation. '*Suzii!* You've got to tell us where you see yourself in ten years' time! Come on.'

Suzii looked at their faces, blankly. 'Ten years? Blimey. Umm, still here, I suppose. Been to uni, come back to Cardiff, hanging out with you guys. I'd like to be an artist, maybe work with Chapter. Be free. Go out to dinner. Maybe have a boyfriend but I don't want to get married till I'm about thirty.' She glanced up at the boy and gave him a look that promised everything. 'Until then I'm young, free and single.' He smiled down at her.

Tamsin leaned forward. 'Why don't we make a plan?' she suggested. 'Why don't we meet up when we're grown up? We can fix it now. And we have to stick to it. We have to meet up when we're really old, like more than thirty. See what's happened to us all. What do you think?'

chapter eleven

I wanted them to see me before I saw them. I held myself rigid, and looked away from the people who were milling around the baggage reclaim. I was swirling with adrenaline, and was fighting the urge to turn and flee. There was a map on the upper level of the airport, a Ryanair map of their destinations. I stared at it, hating myself, until I heard my name.

She said it again, closer. I looked around, and there was Amanda. 'Susie!' Amanda said, a third time. Her voice was warm, pleased.

'Amanda!' I exclaimed. Amanda was twice the size she had been at school. 'Oh, my goodness, sorry, I was miles away. Hey, you look fabulous. Come here!'

I gave Amanda a hug, feeling the surprising bulk of her. Amanda was polished, as I had known she would be, with a deep tan that may or may not have been real, heavy eye make-up, and gold jewellery. But she was fat. In fact, she felt nice to hug. She felt like a mother. We kissed each other on both cheeks, and I realised that I really had missed Amanda, and that I was genuinely glad she had come. Her breath smelt alcoholic.

The children were bigger than I had expected, and this was intangibly annoying. They seemed polite and I knew at once that their parents had them under control. My nightmare – a house full of ADHD kids – was unlikely to be realised. The boy and girl said hello, looking at me closely, sizing me up. I stared them out without any problems.

I kissed Patrick, marvelling at the fact that he had lost almost all of his hair since Izzy's wedding.

'Seen the others?' I asked, suddenly buoyant and confident. I rubbed Amanda's shoulder. Everything about her – her very Amandaness – was as familiar as my own reflection. I was hit by a wave of slightly sickly nostalgia. We should have stayed in touch. It seemed impossible that such a close friendship could be shattered so abruptly. It would be rekindled. I knew it. Something good had already come out of the weekend.

'Mmm.' Amanda frowned. 'We met Izzy at Stansted. Then she and Tamsin were chatting on the plane. Thick as thieves.'

'And here they are!' said Patrick jovially. I looked at him curiously. He clearly had no idea what role he was meant to be playing. 'Excuse me,' he added. 'I'll sort out the hire car. Amanda, do you want to drive, or not?'

'Not,' she told him firmly.

Two women were approaching. I realised, to my horror, that the fat one had once been Isabelle. Her short hair did nothing for her neck or her chin. I sized her up in an instant. Now I understood why she had been worried about everything on the phone. She had no confidence.

Tamsin, on the other hand, had blossomed. She had sorted out her hair, dyeing it almost the same colour as my own, and cutting it into a jaw-length, fringeless bob with plenty of layering, which suited her perfectly. She had traded her glasses for lenses, which revealed her eyes, as wide and suggestive as her little brother's had always been. She was beautifully dressed in classic black pieces. I felt overdressed. I knew the hat had been a mistake.

When Tamsin looked at me, and our eyes met, something inside me recoiled. I inhaled sharply, and then blinked and smiled.

Izzy, Tamsin and Sam had a trolley between them, and Sam was sitting on top of the cases. The women were still chatting as they watched me approaching.

'Hello there!' said Izzy, breaking off. She opened her arms. 'Susie! It's good to see you.'

'You too,' I said, adjusting my hat, and vowing to ditch it when we reached the car. 'And you, Tamsin.' Tamsin's hug was less flamboyant. I rubbed her bony back to compensate. 'And you must be Sam. Hello, Sam.' I didn't quite know how to talk to someone who was three. I probably sounded offhand.

'Hello Susie,' Sam said, gravely. He was a cute-looking child, with blond hair and a button nose.

'Right,' said Izzy briskly, taking Sam's hand to try to encourage him off the trolley. He pushed her away.

'Susie, I'm not allowed to ask if you've got a baby in your tummy,' he said solemnly.

I stared, and took a deep breath.

'Ask, if you like,' I told him, thrown off balance. 'I haven't got a baby in my tummy, because I don't want one.' I looked sharply at Izzy. 'Does that answer everyone's queries?'

The drive home had never felt so long. I had planned to chat airily about this and that; to begin catching up with my friends' lives. Instead, I felt the presence of Tamsin next to me as a kind of black hole. Every time I opened my mouth to say anything, Tamsin stopped me. The fact that Tamsin was next to me stopped me. Izzy and Sam were in the back, but when I tried to talk to them instead, I couldn't get a conversation going. It was stilted, because Izzy was embarrassed at Sam's earlier rudeness, and I was sorry that I had snapped at them, but I didn't want to say so. More than that, though, I was confused about Izzy. I had, somehow, stolen her looks.

We passed through a village. I normally sped through places like this, but today I followed the law and slowed down to a frustratingly sedate fifty kilometres per hour. There was an oldish woman standing on the verge, and she gave me a suspicious look. I waved at her, and the woman held my gaze sternly, as if she knew that I normally hurtled past, heedless of old people, children, or dogs.

'Do you know her?' Tamsin asked, craning her neck back to watch the woman receding behind them.

'No,' I said.

'So why did you wave?'

'Because she was staring and I wanted to make her smile.'

'But she didn't.'

'Worth a try.'

'Mmmm.'

In my rear-view mirror, I watched Patrick, who was driving the hire car a safe distance behind me, ignoring the woman, who was now staring at him and Amanda. Tamsin's existence, in my own passenger seat, was tying my stomach in knots and making my heart race. I gripped the steering wheel. There was no backing out now. I was going to have to go through with this.

As I drove downhill to the turning to the house, I put my foot on the brake. We had passed through countryside and villages, past maize fields and sunflowers, for nearly an hour. I wanted the arrival at my own domain to be dramatic. So I indicated right, slowed to a stop, and turned to Izzy in the back.

'Right,' I said, brightly. 'Here we are. This is it.'

And I swung my car round the corner.

Tamsin had been adjusting the air conditioning all the way back. It was irritating. On a baking day like this, I liked my car to be chilled. I liked slight goose pimples up my bare arms, because then I got to enjoy the heat all over again when the journey was over. I liked to arrive crisp and refreshed, like an iceberg lettuce from a fridge.

Tamsin raised her eyebrows. 'We're there?' she said.

In front of us stood a stone farmhouse. It had three windows upstairs and two windows, a big wooden door, and a smaller kitchen door downstairs. The shutters were bright blue. Everyone except Sam, who was asleep, narrowed their eyes at the glare the sun made as it hit the pale stone. I sighed as I looked at the thick walls. Nobody would have any idea how much expense had gone into them. The scaffolding had been up for months and Roman and I had been forced to spend almost all our time in my tiny London flat, entertaining friends with tales of French builders, aware even as we told them that the stories were clichés incarnate. Roman had had an attack of cabin fever almost immediately. He could happily spend a week in London, drinking, eating Thai and Indian food, and going to the cinema, but after that he hated being away from his waves and his mountains. He was a funny mixture of sports fanatic and hedonist.

The house was rustic and beautiful. It had, now, been gorgeously renovated. It was set a little way back from the road, and the front garden was grassed over, with a small wrought-iron table and chairs, and climbing roses covering the walls.

I drove slowly past the house, and pulled in on the driveway to the side. I looked expectantly at my three passengers. Sam was asleep at an awkward-looking angle on the little booster seat. Isabelle and Tamsin were both looking at me and laughing.

'Good God, Susie,' said Isabelle. 'Is this your house?'

I smiled and nodded.

'Nice one, Susie,' said Tamsin, laughing. 'You win.'

It was a knife through my heart. 'What do you mean, I win?'

'I mean you've clearly beaten us all.' Tamsin pushed her glossy dark hair back from her face. 'I mean it nicely, Susie. It's a wonderful house. Can we see the inside?'

I forced a dazzling smile and told myself not to take it the wrong way. Tamsin had always been slightly abrasive, and God knows she had a reason to be. I unclicked my seat belt and jumped out, into the heat, eager to hear what Amanda had to say.

chapter twelve

Amanda had a headache. The blasted heat didn't help. She sat on the bed and massaged her temples. The guest room was lovely. The walls were rough and white and the view of the trees was almost relaxing. Susie had gone to a stupid amount of trouble. There were budding flowers in a vase, and the whole room was slightly scented with lavender oil. The sheets were white linen. It was like a secret hotel.

If only she didn't have so much on her mind. She closed her eyes and tried to breathe deeply. Susie had told them to meet at seven for cocktails on the terrace. If only she could lie down now and sleep for an hour or so. That would make everything better. She would be able to perk up in time for drinks. In fact the very idea of cocktails was soothing.

Patrick plumped down next to her on the bed.

'All right, old girl?' he said kindly. He stroked her hair. She slapped his hand away.

'Don't call me old girl,' she muttered.

'I'm sorry. Try to relax. This is a great spot and Susie's very nice. We should think about a place in France. It's civilised. I know you can enjoy yourself if you let go a bit.' He started massaging her shoulders. 'We've got a couple of hours until we're needed. Let me try to help you unwind.'

Amanda frowned. This was Patrick's stock response. If anything at all was bothering her, he suggested sex. He did not understand her at all. She shook him off. Now, as well as everything else, she had to feel guilty about turning him down yet again. Ever since their marriage, Amanda had been keeping a mental list of reasons why Patrick might leave her. Her lack of interest in what she liked to call 'the physical side of things' was currently heading the list.

She turned to look at him. 'What do you mean, "Susie's very nice"?' she demanded.

Patrick snorted. 'It's not in code, is it?'

'Do you fancy her?'

He sighed. 'No. I do not fancy her.'

'What if you weren't married?'

'Not even if I wasn't married.'

'If I died, ten years later?'

'No.'

'If you'd never met me?'

'No.'

'You are allowed to say yes, you know.'

'I know I am allowed to, but my answer is no. Susie is nice but I could never have any of those sort of feelings for her, not under any circumstances.'

Amanda hated herself. She knew that Patrick probably did fancy Susie, because he was a man and Susie had become weirdly beautiful. She also knew that he would never admit it because, on one occasion only, he had given the 'what if you weren't married?' question serious consideration and had agreed that yes, if he had never met Amanda, he would have found the woman in question fairly attractive. Amanda remembered vividly who this woman was. She had worked at an exclusive little nursery that Jake had attended as a toddler. Amanda had withdrawn Jakey at once and had not spoken to Patrick for four days. That admission had been Patrick's greatest mistake of the marriage. At least, Amanda hoped it had.

'The kids'll be in the pool,' she said. 'Why don't you take your book down there and keep an eye? Work on your tan? Make them put some suncream on, while you're at it.'

Patrick seemed about to protest, but instead he sighed, and picked up his book. On the way out of the door, he turned back to her.

'You're all right?' he asked. 'Do you promise? No tears when I'm gone?'

'No tears when you're gone,' she confirmed. 'I'm just a bit tired and headachy. I might have a lie-down. Come and wake me at half six.'

She lay back on the impeccable sheets and tried to sleep. She didn't even have much of a headache, and she knew that Patrick probably did. Her mind would not shut down. What would she wear this evening? Everything seemed strange and different from the way she had expected it. Things felt formal. Susie was slightly aloof, and unrecognisable from her old self. All three of them had changed more than she felt she had.

She ought to shower before dinner. It would take an hour to shower, dry her hair, change, and do her make-up. That meant she had to get going at six. It was twenty to five. There was still time for a nap.

She never wanted sex any more. It wasn't Patrick's fault; it was her own. She knew she was too stressed. She hated her body and she could not bear to have it exposed. A bath was depressing enough. She had long ago lost the sexual urge anyway. Nothing turned her on. Patrick never had, not really, not fully. That part of her life was over. From time to time, she did as Patrick wished, but that was purely to stop him from getting it somewhere else.

On paper, her life was perfect. She knew that she was going to spend the evening showing it off. Look: my two beautiful, well-mannered children. Look: I'm the only one with a husband! Look: we have a house in Clapham, yes a house, a whole house with three storeys and a garden. Look at me: I don't have to work, I go to an expensive gym, I drive a huge car, we're off to the Caribbean for Christmas.

Look: my compulsive eating has finally overcome my bulimia and made me fat. I can't be bothered to throw it all up any more. Guess what? I usually do the afternoon school run drunk and

Patrick probably secretly knows that but does nothing to stop me. Look: I cannot settle for one instant because I am obsessed with thoughts of the first cocktail of the evening and I am really, really hoping that Susie has got something chocolatey for pudding.

Look at me: my life is held together by a fraying thread. One day soon, it's going to snap.

She was staring at the ceiling when she heard footsteps on the landing, followed by a quiet knock on her door.

'Hello?' she called.

The door opened and Susie's head appeared. She was smiling. Amanda heaved herself upright and forced a smile in return. Susie came in and sat on the end of the bed.

'Hello,' she said, happily. 'I couldn't wait to see you. Is everything all right?'

'It's fine,' Amanda told her. 'Susie, you look amazing. And all this is . . . amazing, too.'

'Thanks. I can't believe you've got a family. It seems so grown-up.' She looked around and laughed. 'How did it come to this?'

Amanda wasn't in the mood. 'The years passed. It happens. What about Izzy?'

Susie was cautious. 'She seems very happy with motherhood.'

'Mmm. Don't you think she's changed, though?'

'Well, of course she looks different. She's grown up.'

Amanda was longing to be malicious, and she was disappointed. 'We all have,' she said shortly. 'And Tamsin's grown into her looks, just like her mother used to say she would.'

As soon as she mentioned Mrs Grey, she regretted it. She looked away, but heard Susie's sharp intake of breath. Susie stood up and walked to the window.

'Hasn't she just?' she said. 'She seems happy.'

Amanda snorted. 'Lucky her.'

'You're happy, though, surely?'

Amanda stopped herself rolling her eyes. 'People always think that if you're married with kids you have to be happy. Ridiculous, considering the divorce statistics.'

Susie raised her eyebrows. 'Sorry,' she said, sounding offended. 'What, are you not happy?'

'Yes, yes, perfectly happy, thanks. I don't need to ask about you, do I?'

'Ask if you like.'

They stared at each other. Amanda was not sure what to say. She wondered whether she was supposed to be apologising. If that was what Susie was waiting for, she was going to be disappointed. Susie seemed about to say something, but thought better of it.

'Right,' she said. 'I'd better get on. See you at seven.'

Amanda smiled. 'Sure. Looking forward to it.'

She lay back on the pillows, curiously deflated. This was not how it should have been. She listened to the hum of voices downstairs. She could hear the high-pitched whiny voice of Izzy's Sam, and Izzy's lower tones coaxing him to do something. There was a sudden burst of female laughter. She curled around herself and squeezed her eyes shut. She was not a part of this gathering. She did not want to join in. Once she was on the terrace in her dress with a drink in her hand, everything would be all right. She closed her eyes and tried to think of nothing.

chapter thirteen

Lodwell's, 1990

Amanda sat by the window in the sixth-form common room, and stared down at the ground below. She was tingling with her secret; excited by the gulf between what she ought to do and what she knew she was going to do. She looked without interest at the teachers' cars and a couple of token borders with wilting pansies and encroaching weeds. There was a light drizzle which had already made the tarmac shiny. Usually, this was excruciatingly depressing. She scanned what she could see of the sky. There was a patch of cloud which was just a little bit brighter than the others, a clue that the sun was behind it. That was bloody it, as far as daylight was concerned. Usually, February was her worst month.

Dieting was all right in the summer. She could pretty much do it – shorts and swimming costumes were an excellent motivator. In summer she was hugely aware of her pot belly sticking out in front of her, and her arse dangling along behind, and so she could drum up the motivation to avoid food for days at a time. Winter was different, and February was the worst of all. She still had her Christmas fat, and it was freezing and wet, and she could hide her shameful lumps and bumps under navy blue jumpers and crisp pink shirts. Today, however, she simply did not care. She unwrapped a Mars bar and carefully bit the chocolate off its top as she turned her gaze to the builders who were working on the new block of the junior school. She could only just see his outline, but that was enough to make her feel very, very strange.

Amanda had not even hinted at it to her best friends, but she was tingling with sex. She had a boyfriend, but he bored her to tears. Every day this week, the builder, who was only young, and whose name she didn't know, had singled her out on her way past. On Monday, he had watched her walking by, and when she was nearly gone, he whistled and said, 'All right, lovely?' She knew that the proper thing to do was to ignore him, but she hadn't wanted to, so she turned and flashed him her biggest, most suggestive smile. He was ready for her on Tuesday.

'Hello again, darling!' he had shouted, and she stopped, just for a moment, and looked at him, and said, 'Hello,' before walking on.

Today was Wednesday. This morning, he had been braver. 'Hey, love, what's your name?' he said, jumping down from his scaffolding and walking towards her.

'Amanda,' she told him, hearing the crisp poshness of her voice. She caught her breath. She thought that this was probably her sexual awakening. How weird that it was with this scruffy builder, standing outside school, in the rain.

'Hi, Amanda.' They smiled shyly. 'Want to get a drink with me later?'

She knew she should have said no. She ought to have gone straight to Miss Higgins's office and reported him. He would have been sacked on the spot.

She was meeting him at half past six in the centre of town. She had not yet decided what story to spin to her parents, but she knew she'd get away with something.

The day passed agonisingly slowly. Suzii asked, a couple of times, what was wrong. Amanda almost told her at lunchtime, but she changed her mind and said she was depressed at being fat. That was a story Suzii was never going to question, and they wandered off together in a huddle, to talk about the Hip and Thigh Diet,

Callanetics, and something Suzii had read an article about called food combining. They agreed to support each other and give it a try. First of all, though, they had to find out what it was, and Suzii couldn't quite remember where she'd read about it. It might have been in her mother's *Good Housekeeping*. It sounded unlikely to Amanda that eating protein separately to carbohydrates, or something like that, could work, but science was a strange thing and she would give it a go.

'Doing anything later?' Tamsin asked, in the middle of the afternoon.

Amanda was nervous. 'What do you mean?'

'Want to wander into town after? Mum's got a staff meeting. Thought I'd look at the shops and get a train home.'

Amanda considered this. 'I'm meeting someone at half six by Central Station. But I've got to go home first. So I guess not – sorry.'

'Meeting Julian?'

She hesitated. 'I might chuck Julian.'

Tamsin was brisk. 'Good plan. He's too drippy for you. Giving him the elbow tonight?'

'Might do.'

They headed off in different directions, Tamsin to economics, and Amanda to the library, where she spent her study period staring at raindrops on the window, doodling patterns in her rough book, and gazing randomly at the spine of a book on a shelf, called *Physics for the Inquiring Mind*. As far as she was aware, that book had not moved from its spot on that shelf in all the years she had been at the school. She walked over to it, purposefully, and took it down. It smelt musty, and the pages were yellow. The last time it was taken out of the library, it had been due back on 24 January 1974. Clearly, the physics department of Lodwell's did not nurture many inquiring minds, and this did not surprise Amanda in the least.

Eventually, it was the end of the school day. Amanda lived in Llandaff, so she rushed home to shower and change. She told her mother she was going out to History Revision Club at Anne-Marie's house.

'Right,' said her mother, who was just in from work herself, and who, Amanda knew, would welcome the quiet house to do her Open University essay. 'Are you being fed?'

'Yep.'

'Sure?'

'Anne-Marie's Mum's ordering us all pizzas.'

'Take a tenner from my purse to chuck into the pot. Have a good time. Don't be late.'

Amanda changed into her black underwear and eyed herself critically in the mirror. In a way she was glad to be tall, because fat was more obvious on short people. She had read that in magazines. It did, however, make it almost impossible for her to go below nine stone, and if she didn't watch what she ate all the bloody time, she would easily top eleven. 'Eleven stone' was the phrase that struck most horror into her heart, and for now she was edging uneasily around nine stone two. She decided to cover up her bulges quickly, before they made her cry. She was only going for a drink with the builder. He was not going to get close enough to be disgusted by her fat. She dressed in a bright blue miniskirt that was made from some felty material that seemed to make her legs look all right, and thick black tights (slimming), and a dark blue Benetton sweater, tight over a camisole. She wished she owned a pair of knee-high boots, but she didn't, and so she decided on black court shoes with a tiny heel. She let her hair loose, and flicked it over sideways, applying liberal amounts of gel to keep it there. Thick foundation, bright blue eyeliner, light blue eyeshadow, and pink frosted lipstick followed, and she was ready to go. She listened for her mother. When a mutter of 'Oh, botheration' suggested that Mum was safely tucked into Amanda's parents' bedroom, Amanda bolted for the door. 'Bye, Mum!' she yelled, and slammed it shut behind her. Even Amanda's mother, the most trusting parent in the known universe, might have had suspicions aroused by the sight of her teenage daughter heading to History Revision Club in a tiny skirt and full make-up.

He was there, outside Central Station, just as they had agreed. Amanda observed him for a second. He should have been the sort of man she avoided. He was wearing a button-down shirt, pale green, and aftershave. There were creases ironed into his trousers. His light brown hair was spiked up a little on top – like Susie's, she thought.

She normally laughed at people like him. Yet, when she saw him, her stomach leapt into her ribcage and she folded her arms so he wouldn't see she was shaking.

His face lit up with a huge smile, and Amanda felt herself smiling back with the same delight. This was freaking her out a bit; she had never felt anything like it in her life.

'I don't even know your name,' she told him, tingling all over.

'Dai. Amanda, you look superb.'

'Thanks, Dai.' Her smile creased her face in a way that never normally happened.

'Do you want to jump in the van?' He indicated it with his head. 'I know a good place for us to get a drink.'

She adored sitting up in the front of his white van. She felt like his posh girl, his Uptown Girl. She liked having a Bit of Rough. She couldn't stop looking at him and smiling. His face was almost handsome, with the beginnings of laughter lines. His eyes were dark, and she longed for him to turn them back on her. He navigated the city centre expertly, and drove north to Fairwater, a part of Cardiff she had never visited, even though it bordered Llandaff, where she lived.

'Where are you from, Amanda?' he asked. 'Not round here, I bet.'

'Llandaff. Not far.'

He laughed. 'Course you are. Hope you don't mind me bringing you here. It's just that here's where I know.'

'Not at all. It's interesting to see another part of town.'

'Interesting!' He looked at her again, his eyes amused, boring into her. 'It's that all right.'

They sat inside a large, smoky pub. Dai waved to a few people, but he didn't talk to any of them. He bought Amanda a gin and tonic, and then a vodka and tonic, and then three pints of lager in quick succession. She chatted to him and giggled at him, and found herself leaning towards him. He put an arm round her and her stomach flipped over. For dinner, they had two packets of salt and vinegar crisps, and then they went out to the van, which Dai had parked, with some foresight, in the far corner of the car park. He unlocked the back doors and jumped inside, grinning wickedly and motioning her in with his head.

'Cleaned it out for you earlier,' he said, 'just in case.'

'Cheeky sod,' she retorted, and jumped up after him. He closed the doors carefully, grabbed Amanda around her waist, and pulled her close. She kissed him, wrapped her legs around him, and then joyously, if not entirely comfortably, lost her virginity to him, as the van rocked with abandon in the corner of the car park. For the first time in Amanda's life, she completely forgot to be ashamed of her body.

chapter fourteen

Jake sat on his bed. Freya sat on hers.

'Action Man!' Jake said. He widened his eyes.

'Barbie!' said Freya. She tried not to smile.

They looked at each other and laughed. 'It's because she hasn't got any children,' Jake said. 'She doesn't know that Action Man and Barbie are for, like, five-year-olds. I quite like this guy though,' he said, picking up the Action Man figure from his pillow.

'Maybe she's had other children staying who were younger than us,' suggested Freya, undressing her yoga Barbie.

Her brother shook his head. 'I reckon not. Look, you can see these are brand new. They've still got the creases on from the packet.'

'You're right. She got them for us.'

They sat and contemplated Freya's garish duvet for a while. 'I should give these Action Man sheets to the little kid,' said Jake. 'He'd like them, I bet.'

Freya giggled. 'You shouldn't! I'll tell you why. You'd have to swap. I saw his bed, and he's got Teletubbies.'

Jake's jaw dropped. 'No way! Everyone knows Teletubbies are only for actual *babies*.'

Freya shook her head. 'I know that. She doesn't. Shall we go for a swim?'

Jake nodded, and wrapped a towel around his waist to begin changing.

'Don't bother,' said his sister. 'You turn that way and I'll turn this way. We'll both do a quick change. No looking.'

He nodded. This house was cool, and the pool looked brilliant. There was tons of exploring to be done in the garden. He thought this was going to be an all right weekend.

chapter fifteen

The house was full and I had never felt so alone. I hid in the kitchen. Everything was organised, the children's food was almost ready, and I was supposed to be on the terrace. At this point in the schedule, I should have been officially opening the reunion weekend. Instead, I skulked, making work for myself where there was none.

I could hear my guests out there, but I couldn't see them. Roman had brought me a vodka and tonic and made me promise to come out as soon as I could. The kitchen was uncomfortably hot, with the oven at two hundred degrees. I was sweating, which could prove disastrous for my silk dress. I opened the oven door and was greeted with a blast of scalding air. The potatoes were still fine. The chickens were still nowhere near ready. And I already knew that.

The fish fingers were ready to go into the frying pan, when they were needed. I did not have to stand over them.

Everyone was fine out there. They were wittering about how gorgeous it was, about how the early evening sun lit the house up like gold. Roman was pouring drinks so fast I thought he might strain his arm.

I longed to talk to somebody, properly. Amanda had brushed

me off, and I was still smarting. Tamsin was giving me the creeps, just by her very presence. Izzy was the only one of the three of them that I felt able to have a conversation with, and she had been non-stop busy with her little boy. He was, I now admitted, rather sweet. I had misjudged him at first. Earlier, I caught myself staring and smiling when I watched him climbing on the low branches of the little fig tree, laughing with excitement and pride.

My eyes watered as I shut the oven door.

The starter was gazpacho which was chilled in the fridge. The table was laid. The salad was in the fridge, as was its dressing. Pudding was ready to go. I could find nothing, at all, to do.

I could hear them talking. A woman laughed. I didn't know which of them it was. I shook my head and wondered at myself. These people were here because of me. I was wearing full battle dress and warpaint. Every part of me was buffed, highlighted, varnished or plucked, as appropriate. Usually, that was enough to keep me going.

I sidled through the glass door, onto the terrace, without giving myself the option of reconsidering. Nobody noticed me. I gave my studio a wistful glance. I would have given anything to have been in there, creating a gorgeous painting. One, ideally, that did not feature Sarah Saunders.

Amanda had made an effort, in a nice pink Chanel dress that I had tried on in London, though Amanda's was several sizes larger. Like me, she was made up as if for the stage, and she was just as nervous as I was, judging by the way she was knocking back her drink. Patrick looked bored in a short-sleeved white shirt and a pair of slacks, and Roman was carrying off navy linen with his usual aplomb. Tamsin was frighteningly chic in black.

As for Izzy . . . I almost felt a physical pain on Izzy's behalf. Her dress was white, with a pattern of small rosebuds. As I edged closer, I heard Tamsin saying to her, 'But Izzy, you look lovely.'

'Oh, you're being too nice,' Izzy replied, sounding relaxed. 'It's Top Shop, but it was all I could afford. I knew I wouldn't be smart enough, but it covers the worst of my upper arms, and it's the best shape for me at the moment, so that's the most that could be done, unfortunately.'

'No,' Tamsin replied, looking intensely into Izzy's face. 'You look great. You look like yourself, not like some, some *footballer's wife.*'

I told myself that Tamsin was referring to Amanda, but I knew she meant me, too. I put my hand to my mouth, as if remembering a kitchen emergency, and fled.

'You all right?'

I spun round. Tamsin was in the doorway, holding a bottle of gin and another of tonic. I hated gin and I never drank it, ever. Gin was a depressant, and it affected me instantly (so much so that it was certainly psychological). When I drank it, I started to doubt everything. I often wondered why people liked it so much. I thought it was probably not coincidence that G&T was a quintessentially British confection. It chimed with the British character in some way. Gin was probably like cannabis. I had made numerous attempts to develop a cannabis habit when I was living in the squat. It sunk me into paranoid depression, while rendering stronger characters happily mellow. Vodka and champagne, separately, were my tipples of choice. I went for uppers every time. Coffee was my best friend; chocolate my worst enemy.

Tamsin was smiling. She was slender and toned, rather than skinny and scrawny as she used to be, and I realised that she must exercise. She would not have dreamed of that in her teenage years. Through gritted teeth, I told myself that I was glad that Tamsin had grown into herself. It was not Tamsin's fault that her particular brand of minimal stylishness made me feel flouncy. I felt like a royal bridesmaid intruding into the Matrix. I felt – she was right – like a footballer's wife.

It took me a couple of deep breaths to locate some composure. I dropped the fish fingers into the frying pan while I waited.

'Fine, thanks, Tamsin,' I said, serenely. 'Just making sure I've got it all under control.'

'Oh, Susie,' Tamsin said. 'Of course you have. Can I do anything to help?'

'No,' I said, firmly. 'Absolutely not. There's really nothing to do.'

I followed Tamsin's gaze as she realised that, indeed, I was doing nothing. I quickly picked up a spatula and turned the fish fingers.

'Drink, then?' she offered. 'That was, in fact, the purpose of my visit. Your boyfriend's too busy charming your guests to attend to your glass.' She held out the bottles. 'G&T for you?'

I laughed. 'No way. I had a vodka, but I think I might switch. Could you grab me a glass of champagne?'

'Stylish lady. Of course.'

I tried to relax for a moment. A vision of Tamsin and her mother, crushed by twisted metal, sprung into my mind, and I screwed my eyes up to make it go away.

'Is Roman charming Amanda?' I asked weakly. It was the first thing that came to mind.

Tamsin, halfway out of the door, turned and laughed. 'In the most innocent way possible. I don't think you have anything to worry about there.'

'I'm glad he's being a good host.'

I tried to think of other things. I used to have the vision of Tamsin and her mother all the time. It was vivid. It was dark inside the car. There was blood. The teenage Tamsin turned her head to one side, wincing in pain. She tried to say something to her mother. There was no reply.

I forced it from my head, and tried to think about Roman instead. I tried to dwell on the day I met him, four years earlier. We had been at a party in Paris. It was hot and noisy, and I was uncomfortable and about to leave. Then he had wandered over to me.

'Hello,' he said.

'Are you English?' I checked. I hoped so: I was heartily sick of using my atrocious French.

'Yes,' he replied, smiling wickedly. 'And French, too.'

'Half and half?'

'Father English. Mother French. Split right down the middle.'

I forced myself to remember what he had looked like. Young and fresh-faced, but with a certain aura of having lived a little. Blue, loose shirt. Black eyes with a sexy glint. He was twisting his wine glass in his hand, round and round.

'You must be more one than the other, though,' I had objected. 'I mean, where did you go to school?'

'In Paris, until I was fifteen. Then in London. It was a bit tricky swapping language and fitting in halfway through a GCSE course, but my dad did my coursework, so I scraped by. I didn't get going properly until I took A levels.'

'But what do you feel? English or French? They're very different. What are you?'

'A mongrel. Depends who I'm talking to. In England I'm English. In France I'm French. I was married to a French woman until last year. Then I was more French. Now . . .' I wondered whether I was imagining the suggestive look he was giving me. I knew I wasn't. 'Now I feel the English side of my heritage needs some attention. Or should I say British. Where are you from, Susie?'

I laughed at his transparency. 'London. And Wales.'

'The most famous Welshwoman I've met.'

'They hardly stop me in the street.'

'But everyone knows your work. I love your paintings. They brighten up people's lives. I'd say that the person who creates them has a spectacular spirit.'

Roman had charmed me in an old-fashioned way, and I had allowed him to woo me. I was sick of English men who hated me earning more money than they did. Roman loved my success, and this was refreshing. I had no problem with the fact that he had been married, even though he was, as a result, wary of anything approaching commitment. In fact, that had probably drawn me to him. I liked his childish enthusiasm for dangerous sports, as well as the fact that he wasn't fanatical, that he was as happy spending six hours in a pub as he was spending a week on a snowy mountain. He encouraged me to get things done, and he helped me relax.

Within six months, he was showing me farmhouses in Aquitaine that I could buy for a fraction of the value of my flat in Notting Hill. I said I would only buy one if he would live in it with me.

Roman did all the paperwork for the house purchase, escorted me to schmooze the mayor when it was necessary, and made sure we got to know our neighbours. He organised the renovation, and mucked in with the builders when he could. Roman fitted in instantly, even though a Parisian, here, was as curious as a foreigner. He had a social life. He drank beer with men, and watched the local rugby teams. He even, occasionally, played, if they were desperate. I had not managed to integrate, yet. It was not because I was not welcome. It was because I held myself back.

Roman had dabbled in many different professions. He would sometimes shut himself away to write poetry, or else he would spent weeks with his head buried in a book about website design. He did not take any of it very seriously, and I liked that about him. I liked the fact that he didn't have a job. I was glad to have him with me.

'One glass of champagne.' Tamsin handed it to me, and hung around. I had successfully dispelled the unpleasant image, so I managed to smile. 'Remember Janie?' she said, leaning in the door frame.

'How can I forget the lovely Janie. I looked her up on Friends Reunited once. It said she was working for the government.'

'The thought police, probably. She was supposed to dance naked down Queen's Street. I remember it. When Nelson Mandela became President.'

I looked at her and grinned. 'Let's track her down, then. Enforce it.'

'I'm not sure the world's ready. Janie at thirty-two. There's something I can't imagine. You're certain I can't help?' She laughed. 'I must say, you seem almost improbably organised. Not that it's improbable for you. But it would be for any mere mortal.'

'No,' I said, validated and energised by the flattery and trying not to show it. 'Actually, yes. Can you tell the kids their dinner's ready?'

*   *   *

I stayed in the kitchen, listening to the conversation in the dining room next door. I realised at once that nobody had any idea I was listening in, and I kept as quiet as I could.

It started well. The kids were eating fish fingers with oven chips and green beans. Sam said, through a mouthful, 'This is nice! I thought we were going to have funny food.'

I heard Jake laugh and say, 'So did I.'

'Me too,' added Freya.

Izzy was supervising, and soon Patrick came in. I heard him pull up a chair, scraping its legs over the tiled floor. I heard the little bump of his gin and tonic being set, slightly too hard, on my dining table.

'Ahhh,' he said, slightly drunk. 'Better.'

'Cooler,' Izzy agreed.

'More relaxing. Once you get used to the lack of glare it's really rather wonderful. Don't you love the smell of these old French houses?'

'I do. It's terribly evocative.' There was a sound of scraping cutlery before Izzy continued, and I hoped she wasn't polishing off Sam's fish fingers. She needed to preserve her appetite for later. 'I haven't been on a French holiday for years. It takes me right back to when I was a teenager. From this distance, my youth looks rather innocent and lovely.'

'Whereas at the time . . . ?'

'Nothing of the sort. Always longing for the next thing, wishing the years away. Worrying about my bum, when in fact I'd give anything now to have that bottom back.' She sighed loudly. 'Everything was possible, then. We had everything, and we had no idea. I was desperate to grow up and meet Prince Charming and have a fairy tale wedding and live happily ever after. That was all I thought about. I wanted to be at the centre of a blissfully happy family.' She paused, probably to drink. 'What a waste of energy. If I knew then what I know now, I would have revelled in every moment of my youth and beauty.'

This was the first time I had heard Izzy acknowledge what she had lost. My heart ached for her.

'Know what you mean. When I look back at my misspent youth, all I see is hair.' I sniggered at Patrick. 'I had too much of the stuff. It touched my shoulders, if you can believe that.'

'And so I did grow up,' Izzy continued, 'and Prince Charming did arrive, and he did sweep me off my feet. And for a couple of years, I had everything I'd ever wanted. Then it starts to go weird, and then he buggers off. What do you do then? What comes after happy ever after?'

. imagined Patrick stroking the top of his head.

'Buggered if I know. It's the story of our generation, though. Grow up. Find something to do with your life, whether that means falling into what comes along or achieving an ambition. Get the relationship thing sorted, so you don't have to worry about that any more. Start a family. Then what?' he mused. 'Then, you just carry on doing it until you retire or you die.'

'Or you divorce.'

Patrick sounded confused. 'Divorce? Hmm . . .' He pulled himself together. 'Well, yes, absolutely, in your case. But in a way, that's good, isn't it? I mean, your life is not going to be defined for its duration by the choices you made in your twenties. You get a clean slate. You get to recraft your life now, in your thirties, and I bet it's going to be a damn sight more interesting as a result.'

Izzy chuckled sceptically. 'I've never thought of it *that* way. I wish I had time or energy to "recraft my life". It sounds like something I'll mean to do for a few years, but I'll keep putting it off, and then I'll wake up one morning and I'll be sixty. You're sweet, Patrick. I know you're just being nice. You've got everything, haven't you? Your life has worked out perfectly. You're just trying to make me feel better.'

Patrick paused for too long before he replied. 'Something like that,' he said, dutifully; aware, no doubt, of his listening children. 'But we all hanker back to our teenage days. Youth is wasted on the young. One of life's paradoxes. You don't appreciate it until you haven't got it any more.'

'And now we just have to work with what we *have* got.'

106

'Nostalgia, eh?' Patrick said, with a chuckle. 'It ain't what it used to be.'

'Dad,' Freya complained. She sounded both annoyed and embarrassed. 'You *always* say that.'

I swept in and cleared the table.

chapter sixteen

Amanda was uncomfortable. Even though it was the evening, it was horribly hot. She had drunk more gin than she needed, because Susie's unctuous beau picked her glass up whenever she put it down, and smoothly poured a new one and placed it into her hand without her noticing. She had a bugger of a headache. The gin was supposed to make her feel good, but she was stuck with Roman and he was patronising her.

He thinks I'm suburban and boring, she realised. He despises me because I'm not bohemian.

'What do you *do*?' she asked him abruptly, interrupting his monologue on the chicken farm on the hill. She knew he did nothing of any note, and she wondered whether he was going to pretend.

'Sorry? What do I do?'

'Mmm-hmm.'

He answered smoothly. 'I'm Susie's manager. What do you do?' He winked.

'I'm Patrick's manager.'

Roman laughed. 'Surely Patrick is his own manager?'

'Oh, unlike Susie? Anyway, he bloody is not. Let's see, I manage his home, his children, his travel arrangements, his diet. I keep his fridge and his cupboards stocked and I buy his shirts and ties because he has not got a blinking clue. I arrange holidays. I keep the social diary. I'm sorry, but *if* you are Susie's manager, I'm Patrick's.' Roman raised his eyebrows at her. He was, Amanda thought, trying to be sexy. It was not working on her, that was for sure. 'Although,' she continued, 'you have to be a man to be a manager, don't you? I guess that would make me Patrick's secretary. And yes, before you ask, he has already got one.' She glared. Even though Roman had barely said anything, she was furious with him. She had been trying to make a joke, about being Patrick's manager, because she had imagined that she could find some solidarity with Roman in the fact that they were both bankrolled by their partners. It hadn't worked out like that, because Susie's hanger-on boyfriend had been sarcastic, and one thing Amanda could not abide was sarcasm. She was terrible at meeting new people. If only she wasn't so fat, she would be able to wipe the floor with this smarmy Frenchman. 'When you and Susie have children,' she added, 'you'll see what I'm on about. Someone will have to do the drudgery, and it will probably be you. I know you're not really her manager. I know you do nothing.'

Roman narrowed his eyes. 'Did Susie say we were having children?'

'I've barely spoken to Susie yet. I just assumed.'

He shook his head slowly. 'Not a good assumption, Amanda. Excuse me.' And he walked off.

Amanda walked to the edge of the terrace and stepped onto the lawn. The sun was low in the sky now. The grass was yellowish under her feet. There was a soft breeze and, at last, it was almost cool enough for comfort. She inhaled deeply. She smelt figs and herbs and leaves. She made an effort, and unclenched her stomach muscles.

She would never have imagined that Susie was going to end up with all this. In a way she knew she was insane to be jealous. Amanda knew that she and Patrick were rich by anybody's standards. But Susie could use her money to relax. She and Patrick had to drink to do that. They had a garden, but it was small, compared with Susie's rolling parkland. They had children, and school fees, and extracurricular activities, and gym memberships, and three cars, and the congestion charge, and they had no time. Patrick's holiday was limited, so they generally went to a beach resort with guaranteed sunshine, though these days that was harder to find than it used to be. The climate seemed to be going mad. Amanda would only countenance places with kids' clubs. They rarely spent time together as a family, just hanging out. She suspected they wouldn't know what to do with themselves if they tried.

Susie didn't have children yet. That was all it was. Amanda walked across the lawn to the trees beyond it, sipping what she suspected to be the fourth, or perhaps the fifth, gin and tonic of the cocktail hour. She touched the bark of an enormous tree that looked very old. She hadn't a clue what kind of tree it was. It was nice to touch it. The grass between the trees was interspersed with small stones. The soil looked dusty.

'Welcome to les Landes, everyone,' Susie said, beaming. She stood at the head of the table and held up her glass. 'It's wonderful to see you all again. Here's to a fabulous reunion!'

There was a murmur of assent around the table. Amanda lifted her glass and clinked it with everyone else's, carefully noticing who turned to her first, and who turned last. She was certain that Tamsin wanted to leave her out, because she caught a malicious smile playing around her lips, and Tamsin turned to her last, like an afterthought.

Everyone was smiling big sociable smiles, and Amanda assumed that she wasn't the only one taking a huge, grateful gulp of wine after the painstaking toasting. This was undoubtedly going to be a remarkable evening; probably not in a good way. She stared hard at Patrick, sending him telepathic orders not to embarrass her. She had told him to keep nice and quiet this evening and to get up and go upstairs or outside when the food was finished, to give the women some time alone.

She avoided even looking at Tamsin. Everything about the

woman unnerved her, from her black clothes to her slight Australian accent. Amanda knew that Tamsin was giving her sly looks. She knew that Tamsin had never really liked her, and she thought that now she probably hated her. She recalled Tamsin, years earlier, going on about how she would devote her life to South African orphans, and vowed to ask her, when she got the chance, how that was going. She was trying to relax, but she was getting more and more wound up, and when Izzy started wittering on to her about how bloody wonderful all this luxury was, she suddenly wanted to hurt her.

'Oh, do you think?' she said, mockingly. 'I suppose it's all relative to where you're coming from.'

This was supposed to be a scathing put-down, but Izzy just nodded earnestly and agreed that Amanda was right. Amanda noticed Tamsin asking Patrick to pass her the water. She saw Patrick smile as he filled her water glass. She knew that smile. It was Patrick's ridiculous attempt at flirtation. Abruptly, she leaned forward and held her own glass out.

'Patrick!' she said imperiously, and Patrick found himself filling everyone's water. Susie had to send Roman to the kitchen to fetch a new bottle from the fridge. When Amanda leaned back, she saw that the left breast of her dress had brushed the surface of her gazpacho, and she dabbed it furiously with her napkin, daring anyone to laugh.

'Lovely gazpacho,' said Izzy, happily. 'Did you make it yourself?'

Susie nodded. 'Of course,' she said, fiddling with a maroon shoulder strap. 'We make everything ourselves. The culture's different here. It's impossible to get a takeaway – at least, it takes longer to get one than it does to cook, and it's cold by the time you get it home – and nobody really does ready meals.'

Amanda glared at her soup. It was impossible to take anything Susie said or did as anything other than a personal affront. It felt to her as though Susie could see all her failings, and was pointing them up by ostentatiously not having them. Amanda rarely cooked, and when she did she didn't use vegetables.

Tamsin jumped in. 'Susie, do you love cooking? Only I thought that with this lifestyle you've got going on, you'd have someone to cook for you.'

Susie looked displeased for a moment. She sighed. 'I chose to cook for you all this weekend. I wanted to make it perfect. You're right, I could have got someone in to do it. We could easily have gone out. But yes, I do love it, and I love creating meals for my friends.' She didn't sound as if she loved it.

'Well, it's absolutely wonderful,' Tamsin said. 'Well done. We're very impressed.'

The bitch! thought Amanda, and she threw her a dirty look. Tamsin seemed incapable of speaking to Susie without being sarcastic. Amanda wondered why she felt protective of Susie. She supposed she knew. It was all to do with Tamsin.

'Yes, Susie, we are,' Amanda said, belatedly and far more sincerely than Tamsin had managed. 'It's stunning soup. I'd love to take the recipe.'

Susie was gracious. 'I'll write it out for you. Now, girls. Girls and boys, but girls mainly. This is a reunion. So we need to catch up. Let's go round the table and each spill some details. What we did when we left school, to start with.' She looked around. 'Amanda!' Susie said, waving her spoon at her. 'Why don't you start?'

They all turned to Amanda and looked at her expectantly.

Bloody hell, Amanda thought. Why do I have to go first? If Susie had gone first, she would have an idea of what was expected. She drained her glass, and waited for the unctuous Roman to refill it.

'OK,' she said. 'Me. Right.' She breathed a couple of controlled breaths, and started. 'Well, I left school after A levels,' she began. 'I got the grades I needed for Bristol and I went there and studied history.' She nodded, nervous. It felt strange to be leaving Tamsin and her mother out of the story but she could hardly do anything else. Tamsin had been gone by the time she got to uni, anyway. 'Bristol was brilliant. I had the time of my life, I really did. I lived in halls for the first year, and to be honest I can hardly remember most of it because I was pretty much drunk all year.' She caught Patrick's eye and smiled. 'In my second year, I met a very dashing young economics student in the union bar. His name was Patrick. He invited me to dinner at Brown's, which was quite the most upmarket date I'd been asked on in my life. I couldn't normally afford Brown's, but this economics student had an impressive share portfolio on the side and he didn't live like all us normal students did. We started going out and he hasn't managed to shake me off since!' She looked around and everyone smiled dutifully.

As she filled them in on moving to London with Patrick, renting a flat in Clapham, buying a house, and being the first of all their friends to get married, Amanda listened to herself. She was stilted and nervous, and although the skeleton of her facts was correct, she was not telling them the truth.

She remembered her first meeting with Patrick. She had, indeed, been in the union bar, the Epi, and it had been her second year. That much was true.

She was skinny, then, and she was unspeakably miserable. Amanda had always pretended to be happy. She carefully made sure there was a spring in her step when she walked around Bristol. She smiled constantly. She invited people, casually, to come to the bar with her, pretending to be impulsive. Despite her efforts to be pleasant and fun and indispensable, she had not met anyone on her course who was anything other than a casual acquaintance.

She missed Suzii desperately. Suzii was the only one who understood the guilt. Suzii was the only one who would ever understand. Izzy might understand a little. Tamsin, Amanda was certain, she was never going to see again. But Susie had gone to London, without a plan, and she hardly ever answered her letters. When she did, it was obvious that she was busy having a life. She was getting over what they had done. It was only now that their foursome had been torn apart that Amanda realised how dependent she had been on it.

She even missed Dai. In fact, she missed him as much as Suzii. Sometimes she caught a train to Cardiff without telling anyone, to see him. She felt better for a few hours, but she knew he could not be a part of her future, and so, soon after she met Patrick, she wrote Dai a tear-stained letter. Dai was her passion, but Patrick was suitable, and stable, and Amanda knew that without stability, she would collapse.

She overate compulsively. It was her dirty little secret. She spent all her money on cheap alcohol and cheap food, but during the course of her first year she had managed to get down below eight stone, thanks to bulimia. There was a ritual. She patronised fifteen different newsagents, so nobody who worked there would ever realise how gross she was. She'd go to each in turn, buying a couple of chocolate bars at each. It took an hour. Back in her room, she would line up her stash, lock the door, and devour every morsel. For five minutes, timed exactly on her watch, she would sit with it in her stomach, despising herself and panicking as she visualised the fat melting into her body, becoming a part of her. Often she thought about leaving it there and letting herself get fat, but she couldn't do it. The moment the second hand reached the twelve for the fifth time, she rushed to the musty bathroom and emptied everything into the loo. She generally had to flush three or four times to get the bubbly scum of her stomach acid off the surface of the water. She washed her hands meticulously, to banish the sick smell. She scrubbed her nails. She brushed her teeth twice. She cleaned the toilet with the loo brush, and put bleach down it to take the smell away (in a student house, this part of the routine, at least, was a blessing). Then, and only then, was she allowed to feel good. For an hour, she walked on air.

It was after one of these sessions that she met Patrick. None of her flatmates were around, so she went to the union by herself, thinking that she'd pick up a paper on the way and see if she could find someone to talk to. The Epi was almost empty. Amanda sat alone in a sticky corner, her pint of lager in its plastic cup on the table in front of her, and smiled around the room, just so the few drinkers would see that she was nice.

Patrick was there, complete with full head of hair and cricket jumper. He looked like a public school boy, with good reason. He was chatting to two friends, and they ignored her.

When she was halfway down her 90p drink, a middle-aged man lurched into the bar. He was sozzled. Amanda looked up, saw him, and looked back down. People like him turned up from time to time, and she liked it best when the bar staff evicted them straightaway. She glanced at the barman, but he wasn't there.

The man made his wobbly way directly to her table. She cursed herself for accidentally smiling at him. Having a 'please like me' reflex got her into trouble surprisingly often.

'Mind if I join you?' he slurred. His voice was cultured. Amanda wrinkled her nose in distaste.

'I do mind, actually,' she told him bravely.

'Smashing.' He sat down. Amanda tried a withering look, but she felt tears springing to her eyes and she knew it was going to take more than a stare or a sniffle to move this man on. He was dressed in a shabby suit, and his nose was bulbous and pitted. But he looked as if he had once been respectable. He didn't smell like a homeless person. He just looked like a down-at-heel alcoholic; and he was staring at her.

Amanda was reasonably good at fending off unwanted attention in the street, or at parties. Now, though, she looked at her companion and squirmed.

'You're posh, aren't you?' he said, leaning forward. 'I used to be posh.'

Amanda looked away. She knew she should get up and walk off, but something was stopping her. Mainly, she thought, the fact that the man might grab her if she tried.

'Would you get me a drink?' he asked. 'I seem to have left my wallet in the taxi. I'd be very grateful.'

Amanda sighed. 'What do you want?'

'Whisky.'

She didn't know what else to do, so she looked in her purse.

'Or just the price of a drink would be fine,' he interjected hopefully. 'I can see you've got a fiver there. That would cover it nicely.'

At that point Amanda started to cry. 'I *need* that fiver,' she told him. She felt as if she were being politely mugged, and she loathed herself for not being able to tell him to F-off.

At that point – rather belatedly, when she looked back on it, but like an angel from heaven at the time – Patrick appeared.

'Excuse me,' he said. He put a hand on the man's shoulder and borrowed a phrase from a thousand soap operas. 'Is he bothering you?' She watched Patrick registering her for the first time. He took in her hair and her face and her cheekbones, and his manner changed, subtly. He thrust his chest back, lifted his chin, and dealt with the situation in a manly fashion. Within three minutes the drunk had been ejected, celebratory drinks had been bought, and Patrick had asked Amanda to dinner at Brown's.

Three blissful weeks passed before she discovered that Patrick had a girlfriend, or, more accurately, before Patrick's girlfriend discovered that he was sleeping with Amanda. There was a showdown. To Amanda's astonishment, Patrick chose her over the bossy Melanie. They officially became a couple. Once she had him, nothing was going to induce Amanda to let Patrick go. She did not hesitate to choose safety over passion.

'. . . And so Jakey was born,' Amanda continued, smiling. 'I was only twenty-four. We hadn't intended to start a family so soon, but it turned out to be the best thing that could have happened. We had Freya eighteen months later to get it all out of the way. When Freya leaves home, we'll only be forty-four!' She looked round the table, waiting for the approbation that normally followed this revelation. Everybody nodded, without enthusiasm. Amanda pursed her lips, and told herself they were all jealous.

'But what about *you*, Amanda?' Tamsin asked. 'What did you do with your history degree? I know you had your babies young, but you must have worked before that. Did you go back to work when they were both at school? What are you going to *do* when you're forty-four?'

Amanda cast around for the right answer. Typical of Tamsin to hone in on her Achilles heel and leave her feeling stupid.

'Yeah,' she said, noticing that her glass was empty and twiddling its stem to alert Roman to that fact. 'Yeah, of course I worked till I had the kids. Did admin for a PR firm. I was planning to work my way up, but then life got in the way. Now I'm rushed off my feet looking after everyone, to be honest. Sometimes I think I should get a job just for a bit of rest.'

Izzy laughed. 'That kind of work expands to fit the time available, doesn't it? I know I only have Sam, and I live in a teeny flat that definitely wouldn't compare to your house, but I do the minimum of housework when Sammy's with his dad, and leave it at that. Whereas if I had the whole day to do it, I'd be busy all day.'

Patrick leaned forward. 'Guess what, Izzy?' he said, slightly too drunk. 'Amanda has a cleaner who comes three times a week.'

Amanda glared. 'Twice!'

'Twice, then. And an ironing lady, who believe it or not is not the same person. All Amanda does is drive the kids to school and pick them up again. I'm not sure what else she gets up to.'

'What the hell do you mean by that?'

Patrick shook his head. 'Nothing, nothing. Nothing untoward.'

'I go to the gym.'

Amanda heard Roman almost sniggering. She narrowed her eyes at him.

'Do you really?' Susie asked, blandly. The phone rang. Roman headed out of the room to answer it, and, Amanda felt sure, to laugh at her.

'And I wash and iron all your clothes, all the kids' uniforms. I cook and I make the beds and I sort out all the crappy boring admin that you don't even know *exists*.' Amanda caught her breath and tried to control herself. She could not have a public row with Patrick. She would continue this later, in private. 'Anyway,' she said, icily. 'I'm done. Who's next?

chapter seventeen

Izzy cleared her throat and toyed with her spoon.

'OK, well, I should start off by admitting that Amanda's made me feel very inadequate with her house in Clapham and her lovely family life and everything.' She instantly realised that she sounded as if she were being ironic and she hoped that Amanda would know that she didn't do irony very well. She hurried on. 'I went to university, too, as you all know. I went to Sheffield to read English. I was just talking to Patrick about how different youth looks after the event. I was insecure and nervous when I went, even though I was still doing that Pre-Raphaelite thing of wearing tight bodices and flowing skirts and having my hair long. But it was exciting. I settled in and got used to having new friends and new ways of studying, and I enjoyed it. Had a lovely time, in the end.' She swallowed. It was hard to know how much detail to give.

'When I graduated, I moved to London and started working in a publishing house. It was brilliant. I liked the women I worked with, I loved being young in London with endless possibilities before me, and I was really extremely happy. I moved into a shared house in Archway with a friend from university. And . . . well, to cut a long story short, I started going out with one of the flatmates. His name was Martin.'

She looked around the table and made eye contact with each of her old friends. They all smiled, knowing the way the story was going to go. Izzy took a sip of white wine. She had missed her friends, so she was going to tell them everything.

'Martin was ten years older than me, which, yes, meant that he was living in a shabby shared house at the age of thirty-two, the age we all are now. Which at least makes me think my life could be worse. He'd been in a long-term relationship which had ended, and he'd moved into the box room as a temporary measure. He had a daughter from that relationship, by the way, Caitlin, and he used to bring her to the house on Saturdays. He was desperately looking for a bedsit or something so he could have her to stay. She was only one when I first met her.'

Izzy smiled at the memory of the chubby toddler who used to empty the kitchen cupboards and bemuse most of the house-mates when she visited. Nobody had quite known what to do with a baby, but they had mainly found her sweet, if alien.

'Anyway, Martin was keen on me from the very beginning. I wasn't sure. I was young, and I found the idea that he was a father completely amazing. He seemed far, far too grown-up to be interested in me. But the more I pretended not to notice that he liked me, the keener he became. I didn't see it at the time, but he's a very controlling person, and when he decided he wanted me, nothing was going to stop him. My saying no all the time was a red rag to a bull. In fact, if I'd given in sooner I probably wouldn't have had to marry him.

'So it was very flattering. He was a good-looking guy, and he had a reasonably good job with an insurance company. Most of all, though, he was funny. He talked and talked and talked, and he told me things he said he'd never told anyone else before. He loved my hair and my clothes. He said I was unique and he'd never met a girl like me. Anything I said would be fascinating and perceptive and taken as further evidence of my wonderfulness. He was always asking me out for drinks, and normally I said no because I didn't want to owe him anything.

'But then, one evening, I said yes.' Izzy clearly remembered the day it had all changed. It was February, and the rain was coming down in sheets. She stumbled in from work, clutching her Oxfam mac around herself, holding her beaten-up leather bag in her arms like a sack of potatoes. Her hair was sodden, and it stuck to the sides of her face. It took fifteen minutes to walk home from the tube, and she was drenched.

She had had a terrible day. She'd forgotten that she was supposed to be checking numbers for the sales conference and confirming with the hotel. She had been procrastinating over checking the special requirements for weeks. She'd vaguely had it in the back of her mind that she needed to do these things, but it had entirely escaped her notice that the deadline, for the hotel and for the caterers, was that particular day. Trouble had descended at 3 p.m.

Martin arrived home as Izzy was drying her hair with a tea towel, standing in front of the oven, which was turned up high with the door open, as the most efficient piece of heating the house possessed. Their three flatmates were either out or shut firmly inside their rooms.

He stood in the doorway, tall, broad and slightly ginger.

'Jesus Christ, Isabelle,' he said, his eyes crinkling in amusement as he took her in. 'You look like I feel! And I don't feel good.'

She laughed. 'Mmm. Bad day. Bad weather.' She looked at the tea towel in her hands. 'Bad hair. But I'm home now.'

Martin, who was a lot taller than she was, came and stood next to her. He looked down, and she craned her neck to look up at him. And in that instant, something happened. At the time, she thought she had fallen in love. Looking back on it, she thought she had made a decision to take the path of least resistance. Her body suddenly came alive and she saw that she and Martin might have unimagined potential. He adored her. No one had ever adored her, like that, before. At the age of twenty-one, Izzy decided to say yes to his next question, and to see what happened. Martin seemed to be able to read her thoughts. He put a hand on her shoulder, his thumb resting on the side of her neck, and he left it there.

'Come back out in the rain with me,' he said, 'and let me get you drunk.'

* * *

120

'He totally swept me off my feet,' she told everybody. 'Once I started going out with him, it happened so quickly. I was in a haze. I was so happy. He was a real romantic hero. He'd whisk me away for weekends in the country. He took me out for meals all the time, and he was always waiting with some fabulous wine or champagne when I got home from work. It seems like a million years ago now. He stroked my hair, which sounds creepy but it wasn't, somehow. He appeared to worship me.

'We moved in together as soon as we found a place.' She looked at Tamsin. 'You remember how I was always imagining the man I would marry. Some Mr Darcy type. Well, Martin was him. A ginger version of him, anyway. I used to draw pictures of myself in my wedding dress, at school. Suddenly, I was doing it again. I practised writing my married name – Isabelle Allington – even though on principle I wanted to keep my own name. I wanted to give myself to Martin completely, because that was what he wanted. I started to think we were great lovers. I tried so hard to make it a union of souls that I convinced myself in the end.

'When we moved in together, I came down to earth a bit. He could be moody, but I knew he was moodier with other people than he ever was with me. I tried not to take it personally.' Izzy was speaking through gritted teeth. 'When Caitlin came to stay, he'd hand her to me to deal with, and she was so tiny, and I hardly knew how to handle her. Then he proposed. A great, romantic proposal in Paris. We were up the Eiffel Tower. There was a strong wind blowing and I couldn't hear him at first, but I kind of got the message from the fact that he was kneeling in front of me with a ring in a box. Everyone else noticed, too, and there was quite a crowd around us. Oh, I was the most glamorous, luckiest, happiest girl in the world, believe me. They all looked at me, and Martin was gazing with his big dark eyes, and I had to shout "Yes!" so he'd hear me above the wind. Then I looked at everyone around us and shouted, "*Oui!*" even though they must all have known the meaning of the word "yes". And they all clapped. And we held hands and looked down at Paris and Martin put the ring on my finger.'

She sighed, wishing she could leave it there, at the high point of the story. 'I got my white wedding. Most of you were there. And then things changed. I know things are bound to change once you're married. I was on cloud nine for the first couple of months. Always cooking for Martin and somehow actually taking pleasure in ironing his shirts and all that crap, and he was still sending me flowers at work when I wasn't expecting them. But my feet touched the ground, and Martin took me off the pedestal rather quickly, and it started to go a bit weird. He got moodier and moodier. I felt I couldn't do anything right. If I cooked, he was mad because he'd wanted to go out. If I didn't cook, he wanted to know why not. If he wanted to watch something on telly, I'd have to remain absolutely silent throughout. The worst, though, was the jealousy. I'd always gone out after work at least once a week. I met up with uni friends who were in London, or went out with colleagues. It was good fun, and I don't need to tell *you*, as you are all sane and rational people, that it was normal and innocent. First of all Martin started asking about my friends. I was the only one who was married and that upset him. But I was twenty-five, which made the fact that I was married quite a curiosity. Of course my friends were single. He thought it was "inappropriate" for me to hang out with single girls, because of course they were all out to lead me astray. Then he started quizzing me about whether there'd been any men with us. Well, of course there had. I worked with men. My friends had boyfriends. I did, amazingly, have some male friends.

'That was incomprehensible. He would shout at me and accuse me of *horrible* things, things I would just never dream of doing. He once said that he *knew* I'd had sex with some bloke called Paul, on some bins behind a Turkish restaurant in Seven Sisters. He said he'd *seen me*. He'd shout and scream for hours. Then he'd be all right, and he'd hug me and apologise and stroke my hair, and he'd whisper that it was just because he adored me. He couldn't believe that every other man in the world didn't love me and want me as much as he did.

'So things started getting bad, and they stayed that way for a couple of years. I started wanting to leave. On my twenty-eighth birthday, I made the decision. I was resolute. I packed a suitcase, and when he came home, I opened my mouth to tell him I was leaving. *However*. He thought all my nervousness was leading up to something else. He was in a good mood and he started laughing. "I know what you're trying to ask," he said, and he touched my nose like that.' Izzy demonstrated. 'Being all cute.'

'"No you don't," I told him.

'"I do," he assured me. "You think it's time for a baby. And guess what? I agree!"

'And somehow, the thought of a baby hit me right in the stomach. I hadn't felt broody until that moment. But when he said it, I desperately wanted one. I told myself it would be different with a baby. Everything would be fine. I knew it wouldn't, really, particularly since his previous relationship had ended three months after Caitlin was born. But I convinced myself because I wanted it to be true. I rushed upstairs and unpacked my bag, and all the time I did it I was praying that he wouldn't come into the bedroom and ask what I was doing. And I got pregnant straight-away, first month, before I could see sense.'

Izzy paused. She was nearly there. Tamsin touched her arm, gently urging her on.

'So Sam was born,' she said, swallowing. 'Motherhood was over-whelming. Wonderful, but so different from what I had expected. It took me ages to get used to it. I was so focused on Sam that I didn't really notice that Martin was barely about. I preferred it when he was out. He used to swear at Sam crying in the night. It was much easier for me to do it all myself.

'Then, on Sam's first birthday, he told me who he'd been out with all those evenings. Somebody called Jennifer, who was seven-teen. They were, apparently, in love. It was, apparently, my fault for putting on weight when I had the baby and for having my hair cut. Which I did because I didn't have the time to wash and dry it, as a working mother. He packed up and left, and Sam and I moved back to Cardiff.'

Susie leaned forward. 'He's not still seeing the teenager?'

Izzy nodded. 'She's probably twenty by now. But yes. I think that's the way he works, and I cannot tell you how it feels to pack my little boy off to stay with them, knowing that Martin's handing him over to Jennifer for the weekend. But at least Sam sees Caitlin at his dad's. She's twelve and she's lovely. I'm even quite friendly with her mum these days. I suppose that Martin's picked a young one this time so he'll have a few years before the inevitable happens. I hate him more than I can possibly say.' Her voice was calm, matter-of-fact. 'I hope he rots in hell for eternity. I almost believe in hell, specially for Martin. He's a bully and a pig and because I've got Sam I can't even wish I'd never met him, and because I've got Sam I have to keep in touch with him for ever and ever. I have to take him on the train to Swindon every other weekend to hand him over.' She sighed. 'But I'm getting back on track now. I mean, it's been over two years since he left us. We're still not quite divorced. As you can see, he picked me up as a pretty little girl and left me as a fat mother.' She laughed. 'And I do mean mother. I don't mean "mother" in the abbreviated sense. I haven't got the time or the money, or the inclination really, to sort my appearance. I'd rather spend my money on a Buzz Lightyear suit than a Chanel suit. I think Martin only likes pretty little girls who do what he wants, and I imagine he's destined to repeat the cycle for the rest of his life, and I feel stupid for getting caught up in it. I resisted him for ages. I should have stuck with my instincts.' Nobody said anything. 'So there you are,' Izzy said, wanting to stress that her story was over. 'That's me.'

Amanda spoke first. 'Bloody hell, what a fucking bastard!' she said.

Izzy shrugged. 'It was crap but I'm still here. Could have been worse.'

Tamsin squeezed Izzy's knee under the table. 'You've done brilliantly,' she said quietly. 'I wish I'd been around to give you moral support. How has it been, back in Cardiff?'

Izzy swallowed. 'Not too bad. My job's much more boring than the one in London, but I'm glad to be out of the city. Always going to be weird, I think, going back to your origins. I pass Lodwell's on the bus from time to time and I see the girls going in and out, all innocent looking.'

Susie laughed. 'Not that innocent, if I recall correctly.'

'Well, I pass the girls and I'd really rather not see the school, even by accident. Oh, and did you know, they have bloody boys there these days! In the sixth form!'

'No!' chorused Susie, Amanda and Tamsin.

'Christ,' muttered Amanda. 'How much time would *that* have saved? Kids these days don't know they're born.'

'I know. I think that every time I see them,' said Izzy. 'Skinny little blokes with the smuggest faces you've seen in your life. Girls on all sides. But I hate being there. I hate feeling that I haven't moved on from it. But I've got my folks reasonably nearby, still in Dinas, and they're great. Sam loves seeing so much of them. And I have friends, and I have a job, and I just about support us both and pay for occasional treats like this trip, for instance. But it's not what I ever wanted for myself. It's . . .' She screwed up her face and tried to pinpoint what it was. 'Humdrum! That's what it is. It's a humdrum life. I go to work and try to drum up an interest in various trade publications. Enough interest to get me through the editing day, anyway. Sam goes to nursery. I pick him up on the way home. We watch telly. We eat. We read books. We do it all again the next day. I mean, there you are, Amanda, with your exciting London life, and your house and your cars and your gym and the children going to ballet and judo all the time. And Susie, you've got all this, you've got absolutely everything. Tamsin's been living by the beach in Sydney for all these years, which is so amazing I can barely imagine it. All of you have made spectacularly wonderful lives for yourselves. And there I am, five miles from where I grew up, feeling a sense of achievement if I get to work before nine thirty.' She stopped. She didn't want her emotions to get the better of her. 'I'd like to change it,' she said, in a measured voice. 'But I cannot for the life of me imagine how.'

'Get a boyfriend,' Patrick suggested.

Izzy laughed, annoyed. 'Oh, silly me! Single mother, on the

wrong side of thirty, and also on the wrong side of size fourteen, seeks perfect man. They're beating the door down.'

'You've got everything going for you,' Tamsin told her. 'I mean it. It'll happen, and it'll be someone far more worthy than that tosser you married.'

The others nodded. Izzy felt sure they were just being polite.

'Anyway,' she said, with a wave of her hand. 'Susie, it's your turn.'

chapter eighteen

I hesitated. The main course was ready, and Roman hadn't come back from answering the phone. Nobody else seemed to notice: they had all been absorbed in poor Izzy's woes. I wanted to find him. He was being rude and he shouldn't have stayed on the phone for so long. It was probably his mother, anyway. I ought to extract him from the receiver, get the starters cleared away, serve the chicken, and then launch into my tale. Except that I thought I might like Roman out of the way while I spoke; purely for presentational purposes.

'OK,' I said, smiling. 'But I'll just turn the oven off. I'll be quick and then we can get the main course out before Tamsin's turn.' I skipped to the kitchen and made sure everything was all right (I already knew it was). Back in my seat, I tried to decide where to begin. I had practised this monologue for months but, inevitably, my mind was blank.

'Well. I left school after A levels,' I began, echoing the others. 'I didn't really know what I was going to do. We were all knocked for six, really, weren't we? You were, of course, Tamsin, but the rest of us were too, in a much more minor way. I felt terrible about what happened.' I felt Amanda's eyes on me. I knew she was panicking. I met her eyes and smiled an infinitesimal, reassuring smile. Not tonight. 'And I was desperately worried about you, Tamsin. We had no idea what you were up to, and whether you were all right. Anyway, I could have gone to Manchester University, but I turned it down and moved to London. I didn't know what I was going to do. I had no ambitions. I just wanted to do something different, and I had always thought of London as my home. I had a rather rosy view of it, like you do if you leave somewhere when you're young. So I got there, and started waitressing. I lived in a squat. Actually, there were several of them. I still had spiky hair and a fat arse and spots. After a while, I got a boyfriend. He was at art school, and that seemed cool, so I applied too, to the same place, and I did a foundation course and kept up my waitressing in the evenings. It was all a bit hand-to-mouth.'

I swallowed. I considered glossing over this period of my life entirely, but I knew I had to sketch it out, elide it.

'I drifted by, really,' I said. 'Like I said, I had no ambition. Or rather, I was ambitious, but it was unfocused. I wanted a different life, but I couldn't be bothered to work out how to get one, and in a way I didn't think I deserved one. I was one step up from a down-and-out, and I think it was art school that saved me from that. It was full of misfits, and if I'd been a bit wackier I would almost have blended in. I made funny bits of conceptual art, but my heart wasn't in it, and I started to find I preferred still life and figurative stuff. That wasn't something to shout about: it was very uncool.'

I paused, and edited out the most important thing that had ever happened to me; the defining event of my life.

'It was one of my tutors at art school who changed my life,' I was picking up the story later on. 'She used to help me because she said I was good at still life and life drawing. Her name was Janet. She was one of those art school women who drift around in purple clothes and keep their hair much too long and straggly. Now, no one else was interested in figurative stuff. They all learned to draw because you had to, but then they were off, doing wacky installations, you know the kind of thing. Britart, as it wasn't yet called. But I was never interested in blood sculpture or sticking dog turds on photos of Thatcher. And Janet was the only one who made me feel that that was OK. She sat down with me one afternoon in the studio and made me think about my life.'

I shuddered to think what might have become of me if it hadn't been for Janet. I remembered that conversation so clearly: my life was divided cleanly into what had gone before it and what had come after. I had been on the brink when I met Janet. I had lost my future, and I was thinking, seriously, about heroin. I had seen it ruin people's lives; but I had also seen that they didn't care, and I had been drawn to the idea of not caring.

'Where do you see yourself going?' Janet asked.

I blew my fringe up from my forehead. 'God knows,' I said. 'I can't see that anyone's ever going to pay me good money for drawing bowls of fruit.'

'It worked for Cézanne. But seriously, there's plenty of scope for you as an artist. Art is everywhere. Would you like to be a commercial artist?'

I snorted. 'Shh! Those words are banned round here, aren't they?'

'Sweetie, listen,' Janet said, with a hand on my arm. 'You have a pretty and distinctive style. The commercial world will be kind to you. The money folks will adore you. Think about colour. Think about canvases in a Holland Park sitting room. Think about universal appeal.' She leaned in closer, making me uncomfortably aware of the fact that I probably smelled. 'I'll tell you something that worked for me.'

I was still trying to take it in. She was looking at me expectantly. 'Mmm?' I managed.

Janet clapped her hands. 'Pretend you're already a successful artist! Imagine the paintings you create and the pleasure you bring to people. Make them real in your head. Imagine yourself the way you'd like to be. Now, *be* that way! If you behave as if something's true, it becomes true. That works in many different ways, but it does work. Believe me.'

There was nothing to lose: my only other option was heroin. I organised myself. It took an immense effort, but I did it. When

I wasn't working for minimal money, I worked on my art. I stretched canvases, started to master oils, imagined brightly coloured skies and poppy fields. I started creating paintings for rich people's walls. Holland Park offerings, I used to call them. I never painted anything on impulse. I would spend hours at a time staring at a blank canvas, imagining what I was going to fill it with, and when it was completely worked out, to the smallest detail, in my head, then I would transfer it, painstakingly, to the canvas before me.

'Janet made me see that it wasn't morally reprehensible to make a living from figurative art,' I said. 'She helped me approach galleries and get my work in exhibitions. It was a slow process, but after about a year, they started selling, gradually, and then quickly. They were reproduced, and the prints took off. They went onto greetings cards. My parents had been horrified at the way I dropped out, and they'd practically disowned me. All of their friends' children had gone to university and they were embarrassed to mention me. My dad had always wanted me to be a doctor, like him, and it was bad enough for him when I did art A level.' I smiled. 'So when he discovered I was living in a squat, sleeping with someone he classed as a "hippy", and dividing my time between waiting tables and painting, he was utterly horrified. Needless to say, when the art started selling, the parents reappeared in my life. Even Jackie was almost proud of me. I discovered this when she asked me to paint her kids, a few years ago.'

Izzy interrupted. 'Jackie's got kids?'

'Three of them. And doesn't she like to go on about it. She's a GP, which is probably lucky for everyone. A doctor in the family after all. Actually, she's furious with me – she wanted to come out this weekend and see you all but I wouldn't let her.'

They all laughed. 'That is the story of Jackie's life, isn't it?' said Tamsin. 'All I remember of your sister is that she was always wanting to join in and you were always telling her to bugger off.'

'Mmm. She tries to flex her muscles, but essentially that's still the way it works.'

Izzy leaned forward. 'So, then what?'

I thought about it. I was not going to tell them that I had used will power and transformed myself into the person I wanted to be, that it had taken years but that Janet's technique had worked in the end. I acted as if I had always been a naturally thin person with a tiny appetite, and, by sheer will power, I made it come true. I started telling people that I had to exercise every day or I missed the endorphin rush, and, slowly and painfully, it became true. I told myself that I adored Whistles and Ghost clothes, that I had never really liked smoking, and that I had never wanted children. In a way, I knew, Janet's philosophy struck a chord because I had already been using it. It had its limits, however.

'Well,' I said. 'I had long dumped Steve, the hippy boyfriend. I started to care about what I looked like again. Most of my fellow students despised my stuff for being so tame, and I'm sure they despise me even more now for making money out of it. But I can live with that, frankly.'

'What about men?' Izzy asked. 'Come on. Share. I've just told you all about my sad excuse for a love life.'

I smiled, and drank up. 'Roman's the one, of course.' There was still no sign of him. 'Before him I'd had boyfriends. Steve was sweet and I broke his heart. A few after that couldn't hack me being successful. Wanted to get in on the action by calling themselves my "manager". Roman would do anything for me, but he would never, ever style himself as my "manager". I manage myself, thank you very much.' I heard Amanda making an odd noise, but when I looked at her, nothing seemed out of order. 'So, nothing much to report there. The odd episode of mild angst, but nothing unusual. And now –' I looked up as Roman came back into the room and smiled his apologies at everyone. 'Now we've got this house, which keeps us busy, and Roman works on various different projects, and life is just how I've always wanted it to be.'

Amanda held her head on one side. 'But as a childless couple . . .' she began, a finger at the corner of her mouth.

'We're not childless,' I interjected, hastily. I wanted to defuse this topic. Then Roman and I spoke in unison. 'Childfree!'

'Oh, Jesus,' Amanda muttered. 'What's that about?'

Roman stared at her. 'It's about the fact that we don't actually want children, thanks all the same. And not having them in our lives is not a "lack" of any sort. It's a freedom, a positive thing. Hence, child*free*. Not child*less*.' He turned to me. 'Suze, that was Sarah Saunders on the phone.'

'Why?'

'Tell you later. You need to call her in the morning.'

'OK.' I was annoyed with Amanda and I hoped she would shut up now. But she didn't. When I looked at her closely, she was obviously very drunk, particularly considering that we hadn't even cleared away the starter.

'But you must want them really, Susie,' Amanda said, ignoring Roman. 'What about your biological clock? You're thirty-two. You've still got time but you need to think about it.'

I shook my head and clenched my teeth. 'I really don't, thank you. I can't imagine living this life with a baby in tow. And . . .' I paused, then carried on, firmly. 'I don't relate to them. Being an aunt to Jackie's three is enough for me. I don't feel any urge whatsoever to reproduce myself and keep my genes in the world for another generation. The world is overpopulated as it is. There are people who are natural mothers, and people who aren't. You and Izzy clearly are, and I'm not. And I don't want to bring someone into the world who isn't completely wanted, do I? Wouldn't that be a terrible thing to do?'

Izzy interjected. 'Of course it would,' she said, smiling. 'God knows, it's your decision, you two. I agree with you. Don't have a baby if you don't want to.'

'Thanks, Izzy,' said Roman, 'but I wasn't planning on asking your permission.'

Izzy looked surprised. 'I didn't mean . . .'

I silenced Roman with a look. 'I know you didn't, Izzy. Don't worry. You just wouldn't believe the number of people . . .' I looked at Amanda and away, 'who cannot accept our decision. I mean, everybody, from the people in this village to my parents, to Roman's family, to women I meet in the supermarket and the fucking stalker who gets me to paint some woman who might or might not be his wife –' I looked quickly to Roman.

'I'd say, not,' he said.

'Well, *all* of them ask when we're having a baby. And none of them can take "never" for an answer. And just about everybody – particularly women who already have children – gives us that smug look, and nods knowingly, and implies that the "biological clock" will suddenly show up, ticking, on my mantelpiece. As if I am deluding myself. As if they know better. And it infuriates me.'

'Hear hear,' added Roman. 'It is definitely the worst topic of conversation I have ever encountered. It's nobody's business but Susie's and mine.' I looked at him gratefully. 'So, let's drop it,' he ordered. 'Let's clear this table.'

I burned with annoyance as I hooked the apron back over my head and set to work getting food ready to go onto the table. I hoisted the chickens onto chargers using big forks. Amanda had been my best friend. She was the one who was supposed to understand. Amanda was not supposed to make me angry. Amanda and I had nothing to say to each other.

I performed the little test on myself that I often did after any such conversation. 'I'm pregnant,' I whispered. I closed my eyes and imagined it to be true. 'I am actually pregnant.' I believed it for a second. I felt nothing but horror. I was definitely not broody. I inhaled deeply. Definitely. I opened my eyes and found a hand lightly touching my shoulder.

'Oh, Susie,' said Izzy softly. 'I'm so sorry. You have lots of options. If you want to talk, just say.'

I laughed. 'No!' I said. 'You've completely . . .' But Izzy had picked up the green beans, and disappeared.

chapter nineteen

Tamsin didn't start talking until Susie had served up individual
crème brûlées for pudding.

'When I look back now,' she said, abruptly, during a conversa-
tional pause, 'I think I overreacted.'

Five seconds ticked by, and nobody spoke. Tamsin waited for
a response. Amanda was shovelling cream into her mouth as
quickly as she could. Roman was topping up everyone's dessert
wine, raising his eyebrows ostentatiously at the fact that Amanda
and Patrick were drinking twice as much as everyone else. Susie
was staring into space, apparently lost in thought, and Izzy was
watching her.

Then Susie looked at Tamsin. 'You mean, back then?' she asked.

'Yes. By running away to Australia.'

All eyes turned to Tamsin. Amanda looked away again, quickly.
Susie swallowed.

'You can't really overreact to something like that, can you?' she
said, quietly.

'You can.' Tamsin was adamant. 'And I did. That's why I've had
to come back, now.'

'You ran off so quickly,' Izzy said. 'I always felt I should have been
a better friend to you. I should have tried harder to stop you.'

Tamsin put down her spoon. 'Maybe you should, Izzy. It might not have made any difference.' She sighed. 'I knew Mum was dead as soon as I opened my eyes. Instantly. The car flew off the road, and I was going to have to get through the rest of my life without a mother. I was fairly sure that I was fine. I just lay there, next to her. Then we were cut out and it was blue lights and sirens, and everything was going to be different, for ever.

'When I got home, the world felt different. It looked different. It smelt different. It was all defined and hyper real. I think that when someone dies, or . . .' and she smiled at Izzy and then at Amanda, 'probably when someone is born, I wouldn't know – but when a life-changing event happens, it's at those times you truly do live in the present. The way the Buddhists want you to. I went through the first couple of weeks seeing every detail of every part of my life in technicolour. I was suddenly aware of being myself. The fact that I took a breath in, and then let it out again, several times a minute, seemed incredible. The fact that my body worked, that it performed all its functions, was a miracle. I would put one foot in front of the other and walk to the kitchen, and be baffled by the complexity of what I had just done. Physically, I was fine. I was bruised, but nothing else. So I spent a couple of weeks wiggling my fingers and toes and marvelling at the miracle, while my dad was in pieces, Billy was taking to drink, and the neighbours were bringing us dinner every night.

'I could have gone back to school after the Easter holidays. I could have taken my A levels, though I doubt I'd have been able to string many sentences together. Billy did: he did his GCSEs and they became a bit of a life raft for him. He stopped drinking and focused on them instead and he got pretty much As in everything. But I knew. I just knew, as the days went by, that I was never going to set foot in Lodwell's ever again. It wasn't so much that I *wanted* to get as far away from South Wales as I possibly could. It was more that I didn't have the choice. I *had* to get away. I felt that, in some way, I'd lost you three. I'd gone somewhere else, already. It's hard to explain now. A levels seemed fantastically irrelevant.'

Tamsin fiddled with her spoon. She wasn't hungry any more. She drank some water and carried on. She was trying to tell it exactly as it had been. She knew that her friends were missing from the story, and that was because they had been missing from her life when she needed them desperately.

'But I should have done them anyway,' she said. 'Nobody exactly *wants* to do exams, and I think that rushing off around the world because people didn't know what to say to me, because I was shocked and grieving, because you three were awkward with me, was an overreaction. I wish somebody had told me to stay. Still. A couple of weeks after the funeral, I got a train up to London and went to the Australian embassy and applied for a working visa. Which I got, no problem. I had to show some bank statements to prove I had enough money, and I'd nicked a folder of Dad's old ones, so the woman just asked if I would have access to that money in Australia and I said I would. And that was it. My passport came back in the post a couple of weeks later, with this big shiny visa stuck into it, and I bought a ticket to Sydney via Singapore, and I told my dad I was going, and I left. He tried to stop me, but he was pretty half-hearted about it because he was living in his own weird underwater world. Bereavement world.'

Tamsin looked at each of them. 'I feel terrible about it now. I let myself believe that he didn't mind me going, when really he didn't have any fight in him to stop me. Mum would have stopped me, but then if Mum had been there, I wouldn't have been going. Anyway, I pretended to myself that Dad was happy for me to leave, and Billy didn't seem bothered either, and so I went. I didn't say goodbye to any of you. Did I?' Tamsin looked around the room. Amanda was the only one who had finished her pudding. Everyone else had put their spoons down, and they were all staring at her. She didn't say anything else. They all waited. Finally, Isabelle spoke.

'And?'

Tamsin laughed. 'Oh, right. You want to know what happened *next?*'

Amanda spread her hands. 'Of course we bloody do! Come on, woman!'

'Sure. Well, by the time I got to Australia I was feeling thoroughly disorientated. I'd sat for nine hours in a transit lounge at Singapore, staring into space. I hadn't slept at all on the whole journey because it felt as if my life had taken a weird wrong turning. I was expecting it all to snap back to the way it had been, and wake up in my bed in Penarth with Mum opening my curtains and telling me I had to get up for school and me saying I hated school and I wished I'd gone to sixth-form college. And I thought about Lodwell's and the cocoon they kept us in there, and how unhealthy it was to be kept in school like that and treated like children when all the time we could have been doing this, flying to Australia with a working visa and making a new life. And I thought that seventeen was a funny age, because I'd been quite happy to go to Welsh Prayers, and do my homework and for nothing more exciting to happen than a drink in the Railway. But now I knew I was ready to find a job and embark on a new life, on my own. Seventeen is an age when you can be a child or an adult and I knew that my childhood had ended when my mother died next to me, in the Astra.

'I didn't even pretend to read anything on the plane. Sometimes I watched a bit of a film, but never for long. There were people who were interested in speaking to me, but I just answered questions politely with one word and they soon stopped.

'I landed in Sydney sometime in the afternoon, and as soon as I stepped out of the airport I knew it was going to be my home. It's hard to explain this, but Sydney worked for me. The sun was shining but it was bearable, not too hot. It was winter, and even that was good because it made me feel further from the accident: the accident was in spring, now it was winter, so in a way I was six months further on than I'd been two days before.

'People were happy and they looked fit and they smiled at me with my rucksack and my pale skin, because they could tell straightaway that I was fresh from Europe. Sydney kind of opened up to let me in, and closed again behind me and by then I was a part of it. I'd gone from Cardiff schoolgirl taught by her mother, to independent woman with nobody I knew in a whole hemisphere.

I got a bus into town, and I hopped off it in King's Cross and went to a hostel. I told the hostel woman I'd like to stay for a month. So I lay down on my top bunk in a dormitory full of Europeans, and I slept for about sixteen hours. And then I woke up and I was on my own.'

Susie was fascinated. 'You were doing all this when we were revising for our A levels.'

'I know. It seems like a parallel universe kind of thing – like it could not be literally happening at the same time – but it's true. I had my exam timetable in my head. When I was supposed to be taking my first exam, which would have been a maths paper, I was halfway through my first night working in a restaurant across the road from Bondi beach. I loved waitressing because it kept me so busy. I couldn't have borne a job where I had to sit at a desk and stare at a screen because I would have thought about my mum all the time.'

'But Tamsin,' said Izzy, 'you must have thought about your mum all of the time anyway.'

Tamsin shook her hair back. 'Of course. But if you've got your hands full of barracuda and chips, and you have to get it to table five and then rush some espressos to table eleven and try to remember that table three asked you for the ketchup, you can't brood as much. I did plenty of brooding, don't worry. I did *get over it*, in a manner of speaking. I felt close to her in a way, out there, because I was looking after myself and in some way I felt she'd be proud of me. I kind of glossed over the fact that I'd run away from my obligations. And I worked ten-hour shifts, I cleaned espresso machines, I scrubbed toilets, I sprayed tables with disinfectant, I mopped up baby sick and backpacker sick. I did it all gladly. I could never, ever regret it.'

Amanda was accusing. 'What about your father?'

Tamsin sighed. 'Yes. I know. He lost Mum and then he lost me, too. But he didn't quite lose me, did he? I would have left home a few months later anyway. He knew where I was and he had Billy, and I wrote great long letters home all the time and I tried and tried and tried to get him to emigrate with me because I thought that Sydney was everybody's magic answer. He came out to see what this enchanted, seductive city was all about, and I think he did get it, but his life was rooted in Penarth and mine wasn't. I never came back, until now. And now he's getting remarried, to Val, and he's happy again, and I really am pleased about that, honestly.'

'Are you back over now for their wedding?' asked Izzy.

Tamsin smiled. 'I'm back over here because I needed to come. I'm thirty-two. It's early days, but I've met somebody I like, in Sydney. I want to give things a proper go with him. I've never been able to do anything like that, because however settled I've been, I've always been running away. It's been the strongest compulsion, this year. I've been pulled back here. I adore Australia, but when I got there, I was running away. I think, partly, I've needed to check that I didn't secretly belong here. Not here, that is, but in Britain. I didn't want Australia to be a bolthole any more. It's worth more than that. And I can't settle down properly in Australia without saying a proper goodbye to Britain.'

'Watch out,' said Amanda. 'We'll all be visiting.'

'Please do. Life is good. Perhaps it's morbid, but I also needed to go back to where the accident happened, kind of to pay my respects.'

Izzy gulped. Amanda drained her glass.

'And did you?' Susie managed to say.

'Yes. I retraced the journey, from City Hall to the dual carriageway. I'm glad I did it. Somewhere along the way I accepted that I'm never going to know why it happened.' She shook her head, as if to banish the memories. 'So, yes, come and visit. I live in Bronte, in an apartment above my bar, and in summer I sleep with the windows open and the sea air blowing in. It gets noisy sometimes with the British kids but they mainly congregate in Bondi. My bloke, Vikram, lives in Manly, which is miles away from me, but I go to visit him on the ferry. It takes forever to get to the terminal, but once you're there, it's magic, crossing the water to go and see someone who I hope will be a part of my future. That's what I want. That future. That's why I've had to come and lay it all to rest. Your invitation was incredibly timely, Susie. Thank you.'

'You've done stunningly,' Izzy said, with tears in her eyes. 'You're such a survivor. How can you possibly say you overreacted?'

'I did,' said Tamsin. 'I went to the other side of the earth and I never spoke to any of you again. I shouldn't have been upset that you didn't know what to say to me. I probably wouldn't have known what to say if it had been one of you, either. Other people lose their mothers without jettisoning all their friends at the same time.'

Amanda and Susie were looking at the table.

'No, your instincts were right,' Susie said quietly.

chapter twenty

Freya woke first. She yawned, rolled over, and opened her eyes. She was lying on top of her Barbie duvet and her hair was sweaty. There was only a bit of light, squeezing round the edges of the shutters. It made the ceiling look grey. She turned her head towards her brother. Jake was sleeping on his back, with his mouth a little bit open. His Action Man duvet was trailing on the floor. His cheeks were rosy. Freya wondered whether it would be funny if she dropped something into his mouth, but decided she wouldn't bother. She was still tired.

She didn't like the Barbie sheets. They were too pink, and she thought Barbie was meant to be bad, because if she was real she wouldn't be able to stand up. She screwed her eyes shut, and yawned as widely as she could. She snuggled down and tried to make herself go back to sleep. She could hear someone walking around downstairs. Nobody was talking. It sounded like one person walking and that was all.

She curled up. It was definitely Mum downstairs. If there was someone doing stuff when everyone else was asleep, it was Mum. Sometimes, at home, Freya would go down, early in the morning, to see her, but Mum didn't always like that. Normally she gave a funny little smile, and Freya knew that it meant something like,

'I wanted a bit longer on my own but I can't really say that so I'll pretend to be pleased to see you.' Not very often, but sometimes, Mum would shout at her to go back to bed. Then she would say something cross and quiet, something like, 'I can never bloody get you up when I need to, and just when I don't want you . . .' and Freya would go quietly upstairs. Once, Mum had been writing with a marker pen on the whiteboard, and as soon as she saw Freya, she grabbed some kitchen roll and rubbed it all out and shouted at Freya. Later Freya had tried to read what Mum had written, but all she could see was 'Grey'. She'd almost asked Mum what 'grey' meant, but then she hadn't dared.

She couldn't get back to sleep. They didn't have a clock in here, and she wanted to know if it was an all right time to get up, like eight, or if it was a bad one, like five. Jake's watch was probably on the table next to his bed. She sat up and looked around. It was already hot. It must be time to get up. She swung her feet onto the wooden floor, and picked her way over their bags. Jake's watch said it was twenty to seven. Freya couldn't remember whether he had changed it to French time, or not. He probably had. He usually did.

'Jakey,' she said quietly, sitting on his bed. 'Jakey, wake up. Let's go into the garden. It's early.'

The stairs creaked as they went down, as quietly as they could. They had dressed quickly, in shorts and T-shirts, and they had shut their door behind them so no one would know they were up.

They were setting off on an early morning adventure. There wasn't any sign of Mum, or anybody else, downstairs. It was all quiet and shadowy, with the shutters mostly closed.

In the kitchen, a coffee cup was still warm on the side. Jake broke some pieces of bread off a stick and they unlocked the back door and stepped outside, closing it almost silently behind them.

Freya looked at the upstairs windows. Both of the bedroom windows that looked out the back still had their shutters closed. That was Izzy and Sam's room, and Tamsin's room. So they weren't awake yet, probably.

142

The grass was wet and the sky was pink. Lots of birds were singing and there was no wind at all. They walked across the lawn, to the trees. A big bird flew away suddenly from the very middle of a tree, and it made Freya jump.

'Oooooh,' said Jake, laughing at her. 'A ghost!'

'Shut up. It was a bird.'

'It was a ghost bird.'

'You're stupid.'

'*You're* stupid. You were the one who was scared of a bird.'

'Birds can be scary. Like that film we watched with the babysitter.' Freya had had nightmares for weeks after that. She had never dared tell Mum why. She would have told Dad, but he had never asked.

They walked through the trees, and came out next to the pool. Jake opened the gate, kicked his shoes off and sat down on the edge. He dangled his feet in the water. Freya joined him, and he handed her a chunk of bread.

'You know what it feels like?' she said, kicking up a splash of water. 'It feels like we're Hansel and Gretel. Looking after ourselves, without any adults.'

Jake laughed. 'Right. Hansel and Gretel had a swimming pool. Hansel and Gretel lived in a posh house in France. I wish there *was* a gingerbread house somewhere round here. I'm starving, and this bread is boring.'

'It's stale. Jake, if there was a witch here, like in Hansel and Gretel, who do you think it would be?'

He didn't hesitate. 'Susie.'

'Why?'

'Well. Because it's her house and this place could be kind of witchy. Mostly because I keep hearing Mum saying how much Susie's changed and how she used to be fat and ugly and now she's thin and she's got loads of money. I think she did it by magic.'

'She did it by painting.'

'That's kind of magic. I wish I could be so good at painting that I could have a pool.'

Freya threw her bread at him. 'No chance. You're crap at art.'

Jake pushed his sister. She almost fell in the water, but regained her balance in time. She put a hand behind his head and yanked it forwards so quickly that she overbalanced him, and sent him flailing into the swimming pool. She roared with laughter as he resurfaced, spluttering and rubbing the water off his face.

'OK,' he said. 'You asked for it!' He grabbed her by the foot and pulled her. Freya knew she could get away, but splashing around in the water with her clothes on would be fun, so she let him drag her down. Her bottom slid off the edge of the tiles, and she knew she was about to hit water. She took a deep breath before she went under, the back of her head smacking on the surface of the water. Then everything closed in on her. She kept her eyes tight shut and tried to touch the bottom with her feet. Jake was still holding her left foot, so she almost had to do the splits while she sought out solid ground with her right. It wasn't there. She felt she was sinking and sinking, and she had already breathed all the air out of her lungs. Suddenly, she knew she needed to go upwards, not down. She kicked her left leg frantically, but Jake was not letting go. She was trapped underwater. She moved her arms around, trying to push herself to the surface. She couldn't get herself moving, because of her leg. She was going to die. She opened her mouth, even though she knew she couldn't shout. She kicked again, trying to shake him off. He tightened his grip.

chapter twenty-one

Amanda was back in bed. She had walked around the house very early in the morning, and helped herself to a cup of coffee, but then she noticed signs that Susie might have been around recently, so she retreated. Someone had opened the shutters leading to the front garden, and there was a glass of icy water on the table outside.

Now, she leaned out of the open window and tried to imbibe some country tranquillity. Patrick was pretending to be asleep, but she could tell from his breathing that he was awake. He didn't want to talk to her, that was all.

She was pleased not to have a hangover. Last night had not been a particularly heavy one, alcohol wise. She hadn't been properly drunk for ages. Maybe tonight.

Today she might relax a little. When Patrick woke up, she would tell him that he was on child duty all day. It was only fair. She had them all the time. The school holidays had started three weeks ago and there were still five weeks left to go. That was the trouble with private bloody schools. They didn't give you your money's worth in terms of childcare time. Amanda knew that the only thing she liked less than doing the school run all the time was not doing it, and having the children under her feet all day. They ate all her biscuits, and she couldn't get to the gym, and they trailed round the shops with her, sliding chunky KitKats and comics into the trolley when she wasn't looking. Jake was going to some music camp for a week later in August, and Freya had about three hundred sleepovers planned, but that was it. Amanda was going to have to host one of the blasted sleepovers, with all the headaches and responsibility *that* entailed. Yes. Today was going to be *her* day. They would let the children sleep in, and then, later, Patrick could take them for a walk or something. Izzy and Sam might go somewhere with them. She was going to station herself by the pool and read all the magazines she had brought with her.

Amanda was hungry, so perhaps in that sense she was slightly hungover. She had drunk water and coffee already, and what she really needed was a large, carbohydrate-packed breakfast. France, of course, did not generally provide Full Englishes, but Susie would surely be rustling something up.

She leaned on the window sill and looked up and down the narrow road. A figure was approaching the house at a brisk jog. Amanda's heart sank and her mood changed as she recognised her former best friend, out for an early morning run. She looked at Susie's tiny ribcage, enclosed in a tight white vest, and at her legs, skinny but shapely in lycra shorts. 'Witch,' she muttered, surprised at the strength of her own feeling. Amanda did go to the gym every week day, but she knew she barely did herself any good by it. She generally spent twenty-five minutes reading the *Mail* on an exercise bike, then had a quick swim and a sauna. She knew that she was getting lazier on the bike. Sometimes, a member of the gym staff would offer her an appointment to reassess her programme. She always refused without meeting their eyes, and she bristled at the implication that she was lazy.

She gazed at Susie as objectively as she could. Susie's legs were small and toned. Her body seemed tiny, which was odd, since Amanda had always taken comfort from the fact that Susie was 'big boned'.

'It's not her,' Amanda murmured, realising the truth. 'It's me.'

She glowered and turned to Patrick's prone form, ready for a fight.

Susie smiled round the breakfast table.

'Where are . . .' she hesitated for a fraction of a second. 'The children?' she finished.

'Jake and Freya?' Amanda asked, pointedly. 'They haven't put in an appearance yet. They're sleeping.'

'Just hit that age when they start to sleep in,' Patrick said, addressing the table. 'Bless them! Took us eight years to get there but we get lie-ins now. Finally!'

Izzy smiled at Sam, who, Amanda noticed, was shovelling Frosties into his mouth as quickly as he could, giving his mother nervous sideways glances. 'That must be nice,' Izzy said.

'Makes no difference to me,' Amanda said briskly. 'I'm an early riser. I was up before six this morning.'

Izzy looked surprised. 'That's before five in English time! *And* we went to bed after midnight. Blimey! I feel tired because Sam came into bed with me at half seven, and even then we both went back to sleep. You must be *shattered*!'

Amanda gave Izzy her biggest, fakest smile, pleased with this. 'Not at all! I'm usually up at five. It's just the way I am.'

'Really?' Amanda noticed that Izzy and Susie were looking at each other.

'You used to sleep till half past twelve on weekends,' Susie reminded her. 'You said you didn't believe in mornings.'

'And at the beginning of term,' Izzy added, 'it took you two weeks to adjust. You said it was jet lag. Because for the whole of the holidays you'd been getting up later and later, until you were living on Australian time.'

Amanda looked at her bowl. She tipped it up to catch the last of the milk on her spoon, and willed them all to stop talking. It was too late; Patrick had picked up on it.

'Are you sure?' he asked with a laugh. 'I met Amanda when she was nineteen, and she was up with the lark every day. For the first six months I was with her, I was perpetually thinking I'd been dumped, because I'd wake up to an empty bed. I'd be nursing my broken heart and collecting all my things together when she'd skip back in, bearing a bag of croissants. Got me every time.' He looked at his wife. 'Still does, occasionally. So, is that right? At eighteen you were sleeping the day away? At nineteen you were up with the lark? What happened?'

Amanda and Susie met each other's eyes for a fraction of a second. They both looked away as quickly as they could. Izzy turned to Sam and noticed that he was not eating Corn Flakes, as she had supposed. She shook her head. It was too late to do anything about that now. The thought occupied the crucial seconds before everyone regained their composure.

'I grew up,' Amanda said in her briskest voice. 'Where's Tamsin?'

'Still sleeping, probably,' Izzy said quickly. 'Getting into the holiday spirit.' Her smile was forced.

They were finishing the croissants when they heard panting and heavy footsteps on the terrace. Freya appeared in the door frame, closely followed by Jake. She ran across the dining room to her mother. Her shorts and T-shirt, both yellow, were dripping wet and she left muddy footprints on the floor. Her face was red, her eyes were bloodshot, and her breathing was laboured.

'He drowned me!' she cried, pointing a dramatic finger at her brother.

Patrick raised his eyebrows. 'He didn't, happily,' he said. 'What happened?'

Izzy looked at Jake. He was soaked, too. 'We thought you were still in bed,' she told him. He smiled back at her in genuine pleasure at having fooled the grown-ups.

'Jake drowned me,' Freya repeated.

'She drowned me first,' Jake said, serenely.

Amanda got to her feet. 'Are you two telling me,' she began, ominously, 'that you have been in the swimming pool? With your clothes on? Without telling anyone where you were going?'

Freya took a step back.

'You *could* have drowned. And we wouldn't have known

anything about it because we all thought you were asleep. I am very, very angry with the pair of you. You stupid, *stupid* bloody children!'

Jake and Freya backed away from their mother in the direction of the staircase. As they eased themselves out of the dining room, they both said, 'Sorry.'

There was silence as the adults listened to the sound of their feet running up the oak stairs. Amanda got up and started to follow. Then she stopped.

'Oh, what the fuck?' she said. 'I can't be arsed.' She looked at Patrick. 'You go. Make sure they don't leave their wet things on Susie's lovely floorboards. And then someone needs to clean *this* up.' She gestured imperiously to the wet trail they had left behind them, hoping that she was making it clear that the *someone* in question was not going to be her.

After Patrick left the room, she put her head in her hands.

'Jesus, Susie,' she said. 'You've got the right idea. Don't have them. They're swine.'

'I know,' Susie said. She lowered her voice. 'Hey. Tamsin's not up. Roman's shopping. Patrick's upstairs. We need to talk. You might not agree with me, but . . .' She bit her lip. 'I can't bear this. I think we need to tell Tamsin. I can't listen to her any more . . . she practically apologised to us. How can we live with ourselves?'

Izzy coughed, choking a little on her coffee. Amanda's heart started racing. Her palms tingled. Her legs went to jelly. She did not want to have this conversation. She wanted to put her fingers in her ears and sing as loudly as she could.

'Sam,' said Izzy, urgently. 'Do you want to go outside? Don't go near the pool, though. Go and play on the grass.'

Sam shook his head.

Susie leaned towards him and put on a sing-song baby voice.

'Would you like to watch a bit of telly?' she asked. 'I've got lots of English channels and I'm sure we could find something you wanted.'

Sam held her gaze. 'Have you got CBeebies? Or Nick Jr?'

She stood up and held out her hand. 'Let's go and have a look, shall we?' Amanda noticed Susie wobbling as she left the room. To Amanda's dismay, she reappeared almost at once.

'Dora the Explorer?' she said to Izzy. 'Mean anything to you?'

'That's great,' Izzy replied. She looked pale. 'One of his favourites,' she added, fiddling with Sam's cereal bowl, pushing limp Frosties around it with the spoon. Amanda started shredding a croissant, slowly and methodically.

'The thing is,' she said, in a hard voice, 'that what you're talking about is water under the bridge. What could anybody gain from a confession?'

'I don't know.' Susie, Amanda thought, looked as if she could cry. 'We won't know till we do it. And we have to. The whole reason I decided . . .' She broke off as Tamsin came into the room. For a second, Amanda was terrified that Susie was about to turn to Tamsin and tell her everything. She held her breath, but Susie continued smoothly. 'The whole reason I decided to take you to this particular town this morning is because it's market day there, but of course if anybody would like to stay behind, or to do something different . . .' She spread her hands out. 'Morning, Tamsin,' she said, with a weak smile.

'I'd love to go to market,' Tamsin said happily. 'Am I too late for breakfast?' She looked at the table. 'Amanda, you do know you're supposed to eat them, not dismember them?'

Amanda looked at the croissant in front of her. 'Uh-huh,' she said vaguely. 'If you eat it in tiny pieces you don't get as many calories.' She picked up a piece and dipped it in her coffee. 'Mmm,' she said, pantomiming. 'Yummy.'

Tamsin laughed and sat down next to Izzy, pushing Sam's cereal bowl away. She took a croissant from the basket in the middle of the table. 'So,' she said. 'Market? Sounds nice. How far away is it? How did everyone sleep?'

'Great, thanks,' said Izzy.

'Mmmm,' said Amanda. 'Not bad.'

'I slept fine,' said Susie.

Amanda snorted. 'You were up before me, you liar. I saw you

150

running.' She was relieved to be on safe ground, and vowed to keep the conversation as trivial as she possibly could.

Susie shrugged. She looked pleased to have been caught out. 'I always run. I don't give myself the choice. At this time of year it's only the early mornings that work because it's too hot. You wouldn't catch me running when it's forty degrees. But first thing in the morning it's brilliant. It gives you the energy to start the day, and it's a guaranteed hangover cure.'

'Bloody hell, Susie,' Tamsin said, mildly. 'You're nuts. You used to do anything to get out of PE.'

'We all did,' Izzy said. 'Remember the Slackers' Society?'

In spite of everything, they all grinned.

'Of course I remember the Slackers,' said Susie, primly. 'I also remember my huge arse and my jelly belly. Thank you very much, but I think I'm better off without them.'

Amanda caught Susie looking at her, and looking quickly away. She knew what that look meant. It meant, you're fat and I'm thin. She raged inwardly. She should never have come here, and now she was stuck until tomorrow. Suddenly, the big house felt like a nightmare world, somewhere where the worst thing she had ever done was coming back to haunt her, somewhere where she had got fat and Susie had got thin. She knew that Susie was going to tell Tamsin. Tamsin was going to find out that she and Susie had killed her mother.

Amanda stood up, suddenly.

'Excuse me,' she said, and hurried to the bathroom. She closed the dining room door on the way, and locked the bathroom door carefully. She knelt down and stuck her fingers right down her throat. It was something she had not done for years. Her fingertips went as far as they could, before her hand got stuck at her mouth. She had overcome the gag reflex years ago, and she was interested to note that it had not come back. She could only gag when it was going to be productive.

Her breakfast came up easily. Acidic coffee, gloopy croissant, bits of red jam. She tasted the sicky buttery taste as it came back up. She repeated the exercise, tears in her eyes. Then she did it again, to be sure her stomach was empty. She let the tears come.

She could have been somebody different. She could have been brave and let herself have a proper relationship with Dai. She could have done so much, could have been strong, could have been a different woman. If she and Suzii had not been directly responsible for Mrs Grey's death, her life might have been worth something. As it was, despite her marriage and children, she had cowered passively. She was waiting for it to end.

She washed her hands and rinsed her mouth, wishing she'd had the foresight to use the bathroom where her toothbrush was. When she rejoined the group, nobody gave her a funny look. They had barely noticed that she had gone.

'My main memory of the Slackers meetings,' Izzy said, with a glint in her eye, 'was hearing about the progress of Amanda's grand passion.'

'SHUT UP!' Amanda was halfway into her chair, and stood up again, furious. She noticed the way Susie caught Tamsin's eye and giggled. She could see Tamsin trying to bite back her laughter.

'Oh yes,' said Susie, smiling serenely at Amanda. 'I think we all remember young Dai.'

Amanda frowned. 'Jesus!' she hissed. 'Don't tell Patrick! Don't even *hint* to him, OK?'

Tamsin was puzzled. 'About Dai? Why ever not? You didn't meet Patrick for a few years after that, did you? He cannot possibly object to you . . .' She began giggling, and the harder she tried to stop, the less she was able to control herself. Izzy joined in. Susie's mouth began to wobble. '. . . to you humping the school builder, in the back of his van, once a week for the entire sixth form!'

They collapsed.

Izzy managed to add, 'The best part of all my time at Lodwell's was you telling us all about it, in that godawful café, in graphic detail, every sports lesson.'

Susie was clearly trying to stop laughing. Amanda stared at her, stony faced, until she got it down to a spluttering giggle.

'Amanda, there's really nothing wrong with what you did,' Susie managed. 'We were wildly jealous. You were brilliant.'

'Shut the *fuck* up!' Amanda didn't dare shout, because she knew that Patrick was upstairs, that he could, even now, be on his way down with the children. She hissed instead. 'For Christ's sake! Stop it!' She felt compelled to break into monster mummy mode. 'If you don't stop laughing right now . . .' she whispered, terrifyingly, with no idea as to what the threat was going to be. It worked; she was good at that. When she had her friends' attention, she stared hard at each of them in turn. 'When I met Patrick,' she whispered, 'I told him I was a virgin. It seemed easier that way. It went with my image. He liked it. And I *hadn't* slept with any of my boyfriends, I mean there was Piers, there was Julian. Mark. None of them up to the job in hand. So I gave Patrick the official version. A couple of boyfriends, but never gone all the way.' Amanda spread her hands out. 'And so it's not the *fact* of Dai that matters. I mean, you can see what Patrick's like. He's not exactly a jealous monster, and he certainly wouldn't have cared about my past. It's more the fact that I've lied to him for about thirteen years.'

The others nodded. They were still trying not to laugh.

'Do you mean,' asked Tamsin, quietly, 'that the biggest problem in your marriage is Dai the labourer? That seems completely insane.'

Amanda concentrated her energies on being angry with Tamsin, because it was easier than guilt.

'No,' she snapped. 'No, I don't mean that at all. There are no problems in my marriage – it's fine. There's a difference between having a bad marriage and wanting to keep a little white lie hidden away. God, I never give blasted Dai a moment's thought. But I was nineteen when I met Patrick, not that long after Dai, really, and I would hate for him to look back and know I'd lied to him. And faking a first time is quite a big lie. There was never really an opportune moment for setting the record straight. I mean, what do you say? By the way, I wasn't a virgin? At what point do you say that? Before the wedding? After? Then he starts to wonder what else I've been lying about.' She paused. 'Which, incidentally, is nothing.'

Everyone promised that their lips were sealed. Susie was the first to recover her equilibrium. She got to her feet and announced that she would top up everybody's coffee. As she was halfway to the kitchen, Patrick, Jake and Freya came into the room. There were stifled giggles from Tamsin and Isabelle. Amanda glared around the room. Then she looked at her husband. Patrick was a quintessential Englishman abroad today. He was ready for an outing, wearing a pair of cream shorts that were still creased down the front, a white T-shirt through which his wiry chest hair was visible, and a cotton sun hat. Round his neck was a large camera. He was wearing sandals.

'Patrick!' she said, sharply. 'You're wearing sandals with socks! Jesus. Take your socks off, for pity's sake.' She rolled her eyes and managed to stare threateningly, briefly, at Izzy and Tamsin in turn as she did it.

He sat down obediently and took off his shoes and socks.

'Told you, Dad,' said Freya, sadly.

'You did, you did. I had no idea how stylistically unacceptable this practice was. Sorry, love.'

'Do you mean me, Dad, or do you mean Mum?'

'Both of you, I suppose. Sorry to the ladies in my life for embarrassing you both with my attire.'

Susie emerged from the kitchen with a plate of home-made biscuits and a full cafetière. She offered the plate to the children.

'You two haven't even had breakfast, have you?' she said, pleasantly. 'Why don't you start off with one of Roman's double chocolate cookies? They really are . . .' She raised her eyebrows. 'To *Dai* for.'

There was a pause, in which Amanda wondered whether Patrick could really be oblivious to Tamsin and Isabelle's stifled laughter, or whether he was pretending. Was he that obtuse? Could she really have the good fortune to be married to an utter dimwit? Freya and Jake exchanged a puzzled glance.

'There,' said Patrick, balling his socks up and putting them in his pocket. 'Rid of the offending footwear.'

'But Susie,' said Tamsin, innocently. 'You must have *laboured* for hours over these biscuits.'

'Right,' said Patrick. 'Who's coming to town, then? All of us?'

'I can't believe you didn't get one of the *neighbours* to help,' added Isabelle.

'Hmm?' asked Patrick. 'What neighbours?'

'Nothing,' Amanda said, so firmly that nobody dared carry on. 'I'm not going to market. I'm going to soak up some rays by the pool. Read a book. You lot can all go. Patrick, you can take the kids. Maybe see if there's a playground or something you can go to on the way back. Don't rush it.'

Patrick nodded equably.

'If there's a playground expedition,' Izzy said brightly, 'could Sam and I tag along? Sam would be in heaven, and even more so if Jake wouldn't mind letting him trail around worshipping him?' She said it as a question, addressed to Jake.

'Course,' Jake said, gruffly. 'S'fine.'

Amanda smiled at him, pleased that somebody was being nice. She stood in the doorway and let them all leave. Tamsin was unable to resist one parting shot, once she was safely halfway into the passenger seat of Patrick's car.

'Bye, Amanda!' she called. 'Remember, you're on holi-*Dai*!'

Amanda stamped around the ground floor, fuming. They had no respect. She would like to know which of the girls could hold a candle to her. Which of them had what she had. She had money, like Susie, and she had children, like Izzy, but twice as many. Susie had no children, although she was clearly broody, and Izzy had no money. And none of them had a husband. She was a bit miffed that nobody had mentioned the fact that only one of them was married and that it was her. Still, she had the house to herself. Amanda stretched, yawned, and began to luxuriate in the knowledge that she was alone in this huge, beautiful home and that for a few hours she could pretend it was hers. She would use it as a trial run for the day she and Patrick bought a second home. It was ten o'clock. They wouldn't be back before one, at the earliest.

She walked, barefoot, to the kitchen. She poured herself a large black coffee, and added three spoonfuls of sugar to it. Briefly, she considered not replacing the breakfast she had flushed away. It might do her some good to be bulimic again. She would lose weight and it would probably be kind to her liver, too.

She tore six inches off the nearest baguette, pulled it apart longways, and slathered it in unsalted butter. She found some Bonne Maman raspberry jam in the fridge, and spread it liberally on top. Carrying the two pieces of jammy bread, or bready jammy butter, in an open palm, and her coffee in the other hand, she went out to the terrace and sat at the mosaic table to savour her solitude. She could always send this breakfast the way of the first.

She unbuttoned her shorts, put her legs up on a chair, pulled her shades down over her eyes, and looked at the garden. She particularly liked the trees, here. There were so many of them, beyond the lawn. It was like a little wood. A copse. The trees must have been there for ever. One of them was so tall that it was probably a hundred years old. Amanda tried to feel insignificant in the face of this longevity, but she failed. Jakey had told her the other day that the stones in their front garden in Clapham were thousands of years old – 'Even older than you, Mum!' – but she had failed to find this fact interesting. Perhaps she lacked imagination. Maybe she was jaded. She took the wonders of the natural world for granted. The way the world was going, they wouldn't be there for long. There was no point in getting too attached to them.

She bit her bread and savoured the combination of flavours. There was the deliciously gooey baguette, and the way the crust cracked and went squidgy in her mouth. Then there was the slick creaminess of the butter, and over the top of all of that, the perfect sweetness of the jam. It was heaven. Bulimia was definitely better than anorexia.

She closed her eyes, felt the sun on her face, and took a deep breath. She needed to stop thinking about Tamsin and her mother. This solitude might be exactly the tonic she needed.

*   *   *

156

'Enjoying yourself?'

Roman was mocking her. She opened her eyes and craned her head in all directions until she spotted him, looking down at her from the tiny attic window. She glared at him and he chuckled at her.

'Why are you there?' It sounded strange to Amanda as she said it, but that was the way it came out. Why was he there? She had assumed he was out, doing something, earning a living, perhaps. 'I thought you were out doing something, or earning a living,' she added, shouting so that her words would travel to the top window.

'And I thought you were out in town. Where are your children?'

'With their father.'

'Isn't that what divorced mothers say?'

'Oh yes, because you know so much about parenthood.'

'What?'

'I said, you know so much about parenthood.'

'Can't hear you. I'm coming down.'

Roman disappeared. Then Amanda watched in astonishment as he came back to the window and eased himself out of it, backwards.

'What the bloody hell . . . ?' she shouted up to him, but stopped, abruptly, in case she startled him into falling. She watched, horrified, as he stood up on the narrow window sill, two storeys up, at the very top of the solid old house. If he fell, he would land on the terrace. It was concrete, paved with slabs that, Roman himself had told her, had been sourced from some particularly exclusive Pyrennean quarry. She pictured him, vividly, crashing out backwards and breaking his back. She imagined his body, dark blood in his dark hair, limbs splayed at impossible angles. She didn't even know the 999 number for France.

He leapt, backwards, off the window sill. Almost immediately, Amanda saw that he was suspended by a rope, that he was wearing a harness. Nonetheless, she gasped, and her stomach went into knots as he flew out from the house and traced an arc downwards. As his feet came back in to touch the wall, he sprang back out again. He landed on his feet, a couple of metres away from the house, next to her chair, laughing.

'You stupid tosser,' she said, but she was laughing too. She screwed up her eyes at the glare of the sun reflected off the house and the terrace. 'Are you always this much of a show-off?'

Roman unclipped his harness. 'Pretty much. I bet you've never abseiled.'

'What, because I'm such a dull, smug, Clapham mother?' She remembered her shorts, and buttoned them up.

'Have you?'

'Once, actually. Patrick and I went on an Outward Bound weekend when we were at uni. It was organised by the Climbing Club. I abseiled then. So there.'

'Liked it?'

'Terrified. Pretended to be less scared than I was to impress the boyfriend.'

'Would you do it again?' He had a mischievous glint in his eye that Amanda distrusted.

'Jesus, Roman,' she said, quickly. 'When am I going to abseil? I live in London. I have children. Not,' she added hastily, 'that having children makes you put your life on hold.'

'Yeah, right. Your turn.'

'My turn for what?'

'For jumping out, of the attic window. You don't have any children right at this moment, do you? You'd be much better off doing something brave than sitting there eating.'

Amanda glowered. 'I'm on holiday. I was savouring the peace.'

She screwed her eyes tight shut, and forced herself to pay the rope out through her fingers. Her breath was coming in sharp gasps. It was only the morning and she'd already had enough of the day.

'I can't do it,' she said, angrily, through gritted teeth. 'I hate you!'

She didn't look at Roman. She kept her eyes closed, but she knew he was smiling. She knew he was finding her amusing. He was slightly contemptuous, very patronising, and he was torturing her so he could tell Susie about it later. She couldn't believe what she was doing. She could feel the sun on the top of her head. She was mortified that Roman had had to loosen his harness quite as much as he had to make it fit her.

The attic was fascinating. It was the only part of the house that Susie hadn't included on the arrival tour. She had not even alluded to its existence. Amanda would have supposed, had she thought about it at all, that it was a cobwebby, dusty place containing a couple of boxes of junk – containing, perhaps, a sixteen-year-old Suzii, or a portrait of Suzii growing older the way she should have done. Instead, the floor was covered with clean white floorboards. It was Roman's domain. There were pretentious, yet amateurish, abstract paintings on the walls, and they were definitely not Susie's. In one corner, he had a rosewood writing desk, with pieces of paper and a laptop computer on it. By the window, there was his climbing gear. A snowboard and ski-wear were piled to one side, and two skateboards and all their accessories were in the far corner.

'Are you, by any chance,' she had said, looking around, 'a man in search of direction? Christ, you need to get a job.'

'Shut up,' he said sharply, but he was smiling.

'Where are the page-three girls?'

'I hid them. For your benefit.'

'So it wasn't that spontaneous after all? You were planning to entice me up here?'

'Only so I could push you out of the window.'

She leaned back beyond the point of logic, and let the rope, which was half an inch thick, take her substantial weight. Every muscle was in a spasm. She could smell the summer air, could hear the birds and, in the distance, a tractor. She knew she was suspended above priceless, and unforgiving, tiles.

'I'm going to be sick,' she said suddenly. She could taste the stodgy bread in the back of her throat. It was almost ironic, that.

'No you're not,' said Roman. 'You can do this, you know. Come on.'

Amanda opened her eyes and looked at him. She was harnessed

to him. He was going to pay out the rope for her. Apparently he always tied his abseil rope to a beam in the attic ceiling, but this time he had placed himself between her and the beam. He was going to be in charge of her rope, was going to hold her weight. She doubted he could take it. He was probably less than thirteen stone. His body looked strong, because he obviously spent so much time whiling the days away with physical activities, but he was slight, even if he was tall, and she was convinced she was going to pull him out of the window. At least he had tied himself to the beam, as a precaution. She doubted that even her weight would pull the house down.

'I really, really can't do it,' she said again. 'And I really, really hate you.'

'I know. Come on. You're there, now. All you have to do is to pay the rope out and jump. Go on! You're almost horizontal. The hard bit's sorted.'

Amanda spluttered. 'As the actress said to the bishop.'

'Go on! Just fuck off down from there.'

She knew she couldn't go back up, so on an impulse she bent her knees and kicked away as Roman had done. As she jumped, she let the rope slide through her harness, and by the time her feet hit the side of the house again, she was laughing. Another bound, with the wind in her hair, and she was almost on the terrace. It just took a little leap, and she was down with her feet on the Pyrennean slabs.

Roman was leaning out of the window. Amanda realised that she hadn't done anything even slightly exciting for years.

'I love you!' she shouted up at him. 'Can I do it again?'

chapter twenty-two

Lodwell's, 1990

That particular Wednesday, Suzii was longing for the PE period.
This happened every week now, and had done ever since she had
managed to instigate the Slackers' Society by calling in a favour
from Alissa McCall. Alissa did maths with her, and Suzii had culti-
vated her friendship because of the niggling feeling that it would
be good for her to have a friend who was a sports freak. For some
reason, she thought that having friends all over the year group
stood her in good stead, and she made sure she was the least
insular of her little group of friends.

Her friends were relentlessly anti-science. Suzii was taking maths
to please her father, chemistry to ensure her inheritance, and art
to annoy him. Amanda, Izzy and Tamsin would not be seen dead
near a chemistry lesson, and often Suzii was glad.

This week, she was particularly keen to see her friends. She
was desperate to talk to them. She thought that if she could speak
about this thing, it would make it look better, smaller. She thanked
God that, between them, she and Tamsin had managed to insti-
tute the Slackers' Society. One of Lodwell's sixth-form perks was
the introduction of PE 'options'. Sixth formers had an option to
walk down the road to the sports centre and play squash for a
double period before lunch on Wednesdays. Everyone who hated

'games' selected that one. They had all done it for a while: they had messed around in pairs on squash courts for an hour, and jumped up and pretended to play when Mrs Davis appeared in the viewing gallery. But it had been farcical, and boring, and a waste of time. Suzii hated exercise.

Then Tamsin heard from her mother that Mrs Davis had been abandoned by Mr Davis, and that she was, as a result, not at all interested in checking that everyone was playing squash. Suzii bought Alissa's co-operation with a term's worth of calculus, and a course of secret make-up lessons. She liked Alissa, who was tall and strong and sporty, and gruff and boyish and unfeminine. Alissa wore her mousy hair in a straight bob with a blunt fringe, and her glasses were exactly like the old NHS ones, with heavy brown frames that made her look like the school nerd. Alissa was funny and enthusiastic, but not many people outside her sporty circle knew it. Suzii was perfectly positioned to strike a bargain.

'Are you sure?' Alissa had asked, looking worried. 'I mean, what if Davis finds out? She'll come back one day and she'll find me doing the register and marking you all down, and you won't be there, and I'll get in terrible trouble and she'll go and drop me from the netball team or something.'

Suzii had laughed. 'She won't! If that happens, if you've already marked us down, we'll say we did a runner afterwards. If you haven't, then there's no problem – we'll be the only ones in trouble.' Suzii threw in a shopping trip to Cardiff one Saturday, and cut some photos out of magazines for Alissa to take to her hairdresser, and the bargain was made.

As the bell rang for the end of break, three-quarters of the sixth form picked up their sports bags and headed across the school forecourt and out of the imposing front gates. It was the only time they were allowed to leave school during the day, and so the only time they ever left by the front entrance. At other times, a locked gate at the end of the playing field was the most conven-ient, least obvious exit. It was easily hurdled except by those in short, tight skirts, who had to perform an ungainly scramble. On Wednesdays, the sixth form walked in groups and gaggles down

Cathedral Road, which ran alongside the park. They smoked, burped, and shouted lewd things at passing male cyclists.

Suzii, Amanda, Izzy and Tamsin had become complacent, so they blatantly turned the wrong way out of the front gate, and walked into Llandaff, where they went straight to the back room of a greasy café and self-consciously ordered white coffees all round. They were engaged on a joint project to get to like coffee, and the coffee here came with little plastic filters that sat on top of the cups. That, Suzii felt, was one step up from the kind of own-brand instant that was the standard fare in the common room. It was still rank. She tried to pretend to like it, but she had to get a Coke afterwards to take the taste away.

This particular Wednesday, Suzii could not even look at coffee. She couldn't think about it. It was the beginning of the summer term, and she was worrying about a lot of things. She ordered herself a diet Sprite.

She looked wistfully across the formica table at Isabelle. Izzy never seemed to have the sort of problems she had. Izzy didn't care about food, so she never overate and never dieted. She genuinely appeared to like coffee. She looked just right all the time. Whatever she wore, she looked like a goddess. She never had spots, never had crap hair, and she never took stupid risks because she knew her boyfriend would be angry if she kept saying no. Sometimes Suzii thought she hated Izzy. Most of the time, she worshipped her.

'I feel sick,' she announced. Her glass left a transparent ring on the table. She dragged the glass along a bit, smearing the lemonade around.

Izzy looked at her, with concern in her big green eyes. 'Are you ill?' she asked. Her hair was thick and loose, and Suzii was more aware than ever of her own limp black mop that was between styles.

'Not infectiously,' Suzii said. 'I took the morning-after pill this morning.'

Tamsin's head jerked up. Suzii thought she was looking at her with a little bit of admiration in her eyes. 'Really?' she said. 'What happened?'

163

'It was Jonathan.'

'You and Jonathan did it?' Amanda was excited on her behalf. In fact Amanda had appeared to be constantly excited ever since she had started screwing the builder.

'Yes.' Suzii felt tense, hoping someone was going to keep asking questions.

'Hey, that's great!' said Izzy. 'I'm thinking of losing my virginity to Jasper. What was it like?'

Suzii shut her eyes and wished the ache would go away. 'I'm sure it'll get better,' she said, nausea rising in the back of her throat. 'I hated it. It's sore and I bled.'

'And he didn't use a condom?' Amanda asked. 'Or did it split?'

Suzii stared at the table. 'We got a bit carried away.'

Tamsin tried to catch her eye. Suzii could feel her trying, and she refused to look up.

'You mean, *he* got carried away,' Tamsin said, heavily.

'I said yes.' She was utterly miserable. If this was sex, she didn't know what she was going to do with the rest of her life. It had been crap and she never wanted to do it again. 'It wasn't rape,' she added, although it felt like it.

'Did he pressure you?'

Suzii smiled down at the table, not because anything was amusing, but because the only alternative was to cry. 'Of course he pressured me,' she said. 'He said I was cold and he was going to find what he was looking for somewhere else.'

Nobody said anything.

'Oh, Suzii,' Izzy said, after a while. 'You have to chuck him, you know. You're *not* cold. Not at all. He's not the one, that's all. And he has no fucking right to speak to you like that.'

Amanda agreed. 'Julian wanted to do it with me,' she said, 'but I didn't want to. He didn't say I was frigid but he nearly did. But when I met Dai, I couldn't wait, I mean, I literally couldn't get my knickers off quick enough.'

They all laughed, even Suzii.

'We did gather that,' Tamsin said.

'But it's true,' Amanda continued. 'My point being that you

164

shouldn't give Jonny Fartpants the time of day. Tell him! Tell him
he's crap in bed. Tell him you've told all your friends. It's not you.
It's him. When you meet someone you fancy the arse off, it's going
to be completely different.' She smiled to herself. 'Believe me. I
don't even care about diets any more. Because Dai fancies me
rotten.'

'Amanda?' Suzii asked, uncertain of herself and worried she was
going to look a fool. She looked at her lap. 'Erm, this is probably
a silly question. But do you have . . . orgasms?'

Amanda smiled. 'Do I hell!' she said. 'Lots of 'em.'

'How do you know?'

'Oh, you know. Believe me, you know.' She leaned towards
Suzii. 'And if you have to ask, you didn't.'

'Hmmmm.'

Tamsin turned to Suzii. 'Suzii,' she said, her words tumbling
over each other. 'I know this is a really crass thing to say but, if
it's any consolation, even though you had such a horrible time,
I still envy you a bit. I kind of wish I had the chance to try sex.
But nobody's interested in me. Ever.'

Isabelle shook her head. 'All those boys at the Square Club
think you're fantastic,' she told her friend. 'It's you that's not interested in them.'

'They don't. They like me but they don't want to go out with
me. Let alone Have Sex. They just want to get pissed with me.
I'm like one of the lads. They would walk across hot coals for
you, Izzy. Not me.'

Suzii tried to enjoy her new, experienced status. It was true
that sex was a divide, and that she had crossed it. That meant
something. It meant she was soiled and spoiled, that she could
never be a royal bride, and that in some countries she would now
be unmarriable. She was no longer innocent, and she wondered
if that meant she was guilty. It felt that way.

'Morning-after pill?' said Amanda. 'You got a GP's appointment
before school?' She sounded impressed.

'Yeah. Well, with the nurse. I didn't catch the bus, so I had to
bribe Jackie not to tell Dad, and I turned up at the surgery crying

and saw a nurse, and she nipped into one of the doctors and it was a horrible man, and he gave me a withering look, but he gave me the prescription. I had to take two pills, and some anti-sickness stuff which doesn't appear to be working very well.' She swallowed back some bile. 'And I have to take two more this evening. Then I caught the train in and just made it for registration.'

'What did you tell Jackie?'

Suzii laughed. 'Not the truth. That's for sure. She'd blackmail me for ever. Just some rubbish about a row with Jonathan and needing to see him to make up.'

'Amanda?' Izzy said.

'Mmm?'

'Are you still going out with Julian?'

Amanda shrugged. 'I guess. I'm not exactly ready to take Dai home to Mum and Dad, so Julian's useful cover. We see a film from time to time. Or he comes over for dinner. I think he's probably gay and I think we're each other's disguises.'

Tamsin looked into her coffee cup. 'Eee, look at that,' she said, tipping it up to reveal previous drinkers' brown rings below the level of her own liquid. 'I knew they didn't wash up properly here. Gross. Amanda, you're so into Dai. You must realise how lucky you are. Jeez, look at the rest of us. Why don't you just come out and let him be your boyfriend?'

Amanda smiled the secret smile which always infuriated Suzii; every time she saw it she felt her best friend slip a little further away.

'I'm not ready to do that yet,' Amanda said calmly. 'All in good time. There's a bit of a gulf between us, you know? Sure, we shag, but when that's not happening, we don't exactly have common ground.'

Suzii smiled, trying to imagine it. 'What do you talk about when you're not having sex?'

Amanda waved a hand, airily. 'Oh, you know.'

'No we don't.'

'Stuff.'

Tamsin leaned forward. 'Amanda! Answer the question. What

166

do you and Dai talk about, or do you sit in stony silence?'

'Well.' She took a deep breath. 'OK. OK, I'll tell you, but you must promise not to laugh.' They all muttered and nodded their promises. 'We talk about *Neighbours*. *Neighbours* is the biggest thing we have in common. We both watch it, so we talk about that. Once I went to his house and we watched it together.'

Tamsin laughed so loudly that the woman behind the counter popped her head into the back room to check that everything was all right.

'Sorry,' Tamsin told her, wiping a tear from her eye.

When she had retreated, Tamsin leaned forward to Amanda. 'You mean to say,' she spluttered, 'that you and Dai are at it hammer and tongs, and when you're not at it, you're talking about Paul and Gail and their marriage of convenience? And Madge and Harold, and Mrs Mangel? Plain Jane Superbrain?'

Amanda giggled. 'Uh-huh. He doesn't reckon Paul and Gail are going to fall in love properly, but I say to him, come on! It's obvious, isn't it – they've been in love for ages, they just haven't faced up to their feelings yet because they're scared of the consequences.'

Suzii looked at her best friend. She had thought that if she lost her virginity to Jonathan, it would bring her and Amanda closer together. She had hoped it would bridge the gulf that had opened between them. That was mainly why she had done it. But now they were further apart than they had ever been. It had all been for nothing.

chapter twenty-three

I drove Izzy and Sam to market, chatting in a brittle way, pointing out local landmarks, and hoping Izzy wouldn't guess how much I wished I was alone. I longed to be alone, and at the same time I thought that if I was, I would probably cry.

Tamsin lived in Australia because of Amanda and me. Mrs Grey was dead, because of us. We had done it. I dreaded telling Tamsin, but I dreaded not telling her more. The years had evaporated. I felt it was yesterday.

'Look,' I said to Isabelle. 'See that little church on the hill there? Actually you can hardly see it at this time of year because of all the vegetation.'

'Oh yes,' she said, craning politely.

'It's dedicated to Our Lady of Rugby, the virgin supporter of rugby teams from the Landes.'

'How fabulous!' She laughed. 'That's brilliant.'

'It's full of rugby shirts. We could call in on the way back. Depending how we're doing for time.'

'Great.'

I drove along, wishing all my friends away. I didn't care that I had run my circuit three minutes faster than my previous personal best time. I didn't care that I was wearing my expensive new dress and that I knew the shape of it flattered me. Everything that usually preoccupied me was abruptly revealed as trivial and narcissistic. I wished I cared more about important things, like we used to.

'Do you still boycott Nestlé?' I asked Izzy.

She smiled. 'I did for ages. They raised the stakes when they introduced the Chunky KitKat. My resolve wavered.'

'Crafty buggers.'

'It's big corporations. They play dirty. How about you?'

'Actually, I think I more or less boycott them. Sometimes they slip things past me. You very rarely come up against a Chunky KitKat in France, so I don't have that temptation.'

'Oh, look at you. You could resist that temptation easily. I don't even know if we're still supposed to be boycotting them, are we?'

'Not really sure if they're worse than everyone else. But by avoiding Nestlé products, I don't really think I'm exactly doing my bit. I know I ought to resolve to stop air travel, convert my car to run on sunflower oil, get the house solar-powered . . .' I sighed. My burden of guilt about the world had been growing, lately. 'But it's so difficult. I mean, I could do all those things – apparently there's a guy not far away who could sort my car out for me so it ran on biodiesel – but what the hell difference would it make? It would be a drop in the ocean. If I had a totally green lifestyle, all I would do is balance out one single person who drives an SUV and takes six long-haul flights a year . . . But I know that's not a reason *not* to do it.' I looked at Izzy, feeling pathetic. 'Do you know what I mean?'

Manslaughter. We were drunk, but not that drunk. And then there was Sarah Saunders.

She smiled. 'All too well, believe me. And when your . . . well, if you ever have a baby, there's the thorny issue of nappies and the guilt of using disposables, versus the fact that cloth nappies gave Sammy a terrible rash. I suppose it's a blessing in disguise that I never learned to drive.' She laughed. 'Heavily disguised, sometimes, when we're stuck on a train going nowhere, trying to get him to Swindon station to be picked up by his dad.'

I looked at Izzy, refreshed at the normal nature of our conversation. 'Remember when you first took your test?' I asked her.

'How could I forget that?' We both laughed at the memory of her faked confidence beforehand, and the oceans of tears she had cried afterwards.

'You knocked someone off a moped,' I reminded her.

'And he made me finish the test! The sadist.'

'It's good to see you,' I told her.

'You too. You know, you're insane, hosting this weekend. It must be driving you demented.'

'No!' I said, brightly. 'Not at all. It's . . .' The pretence was pointless. 'It's terrible. Completely different from how I imagined it. I can't look at Tamsin. I'm so on edge. I'm going to tell her.'

'I know. Don't think about it till we can talk to Amanda.'

'And Amanda's a nightmare, isn't she? Talk about a princess. And I've got this woman on at me, who I painted – it's a long story. Basically, she says the guy who commissioned the portrait is stalking her, and he says he's married to her and she's having a breakdown. She called when we were eating last night, which is where Roman disappeared to. He spoke to her, and he says she was crying, saying she was scared, and that she sounded really scared. So Roman called the guy's mobile, and he says his wife is deluded and psychotic. Paranoid schizophrenia. One of them is lying and for some reason they both like to talk to *me* about it.' I sighed. I was due to phone Sarah when we got home, and I wasn't looking forward to it.

'Don't answer the phone to either of them,' Izzy said, sensibly. 'You've done the portrait, right?'

'Three of them.'

'And been paid?'

'Yes.'

'So, they sound like trouble. Whatever's going on, it's got nothing to do with you. If he's stalking her, the police are in a far better position than you are. Let them help her. I don't mean to be unsympathetic to the poor woman, but please. Strike that from your list of problems.'

I managed a smile. 'You're right. It's not my fault, is it?'

'Hardly! Hey, Susie, what about you and Roman? He's gorgeous. Do you think you'll get married? Or anything?'

This was what I had missed. Ordinary friendship. 'Well,' I said to her. 'We've talked about marriage and I think we probably will. I don't want to do it for the hell of it, because you do hear about couples getting married when they've been together for years and then splitting up a month later, but yes, if he wanted to, I would too. He's been married before, you know, and that made him a bit reticent.' I sighed. 'Izzy,' I said. 'I'm not pregnant. I know you thought I was but . . . I'm not. I just test myself from time to time, to check that I'm not broody.'

Izzy looked at me, then suddenly laughed. I joined in. Laughing felt good. In fact, it felt wonderful.

chapter twenty-four

Patrick was strolling round the market by himself. The kids were
tagging along with Izzy and Tamsin, for some reason. He supposed
they just didn't want to be seen with him, their boring, bald old
dad.

It was fine by him. The bloody sun was probably hotter than
yesterday, but he had his hat and his sunblock on, and he was
sticking to the shade as much as possible. His head was throb-
bing, but he suspected that had nothing to do with the sun. He
had taken his codeine; there was not a lot else he could do, now.
It was funny to think how used he had become to his head hurting.
There would be scans when he got home, but he couldn't bring
himself to think about that just now. They were in a biggish town
quite a long way from Susie's house. The streets were narrow,
and they were all pedestrianised (parking had been a bugger). It
was crowded. Small middle-aged women with determined faces
were all around him. They shouldered past him to get to the cour-
gettes, and he let them without complaint. He was working at a
different pace, and he had nothing to buy but a few souvenirs, if
he spotted anything.

It was strange, Patrick thought, that he spent quite a lot of time
on his own, but it never felt like enough. He left the house, feeling

pathetically liberated, early every morning. He resolutely spoke to nobody on the way to work, even though he saw the same faces on the train every day, had been seeing some of them for eight years. He sometimes left the office to get a sandwich at lunchtime, although, more often, he got supplies from the trolley that came past his open door every couple of hours. A bland ham sandwich, a packet of salt and vinegar crisps (crisps to be tucked into sandwich to perk it up), a Twix or Mars bar, a can of lemonade, and a coffee. He would take his paper out of his briefcase, divert his phone, and spend ten happy minutes savouring his bad food, and being alone. Of course, it wasn't always possible, and he knew that he was regarded as quaint and out of touch for taking ten short minutes at his desk. His younger colleagues looked on him as an old man, even though he would be thirty-four in November. He knew that he acted like an old man. He even spoke like one. He was not quite sure when, or why, that had started happening. Every now and then someone would discover his age, and would be astonished at his youth. He thought of thirty-four as his biological age. His other age – his 'adoptive' age, he supposed – was mid-forties, at least. Somebody had once told him that everyone had their correct age, an age at which they suddenly felt comfortable in their body. Most people seemed to reach it at around twenty-eight, but he had definitely not caught up with himself yet. He had been looking forward to being in his forties for years.

He walked past a cheese stall and decided to ask the young lady's advice about a cheese or two to take home. There was quite a crowd there, but he could wait. After this he would find a quiet café. The cheese stall was on the edge of a little square. Other stalls were round the edge, and in the middle there was a little square of green with flowers on it. The buildings that surrounded it were imposing grey edifices with little wrought-iron balconies, high up. He imagined himself inside one of those apartments, with a view over the small town. Just him.

The thing was, he was happily married, and he loved his kids. It was odd, this melancholy that had afflicted him recently. This yearning to get away from Clapham, from domesticity, from

Amanda's misery, from Jake and Freya's complicated routines. Some days he thought he might just pack a bag and wander off. It wouldn't be as dramatic as leaving his family. He wouldn't be being a bastard – at least, he wouldn't feel like one. He simply craved a little meander.

He took an assertive step forward in the cheese throng. Not that it did him much good. He was sick of this jolly, clueless persona he seemed to have adopted, but he had no idea who he would be without it. He was always aware of his duties as provider. He looked after the family, funded Amanda's shopping, gym and car habits, paid extortionate school fees that were only going to get worse as the children got older, bankrolled so many varieties of extra tuition, dancing, music, sports, that he couldn't keep up with them, and had no idea who did what beyond a vague feeling that the ballet bill probably didn't concern Jakey. He didn't have time to be anyone except the family banker. When they were on holiday, he always looked after the children to give Amanda a break, and that was fine. Sometimes he and Amanda would dump the kids with friends or family and have a little break together, but even then, it was all about money and status. Amanda became obsessed and stressed about where they were going for dinner and what she should wear. In Venice she had dragged him around every church on the list in her guidebook, when he would have preferred a leisurely stroll and a café. In Paris she had dragged him from Eiffel Tower to Louvre and from there to the most exclusive restaurant she could find. Their breaks were never about peace. Once, and only once, he had gingerly suggested a walking and camping holiday in Northumbria, or trip round the Cornish coastal path. He smiled to himself as he remembered her reaction.

The trouble, although he never dwelt on it, was that he and Amanda could have been happy together but, somehow, they weren't. They were strangers. He had never quite fathomed her out, even though he tried extremely hard. However he tried to cheer her up, he only ever managed to annoy her. He had read in one of her magazines, once, that if things were all right in the bedroom, they were all right full stop. This seemed to make sense to him at the time, because if he and Amanda weren't getting on, sex was out of the question. So he made it his business to try to initiate things whenever he felt it might be a good moment, but she almost always pushed him away. This led him to believe that their marriage was not a particularly happy one. Nothing he did ever excited her any more, in or out of the bedroom. She was worse than ever at the moment, and Patrick had no idea why.

He was almost at the front of the queue now, or he would have been, had there been a queue. A woman was being served who, Patrick knew for certain, had arrived after him. He watched her tasting the slivers of cheese she was being handed, and tossing the rind into the little bin by her feet. It looked to him like a good way to shop.

Patrick knew that several of his colleagues had had, or were having, affairs. He never had, and he knew that he never would. It wasn't in his nature, and he never met women who interested him anyway. He knew that Amanda half expected him to be bonking his secretary, and that this was making her more edgy than ever. He wished he could get her to believe that he had no interest in cheating on her, and that what he wanted was to make her happy, because if she was happy, all the family would be happy. But he could never find the right words to get it across to her. They were probably destined to carry on living like this until one of them died. He wondered what Amanda would do if he died first. Whether she would remarry.

'*Monsieur?*'

The cheese seller was smiling at him. She was a pretty woman, early twenties, with a wide smile and long brown hair in a pony-tail down her back. She was dressed for her trade in a white overall and a little white hat. Patrick knew he had an impatient audience, and he became flustered.

'Er,' he said. French was not his strong point at the best of times. 'Erm. *Je voudrais du fromage. S'il vous plait.*'

She said something fast and a few people around him smiled. He looked at the cheese ranged in front of him, and pointed at a goat's cheese.

'*C'est bon?*' he asked.

175

She nodded. '*C'est fort,*' she warned, and cut him off a sliver. He tasted it. It tasted of goats. Lots of goats. Lots of unwashed goats. (Did goats ever get washed? Probably not.) Lots of unwashed goats at the height of summer. He coughed, and his audience laughed, but not unkindly.

'*Quelquechose un peu . . .*' He tailed off.

'*Plus doux?*' She sliced a piece from a hard cheese and handed it to him, telling him it came from the Pyrenees. He tasted this one nervously. It was perfect. It was exactly what he had been looking for. Gentle, but flavoursome. Soft but memorable.

He tasted cheeses, and bought big chunks of them, a piece of each one he ate. For a few moments, everything in the world seemed harmonious. The people around were apparently friendly, and seemed to be entertained by his buffoonish manner. Each cheese he sampled was better than the last, and before long, he had so many purchases that the lovely young woman had to load them into three flimsy carrier bags for him. Everyone else seemed to have a basket. Susie, he thought, must have baskets. To be carrying these bags must mark him out as not being local. That, and everything else about him.

Patrick sat down at the café with his bags of cheese at his feet. He ordered a large white coffee, and leaned back, trying to stay in the shade because the heat was not agreeing with him. He pulled his T-shirt away from his armpits, conscious of spreading sweaty patches. It was extraordinary, this heat. The people in this square – some of them walking purposefully, others idling and gossiping – seemed to be living in a different climatic zone. A couple of hard-core women even had long sleeves. Yet he was sweltering. Sun, cheese and coffee; the three things doctors had advised him to avoid. He had ordered the coffee out of habit. Stupid to have chosen something both hot and dehydrating, which was also a peril to his brainache. He may as well have gone the whole hog and had a Pernod.

Freya spotted him before he saw them. He heard her high, clear voice across the square.

'Look!' she said. 'There he is! There's Dad!'

He sighed and closed his eyes. Was it very bad of him to want his solitude to last just five more minutes? They were all at his side in no time. First Freya, then Jake and little Sam, and finally Izzy and Tamsin. Tamsin, he noticed, was carrying an authentic looking shopping basket.

'Nice basket,' he said. 'Did you bring it with you?'

She laughed. 'Of course not. I bought it. Then bought stuff to put in it.'

'Dad,' said Jake. 'What's that?'

Patrick looked at the table. 'Pernod.'

'What's Pernod? Can I try some?'

'No. It's a grown-up's drink.'

'You mean alcohol.'

'Yes, Jake, I do mean alcohol.' He looked at Izzy and Tamsin. 'It comes with a little jug of water, so how bad can it be?'

'Can I have an Orangina?' asked Freya, sitting down next to him.

Patrick rolled his eyes. 'Yes!' he said. 'I can hardly sit here drinking by myself, can I? Everyone, grab a seat and let's see if we can find a waiter.'

The children drank sticky drinks through straws. Wasps hovered with intent. The women ordered beers, even though it was still early, because they were on holiday. Freya showed him her pocket money purchases, which seemed to be mainly tat, and Jake said loftily that there was nothing that interested him in this town.

Tamsin had bought honey and fruit. Izzy seemed to have limited her activities to knowing where Sam was, and helping Freya make her purchases.

'Thanks, Izzy,' Patrick said, holding up his glass. 'Much appreciated. Frey, did you say thank you to Izzy?'

'Thank you, Izzy,' said Freya.

'You already said it, sweetheart,' Izzy said, brushing Freya's hair back from her face. Patrick looked at the way Izzy was looking at his daughter – fondly, uncomplicatedly, caringly. Freya pulled her chair closer to Izzy's. 'Freya did brilliantly with her French,' Izzy added. 'I didn't need to help her at all. Just to encourage her.'

Tamsin looked interested. 'Do you do French at school, then, Freya? In our day we didn't start it until about ten at least. It's wonderful if you do it sooner. Finally Britain starts moving in the right direction.'

Freya sucked the last of her Orangina through a straw. 'No, not at school. We start that in year six at school. I do languages on Saturday mornings.'

'Really?' Tamsin asked. 'How many languages?'

'Two at the moment. French and Italian. But some of the others are starting Japanese soon so I might have to do that as well.'

'Wow,' said Tamsin. 'Loads of kids in Australia learn Japanese. One of my waitresses taught me a bit. *Konnichiwa. Watashi wa Tamsin desu.* It's my party trick when Japanese tourists come to the bar. You must really enjoy languages to give up your weekend for them.'

Freya shook her head. 'Not really. Sometimes it's fun. It's at a little college which does all sorts of coaching, and lots of the girls from school go because it's important to get ahead for all the SATs and exams. Everyone says you have to have all A stars at GCSE or the Oxbridge colleges won't even consider you for interview. I quite like French. Mostly I think I'd like Saturday morning at home more.'

'And you're, what, seven?'

Freya nodded.

Izzy was intrigued. 'What other out-of-school activities do you do?'

Freya started to count them off on her fingers. 'Ballet, tap and modern, piano, violin, and I do extra maths and English, as well as French and Italian.'

'And you do gymnastics club,' Jake reminded her.

'Yes, gym club. Jake does judo, trombone, orchestra, piano and drama, and extra maths and English and he does French too, and German.'

Tamsin laughed, appalled. 'Freya!' She looked at her closely. 'You're not joking, are you? When do you get to slob out in front of the telly with a chocolate biscuit? When do you veg?'

Freya looked at her father. 'Sunday afternoon, sometimes?'

Patrick laughed. 'What Freya is trying to say is that occasionally her mother goes out on a Sunday and the three of us partake of some guilty pleasures. Like biscuits and telly and laziness. Otherwise, their lives are pretty full.' He thought about the sense of joyous release that infected the three of them when the door shut behind Amanda. They never mentioned it, but they had a lot of fun without her. He wondered whether it would be like that if he was on his own; if they visited him at weekends, without their mother.

'I'm sorry,' said Tamsin, 'but I think that's fuc— absolutely awful. What about the pleasures of childhood? What about just messing around in the garden or the park, or lying on your bed reading a book? What about *playing?*'

Freya looked at her father. Nobody answered.

'I have to agree,' said Izzy. 'I know Sam's only three.' She saw him running off towards a small boy at a nearby table, and kept her eye on him, ready to run and intervene if necessary. 'But I wouldn't get him extra coaching unless he had big exams coming up and he was really worried about the subject. And that means when he's fifteen at the earliest. But really, we got through without cramming. I don't see why he can't.'

Patrick snorted. 'You try living in bloody Clapham. They all want to go to ballet, judo, whatever it is, because all their friends do it.'

'I don't want to, Dad,' Jake said immediately. 'I really don't. I hate trombone and it's heavy to take around with me, and it makes a horrible noise. I feel stupid playing it and when the orchestra plays in assembly everyone laughs at me because it sounds like farts. And I hate extra tuition. There are boys at school who don't have it. They do well in exams. And I really, really hate German.'

'Well, if you don't like it, stop it,' Patrick said, instantly. As he said it he knew he had invited great wrath to fall upon his head, but he didn't care.

'Can I stop extra maths?' Freya asked quickly. 'And tap and modern?'

'Of course you can, sweetheart. I thought you loved it all.'

'Patrick,' said Izzy, taking Freya's hand, and fixing Patrick with an amused look. 'Did you really just sit there with a straight face and tell your seven-year-old that you thought she loved extra maths? Do you know *anything* about children?'

He waved a hand. 'Amanda organises that side of things. But they only do it if they want to do it. That's the rule.'

'Does Amanda know that rule,' Tamsin asked, 'or did you just make it up?'

Patrick caught her eye and smiled. 'It's the newest rule.'

Freya beamed at her father. 'I love you, Daddy,' she said. 'If I can stop doing tap and modern and maths, I really *really* love you.'

He spread his hands. 'What can a father say to that?' He leaned back, feeling pleased with himself.

'Do you get very tired, you two?' Izzy asked the children.

'Mmm,' they said together, nodding in unison. Jake continued, 'We always have homework and stuff. It's nice to be on holiday.'

Tamsin leaned forward. 'You sound like a stressed chief executive, or the Prime Minister. You two should make the most of this weekend. Just mess around and don't think about maths or judo or tap and modern for one instant. Be children. Have fun.'

Patrick was tense as he pulled out of the parking space and started the drive back. He had had a marvellous time, and he was pleased to be bringing his cheese back for everyone's perusal. Susie had been delighted when he handed a bagful over to her, after she eventually found them laughing over second drinks at the café. All the same, she had immediately rushed them home. Lunch was, apparently, scheduled, and they were not supposed to dawdle.

He tried not to analyse anything. He probably shouldn't be driving. In fact, he knew he shouldn't, after two Ricards. He felt slightly wobbly, and he had his son in the back. Freya had insisted on riding home with Susie, Izzy and Sam. Patrick was ferrying Tamsin and Jake. He was responsible for them and he was breaking the law. He slowed down as he passed through a tiny village, and concentrated on the road as hard as he could. He felt slightly dizzy.

'Patrick?' Tamsin asked, putting a hand on his arm. 'Are you OK?'

'What? Oh, God, yes, fine,' he said, going down into second gear.

'What's the matter? You've almost stopped the car.'

'It's nothing.' He turned and looked at her. As his eyes met her clear brown ones, he remembered about her mother. 'Oh, Jesus,' he said quietly. 'Tamsin, I've had too much to drink. I shouldn't be driving.'

She took a deep breath. 'You're right,' she said. 'I'm stupid not to have noticed. You had a lot of pastis, didn't you? You definitely shouldn't be driving. Stop a moment. We'll swap. I only had one beer and a coffee.'

He stopped. They were outside the *mairie* of some village or other. 'You're not on the insurance,' he told her.

'That's fine. I can drive. I think I'll manage the wrong side of the road thing. The police aren't out in force, are they, not out here in the back of beyond. We're only a few miles from Susie's place, and anyway I'd rather be done for driving uninsured than have you . . .' She tailed off.

'Indeed,' he agreed, and they got out and swapped places. Two elderly women were watching from a garden over the road. They stared without any shame, and when Patrick looked back at them, they were unembarrassed. They just kept staring. One was very stooped, with a stick. She was lifting her neck at a ninety-degree angle to see them, like a tortoise. The other was robust; tall and healthy with short grey hair and a creased face. The garden was meticulously cared for, with rows of vegetables and plants and not a single weed.

'*Bonjour*,' Patrick said nervously.

'*Bonjour*,' they replied, with curt little nods. They did not take their eyes off him for a moment.

He got into the passenger seat and looked over at Tamsin. She was a beautiful woman. Her glossy dark hair fell across her face.

He liked the way it was cut, shorter at the back than at the front. Her eyes were big and chocolatey. Her skin was clear. And he liked her clothes. She was slender but curvy. The knowledge that the two old women must assume that he, Tamsin and Jake were a family suddenly excited him.

He got a grip on himself and hoisted a bag of cheese up onto his lap.

'I'm sorry for that,' he said, feeling inadequate and suddenly, unprecedentedly, infatuated. 'I didn't mean to upset you. I just hadn't thought.'

'That's fine,' she said, keeping her eyes on the road. 'Really. Good on you for sorting it out when you did.' She looked at him. 'You know, I don't think I'm any more sensitive to drink driving than any normal person. The years have passed, you know?'

He turned and looked out of the rear window. 'Those women are still watching us.'

'Lucky them.'

'Dad?' asked Jake. 'Are you drunk?'

'No, Jake,' he said firmly. 'Just had one too many to drive the car.'

They sat in silence as Tamsin navigated the country lanes and brought them, after only two wrong turnings, to Susie's house.

Patrick was full of trepidation about Amanda. He desperately wanted her to be happy, and he knew she wasn't. He steeled himself to see her miserable as ever, and prayed that she hadn't started drinking yet. He wanted her still to be in the coffee phase of her day. At some point around lunchtime, at least when they were on holiday, she invariably moved seamlessly from coffee to aperitifs. Aperitifs had the potential to stretch out until dinner, when she moved on to wine. It was a mystery to Patrick how Amanda's body stayed hydrated enough to function. She rarely, if ever, touched water. But this was one of those things he could not ask her about. He knew that, one day, he needed to find out when, in the course of a normal week day, she had her first drink. For years, he had shied away from the certainty that she picked his children up from school after three or four cocktails. For years he had told himself that she would never be so irresponsible, which was a cover for the fact that he didn't dare ask her. He realised this, and loathed himself.

'Thanks for driving,' he said to Tamsin, looking for a moment at the way her hair fell across her face, then worrying that he had looked too long, and looking away. 'Sorry about all that. Many apologies.'

'Sorry about my dad,' echoed Jake.

Tamsin smiled at them both and shook her head, dismissing it.

He stepped out into the heat. It was baking, boiling, scorching. He tried to find more adjectives. It wasn't really boiling, because that implied water. It was certainly roasting, toasty. It was like a furnace, like an oven. Like a microwave? The trouble with microwaves was that you could never know what it was like to be inside one. It was, at any rate, extremely warm.

'It is extremely warm,' he said to Tamsin.

She gave him a puzzled smile. 'Yes,' she said. 'I'd say.'

Susie's car was already in the drive. They found her in the kitchen, frowning as she arranged cheese on a plate at the same time as grilling pieces of chicken and spinning lettuce leaves.

Tamsin stopped. 'I'm helping with lunch.'

Susie tried to shoo her away. 'You go and sit down. I'm fine. All under control.'

'No, no way. Come on. Let me do the salad.'

Patrick continued outside, expecting to discover Amanda drinking vodka by the pool. He strode across the terrace, seeing evidence, in the form of a copy of *Elle* open at the health pages, that she had been there recently. Izzy, Freya and Sam were playing hide and seek amongst the trees, for Sam's benefit.

'Seen Mum?' he asked Freya.

'Nope!' she said. 'Sam, I can see you! I'm coming to get you! You'd better run!'

Sam ran past him. Patrick felt the breeze as he rushed by.

'He must be hot,' he remarked to Izzy.

'He's in heaven,' she countered. 'Your two are being so sweet to him. They really are a credit to you both.'

Patrick was surprised. 'Thank you, Izzy,' he said.

He continued. Jake hurtled past him, ignored the open gate, vaulted the fence and dived into the swimming pool in one fluid movement. Patrick waited tensely for him to resurface. He did, spluttering and laughing, checking that his father had seen him.

'Good stuff, Jakey,' he said. 'Seen Mum?'

'I thought she'd be here,' Jake said, checking the sun loungers. 'She isn't, though.'

'No,' his father agreed. 'Oh well. Maybe she's gone for a walk.'

There was a brief pause before father and son burst out laughing.

'Or maybe she's gone to the moon,' said Jake. 'More likely.' And he dived underwater, and swam to the deep end. Patrick thought he might as well go and fetch that *Elle*, take up residence on a shady sun lounger, and keep an eye on his son.

chapter twenty-five

Amanda and Roman were drinking in the attic.

'This feels naughty,' Amanda said, rifling through his CD collection. 'I bet you're the kind of guy who has a top of the range stereo and I bet you're really obsessive about it.'

'It's important. But I put everything on my iPod. That's my baby at the moment.'

'I've never heard of all these people. Not surprising. We know nothing about music. We think ourselves hip if we buy a Coldplay album from time to time. Patrick bought me Robbie Williams for my last birthday but I got him to change it.'

'For?'

'Oasis.'

'Hmmm.'

'I mean, who's this? Glove? Glove and Special Sauce – funny name. What are they like?'

Roman took the CD from her hand, laughing. 'It's not Glove. It's G-Love. You'd like it. Look, I'll put it on for you.'

Amanda picked up her drink, a vodka and cranberry juice, heavy on the vodka and light on the cranberry. 'Are you sure it's G-Love? It looks like Glove to me. What's the G for?'

Roman shrugged elaborately. They were both slightly drunk.

Emily Barr

'Drink up,' Roman told her, putting the CD into his stereo and standing by the window. 'They're all home. I can see your girl outside. Your husband's taking your magazine off the terrace. It's time for your grand entrance.'

She giggled. 'I'm going to feel silly. I never ever do anything like that.' She was excited. She liked the idea that she was going to surprise everybody.

'I know you don't. But that's why you're going to today.'

The music started. It was funky and funny and it had whistling on it. She liked it. It was retro, she thought. She danced a little, embarrassed even as she did it, and downed the rest of her drink. She picked up the harness and waved it at Roman. 'OK,' she said. 'Saddle me up then, cowboy.'

Roman laughed. 'Now, that sounds like an invitation a man can't turn down.'

'Are you flirting?'

His smile froze for a second. 'No,' he said. 'I'm being friendly.'

Amanda was feeling strange. She was happy, and she was enjoying herself, and she had met someone she liked. This was an unfamiliar state of affairs. She had had more fun that morning than she could remember having since . . . well, since the days of Dai. But this, she knew, could not be good. She was happy with another man, and, whatever he said, she was attracted to him. Roman was beautiful – toned, fit and handsome. He was far out of her league. She was far too fat to be flirting with him.

'Do you adore Susie?' she asked, suddenly. Roman squinted at her, harness in hand.

'That's a weird question, Amanda. Of course I do.'

'But do you? Do you think about her all the time? Is she your ideal of female perfection?'

'Yes, she's gorgeous. She's wonderful. What are you on about?'

'Are you faithful?' As she asked it, she wished she hadn't.

'Yes,' he said. 'Amanda, don't mistake us messing around today for anything else. I can assure you there are no ulterior motives. I like it when there's someone to mess around with.' He thought for a moment. 'Fuck, you must think I'm sleazy!'

186

'Not at all.' She said it too quickly. 'Of course. I mean, for Christ's sake, I'm married, with kids. I'm just being silly.'

'Let's get it straight,' he said decisively. 'You think I'm a complete and utter bastard. Jesus! You're one of our guests. You're the only one who stayed home this morning. I thought it would be friendly to get to know you a bit, and we've had a good time, haven't we? I love Susie. Last night you seemed seriously uptight. This morning you've relaxed. You're funny, and you're not ashamed to be yourself. I like that. It doesn't have to be about sex.' He looked at her. 'It definitely isn't about sex. Now, are you going to abseil out of that window, or not?'

Amanda thought about it. 'Not,' she said.

'Yes you are.'

'No, I'm not.'

'Yes, you are.'

'Not.'

'Come here.'

She rolled her eyes elaborately and let him put the harness on her. She was nervous about the idea of doing it again. It had been Roman's idea for her to make an entrance. She was as scared as she was excited. She hoped the kids saw her.

'All right, then,' she said, and she climbed on to the window sill. This was the third time she had done it, and she felt reasonably competent. Roman had told her to ditch her useless gym habit and join a climbing centre. This abseiling was making her so happy that she might just do it.

'Off I go!' she said, with a shrill, scared laugh. Her heart thumped and her stomach tied itself in knots as she leant back. 'Are they watching?' she asked, too scared to look round.

'Can't see, you're in the way,' Roman pointed out. 'Don't worry. They'll spot you.'

She listened out for reaction as she bounded down the wall, concentrating on the rope that was holding her up. They were silent. She remembered how scared she had been watching Roman doing this. She landed with both feet on the terrace, and turned round, exhilarated.

There was nobody in sight. She could hear Sam shouting beyond the trees. She looked up. Roman was leaning out of the window.

'They've all buggered off!' he said, half laughing.

'Bastards.' Suddenly, she was humiliated. She ripped the harness off, unclipped everything, and left it on the ground. Then she ran upstairs and shut herself in her bedroom.

She lay down on the bed, fuming but happy, and was still there when Freya edged nervously around the door to tell her it was lunchtime.

Amanda was chastened, but she was still high on the morning's adrenaline. There had to be a climbing wall in Clapham. She would love to have this buzz on a regular basis.

'Hello, Freya,' she said, with more enthusiasm than usual. 'Come and tell me about your morning.' She sat up and patted the bed next to her. Freya arrived with a jump and snuggled up to her mother. 'What was the market like? Did you go to a playground?'

Freya smiled up at her. 'The market was nice. We were with Izzy. She helped me talk French.'

'I know you can talk French perfectly well by yourself.'

'Yes, but I felt shy. I didn't think they'd understand me. Real French people. But they were sooooo nice. Izzy's sooooooooo nice. And guess what, Dad said I can stop doing maths and tap and modern!'

Amanda frowned. 'Did he? Well, he's wrong. He had no business telling you that.'

'And he said Jake can stop trombone and German.'

Amanda felt her black mood descending again. Patrick was always undermining her in front of the kids. He always made her be the bad guy.

Freya continued, oblivious. 'Tamsin said we should watch telly instead and eat chocolate biscuits. She said we need to be children. Izzy said it's terrible that we do all the activities.'

The rage bubbled up. Amanda leapt to her feet. 'Right. Is that what they think? I'm going to set them straight.' Freya tried to take her hand, but Amanda pushed her back onto the bed, harder than she had intended. Freya got up again and ran out of the room after her mother.

'They weren't being nasty, Mum!' she called, feebly. 'They were only trying to help!' But her mother was long gone.

chapter twenty-six

Freya decided to avoid the confrontation she had provoked. She tiptoed downstairs and out of the front door. She felt her arms and legs getting hot and heavy as soon as she was outside. She walked quickly through the grassy front garden, out of the gate, and down the road. Then she climbed over a side gate, which brought her into the very far corner of Susie's garden. She and Jake had spotted it yesterday, and she was pleased that she was using it.

This part of the garden felt as if no one ever went into it. There were a few trees, so it was nice and shady. The grass was scratchy on her ankles. It was completely silent. There was a ditch on her left, which ran all along the side of the garden. Past the ditch was a huge field of very high plants. Susie had said it was maize, but until she looked closely, Freya hadn't realised that meant corn on the cob. She thought it was funny how something as small as corn needed a plant that was twice as tall as she was to grow on.

The plants were far enough apart from each other for her to walk into the field. She smiled, and ran all the way across the garden, to the pool, to fetch Jakey.

Jake was treading water in the deep end while Dad was timing him on his watch.

'Six minutes!' Dad said. Jake said nothing. His mouth kept dipping below the surface.

'Hey,' Freya said, urgently, checking to see whether Mum was coming through the trees yet. 'Mum's mad. Let's go!'

She saw her father's face fall. 'Mad about what?' he asked wretchedly.

'Sorry, Dad. I told her about stopping maths and tap and modern, and she went crazy. Come on, Jake. Let's go. This way.'

Jake grabbed the side of the pool. He looked pleased with himself.

'It's lunchtime, isn't it?' he said.

'We'll just have a wander round the garden. I know some good exploring. Then we'll go in for lunch after the others. That means we'll be really hungry. And I know you pigged out on *pain au chocolat* at the market, because I did too.'

Jake climbed out of the pool and dripped water over to his towel. He quickly changed into his shorts as modestly as he could. 'OK. Let's go. See you, Dad.'

They hurried off together. Freya led Jake to the best place she had seen for getting into the maize field. They leapt the ditch, side by side.

chapter twenty-seven

Lodwell's, 1991

During the Easter holidays, Izzy drew up meticulous revision timetables, read as much of Alexander Pope's oeuvre as she could, and busied herself on numerous side projects to make her forget about her A levels. She felt supercharged all the time. Everything was about to happen. She was going to leave school. The magical last day of term shimmered on the near horizon. If she managed to get three Bs in her exams, she would be going to Sheffield to study English. She was going to be a student. The excitement of it all propelled her through revision and clarinet practice, through the mechanics of preparing for a music history paper and a French oral. She wanted to be busy all day long. She decided to make herself a dress for the ball, because she certainly couldn't afford to buy one, and nobody else was likely to make one for her. It was surprising how many of the girls at school were suddenly able to produce mothers or grandmothers who were apparently able to whip up yards of netting and satin and tulle into a bona fide gown. Izzy's mother didn't even bother to laugh when she asked her.

'Of course not, darling,' she said, frowning out of the window, her mind clearly elsewhere. 'We'll give a contribution if you like.'

Izzy had taken the contribution and bought herself a Vogue

pattern and a lot of soft burgundy stuff. She had no idea how to sew, and was scared of the old sewing machine that lived in a corner of a box room, so she was stitching it all by hand. She listened to her set work, a cassette of Haydn quartets, while she sewed, trying to remember to keep her stitches tiny. This was an interesting project. The dress she was making was going to be skin tight, but long, with narrow straps at the shoulders and an extremely long slit up the back. She was, she hoped, making it to fit her curves perfectly, although she was a little worried about that part of it. Still, she had stood in her underwear and made Tamsin take all the relevant measurements three times, and she had personally written them all down and chalked the outline onto the back of the material.

She had no idea why she was bothering. Other schools, even private schools, had discos. The fact that Lodwell's had a ball instead crystallised everything she hated about the place. It was pretentious and elitist. She had gone last year, drunk too much, snogged someone and been sick, first in the loos, and then in the bushes outside City Hall. Last year she had worn a black dress from Warehouse, and it had been fine. Somehow, her new dress was connected to her new identity, as Izzy the English student. When she went to university, she was going to be someone a little bit new. *Izzy who makes her own clothes* was an appealing persona.

Tamsin hated the ball, and Izzy could understand that. She hated it too, and if, like Tamsin, she hadn't been interested in dancing or snogging, she would have refused to go. Tamsin had to go because Mrs Grey was in charge, and she claimed, 'I can't sit at home watching Saturday night telly while my mum's at the fucking school disco! I have to *pretend* to be normal.'

Izzy sat listening to the quartet, mentally noting the recapitulation of the theme and picturing the notes on the score. It was nearly lunchtime. After lunch she was going to start re-reading D.H. Lawrence. *Sons and Lovers* was her least favourite of the A-level texts, which was why she was forcing herself to do it when she would much rather be going over *Othello* or *The Rape of the Lock*. She pushed her hair back behind her ears and down her back, annoyed at the way it kept sticking to the material, and getting tangled up in the thread. If she was braver, she would cut it all off. It was far too long and it annoyed her. It took her hours to wash and dry it, and she was always having to brush it through. It had recently occurred to her that all Susie did to her hair was to run some gel through with her fingertips, and stand it up on end. Then she was ready. Amanda applied various styling products liberally, close to her scalp, so it held its position when she flicked it into place, and blow-dried it to within an inch of its life. And Tamsin did nothing whatsoever to her hair. Izzy tried to imagine what it would be like to lose her mane. She tried to picture herself with a jaw-length bob. Her hair was thick, and it would probably look quite good short.

She could not do it. Her hair was herself. She knew that everybody would think it was a shame if she cut it off, and she knew for certain that every single person she had ever met would sidle over to her and ask whether she regretted it.

She heard footsteps on the stairs. She hoped it might be Tamsin or Suzii or Amanda, but she knew, from the heaviness of the tread, that it was actually Jasper. She was fed up with Jasper. He was funny and nice and adorably polite to her parents, but Amanda's grand passion with Dai had thrown Izzy's little relationship into stark relief. She did not particularly fancy Jasper, and although he was a good friend to her, she was bored of their relationship. She was already thinking about men she might be going to meet at Sheffield. She created them, sometimes, as she lay in bed. Men with dark hair and round glasses and baggy jumpers. Men who liked books and opera and cooking.

'Hello, Iz,' he said, poking his head round her bedroom door. Izzy looked up and smiled. Jasper had shiny hair that almost reached his shoulders, and this was what had drawn her to him. She'd thought he had an interesting face, but now she was not so sure.

'Come in,' she said. 'I'm sewing.'

'So I see. You really know how to party. Nice music.'

'Thanks. It's the recapitulation.'

'My favorite band!'

'Shut up.'

'Are they in the top ten at the moment?'

'In this house they are.'

Jasper flung himself down on Izzy's bed and looked at her suggestively. That was why she was going to have to finish with him. She wanted to have wild abandoned sex like Amanda and Dai. She didn't want it to be sore and resentful, like Suzii and Julian. She knew that the issue was at the very top of Jasper's mind, and she knew that she was soon going to have to confront it.

'Iz,' he said.

Her heart sank. She didn't want the confrontation to take place this instant. 'Jass?'

'We're eighteen.'

'Aren't we just?'

'And we've been seeing each other for quite a while. And I, like, well, I'm pretty sure I, like, love you and everything. You're the greatest girl I've met in my life and you're, well, you're really beautiful. I think we should maybe think about, you know, taking our relationship to the next level. You know?'

Izzy looked at him and smiled. She felt maternal towards him, which was probably not good. That little speech had not been easy, and he had done it well.

'I'm not sure,' she said, and waited to see how he responded.

'Your friends, though – they must have done it by now?'

'My friends? I don't really base those kinds of decisions on what they're up to.'

'Have they, though?'

'Well, yes, Amanda and Suzii have. Not Tamsin.'

'No surprises there.'

She looked at him. His hair was flopping over his face, and she remembered her six-month crush on him when he was just a boy she used to see across the pub. She had been smitten, had written 'Isabelle Wilson' over and over again, in different types of handwriting. She had dreamed about his glossy hair and the soft stubble on his chin. She had loved the granddad shirts he wore. But now they had been together for six months, and she was bored, and the shirts had got a bit predictable. She was determined not to screw him for the sake of it, because it would be the path of least resistance. Izzy was a romantic, and she wanted it to be true love.

'Jasper,' she said, with some trepidation. 'I'm very fond of you, you know that. These last six months have been great.'

'Seven months.'

'Yeah. But, you know, because we've spoken about this before, that I want to save, you know, sex, for a time when it really feels right, when it feels like the only thing to do.'

He stared at her. Consternation, she thought. That was the word.

'Doesn't it feel right?' he said quietly. 'Doesn't it feel like the only thing to do?'

'No. Sorry, but no.'

She looked at him, and he looked at her with eyes that had once made her melt, and a sudden impulse urged her to change her mind, to strip off her baggy cotton trousers and her tight black T-shirt and present herself to her boyfriend. It was what, she was sure, her parents imagined she was doing. She could be married, could be a mother of several children by now. There was something geeky about an eighteen-year-old virgin.

But she did not do it. Instead, she watched Jasper get up, give her a last, pleading look, and leave the room without another word. She heard his footsteps on the stairs and then, a minute or so later, she heard the front door slam. She imagined him getting on his bike and cycling back home, to Penarth, calling her terrible names under his breath. She supposed they were finished. She was sad, but she was excited at the same time. Jasper had definitely not been The One. In six months, if she worked hard, she would be in Sheffield. Unencumbered.

She changed tapes, putting *Othello* into her cassette player, and she picked up her sewing again.

chapter twenty-eight

Patrick knew he had to find Amanda and get the row over with. He started walking towards the house, but when he saw his wife on the terrace, leaning her face in towards Tamsin in her most aggressive fashion, he paused. He hoped she would see him by the trees and come over to him, taking the row away from their friends and keeping it private. But she just carried on arguing with Tamsin, who was clearly holding her own. *Mistake*, he thought. He tried to convey it telepathically to Tamsin. *Don't argue with her*, he urged. *Fighting back makes it worse*. Tamsin didn't know Amanda, so she didn't know that the only way to defuse her was to capitulate, to tell her she was right, to cave in entirely.

He walked as slowly as he could towards them, dreading the moment when his wife would turn on him.

'And what about you?' Amanda was yelling. 'You were the one who was supposed to be rescuing the African orphans! Where does a nice apartment in Sydney fit into that?' She saw him coming and barely paused for breath. 'Oh, and here he comes,' she shouted. 'That's right. Saunter over looking mortified. Come on. Now you can join the fucking frog chorus telling me what a terrible mother I am. Because I want my children to do well. For Christ's sake! If you have to talk about me behind my back, try not to do it in front of my seven-year-old daughter, would you? Patrick! You tosser! You undermine me *constantly*. You take bugger all interest in anything either of them do, but when someone who has no children of her own –' she thrust her face into Tamsin's – 'when someone who knows nothing whatsoever about it decides to weigh in with her great expertise about the kids' extracurricular activities, you instantly agree with her and tell them – *tell them!* – they can do whatever they like. Jesus!' She turned and stormed off.

Patrick took a couple of steps after her, then faltered. Instead, he turned to Tamsin, trying to gauge how upset she was.

'I'm sorry about all that,' he told her, awkwardly. He was excited, partly by Amanda's anger, and partly by being close to Tamsin. 'I seem to be constantly apologising to you. But I really am sorry. It was a chance comment from Freya that sparked that off. It's my fault. Amanda's right, I shouldn't make promises to the kids without consulting her first.'

To Patrick's secret pleasure, Tamsin touched his arm. 'Don't be silly,' she said. 'It's not your fault. You were perfectly reasonable. Amanda doesn't seem very . . .' She looked at him, clearly unsure whether to continue.

'Very what?'

Tamsin took a deep breath. 'Very happy. In fact she doesn't seem at all happy. She seems to be thoroughly miserable. Always half drunk, always on the offensive. Sorry to say this, Patrick. I don't want to pry, but what's going on with her?'

His shoulders slumped. 'Oh, God, Tamsin.' He reminded himself that he had to be loyal. He should not confide in Tamsin. But who in the world *could* he confide in? 'I wish I knew,' he admitted, and as he said it he felt his world crumble. He had never shared his fears about Amanda before. 'I don't think I've been the greatest husband to her,' he admitted. He saw Tamsin's face. 'Oh, Christ, not like that. I've never played away or what-have-you. I've just, I suppose, always known that she was a bit miz, and I am, it seems, not the right person to perk her up, because if I was she would be happy by now, but instead she seems to get worse all the time.

She seems to blame me, and I think she's probably right.'

Tamsin started to say something, and then stopped. 'Has she . . . I mean, I can't say I know Amanda any more. But at school, when I used to know her, she would drink, because we were all experimenting with alcohol at every opportunity. I don't think it was called binge drinking back then, but that was what we did on Fridays and Saturdays. We were all in it together – there was nothing unusual about Amanda's drinking. Her eating, though. Now, that was a different matter.' She looked at Patrick questioningly. 'It was really screwed,' she added.

He laughed, slightly in horror at Tamsin's broaching of the forbidden topic. 'Oh, good Lord, yes.' He said it as quietly as he could, just in case. 'I would never, ever mention food to her. She would be one hundred per cent guaranteed to blow up in my face and I'd only succeed in making things worse. She's hung up about that, and yes, you just alluded to her drinking, and yes, I am very well aware that she has a problem with alcohol and I am also aware that by ignoring it – or possibly encouraging it – I do nothing but exacerbate it.'

'Do you encourage it?'

'Mmm. I think I legitimise it. I take her a G&T when I can see that she's gasping for one. I drink with her, most days. I freely admit that I like a drink when I get home from work. But most evenings I could be happy with that, with my one tipple on getting home, unless it's a special occasion. Except that Amanda just keeps pouring. We're constantly having cases delivered from the various wine websites she's signed up to. She's always got a red and a white on the go, and she has this idea that you shouldn't leave any wine in the bottle, that if you open one you may as well finish it. She says that it goes off by the next day. And it's not the first bottle she's insisting on finishing. More like the third.'

'You know that's bollocks.'

'I do. And I should tell her that. I should just say "bollocks" like you did. But I can't. When I met her, she was a drinker, and that was one of the things I liked about her. You know, everyone drinks at uni, like you just said they did at school. I thought she was the coolest girl I'd ever met, because she'd drink lager and match me pint for pint. All the lads adored her. But then it just carried on. Got worse, rather.'

'And the food?' Tamsin asked gently.

Patrick shook his head. He felt disloyal even thinking about this. 'I daren't go there. If I so much as hinted at all about her eating, it would mean I was saying she was fat and I didn't find her attractive any more. Amanda would be furious and my life wouldn't be worth living.' He drew in a sharp breath, imagining it.

'But she *is* fat.'

Patrick shook his head and knitted his eyebrows together. 'Shhhh!' he said furiously. 'We should stop this conversation right now!'

Tamsin was undaunted. 'Amanda's always had a strange relationship with food,' she said, ignoring Patrick's interjection. 'At school she'd drink on Friday and Saturday nights, like I said, but she'd never touch a drop the rest of the week because of the calories in it. But food was a major stumbling block for her and Suzii.' She smiled. 'It's funny, thinking about it. They've swapped roles. Susie was the larger one who was always giving in to temptation. Amanda kept herself stick thin. She was a rake. Bones jutting out everywhere. She'd go for days without eating, and then . . . Well, I shouldn't say much more, really. It's not fair on her.'

'No it's not,' Patrick agreed hastily.

'I wonder what happened,' Tamsin said suddenly. 'Something happened to her. She stopped sleeping. She started drinking insanely. Do you know what it was?' Patrick thought there was a faraway look in Tamsin's eyes, as if she were trying to work something out.

'What do you mean?' he asked.

'Sometime before she met you? I don't know what.' She suddenly looked depressed. 'Anything?'

'I have no idea what you mean,' Patrick told her, and he really didn't. 'And the thing with all of this is,' he added, 'that I haven't the strength for any of it.' He looked at Tamsin, trying to gauge how much she despised him. 'I'm not cut out for it. I can't stand up to her. Can you imagine? Imagine if I confronted her with her drinking problem, with her . . .' He paused, unable to articulate the word *alcoholism*, still feeling that the word was too strong, that it applied to other people. 'Well. She would fight me tooth and nail.'

Tamsin sighed. She put a hand on his arm. 'If you like, I could say something. She already hates me so I've nothing to lose. Because I don't think she's going to have an epiphany of her own accord any time soon.'

'Are you serious?'

She laughed. 'Patrick, I'm not scared of Amanda. And you shouldn't be scared of her either. I just want to know where my funny, sweet, passionate friend went.'

Patrick shrugged. 'You see, she has friends,' he said. 'Kind of. She has these women she does school stuff with, a few other mothers who live in the streets around us. But she doesn't have that sort of relationship with them. I'm sure they gossip about her drinking, but they certainly wouldn't have said anything to her face. It's not like that, in the circles we move in. Everybody's sweet as pie on the surface, and nobody would put themselves out to help someone like Amanda. Her mother drifts around in her own little world most of the time, and Amanda's dad has never been a communicator. He's like me, I suppose.' He paused and ran a hand over his bald head, which was aching in a nagging, low-key way. 'Depressing thought. There's no chance of any input there. I'm the one with the responsibility and I have failed.' He looked around, at the thirsty garden. The sun was directly over-head and he knew his head was starting to burn. He needed more codeine. 'We shouldn't be having this conversation,' he said, quickly.

'We should! We have to,' Tamsin said urgently. She stared at him with her liquid brown eyes. 'It bothers me to see her like this. I had no idea. Susie said Amanda had a husband and two kids and lived in London, and I imagined everything being rosy. Not sure why. Take away the money and she'd be a down-and-out. Does she pack the kids off to all their activities because she can't deal with them?'

But Patrick was regretting his openness. 'Oh, you have no idea how competitive it all is, when it comes to the children. Amanda deals with them very well. It's her territory and she does a superb job. But if you want to talk to her, good luck.'

He felt Tamsin's scrutiny. Before she could say any more, Susie stood on the terrace and clapped her hands.

'Everybody!' she called. 'Lunch is ready! Come and get it!'

Tamsin inclined her head. 'Shall we?'

'I'll say.'

chapter twenty-nine

I made sure my guests had full plates of food before I disappeared inside. Amanda had run away, and I wasn't sure what she was angry about this time. I was annoyed by her tantrum, so I didn't go upstairs to invite her down for lunch. She would smell it. She was an adult.

I felt myself jigging around, so nervous that I did not know what to do with myself. I was jittery and ill at ease as I watched them fill their plates. I put the free-standing parasol up on the terrace, so it shaded the lunch table completely.

'Sit down,' Izzy said, with a friendly smile. 'Come on, Susie. Come and relax. Let us enjoy your company.'

I grinned at her. Izzy was, now, the only person I was pleased to have back in my life. 'I will. I've just got a phone call to make first.'

'To the stalker lady?'

'That's the one.'

'What stalker lady?' Tamsin asked, as she sat down between Patrick and Sam. 'You've got a lady stalker?'

'No,' I told her. 'Long story. And really nothing to do with me, as Izzy has pointed out. Back in a minute. Hey, Patrick, where are your children?'

'Last seen playing in the garden.' He pointed to the far corner, beyond my studio. 'They were going to climb some trees, I think. Full up from the pastries they ate this morning.' He looked at me and I saw a dawning realisation that he and his family were not being considerate guests.

'Tell you what,' he said, quickly. 'How about if I make them each a sandwich now, for them to have later? To save them annoying you.'

I was eager to get my phone call over. 'Wrap them in foil and put them in the fridge.' I started heading for my shed.

'Susie,' asked Sam, chewing on a piece of chicken. 'Have you got any ketchup?'

'In the fridge.'

'I'll get it,' said Izzy, standing up. I looked at her gratefully, then turned and went into my studio, to use the phone in there.

I stared at three photos of the paintings I had done of her. I had been pleased with each of them. They looked vibrant and happy. I almost wanted to step into their sun-soaked, tranquil worlds. I also wanted to tear them into shreds and burn them slowly in the flame of a candle. I thought I would probably put them in the bottom drawer and try to forget about them.

'You can see, can't you?' I said to her. 'This is a very bizarre situation for me. I don't know what's going on, or why, and . . .' I steeled myself, wishing I was better at confrontation. 'And I don't want to play any part in it. Quite honestly.'

Her voice was tight. 'Yes, I realise that this is your position. Your husband made that very plain, not nearly as politely as you have.'

'He's not my husband.'

'Not you as well.' We both laughed, even though it wasn't funny.

'He's my boyfriend,' I explained. 'And I'm sorry if he was rude. I was in the middle of dinner with my oldest friends, and you know . . . school reunions aren't always straightforward.'

'Did he tell you I was ringing because I was scared? I don't know this man. But I think I know who he is. And I'm scared of him and what he could do to me.'

'But he commissioned paintings of you! It's hardly a knife to your throat. Sounds more like he's trying to woo you, and admittedly not doing a very good job of it.'

'Or else that he's letting me know that he has money to get these very expensive artworks made for me, and that he has the advantage over me in oh-so-many ways.'

I was intrigued. I stood by the window and looked out at the garden. I thought Freya and Jake were supposed to be playing there, but there was no sign of them. 'So, who do you think he is?'

She sighed. 'My friend's ex-husband.'

'Is his name Neil Barron?'

'Sean Barron, actually. Though he seems to have changed it since they split up, for some reason. I've heard that he's calling himself Neil some of the time.'

'If this is true,' I said cautiously, 'why would he be doing this to you? What's your connection to him? Why's he set his sights on you?'

'Oh, he hasn't set his sights on me. He's threatening me.'

'Because . . . ?'

She laughed slightly. 'Because he hates me. Because I saw him out with some young girl and of course I told my friend. You do, don't you? For her it was the last straw, and she kicked him out. He blamed me for the whole thing.'

I wasn't sure how plausible this was. 'But why would he? I mean, I can imagine that he'd be pissed off with you for telling his wife, though equally if he's out with a girl and he meets his wife's friend he must have known he was rumbled. In any case, it's between him and his wife. Why on earth would he be spending tens of thousands of pounds of portraits of *you*? It doesn't make sense.' I thought about it. 'You see, if that scenario you'd just told me was true, but if you were his wife, rather than his wife's friend, then it all fits together perfectly.'

'Susie,' she said, sounding defeated. 'Things rarely fit together perfectly. He turned all his anger on me, and he's a very angry man. He's threatened me in various ways. He's got money. He's plausible. You know.'

205

'I don't know,' I told her. I worried that she might be telling the truth. 'I don't know,' I said again.

'Of course you don't,' she said, and hung up.

I waited a moment, then picked the receiver up and left it off the hook. If either of them tried to ring me, I would not speak to them.

I sat down at the lunch table, but I wasn't hungry. Sam had nearly cleared his plate, and he was playing with what remained of his food. I presumed Roman was upstairs, since his car was parked in the drive. I was annoyed that he was shutting himself away in his attic. These were my friends – this whole godawful weekend was my project – but I was always extra nice to his friends, even when I didn't like them.

Sam picked up a piece of ham from his plate and dropped it on the floor.

'Sam!' said Izzy. 'Don't do that. Pick it up, please.'

'It wasn't me,' Sam said, reaching down to get it.

'Then who was it?'

He smiled triumphantly. 'Gravity!'

I smiled, in spite of myself. 'Gravity was keeping it on your plate until you picked it up,' I pointed out. 'So it was you.'

'Gravity put it on the floor,' he insisted.

Izzy looked at me. 'Consider yourself lucky,' she said mildly. 'Childfree, indeed.'

I smiled and nodded. I was annoyed with Sarah Saunders, because I knew I should do something to help her, and pissed off with Amanda, and agitated about Tamsin, who was contentedly eating and talking to Patrick. I tried hard to ignore Sam, but there was something about his innocence and his pride in himself that broke my heart.

And suddenly, it was too much.

I leaned to Izzy, and spoke quietly so no one else would hear.

'Come to the kitchen with me,' I said. 'I want to tell you something.'

She looked at Tamsin. 'Could you guys keep an eye on Sam for a sec?' she said.

'Sure,' said Tamsin, turning back to the intense conversation she was having with Patrick. It seemed to involve the disparity between Sydney and London house prices.

I led Izzy into the kitchen, desperate to share this thing that I thought I had long since left behind. Of all my recent worries, I had thought that this was the least pressing. The oven was still hot and the room was uncomfortable. I never spoke about the baby, or thought about it, these days. That, though, was not completely true.

I composed myself. I took a few deep breaths, lifted my chin, and pulled in my stomach. I was exhausted. It was hard work looking after all these people. I reminded myself that I was a famous artist, that I looked lovely in my dress, that I had good hair and a delectable tan. I wondered why I had ever thought things like that were important.

'Urgh,' I said, pulling a face. 'It's unbearable in here. Shall we go out the front?' Izzy nodded.

She pulled out a chair at the wrought-iron table in the tiny front garden, but I looked up and saw that Amanda had her bedroom window open. I was not going to allow her to eavesdrop. I pointed to the open window, and set off down the road, with Izzy following me, looking apprehensive.

We walked slowly away from the solid stone house. The midday sun was unforgiving, and our pace slowed further. We passed the boundary of my garden, and walked alongside a huge field of maize, which was turning from green to a dry, dusty brown. Patches of tarmac on the road were melting, squishy. I was nervous. I had never told anyone this story, not properly. It seemed, suddenly, that my life was full of shameful secrets.

'About Tamsin,' I said. 'I'm going to tell her tonight.'

'Susie,' Izzy said quickly, 'I know that's what you want. But do you think it's wise? Really? What good could ever come from it?'

I shook my head. 'I don't know. I just think she needs to know.'

'She doesn't. She wouldn't want to.'

'I'll try to talk to Amanda first. But otherwise, I'm going to do it anyway. She's being so difficult.' I swallowed. Amanda had been my best friend. I was disturbed by the fact that I didn't even like her any more.

'Is that what were you going to tell me?'

I shook my head. My mouth was dry. 'It's to do with babies.'

'Babies? So you *are* pregnant?'

I huffed a little. 'Not at all. It's something else. I really don't talk about it. But, I don't know what it was. Sam is adorable, and I can suddenly see why you'd buy a Buzz Lightyear suit rather than a Chanel one. And that's something I've never understood before. And I can see how your priorities have changed. Everything's looking a bit hollow in my life at the moment, and there's all the worry about Tamsin, and then that Sarah woman has been spinning me some crap story.'

'And . . . ?'

I picked a daisy from the verge, and put it behind my ear. 'I've never told Roman this,' I said. 'Here goes. There's a bit of a story leading up to it. When I was in London, you know, after we all lost touch, I was drifting. You know that. But drifting is a polite way of putting it. I was living the crappiest, most miserable life you can imagine. We'd move around, me and this bunch of losers I'd fallen in with. We'd live in squats, which I shudder to think about now. Word would come of a house which was empty, and we'd just go and move in, use all the tricks to get in with no apparent damage, and we'd live there, in these people's homes, and then we wouldn't leave again until they got the police. Paint graffiti on their walls and hang banners in the windows. It seemed exciting at the time. There was an adrenaline thrill in the idea that we were breaking the law.' I could remember it all so clearly. Now Izzy would know that my current life was a sham.

'Mmm.'

'I had that boyfriend, Steve. I was in such a state. You know why. Because of Mrs Grey, and Tamsin, and that total, consuming guilt . . . I think I was very depressed, which was only right, but I would never have put a label on it. I wasn't even articulate enough to realise that there was something wrong, that feeling like I did wasn't normal. I knew that Amanda and I had murdered Mrs Grey, as surely as if we'd cut her brake cables. I knew that I didn't deserve to be happy, so I thought that this was how my life was going to be as a result.

'I met Steve because we were in the same crowd. He was good-looking, in a stinky sort of way. He had a wispy beard and round glasses, but behind all that there was a nice face. He wanted to move to Cornwall and be a gardener. For ages that was our dream. We kind of drifted together, slept together, abused various substances together. It was him that got me to art school.' I laughed. 'God knows what he must think of me now, wherever he is! Anyway, he was my boyfriend, in a casual sort of way.' I remembered Steve as if it had been yesterday. He was earnest, always dreaming of a miraculous future built around a rural idyll. He had been skinny, because he never ate. I remembered, once, trying to put on a pair of his jeans and finding I couldn't haul them above my knees. But he was kind, in a slightly pathetic way, and he was, for a year or so, all that I had. I never even mentioned my private education, or my school friends, and when Amanda wrote me letters, I ripped them up and threw them away without opening them.

'And one day,' I continued, 'I realised it had been ages since my last period. And so I went to the doctor's for a pregnancy test, because I couldn't afford to buy one, and found that I was having a baby. It turned out I was already three months gone.'

I didn't look at her face. I remembered being twenty, and miserable. I remembered asking about abortion. I remembered the doctor making me an appointment with a counsellor. Then I remembered Steve's reaction. His face had changed. He had been overjoyed at the idea of a baby. And, gradually, I came round to the idea.

'I decided to have the baby,' I said, still avoiding eye contact. 'And I was pleased about it. Very pleased. And, you know, as the months went by, the pregnancy changed me. It gave me a bit of focus, and I started to think that, even if I'd been lost myself, I needed to get myself together for the baby. That responsibility was an amazing feeling. And because I'd come from a nice stable home – and of course my parents had no idea how I was living in London because I was barely in touch with them – and because I'd got good A levels only two years earlier, I was actually reasonably well set up to pull myself together. I started thinking of the life I wanted my baby to have, and it made me make some changes that I'd never have been able to make otherwise.

'And I thought about Mrs Grey, and I knew that I would always live with it, but I felt my baby didn't deserve the guilt, so I thought I had better try to move on, although I didn't quite know how I was going to do that.' I looked at Izzy. 'I still don't, as you will have noticed. I wanted to include Steve in my plans, and he was desperate for us to be a family unit, so we started looking for a proper place to live, and we went on the council waiting list. I was at art school and I got a job in the Body Shop on Saturdays, which was a big step for me because it meant I had to look presentable and be at work on time. At the Body Shop you even have to *smell* presentable.'

'But Susie,' said Izzy, peering into my face and forcing eye contact. 'I can't believe you ever had a problem with looking presentable. Look at you now!'

'Oh, I did, believe me. I was fatter than I had been at school – size sixteen I think, at that point – and I didn't have any money for clothes. So I just wore any old crap. Remember those faded black skirts with tassles on the bottom?'

'And a band of black embroidery just above the tassles?'

'I wore those because we knew someone who sold them on Camden Market so I got them practically free. And other stuff like that. Cast-offs. Oxfam stuff. Things people had died in. Clothes that belonged to the squat owners.'

'I get lots of my stuff from Oxfam.'

'But you don't get old men's cardigans or enormous lumberjack shirts.'

'No.'

'And you wouldn't have worn such items as maternity wear, either.'

210

'I might.'

'Anyway, the Body Shop made me dress well, because wearing a Body Shop sweatshirt counted as dressing well for me, then. It was a big thing just to buy some reasonable looking clothes that fitted me. Correctly gendered and everything. And I started wearing a little bit of make-up for work. I'd go in early and the girl who did the make-up demonstrations would do it for me. Then I bought what she used and practised.'

'But you already knew how to wear make-up. Remember you at the ball?' As soon as she'd said it, Izzy obviously regretted it, but I didn't care.

'You have to remember, Izzy, I'd sunk really low by this point. The Suzii I used to be at school was gone. I was in a terrible state. I had to learn some of that stuff all over again. So, I started to do it, to get my act together. And the pregnancy was brilliant for me.' I took a sharp breath and felt the hot air in my lungs. A trickle of sweat ran down my back. It was a moment before I could speak. 'Sorry. I've never talked about it. But I do remember what it's like, feeling a baby kicking you from the inside, and the heartburn, and that exhaustion that's unlike any other kind of tiredness. All of that. I do remember it, so vividly.

'By the time she was born, we had our own place. Steve was working as a waiter and for an office temping agency, and I was still at art school and had my Body Shop job too, and we were getting there.'

'She?'

I forced myself to say the word. 'Stillborn.' I breathed deeply. That was a word from which I recoiled. Midwives and my mother had tried to substitute 'born asleep', but I had never gone for that. A brutal fact needed a brutal word. 'I knew there was something wrong,' I continued, speaking blankly. 'I hadn't been feeling much movement for a few days, but people said it was because the baby was so big that it didn't have space. I tried to believe that. I had a thirty-eight week midwife's appointment, and she couldn't find the heartbeat, and I was in an ambulance and having a section. Even then, I was waiting for the cry.' I stopped still and used my powers of self-control. 'Steve kept telling me it would all be all right,' I explained. 'And I was letting myself believe him. She was blue.'

I looked up at the deep blue sky. How could I ever have thought I could get over this, and leave it all behind and never speak of it again?

'Susie,' said Izzy. 'I don't know what to say.'

'Don't say anything,' I said quickly. 'It's OK. It was ages ago now. Steve and I crumbled instantly. I never wanted to see him again and I barely did. I was horrible. I told him to fuck right off and never try to contact me ever again. I had that chat with the woman at art school, Janet, that I mentioned yesterday, because she knew what had happened. She was the only one who sought me out to talk about it. And I channelled myself into succeeding.' I wanted to laugh, for some reason 'The weirdest thing is that it worked.'

'And you truly don't want another child?'

I shook my head, trying to look more certain than I felt. 'I've got one child, and that's Roman. I couldn't take the pain of anything else. I've locked it all away. I never imagined that seeing you and Amanda with your children, and having Tamsin here and thinking about Mrs Grey . . . I didn't imagine that it would bring all this to the surface.' I swallowed and looked up at the blue sky. 'I know, Izzy, I absolutely know that losing my baby was my punishment for what I did. And I think Amanda's suffered, too, in a different way.'

Izzy put a hand on my arm, and I turned towards her, desperate for comfort. 'But Susie,' she said. 'That's ridiculous. You must know that. What you did was *not* murder. You're not being punished. And it wouldn't happen next time. And you have so much to give as a mother.'

I felt despair. 'It wouldn't happen next time? Do you promise? Can you give me a one hundred per cent cast-iron guarantee? Can you protect it from illness, too, and cot death, and heart conditions and everything else that can happen?'

Izzy put her hands on my shoulders and hugged me close to

her. I closed my eyes, and let her. Izzy was the only person who knew my secrets, and she still wanted to hug me. That gave me more comfort than anything else in the world.

'Of course not,' she said. 'It's the risk you have to take, and the odds are stacked in your favour, and the risk is worth it, Susie, believe me.'

'It's only worth it for you because Sam's fine.'

'It would be worth it anyway. Sam is so great, such an enormous source of joy, that even if the unthinkable happened to him tomorrow, I would never, ever wish that he hadn't been born.'

I shook my head.

'What did you call your daughter?' Izzy asked. She looked nervous, as if she were asking a deeply personal question, which she was.

Here was another word I avoided. I took a deep breath.

'Natasha. Though I've almost never talked about her. I told my parents that I didn't want them to mention her, ever. I cut ties with everyone I'd known in my pregnancy – everyone except Janet. I still see Janet. I don't tell people.' I looked at Izzy. 'Until now. I never imagined that this would surface. If anything, I would have thought I'd be confiding in Amanda. But Amanda's completely nuts, isn't she? Poor thing. You know, I like Tamsin. I'd really like to get to know her again. But I can't.'

'We don't need to tell her,' Izzy said, with conviction. 'It would stir things up. It wouldn't accomplish anything. I can see that you feel you need to confess, but you don't. Tamsin's coped, hasn't she? At the moment, she's probably the most balanced of all of us.' I started to speak, but she stopped me. 'We'll talk about it later,' she said, firmly. 'But did you say you haven't told Roman about Natasha?'

'That's right. I just . . . I don't tell people, you know? It's just not what I do. I thought about it when he moved in. I decided not to. Roman likes life to be fun and easy. He likes freedom. He doesn't go in for dead babies. I was sure that it would scare him off. He doesn't have any interest in kids, so that works out fine. If he'd wanted children, I'd probably have told him.' I drew a breath and thought about telling Izzy that, just lately, I had been half wondering whether I might still want children. I decided not to. I had to stick to my line, or anything might happen. And Izzy didn't know Roman. I knew that nothing would send him running in the opposite direction faster than my mentioning the word 'baby'.

'And you feel that it's OK, having such a big secret?'

I was pleased to be on firm ground. 'Yes I do,' I said, as briskly as I could. 'I have lots of secrets. You must have noticed that my life is about image. It's all pretence, Izzy. I shouldn't talk about that, but you know it and I know it. Your life is real. That's what struck me yesterday, when you were talking about Martin. Your life is real and flawed and honest and that counts for more than you can possibly imagine. You wouldn't think that I'd envy you, but I do.' I looked her in the eyes. 'I really do.' I was trying so hard not to cry that my face was screwed up in a bizarre grimace. 'I don't even like living here. I only do it because it goes with my image.'

'Susie,' said Izzy, wiping the sweat off her face with the back of her hand. 'My life is crap. You have no idea how fucking awful it can be. I work full time at a rubbish job, I look after Sam, I miss him when he's with his dad. I'm a whale next to you and Tamsin, I eat badly, I don't exercise. I don't have space to breathe. I never have two pennies to rub together. Being a single mother is rubbish.'

'Well, at least I avoided that.' This was empty comfort, and we both knew it. We smiled at each other, sadly, and turned back.

'I think I'm going to call the police,' I said suddenly. 'In England. Try to do the right thing for once. If Sarah Saunders is telling the truth, if this man's threatening her, I have to do something.'

'Good idea. Just tell them what each of them has said. It won't take much detective work to find out if they're married.' Izzy paused. 'Something just moved in that field,' she said. 'I saw it, it rustled. There's something big in there.'

I waved a dismissive hand. 'Deer. They drive the farmers mad. That's why they all get shot. They go out hunting every weekend round here and deer are one of the top targets.' I looked at the forest of maize. The only way to see a deer was if it emerged. The crops were too thick. 'It's a shame it didn't come right out. Often they run right across the road. I see them when I'm running. They're beautiful. But the farmers don't agree.'

'Poor old deer.'

'Yeah. You can't be too sentimental about animals round here. Animals are either pests, or they're food on legs. Deer are both.'

'Still, poor things.'

'I know.'

chapter thirty

Jake and Freya crept away, hidden by the maize, which was over six foot tall. It was like a scary film, Jake thought, but he didn't tell Freya because he knew she was a bit scared already. They had both heard a lot of what Susie and Izzy had said. Freya was starting to cry.

'Susie had a dead baby, didn't she?' she said, looking to Jake with teary eyes for confirmation. 'That's so sad. That's what still-born means, isn't it? Otherwise the baby wouldn't have been blue.'

'Mmm,' he said. 'Think so.'

'Poor Susie. I'm going to tell Mum. Then Mum can cheer her up.'

'Don't tell Mum, Frey,' counselled Jake. 'Mum's mad today. She wouldn't cheer Susie up at all. And Susie said she hadn't told anybody, not even Roman. So you can't tell because it's secret.'

'Oh. OK.'

They trudged on, along rows and pushing through the strong stems of the maize plants. They had already noted that most had one corn cob on, and a few had two. They had each picked one to take back to show everyone. Now they were heading away from the road, to the middle of the field.

216

'They said Mum was completely nuts,' Freya remembered, as she trudged along.

'They got that right.' Both of them laughed.

Twenty minutes passed. Jake was leading a random, zigzag path through the plants. It was extremely hot and they were tired. Every time Jake wanted to move between rows they had to squeeze between tall, thick stems. The leaves shaded them from the sun, but the air that was trapped between the green leaves and the cracked earth was baking. Freya was finding it hard to breathe. She thought she might be suffocating.

'Let's go back, Jake,' she said. She held the stem of a maize plant, because she was starting to feel dizzy.

Jake looked round at his sister. Her fair hair was plastered to her head, and she was very red.

'OK,' he said. 'Good idea.' He looked around. There were endless maize stalks in every direction. 'This way,' he said firmly. 'We'll just walk in a straight line and that'll take us to the edge of the field. Even if it's the wrong side of it, we can go back to the road and walk round. Come on. Just think about getting back to Susie's house and drinking lots and lots of cold water. We're going to follow this row so we know that sooner or later we'll get to the edge.'

Freya nodded. She was still feeling a bit faint. But she instructed her feet to move, one after the other. And they did, slowly.

chapter thirty-one

Izzy and I dawdled back to the house. I felt strangely peaceful. I had never shared that story with anybody who didn't already know it.

'It's not something to be ashamed of,' Izzy said quietly, as we approached the house. 'Have you thought about why you keep it a secret? From Roman, in particular?'

I looked up. Amanda's window was still open.

I shook my head and tried to answer her question. It was hard to think about it, and I felt myself closing up. I tried not to.

'It's not "shame", exactly,' I said, stiffly, and very quietly. 'It's because I don't want it to be a part of me. I want to be a successful, rich woman with a gorgeous lifestyle. I want to be childfree –' I looked at Izzy, and we both laughed at the memory of Amanda and Roman's stand-off – 'as a choice I have made. I want to be too selfish to have children. I don't want to be "poor old Susie whose baby was born dead".' I looked at Izzy. 'It is terrifying to be talking about it. Liberating, in a way, but scary. It makes me see that I've kept everyone at arm's length, ever since it happened. The hospital arranged all sorts of counselling for me afterwards, and I went along because they told me to, and I was a bit dazed, but I didn't join in. This woman just sat there asking open-ended questions in a soft voice and I answered as briefly as I could, with one eye on the clock. I just didn't know what to do, so I tried to shut it away. So you can imagine that when Janet came along and told me I could be rich and successful, and leave everything bad behind me, I leapt at the chance. And when she said I could be whoever I wanted to be, well, there was my escape route. So here I am.' I looked at her. 'I always thought about looking you up but I was scared. The only person I'm in touch with from school is Alissa.'

'Alissa McCall?'

'She's good. She's been a good friend to me, even though she doesn't know any of this stuff.'

Izzy looked almost hurt. 'Really? But you and Alissa are so different.'

'Not really. Not now.'

'Do you think you and Roman will stay together for ever?'

I thought about it. 'I don't know.' I looked at Izzy and wondered what to say. I wanted to be honest. 'The *correct* answer is yes. But I'm not sure. I hope so. I love being with him. We have fun and we understand each other and we never run out of things to talk about. I feel completely comfortable. But I have these two big secrets. And I think we could only really stay together for ever if he knew them. And I don't know what he'd think of me, then.' I tried to imagine it. Roman would be horrified by the fact that I had once had a baby; and he would be horrified all over again at the fact that I hadn't told him.

'What about you?' I asked Izzy. 'Would you marry again?'

Izzy laughed, then stopped abruptly. 'I would, Susie, if anybody was interested in me. I should start internet dating or something. God knows.'

I was barely listening. I knew that Izzy's story was going to end well. I had read it in books and seen it on television often enough. She was going to meet someone new, someone who would recognise her wonderful qualities, and she was going to live happily ever after. She would probably marry somebody with wild hair, or with a beard; someone who did not judge on appearances.

219

Someone who would consider me to be tiresome and shallow, who would ask Izzy why I was her friend.

I hoped that, at that point, I would still be her friend.

We walked in through the kitchen door, and out to the terrace. I stopped still in the doorway, so suddenly that Izzy walked into my back. Patrick and Tamsin were sitting where we had left them, laughing. He touched her arm. She patted his leg. They were flirting: Sam was nowhere to be seen.

Izzy and I exchanged alarmed glances, and together we walked to the table as loudly as we could, which, in flip-flops, was not particularly loudly. We watched them move slightly apart.

'Where's Sam?' Izzy asked, as I clattered plates together accusingly.

'In the garden,' said Tamsin, waving a hand in the direction of my studio. 'He went off to look for Jake.'

Izzy set off across the grass. 'How long ago?' she asked, over her shoulder.

Tamsin shrugged. 'Five minutes? Sorry, I should have gone with him, shouldn't I? Patrick says Jake's just behind that barn so I'm sure he's fine.'

I stood still and gazed after Izzy as she set off to find her son, slightly anxious, hot, resigned, and completely at home with her responsibility for another life. I remembered that Jake and Freya hadn't been behind my shed when I had been in there, half an hour ago, and I hoped Sam had managed to find them. For a moment I allowed myself to wonder what it would be like if I still had Natasha. I pictured my eleven-year-old daughter, playing with the younger children. It was too easy to imagine. Yet if I'd been allowed to keep Natasha, I wouldn't be here now. I would probably be stuck in a dead-end job in a bad part of London, claiming benefits. I would be poor and unfulfilled, reading celebrity magazines and dreaming of fame and fortune.

I would have cared for Natasha like Izzy cared for Sam. I would have been the person my daughter turned to, for ever. I would have swapped lives in an instant.

Izzy was huffing in the heat, and she was a world away from

the elegant, head-turning teenager she had once been. I envied her fiercely. I often wished I was no longer young enough to have children. I looked forward, in a perverse way, to the menopause. If pregnancy were not a possibility, I would not have to consider it, to feel the time running through my fingers.

I turned indoors and decided to make that phone call.

I had Neil Barron's address, so I found the number of his local police station from international directory enquiries, and phoned them. I felt silly, but the woman on the end of the phone did not tell me to stop wasting their time. She wrote it all down and said they would look into it when they could. I smiled as I hung up, and then left the phone off the hook again in case Neil Barron tried to ring me. I had done my bit, now. It had taken three minutes. I decided to try to do the right thing more often.

I was angry with Tamsin, and frowned as I cleared lunch away. Neither Patrick nor Tamsin got up to help. They didn't even seem to notice that I was glaring. I rarely frowned. I had consciously stopped doing it when a woman from a glossy magazine had told me, at a private view at Tate Modern, that I could give myself 'DIY Botox' by keeping my face as still as possible. 'It's fabby,' the woman had insisted. 'Once you get in the habit, it's easy and it gives you this wonderful air of mystery.'

Since that conversation, I had tried not to frown, and not to smile. I did not want lines of any sort appearing, so I wore my face like a blank mask, and sometimes sellotaped my forehead smooth at night, but only if Roman was away. Right now, though, I was pulling my eyebrows together and pursing my lips slightly at Patrick and Tamsin's joint behaviour. They were ignoring me.

'Did you make the children's sandwiches?' I asked pointedly. I knew the answer.

'What's that?' asked Patrick. 'Oh, sandwiches. Forgot, I'm afraid. Don't worry, though, Susie. I won't let them bother you when they finally decide they're hungry.'

'Very good of you,' I said sharply.

221

'Not at all,' he said, and when I saw him glancing at Tamsin, with what looked like lust and complicity, I was suddenly furious.

'I'll go and ask them if they're hungry,' I said, tightly, 'before I put all this away.' I stalked across the grass, to my shed. The sunlight made me blink, and black blotches clouded my vision briefly. I carried on, wondering where Roman was, and whether our relationship was a sham. I longed to see him, to feel his physicality, to find out whether it still made me feel safe. The grass was brittle, the ground hard, and I could see that all the farmers whose fields surrounded my house were brazenly flouting the water restrictions, as ever. The trouble was, the penalties were too low. Even though it had rained at the beginning of August, the crops would die without extra irrigation, and a farmer could afford a thousand euro fine for the sake of a twenty thousand euro field. Roman and I had been flouting water restrictions, in our own small way, this summer. Roman was for ever topping up the pool, claiming it was evaporating away.

The heat was strong on the top of my head, and I touched my hair, which was strangely hot. When I walked round the side of the studio, I heard a child crying. It sounded like a serious cry, a cry of pain. It was not just a grizzle.

When I got past the old oak tree, I saw that it was Sam. He was sobbing in his mother's arms, and Izzy was hurtling towards me, carrying Sam on her front. His arms were clasped round her neck. Her face was transformed by worry.

I jogged over. 'Is he hurt?' I asked. I touched Sam's hair, and felt my loss.

'He says a bee stung him,' Izzy said, 'but he seems really ill.' She kept running.

'How's he ill?' I tried to look at him, but his face was buried in his mother's neck. His cries were getting louder. It was unbearable. 'Is it shock?'

'I don't know. His leg looked pretty red. Let's get him inside and have a look.'

We sat Sam on the table, indoors, and examined his leg. I could see the big red patch with the sting in the middle of it. The swelling was getting bigger every second. Patrick had vanished, but Tamsin came and looked.

'Take him straight to hospital,' she said at once. 'I've seen this. It's a reaction. There's no telling how bad it's going to be. Seriously. Get in the car this instant and take him to hospital. Actually, got a credit card or something? I can get the sting out first.'

I drove. Izzy sat in the back and held Sam on her lap. Tamsin jumped into the front seat. The brakes squealed as I reversed out of the drive, and set off on a course for the nearest hospital, which was, unfortunately, seventeen kilometres away.

chapter thirty-two

Patrick was bemused by the exodus. One moment he'd been sitting with Tamsin having an extremely pleasant chat about Australia, and an ill-advised second glass of rosé, and then he'd popped to the loo. When he came back, they were all clustered around the dining table. Then they rushed off, out of the front door, and he'd stood in the doorway and watched Susie driving her car off at a hundred miles an hour. He had just about picked up that it was about Sam, and possibly to do with a reaction to a sting. He hadn't got close enough to see whether they were in the grip of a collective gender-related panic, or whether there might actually be something in it.

As he listened to the silence, he remembered, guiltily, that Amanda was upstairs. She was, without a doubt, waiting for him to arrive with a peace offering. He sighed. Tamsin's words sounded in his head. 'If it wasn't for the money, she'd be a down-and-out,' Tamsin had said. He wished he could go and live in Australia, away from it all. He smiled as he remembered snippets of his delicious lunchtime conversation.

'When I left, John Major was in charge,' Tamsin had said, reminiscing. 'But everyone thought he'd be booted out by Kinnock at the next election. And everyone was up in arms about the poll tax. And Diana was on the front of all the magazines, and that

Andrew Morton book hadn't quite blown the lid off the Camilla stuff yet. So I knew that Britain would have changed. I knew that Diana was dead – you could hardly escape that; the mawkishness was probably worse in Australia than it was in Britain. I knew all about Tony Blair. I even had an idea that there was Starbucks everywhere and everybody had mobile phones and everyone sold their old stuff on eBay. What I wasn't expecting was for it to be so fucking busy. And so crowded. You can't move in Britain. Everybody's rushing somewhere.'

He had sighed. It would be wonderful to have missed that happening. Imagine being surprised by Britain's crowded roads and jostling crowds! Now he could see why expats retained a rosy view of their homeland.

For half a moment, Patrick allowed himself to dream. He pictured himself and Tamsin, boarding a Qantas jet at Heathrow and soaring off into the sky, around the world together to start a new life. It could never happen. He had the children to consider. He also had a wife.

'Buggeration,' he said to himself, and he set about collecting a lunch for her. Susie had dumped everything on the kitchen work-tops, and he easily put together a large slice of onion tart, a selection of cheeses, a wedge of butter, half a baguette, and some token pieces of salad. It was a gourmet ploughman's, without the pickle. He took the rosé from the fridge and filled the largest wine glass he could find. A linen napkin – Amanda insisted on a napkin – and a flower from a vase on the mantelpiece of one of those interminable sitting rooms, and his tray was ready.

He knew he was being weak. He knew he was allowing her destructive behaviour and her depression to grow and thrive by feeding it like this, but he did not have the stomach to see the fight through right now.

The door was firmly shut, and Patrick tried to open it with his elbow, but just succeeded in spilling rosé onto the tray. He knocked with his foot. After a loaded pause, Amanda's voice called a conde-scending, 'Come in, Patrick.'

'Actually,' he said, 'I need you to open the door.'

He was full of dread as he waited. She was going to be mean to him, without a doubt. Sure enough, she stood in the doorway, wearing enough make-up to sink the *Titanic*, smiling menace.

'Too little too late,' she said sharply, motioning to him to put the tray down on the bedside table. He saw her looking him up and down and sneering, and Patrick knew that he made a silly sight, that he was never going to be a great romantic hero. He was probably lucky to have a wife as feisty and well-dressed as Amanda was. It was just as well, really, that he had such an ugly mug, because as things stood, Tamsin would never in a million years be interested in him, and that would save everybody an awful lot of trouble. She had let him touch her arm, but she'd only been being polite, he knew that.

Amanda took her wine glass and gulped. 'Nice and cold,' she commented.

'Straight from the fridge.'

'What was all the commotion?'

'Sam was stung by something, as far as I could tell. It was swelling up so they've taken him to hospital.'

'Fuss about nothing, no doubt.'

'You never know.'

'Where's our two?'

'Oh. Outside, I think. Or maybe indoors helping themselves to a late lunch.' He knew he had to broker a peace deal. 'Erm,' he added, with what he hoped was a rueful smile. 'I'm sorry about what I said to the kids. Wasn't really thinking, somehow. Last thing I wanted was to undermine you.'

She rolled her eyes and torpedoed contempt at him. '"Not really thinking." Just for a change. Patrick, you know the way the family works. You do your job and I'll do mine. Mine is the kids, for my sins. You don't know the first thing about what they do and why they do it. So do us all a favour. Leave it all to me and for Christ's sake, don't jump in and make random promises to Freya just because you want to look good in front of Tamsin and Isabelle.' She glared through narrowed eyes. 'Tamsin, mainly.'

'That wasn't what I was doing.'

She raised her voice. 'Oh no, not much it wasn't! Jesus, Patrick, what *were* you doing then? You wanted to look good in the kids' eyes and everyone else's. That was it.'

He coughed. 'Actually,' he said, 'it didn't really seem fair. I had no idea exactly how much extra gubbins they did. And they are so young. They seem happy here, just relaxing. And that's how I feel and it seems a bit . . .' he tailed off.

'A bit what?'

Patrick took a deep breath. Both he and Amanda wondered whether he would dare to continue. 'Well, a bit sad, to be honest, Amanda. They're tiny little things, still. Do they really need maths lessons on Saturdays, for instance?'

'*Yes they fucking do!* Now, fuck off and leave me alone.'

chapter thirty-three

Freya was confused. She didn't understand why they were still walking. It was getting harder and harder for her to keep going, because she was hotter than she had ever been in her life before, and she was very, very thirsty. They were still struggling through the thick stalks, and they were still not in the garden. They had both dropped their cobs of corn long ago. Freya never wanted to see sweetcorn in her life again. Still, maybe it would come up in biology or geography one day. At least she knew how it grew.

'Jake?' she said. 'We should be there by now, shouldn't we?'

Jake turned round and Freya decided that he looked scared but that he was pretending to be brave. 'I thought so,' he agreed. 'The thing is, even if we're going the wrong way, we just have to keep going, along the same line of corn, and we'll get there in the end. We'll get out of this field because we're walking straight and very, very soon we'll get to the edge. It can't be far away.' For a moment, his fear showed on his face. 'It really can't,' he said, more firmly. 'We just keep going this way and we'll get out.'

'Can we just sit down for five minutes?' Freya asked. 'Please? I'm too tired to keep going.'

Jake paused. Freya sat down, pushing some stalks of maize aside, and looked at him challengingly. He smiled and sat next to her.

'We definitely shouldn't split up,' he said knowledgeably. 'That would be the worst thing to do. So it looks like I have to wait for you.' He sat down next to her. Freya leaned back on her hands. The earth was cracked and dry, and it made her palms sore. It was like being in a weird tent. She tried to breathe deeply, but she felt hot inside.

'Are we suffocating?' she asked.

'No,' Jake assured her. 'We're just overheating. We might have the opposite of hypothermia.'

They relaxed for a few minutes. Freya started to feel drowsy. She lay back, crushing a few more plants together, and closed her eyes.

chapter thirty-four

Amanda tried to savour her lunch, but it didn't work. She wolfed it down. She was confused by her strong feelings, and since she was unsure what exactly she was feeling strongly about, she channelled it all into rage and indignation. What she deserved, she decided, was an outing. It was high time she had some fun.

She tiptoed to the bathroom, hoping not to meet Patrick on the way or, worse, in there. His clothes were folded neatly on the wicker chair. The car keys were in the pocket of his shorts. This meant, she imagined, that he was in the pool, presumably with the children, probably making them all sorts of stupid promises to make them like him better than her. She was pleased that she didn't have to make him hand the keys over. He wouldn't have wanted to do it. She would have forced him and there would have been a scene. Yet another scene. She was sick of trying to pretend that their marriage was fine. The crisis was impossible to ignore, now, and their friends knew about it. Everything about him infuriated her, at the moment; from the pink dome of his stupid bald head to his ugly hairy toes. She hated the craven way he tried to reason with her. If he had a problem, she would respect him far more were he able to come out and say it. A real row, a shouting match, would be cleansing. This passive-aggressive tiptoeing was driving her barmy. She hated having to do all the shouting, while he spinelessly agreed with her, and didn't mean it.

She folded his shorts again, as anally as he had done it in the first place, and swung the keys from her index finger. She was off to have an adventure. She had been happy that morning, when Roman took her abseiling. Already, that episode had the air of a fantasy. It was her bloody domestic situation that was making her miserable. Roman had shown her that. Dangling from a rope, with her life in his hands and those expensive tiles waiting for their chance to crush her skull, she had been happy. With Patrick snivelling at her and messing around with the detail of their dull-as-fuck married life, she had been instantly miserable again. Therefore, Patrick was the problem. She would not leave him, of course. She wouldn't deal well with the fallout of a divorce, and Izzy was hardly an advertisement for single parenthood. But something had to change.

It was not the business with Tamsin. That had happened years ago, and it hadn't been her fault. Suzii had been the ringleader, and anyway, they were too drunk to be responsible for their actions.

She changed quickly into a dark olive Ghost dress, which was sack-like but forgiving, and matching Birkenstocks. She put her shades on her head, to keep her hair off her face, and gave herself a shiny red lipsticked mouth. The rest of her make-up was still in place.

It was oppressively hot outside. Amanda unlocked the car and sweltered in its interior. Typically, Patrick could have parked it in the shade but hadn't bothered. He had parked in the full glare of the August sun, and the car was a furnace. She knew she wasn't insured to drive it, but got behind the wheel anyway, pulled the seat forward, and adjusted the rear-view mirror. She had rarely driven on the wrong side of the road, but she imagined she would manage. She reversed out onto the road without any problems, and drove slowly, remembering to stay on the right, getting a feel for the car.

After two hundred yards, she saw Roman at the village re-cycling bins, chatting to some swarthy looking Frenchman with a moustache. Awash with relief and excitement, she slowed to a halt. Exactly the person she wanted. She located the correct button, and buzzed down the passenger window.

'Hey, gorgeous!' she shouted. 'Need a lift anywhere?'

Roman turned, surprised, and smiled at her. He said something to the man next to him. 'Where are you going?' he called.

'Anywhere you like.'

'OK.'

He disposed of the last few champagne bottles, and parked his wheelbarrow neatly at the edge of a field of sunflowers. Within seconds he was sitting next to her, in the passenger seat, looking at her expectantly with that arrogant face of his.

'Wow,' he said. 'You're all dressed up. Where's Susie?'

'That kid got some sting, and they've taken him to hospital.' Her voice dripped with disdain, which she imagined Roman would share.

'That kid?' he said, mockingly. 'Meaning the one that isn't yours, presumably?'

'That's the one.'

'Is he all right? I saw Susie hurtling through the village at three hundred K an hour. She got some stern stares from the villagers for that.'

Amanda shrugged. 'I missed all the excitement. Patrick told me what happened. Everyone's gone except him and my kids, and they're all swimming, so I'm having a little explore.'

'Right,' he said. 'Let's do it. We'll go somewhere good. I don't suppose you're up for a surf, so we'll go for a drink.'

He directed Amanda through country lanes, past interminable fields of maize, interspersed with cows and occasional seas of sunflowers that were all decidedly past their prime. Whenever a car came towards them, he reminded her to drive on the right. The rest of the time everyone seemed to bumble along happily in the middle of the road, so it was immaterial. They had the air conditioning on at full blast, and Roman soon located a radio station that was playing Frank Sinatra.

'This is cool,' Amanda remarked. She listened. '"My Way" in French. Is it a direct translation?'

Roman listened for a second. 'No,' he said. 'Not *I did it my way* at all. *As usual*. It sounds better in French. I'd have taken my iPod with me to the bins, if I'd known. Played you some real music.'

Amanda nodded and hummed along. She felt her mood lightening, aware that a large component of what she was feeling was a rather delightful malice. She was being naughty, and now that she was an adult, nobody could stop her. She was overjoyed to be away from Susie's house. It was pretty enough, but the atmosphere was heavy.

She had always got more pleasure than the others had from breaking the rules. She had adored their Slackers' Society meetings in the crappy café, not least because she was generally the centre of attention. She'd loved mitching off school and cheating in exams and copying essays, and she had happily let her essays be copied in return, whenever she had done them. In her married life, she had been the archetypal bored housewife. She had never driven off in a car for which she was not a legal driver, very slightly tipsy, dolled up to the nines, with a man who was not her husband. No, she had never done anything remotely like that. Although she had driven drunk more often than not, but she tried not to think too hard about that.

'What would you have done,' asked Roman suddenly, 'if you hadn't met me?'

She was incredulous. 'What would I have done if I hadn't met you? I've only known you five minutes, you wanker. Oooh, I wouldn't have abseiled out of the window. My life would have been meaningless.'

He was laughing. 'I didn't mean that! I meant, right now. Where were you going to go, on your own, with all that lipstick and all?'

She smiled. 'Oh. Nowhere. Somewhere. Wherever. I don't know. I was just going to drive around and see where I ended up. I'm sure me taking off on my own wasn't on Susie's agenda, but since she's out, I thought I was probably allowed.'

Roman smiled. 'She's been very nervous about having you all here. I've never seen her like it before. Every moment accounted for. There's a certain military precision to it.'

'Why?'

Roman shrugged. 'No idea, really. She admits it's partly to show off, or rather to "share our good fortune". But I'm sure there's another agenda going on and I haven't the faintest idea what it is. Which is unusual because normally I can tell exactly where she's coming from.'

This made Amanda nervous and she changed the subject.

'You know, I had to get out because I was alone with Patrick, and . . .' She took a breath. 'He was doing my head in, and I hate my marriage and I can't think of a single thing to do about it.' She stared at the road. A purple Peugeot came speeding around a corner towards her, and she swung the wheel abruptly to the right. They were almost in a ditch as the car flew past. Amanda gasped and then laughed.

'Fucking hell,' she said. 'Do they all drive like that? It's worse than London.'

'It's not, actually,' said Roman, lazily. 'That was a boy racer. You can tell because he was about twenty, he was driving a purple car with a spoiler. He had two exhaust pipes and a low trim, and of course he was driving like he had a death wish. But he was just having fun, on his way to cruise one of the towns, no doubt. The thing here is that the roads are probably more dangerous than they are in the UK, but you don't have the rage. Round here, at least. Paris is different. Here, everyone stares at you as you pass and that's because they're trying to see if you're someone they know, so they know whether or not to wave at you. Then, if they don't know you, they keep the stare going to try to work out who you might be. A lot of people have no idea it looks rude. They don't mean to be rude.' He thought about it. 'Although they equally wouldn't particularly care. And they drive round corners too fast, and they drive right up close behind you, which is the thing that Susie hates. But for all that, it doesn't get *personal* like it does in Britain. No one would dream of chasing you and winding down their window to scream abuse. The worst you're likely to get is a shrug.' She looked at him as he performed the exasperated gestures of a frustrated French driver. 'Not "you fucking wanker cunt I'm going to fucking shove your head right up your arse . . ."'

Amanda wasn't sure whether to admit to it. 'Mmm,' she said non-committally. 'I must admit, I drive the kids to school and back every day and I have been known to have a spot of road rage myself. I may have uttered the c-word to a perfect stranger on occasion.' She saw that he was unimpressed and changed the subject. 'Doesn't it drive you mad, all this quiet? I mean, what in God's name do you do?'

He looked at her slyly. 'Oh, we make our own entertainment.'

'You mean, Susie paints her nice little pictures and gets paid a bloody fortune and keeps you in the manner to which you have become accustomed?'

'While I try all the dangerous sports going to try to entertain myself in a pathetic and risible manner? Yes. I bake biscuits too. And I drink wine. So, are you going to leave your husband?'

Amanda shook her head. 'Nu-huh.' She looked at him, sideways, unsure whether to ask. 'What do you think of Patrick, Roman?'

Roman rocked back and forth in contemplation. 'Turn right over this bridge, yeah? Then follow the road round. I'm sure he's a nice guy. I think you've got the worst marriage I've seen in my entire life. We have *divorced* friends who are happier in each other's company than you and Patrick are. I mean, you've got a spark to you, and Patrick's obviously a good guy, although I think I'd struggle to find common ground with him if I tried. But together, you seem . . .' He looked at her, and she nodded curtly for him to continue. 'Well, you seem to hate each other. You obviously want someone more challenging, and he'd probably be happier with someone less challenging, because let's face it, Amanda, you are pretty fucking challenging.'

Amanda was unexpectedly torn. This was the very first time she had hinted at marital difficulties to anybody, ever. She had hoped, and assumed, that she and Patrick put on a united front, but clearly they didn't.

'That's a bit nasty,' she said, as mildly as she could. 'I'm allowed to moan about it, and you're supposed to gasp in astonishment and say we seemed the perfect couple.'

'No, because if I did that I'd be a woman. I'm a man, so I can't manage the pretending part. But if you don't want me to say anything, I won't. That's fine.'

'No, you can say what you like.'

'All right. While we're being honest, why do you and Patrick both drink so much?'

Amanda glared. 'I've noticed you like a drink or two as well, Mr Perfect. You just said so yourself.'

'Oh, I have never claimed to be Mr Perfect, have I?' Roman looked across at her, and then back at the road. 'If I was Mr Perfect I wouldn't be here.'

'Wouldn't be where?'

'In your car, directing you to a nice little bar by the river. Helping you storm off from a marital row. What would Patrick say? What will he say? What would Susie think about us heading off together? OK, you stormed off because you're having your little crisis. But me? I was talking to Serge by the bins and then I jumped in your car. The village will know about it already.' He looked at her with a sly smile. 'I may as well take you to a hotel and be done with it.'

She stared. 'You're joking.'

'Of course I am. But you know, everyone's going to think we were up to no good. So in that sense, I really shouldn't be here.'

She tutted and went down a gear to overtake a tractor. The acceleration scared her, and the corner was closer than she had thought. She cut back in as quickly as she could, praying that no car would appear around the corner at the crucial moment.

'Jesus, Roman,' she said, suddenly angry. 'You do talk some fucking crap, don't you?'

'You think so?'

'You know it as well as I do. Arsehole.'

Amanda speeded up, eager to leave the heavy tractor far behind. She was angry with Roman and, suddenly, exhausted. She was tired of being angry, angry with being tired. Speeding recklessly around the edges of maize fields and past fat white cows and through tunnels of trees, she decided that she had had enough. Something was going to change.

'Slow down?' Roman suggested, lazily.

She put the brakes on and performed an emergency stop. To her satisfaction, her passenger banged his nose on the dashboard. He rubbed it and looked at her quizzically.

'Are you all right to drive?' he asked. 'You're fucking drunk, aren't you?'

She raised her eyebrows. 'Probably. We'd better go back.'

Roman pulled a hurt face. 'You mean you don't want to pursue our little adventure?'

'I've had enough of it all.'

'Oh, come on. You owe me a drink now. We're nearly there.'

'I think I want to go back.' Amanda's mind was blank. She had no idea what she wanted, except for a drink.

'Well, make your mind up. We go onwards, and soothe our nerves with one small drink before heading home before we're missed, or we wimp out and go back. Bearing in mind that Susie and the girls are out anyway.'

Amanda frowned.

chapter thirty-five

Lodwell's, 1991

It was a cold evening. Spring had not yet arrived, even though it was April. The sky was cloudy but at least it had stopped raining. The pavement outside City Hall was slick and damp. Tamsin stopped to savour the city smells. Chief among them was exhaust. Cars were roaring by on the roads all around, rushing into town, or out of it. As well as that, she could dimly smell fast food, from far away. There were distant voices, a laugh.

She sighed and followed her mother into the building. They had found a parking space just outside, which, she supposed, was good. Leaving this disco was going to be the best part of the evening.

She insisted on thinking of it as a disco, because it was wildly pretentious to call it a ball. Balls were from fairy tales. Cinderella's ball was a real ball. Balls were Viennese, or royal. At a ball, beautiful people danced to waltzes played by string orchestras dressed all in white. If this was really going to be a ball, Tamsin thought she might quite enjoy it. She could carry an engagement card and allow young men to book her for particular dances. She would learn to quickstep and foxtrot.

A real ball would not involve anybody slow dancing to the Righteous Brothers. It would not be peopled by teenagers on

238

heat. Nobody at Cinderella's ball would have sex under a table, or vomit all around a loo. There would be nobody rushed to hospital to have their stomach pumped. The correct name for the party she was reluctantly attending was a disco, so that was what she was going to call it. Izzy was the only one who concurred.

The ball, the disco, the event, was a source of feverish excitement for everybody but Tamsin. Izzy had been hand-stitching her dress for months, as a distraction from revision. Amanda and Suzii had taken the more conventional shopping route and, although Tamsin had heard about their dresses in the minutest detail, she had not yet had the pleasure of seeing them. She pulled her grey mac tightly round herself and feared the worst.

She was wearing a black shift dress that her mum had bought her from Laura Ashley. It was inoffensive. It was plain. It finished just above her knees, which knobbled out below it in an ugly manner. She felt gawky and stupid, and she wondered why she was going to be the only girl in the whole sixth form who was in this predicament. There were a few fellow 'tomboys', who would be staying at home wearing their Metallica T-shirts. The other geeks, people like Izzy's hanger-on, Mary-Jane, would be at the disco, being wry about their imagined wildness and wearing shiny dresses that had been run up by great-aunts, or bought from the elderly section of M&S. She pictured Mary-Jane last year, shimmering in unflattering yellow, and she almost felt sorry for her at the memory.

But MJ would enjoy herself, as would Izzy, and horrible racist Janie and her friends, and the Goths, Beth and Bobby (who had turned up last year resplendent in tight black and purple dresses and full make-up). Tamsin's mother, who had supervised the evening for years, admitted that she generally had a reasonably good time. Tamsin knew that most of her enjoyment came from laughing at her charges, and she wished she had enough distance to laugh too. Even Mrs Spencer, Izzy's least favourite teacher, had apparently been known to dance. Tamsin was the only person there who was going to be checking the time for the entire evening. She should have stayed at home and watched *Noel's House Party* with Billy.

But she was here, and she was here ludicrously early.

'Come on, Tamsin,' said her mother, turning to wait for her.

'Do I have to?'

'Well, no, you know you don't have to. But your friends will be here – what's the problem? People always seem to manage to have a good time.'

'Yeah.'

They put chairs out around the edge of the hall. They checked the bar was stocked and ready, and that there were plenty of soft drinks. They sat down, side by side, on plastic chairs, and waited. Tamsin looked sideways at her mother. She was in full teacher mode, in a paisley blouse and a sensible skirt, with her hair in a spinsterish bun. At the weekends, Mum wore jeans and sweatshirts and she looked just like a normal person. The moment she had anything to do with school, however, she suddenly appeared in flesh-coloured tights and thick pleated skirts. Blouses with brooches materialised, and her hair, normally longish and messyish, was scraped back and fixed firmly with spray and combs. When Tamsin's mother was with her husband, she was tactile and smiley, with rosy cheeks and a loud laugh. At school, she was a frump.

'Don't you want to dress up?' Tamsin asked her, curious.

Mum smiled. 'Don't you?' she asked back.

'No, I don't. But I know you do. Don't you want to put on one of your dresses and look glam and have everyone saying to their boyfriends, *actually, that's a teacher*?'

'Jesus Christ, no! I'm not here for a party. God forbid. I'm on duty. I want to look as much like a teacher as I possibly can. Because if I dressed up as if I was going to a real party, I might suddenly forget myself and start drinking wine and dancing, and before I knew it I'd be neglecting my duties *and* losing the respect of you girls *and* on top of that I'd be shelling out for a cab home for us both.'

Tamsin laughed.

Mrs Spencer came into the room and looked around with a broad, chilling smile.

'Evening, both,' she said.

'Hello, Mary,' said Mum.

'Hello, Mrs Spencer,' Tamsin said to her shoes.

'Looking forward to tonight, Tamsin?' Mrs Spencer asked.

'Oh, I can hardly contain my excitement.' Tamsin spoke in a monotone, still staring at her shoes.

'I can see that.'

Tamsin's mother rolled her eyes ostentatiously at her colleague. 'Tamsin,' she said. 'Why don't you go to the toilets and do your hair and make-up?'

Tamsin raised her eyebrows and spread her hands wide. Mum rummaged in her handbag and retrieved a make-up bag. She threw it over. 'Just get some colour on your lips at least. A bit of mascara. Red lipstick. Be a devil.' She shook her head. 'You've always been a tomboy.'

'Aren't you glad, though?' asked Tamsin. 'Aren't you pleased I'm not a slapper? You wouldn't believe what I could be doing.'

'Yes I would believe it.' She looked to Mrs Spencer. 'We would believe it, wouldn't we?'

'Oh yes, indeed, we would.' They laughed at a secret memory. Tamsin's mother always refused to share stories from the previous eleven balls, but she smiled at the memories when Tamsin asked. It drove Tamsin insane.

'Oh, Tamsin,' Mrs Spencer said as an afterthought. 'Would you like me to take care of your hair? I could give you a lovely chignon.'

Tamsin fingered a strand of her loose, lank locks. She thought this had to be the low point of her life to date. Mrs Spencer – Hairy Mary – was going to do her hair. It was dreadful on many levels, but the worst was the fact that she knew Mrs S would do a better job.

'Oh,' she said. 'Yes. If you wouldn't mind. Why not?'

People began to arrive at half past seven. Tamsin hated being the first. She hated the giggly girls coming in tarty clusters, with their boys. She hated the fact that she was invisible. It was a toss-up over which was worse: sitting on one of the chairs she had lined up around the edge of the room, all on her own without even a book to read, sitting at the bar with her mother, or sitting by the toilets with Mrs S.

She could not possibly hang out with the teachers. She sat by herself, in a random chair halfway down the long room, and stared around, and waited.

There were, she decided, two girls arriving for every boy. When you took the Mary-Janes and the Tamsins out of the equation, that meant, she decided, that every boy was guaranteed a snog, and every girl who had basic social skills would probably pull. As the partygoers continued to arrive, Tamsin mentally divided them into two camps: the slappers and the virgins. The typical virgin wore a Bo-Peepish dress with a full skirt and gathers at the top of her sleeves. She clutched a matching bag, which contained a brown lipstick, a twenty pound note, and ten pence for the phone. Bo Peep stood self-consciously with her friends, looking warily at boys who did not look back.

The slapper, on the other hand, was in a skin-tight concoction, with cleavage spilling over the neckline, and almost her entire thighs exposed. Her money was kept in her bra or, stripper style, tucked into a stocking top (which was all very well until the barman gave her change). She eyed up the boys and they eyed her right back, discussed her with their mates and, depending on exactly how slapperish she looked, placed bets.

Tamsin's Laura Ashley dress didn't cover her arms at all. She pulled at the strappy sleeves, contorted with self-consciousness, knowing that nothing she did would make a thin strap cover a bony shoulder, still less an ugly elbow. She rubbed her cheek, trying to take off her mother's blusher which, she felt, was making her look like Aunt Sally from *Worzel Gummidge*. She pulled at her hair. Mrs Spencer had been businesslike and had produced a tin of hairpins, and the results of her handiwork were depressingly impressive, but Tamsin was not a chignon kind of girl. She was dubious about being beautified by her old biology teacher. She was about to pull her hair loose when Izzy appeared.

'Hey,' said Tamsin, smiling in spite of herself. 'Nice dress.'

'Do you think? Is it OK?' Izzy sat down beside Tamsin.

'Yes, I think. Yes, it's more than OK. Bloody hell, Izzy. You look stunning.'

Izzy smiled in delight. She was ravishing. Her dress finally fitted her slender body perfectly. She had been up until three, pinning it against herself, taking in seams and sewing them, changing her zip for a longer one so she could fit her hips in, and once, painfully, sitting on a needle. Now she was beautiful, and tired. Tamsin quickly scanned the room, to judge how much attention Izzy was attracting. The answer, inevitably, was plenty. Every male eye in the room seemed to turn to Izzy at the same moment.

'Thanks,' Izzy said. 'Hey, you have to cheer up. You're not allowed to be depressed. It's a party, remember? I like your hair.'

'It's the bloody school disco and my mother is propping up the bar. And I'm not even going to tell you who's responsible for my bloody hair.'

'And now your best friend has arrived. So things are looking up. I know it's horrible. I didn't want to come either, but we may as well have fun.' She sprang to her feet. 'I get nervous sitting down. I can feel the seam straining. Drink?'

As they headed towards the bar, Tamsin looked around. Nobody here was interested in her, and she shuddered at the idea of getting off with any of these pigs. No man of any interest to Tamsin would turn up at a girls' school disco. Robert Smith of the Cure would not be seen dead here. Instead, there were identical boys from Cowbridge, poncing around in their dinner jackets, practising their sleazy smiles on girls with porcelain skin and indulgent daddies. Shouting close to their ears with stinky cigarette breath. She grimaced, and steered Izzy to the end of the bar where her mother was not stationed.

Amanda and Suzii arrived, tarty and giggling, an hour later. Both of them wore tight-fitting satin. Suzii's blue dress was so short that the curve of her buttocks was just visible, beneath the hem, in lacy white knickers. Amanda's legs were long and slender, and in her cream dress she might as well have been naked. Her shoulders were back, her chest was out. Her collarbone jutted out so far that it cast a shadow, and Tamsin suddenly wondered whether Amanda might be anorexic. Her make-up was impeccable. Every boy in the room noticed her. A few began to circle.

Suzii pushed her hair up with her fingers. It was stiff. 'We've had half a bottle of vodka,' she confessed, clutching Amanda's arm.

'Let's start on the other half,' Amanda shrieked, steering her friend towards the bar. Five men followed. Drunk Lodwell's girls were notoriously enthusiastic. Tamsin thought that Suzii did herself no favours by dressing as she did. She was forever getting into sticky situations.

Tamsin and Izzy looked at each other. 'I don't think we'll be seeing much of them this evening,' Izzy shouted.

Tamsin raised her eyebrows. She was convulsed with the contrast between her gawky plainness and her friends' sexiness. Flagrant, overstated tartiness was surely more healthy for eighteen-year-old girls than the apathetic lack of energy that dogged her. She wished she cared. She fingered the beginnings of a spot on her chin. There were some boys on the dance floor who were talking about Izzy, and Tamsin knew for certain that they were arguing over who was going to get the ugly friend. She scowled at them. They looked at each other and laughed. Tamsin looked down. She detested the fact that the boys dressed in black tie, as if they were sixty and going to the opera. She loathed the conspicuous excess, the show of affluence. She tried to imagine what it would be like in the Third World. What would African women their age, burdened down by children and having to fetch the water every day, make of this party? She was ashamed to be a part of it. She wished she'd stayed home and donated the cost of her ticket to Oxfam.

Tamsin couldn't relax at school. If she was in the pub, she was fine. If she was at the Square Club, she was fine. At home, fine. Anywhere but Lodwell's she felt reasonably comfortable. At school, though, she just could not be bothered. It was unnatural to spend so much time in such a high-pressured female environment. The bitchiness was unbelievable. The bigotry scared her. Now, to be at school and yet not at school, to be officially Having Fun, but with the whole of the sixth form in the room – this was hell. And she was about to lose Izzy.

'Hey there,' said a boy with black hair carefully styled around his face. He was ignoring Tamsin.

'Er, hello,' said Izzy, with a fresh and friendly smile.

The boy held out a hand. 'Like to dance?' he asked.

Izzy looked at Tamsin. 'Go on,' Tamsin told her. 'Here, give me your bag. You don't want to dance around it.'

Izzy handed over the bag, and her drink as well, and the boy led her, by the hand, onto the dance floor. Tamsin watched them. They stood opposite each other and jiggled around for a bit. The DJ was playing 'I Wanna Give you Devotion'. Somehow, Izzy had the hang of jiggling gracefully. She even managed to mouth the lyrics without looking silly. Tamsin sighed. She checked the time. She finished Izzy's wine.

The evening passed. Tamsin refused to dance, even with Isabelle. People were sick. Twice, Mrs Grey was called to the girls' toilets to help Mrs Spencer tend to the extremely ill. Izzy kissed the black-haired boy for the entire evening, rosy-cheeked and happy to have replaced Jasper, temporarily. Amanda and Suzii flirted with all the contenders, and only chose their partners in the last hour. Tamsin was surprised they could see straight enough to pick them. Eventually, one o'clock came. Couples emerged from under tables and inside cupboards. Boys rubbed lipstick off their faces. Girls asked their friends for objective assessments of love bites, and made optimistic efforts at covering them with make-up. A young man picked up half-empty glasses from the bar and from tables, and even the floor, and drained their contents until Mrs Grey shouted at him to stop. Coats were retrieved. Lights went on. People left.

Izzy clung on to her boy, giving him a last kiss, until Mrs Spencer coughed very loudly. Then she said goodbye to Tamsin, clutching the back seam of her dress.

'It's started tearing,' she said, giggling. 'The taxi driver might get more than he bargained for!'

'Sure you don't want to stick around and come home with us?' Tamsin asked. She had to wait till the very end and she wanted Izzy to wait with her. 'No problem dropping you off.'

'Thanks, but I've got to dash,' said Izzy. 'Sharing a cab with the other Dinas girls. All booked. See you on Monday. I'll call tomorrow.'

'Bye.'

Tamsin stood around, repetitively banging the toes of one foot on the ground. She had remained an observer, unpopular and unnoticed, for five long hours. She hated everyone and everything. Mrs Grey shooed her drunk charges away. Mrs Spencer made sure they got into the cars of their waiting, long-suffering fathers, or into taxis.

As they were leaving, Tamsin's mother said, 'I feel a bit light-headed. That's the trouble with these things. You can drink orange juice all evening and still feel drunk by osmosis.'

chapter thirty-six

I drove as fast as my car would go, with my foot flat on the floor.
I tried to shut myself off from the panic, and just to drive. I had
no worries about speeding, and I almost wanted to get stopped
by the police so that they would escort me to the emergency
department.

Tamsin had climbed over in the back to be with Izzy and Sam. I
was trying not to use my rear-view mirror to check on him, because
when I had last looked, his face was swollen and red, and this, I
knew, was not good. It had distracted me from the road. I could hear
Tamsin and Izzy conferring in urgent, low voices. They were all
crammed together. The back of my little Merc was not built for three.

'Was it a sting? You're sure it was?' Tamsin asked, as I pushed
out onto the roundabout, forcing a blue Renault to stop suddenly.
I took no notice of whatever signals the driver might have been
making at me, spun round the roundabout, and overtook another
car as I exited.

'Sam said so,' said Izzy, who was holding her son on her lap.
'But he's been stung before and it was fine. So I wouldn't have
thought he could be allergic.'

'He could. He's having an anaphylactic reaction, and that can
happen if you've been exposed to the allergen before. So if he's

247

had a normal bee sting, his system reacted weirdly to it and now it's massively overreacting to the same poison this time.' For a few moments, I drove in tense silence. 'He needs epinephrine,' Tamsin said. 'A shot in the thigh and he'll be fine. Suse, how far are we?'

'Ten minutes. I'll try to be quicker.'

I clutched the steering wheel and realised that I had to stop driving simply dangerously and start driving like a racing driver. I needed to be insane. If I managed to get pulled over, so much the better. I had to get through part of Mont de Marsan to reach the hospital, and that meant traffic lights and junctions and queues. Sam's life, and Izzy's future, were hanging in the balance. I could not bear the idea that Izzy might be heading for my own particular brand of loss. I could not let that happen.

If he died I would always know it was my fault for holding back. That could not happen.

I swallowed hard and put my hand down on the horn. I drove as aggressively as I possibly could, making as much noise as I could in an attempt to make it safer. The road through the outskirts of town was long and straight, and I put my foot on the accelerator, kept my hand on the horn, and blasted my way along it. At a red light, I jolted onto the pavement to pass the queue, and swerved back onto the road at the corner. Cars pulled out of the way. Pedestrians stared. I was fixated on saving Sam. He might die. The reality of it propelled me round the inner ring road, through junctions, past cars, and along whichever side of the road was emptier. I shut myself off from the conversation behind me, did not want to know how the child was doing. I dreaded hearing Tamsin or Isabelle telling me to stop.

I pulled onto the pavement outside the hospital, and we ran in, Sam in his mother's arms. I stole a quick look. He was floppy and seemed unconscious. The hospital was large and confusing, but I knew where they needed to go, and so I ran ahead of Izzy and in through the main entrance. A woman sitting behind a reception desk looked up at us calmly, and I rushed over.

'A little boy,' I hissed urgently, in French. 'A bee.' My words fell over each other, and I couldn't manage to get 'was stung by' out of my mouth. The woman understood. She got to her feet and ran to meet Izzy and Sam, and she called, and two medical staff arrived and took Sam from Izzy's arms, and everyone rushed away.

I followed, but I walked. Tamsin walked faster, then started trotting, catching up. I forced myself to take a couple of deep breaths. I was shaking. The smell of the hospital was reassuring. This hospital was clean and efficient, reliable. I was relieved that Sam's life no longer rested in my hands. He had not, however, looked good when we delivered him to the professionals.

That, I reminded myself, was why I was going to remain childless. And I was childless, and not childfree, whatever Roman had to say about it. Sam's accident was a cosmic reminder of why it had to be that way.

I walked to the accident and emergency department, and found Tamsin standing outside a treatment room.

'What's happening?' I asked, not really wanting to know.

Tamsin shrugged. 'They're making him better. I hope.'

We looked each other in the eye. I saw my own hollow sickness reflected in Tamsin's eyes.

'What were you doing flirting with Patrick?' I asked.

'Oh, Jesus, Susie. What was I doing? I have no idea. I was being stupid.'

'That's what I thought.'

We stood together in silence.

'Is Izzy with him?' I only said it for something to say. Of course Izzy was with him.

'Yes.'

'How about I get some drinks? Sweet tea or something? Something for Izzy when she comes out?'

'Is there somewhere?'

'There's a drinks machine. And a little café. Maybe I'll go there. Chances are it would be nicer. I don't know if they'd do takeaways though. Lots of places don't, in France.'

'Susie, let's just wait. I think they only have to inject him and then he should recover.'

I swallowed. 'Why's it taking so long?'

chapter thirty-seven

'OK,' Freya said, sitting down on the cracked earth. 'Now I'm really scared, Jake. I'm so thirsty.'

'I know,' Jake told her. He drew a deep breath. 'Me too. I'm hot and thirsty and I don't understand what's going on here. We should shout.'

'No one would hear us.'

'How about if you get on my shoulders?'

Freya thought about it. 'That's a good idea,' she agreed. 'I'll get up and have a look around and shout as loud as I possibly can.'

'And that's loud,' Jake said. She poked him.

'Shut up,' she said. 'And help me up. What if we're right in the middle of the whole field and I can't see anything?'

'Then you shout even louder.'

Freya didn't want to admit how weak she was feeling. Her head kept feeling dizzy, as if she had been spinning around for five minutes without stopping. She was starving, and she was so thirsty that if she started thinking about water she thought she would die. She had to concentrate hard to climb onto her brother's shoulders, because there were black and green and pink blotches everywhere. She felt very, very sick. She took two handfuls of his thick blond hair and held tight. Slowly, Jake stood up, holding her calves tightly.

Freya craned her neck. It was no good. She burst into tears, and once she started, she couldn't stop sobbing. All her fear came out in choking gasps.

'Frey?' Jake was puzzled and annoyed. 'Frey, what's the matter? What is it? Frey, what can you see? You're supposed to be shouting, not crying. What can you see? What?'

She struggled to catch her breath. 'Nothing. I can't see anything.' Jake tried to look up at her, and she almost fell off his narrow shoulders. 'Put me down,' she said. 'We're not tall enough. I can only see the top bit of the maize.'

'Oh,' said Jake, and he knelt down so Freya could climb off him. 'Well, if I stood next to a strong kind of plant, could you hold onto a couple of them and maybe stand up on my shoulders? Or we could build a ladder or something.'

Freya shook her head. 'We've just got to walk,' she said, wiping her nose on the back of her hand. 'And let's shout anyway. They must be looking for us by now. I bet they're going frantic.'

Jake thought about it. 'Yes, it's *ages* past lunchtime, isn't it? They must be out trying to find us. Mum'll be going ballistic.'

'Do you think they'll call the police?'

'Maybe they'll come with helicopters.'

'Then we'd need to flatten some of this corn down so they'd see us.'

'Let's wait till we hear them, though.'

On an unspoken agreement, they carried on walking in the direction in which they had been going. There was no point turning back. Freya tried out her voice as they went.

'Help!' she shouted. Her voice sounded silly the first time, but after a few more goes, yelling at the top of her lungs began to feel normal. 'Help!' they shouted. '*Au secours!* Help! *Au secours!*'

If they kept trudging, by the laws of science they were going to reach the edge of the field.

* * *

251

It seemed as if hours passed, but really it was only fifteen minutes. At first, Freya thought she was imagining it. A few steps later, she knew she wasn't.

'Jake?' she said, hardly daring to believe her eyes.

'Mmm? *Help!*' said Jake, unwilling to break the rhythm of his shouting.

'Look, Jakey! It's light. We're walking towards the daylight!'

'*Au secours!*' he said. 'Oh God, Freya, you're right.'

They looked at each other, amazed and exhilarated. 'We did it!' Freya shouted. 'We did it! We're here!'

'Where are we?' Jake asked.

They stepped cautiously out of the tunnel of maize. They were certainly not in Susie's garden. Nor were they on the road that ran along the other side of the field. They were on a track which looked like a tractor path. It was brown and dusty, with a strip of parched grass in the middle. In front of them was another field of tall, brownish maize. They looked both ways.

'Which way shall we go?' Freya asked.

'Well. We must be either on the top of the square that is the field, or on the left-hand side,' Jake decided. 'So, if we're on top, we should head this way.' He pointed right. 'Because that should bring us to the back of the garden. But if we're on the side, we should go this way.' He pointed in the opposite direction. 'Because that will take us to the road.' He looked expectantly at Freya. She thought about it.

'So we should go left,' she said confidently. 'Because there isn't a path like this leading to the back of Susie's garden.'

'OK,' Jake said, equably. And they set off, their energy renewed, in what they hoped was going to be the direction of the road.

chapter thirty-eight

Patrick was mildly surprised to discover that he appeared to have the entire house and grounds to himself. After his dip, he went back to the bedroom, confidently expecting to find Amanda sulking on the bed. He had considered their situation, as he swam, and, after some reflection, he felt ready to confront her. He had never mentioned her problems to anybody before, although he knew that everybody must have been talking behind his back for years. It was liberating to have discussed it, even sketchily, with Tamsin, and he was determined to prove himself worthy, and to take action. He was going to force Amanda to confront her drinking and get some help. He was going to be firm but fair; the best friend she would ever have. She would fight him in the short run but ultimately it would bring them together. This was what he was telling himself. He took the stairs two at a time, hoping to make his speech before his nerve went.

Only she wasn't there. The shorts she had been wearing earlier were crumpled on the varnished pine floorboards, and her blouse had been thrown over the end of the bed. She had, he imagined, changed into her bikini. Except that she was not by the pool, because he had just come from there. And anyway, her bikini was on the bedside table, its straps dangling down in what appeared to Patrick, for some reason, to be a suggestive manner. He tried to work out why she would have changed. Then he laughed. Amanda changed her clothes all the time. She was a woman.

He had left his own clothes in the bathroom, because he hadn't wanted to disturb her. In truth, he had left them there because he hadn't wanted to cross her path. He quickly changed back from his swimming shorts into his normal clothes and wondered what to do. He supposed he would locate his wife somewhere in this house, and . . . Yes, he was going to confront her. He practised what he would say, in his head. *Amanda*, he would tell her, and he said it aloud, trying to say it in a tone that signified that he jolly well meant business.

'*Amanda*,' he said, heavily. 'A-*man*-da.' He needed to say it in a way that would make her stop whatever she was doing, put down her magazine, and look at him quizzically, perhaps wondering who this masterful man was and where her silly little husband had gone. A-*man*-da, we need to talk. We need to talk about your drinking. Your drinking *problem*. Enough is enough. Together we're going to get you happy.

He sighed. Nothing he said could possibly make her change her ways. He walked around despondently, knowing she hated him because he was bald and short and that she despised him for letting her get away with everything. He checked rooms, increasingly relieved to find them all empty.

When he saw the car was gone, he cheered up a little. He recognised that this was bad: it was depressing how easily he could make himself overlook the fact that he had, himself, presented her with an enormous glass of rosé with her lunch, and that her breath had already smelled alcoholic. But the fact that she had obviously taken the kids out somewhere lightened his heart. That, he was sure, was a good sign. Amanda never spent time with the children unless she couldn't avoid it.

It was a sorry state of affairs when he was glad that his wife was drink driving with his kids in the back. That was why he had to take this blasted action.

He fervently wished that Tamsin hadn't gone to the hospital.

He and Tamsin could have had the place to themselves, probably for hours. Patrick laughed at himself, a little. It was a strange feeling, having a crush. It had rarely, if ever, happened to him before. Certainly, it had never happened in his adult life. He was energised by Tamsin. When he thought about her, a thrill ran through his body, like a pleasurable electric shock. He thought again about her hair. Was he strange to find glossy dark hair sexy? He liked the way it emphasised the curve of her neck. He liked it that Tamsin was fit and healthy and knew how to enjoy life. He loved the simple way she dressed and the slight Australian twang when she spoke. He liked her moderation.

Amanda had said that Tamsin used to be the geeky one without a boyfriend. Now that he'd met her, Patrick thought his wife was probably just jealous. He decided to spend his free time lying by the pool with a glass of water and a good book, hoping that the object of his awe would come back before his wife turned up.

chapter thirty-nine

Lodwell's, 1991

Amanda was planning to stay in bed all day. She had a bugger of a hangover, and it was Sunday, and there was no chance she was going to do any revision today, not the day after the ball. She half woke, noticed it was light, drank half a pint of water, and curled up to go back to sleep. A swathe of her brain seemed to be pulsing in rhythm with her heart. She decided to take some painkillers. She levered herself up out of bed, and put a foot to the floor in some trepidation. The room spun and bile filled the back of her throat. Sometimes, she remembered, it was not a good idea to drink so much water so quickly, when she was feeling delicate. Sometimes even water could upset the fragile equilibrium within.

Nausea struck. Amanda swallowed hard and ran to the bathroom. Not for the first time, she thanked her lucky stars that she had her own bathroom, up here on the top floor. She made it in time. She doubled up over the loo, and vomited an acidic mix of semi-digested alcohol and chips into the porcelain bowl. Even when she was certain that everything was out, she stayed in position for a minute, gathering her strength and preparing herself to stand up. Sometimes she thought she knew the inside of her loo better than any other part of the house.

Holding the edge of the basin with one hand, she splashed

water over her face, then brushed her teeth. She took two para-cetamols.

The world felt marginally better. She was glad to have the vodka safely flushed away. Not to mention the chips, which had been ill-advised. She and Suzii had made their taxi stop at Caroline Street so they could fill their stomachs before going home. It had been an entirely unnecessary loading up of thousands of calories, and now some of them were gone. A positive development. Her mouth felt fresh and minty, now. She would have a shower later.

Back in bed, she pulled her duvet back over herself and started drifting. She felt a nagging remorse. What had she done? She had got off with some boy. She did not think she had gone very far with him – certainly not all the way – but she felt guilty about it. She knew she would be hard pushed to pick him out of a police line-up this morning and she had no idea what his name was. She was still nominally going out with Julian, and he would probably hear about this, but that didn't matter. She was more worried about Dai.

And that, she told herself, was silly. It was ridiculous. Dai would never know that she had pulled after midnight at the school disco, and he probably wouldn't care if he did know. He knew she still had a nominal 'boyfriend'. He knew that he was never going to be her boyfriend because of the social gulf between them. He probably got off with other girls. She didn't want to know about it.

So why, as her head split in two and she waited for the para-cetamol to kick in, did she feel that she had just betrayed him? Conversation between the two of them flowed, these days. They no longer just talked about *Neighbours*. He laughed at her for being posh and took the piss out of the way she said 'loo' instead of toilet, and 'sofa' instead of settee. She copied his accent, his 'over by there' and his 'where to is it?' She liked him more than she wanted to like him, and that, she felt, meant trouble.

Everybody in that room had expected her to pull a Cowbridge boy. Suzii had expected her to. She had dressed to pull and drunk to pull, and she had gone through the motions. But in a way she envied Tamsin, who had made no secret of the fact that she hated everything about the ball and had sat grumpily to one side looking at her watch until it was over. Amanda wished she had been strong enough to sit with Tamsin, or to take Dai, or not to go.

She closed her eyes and tried to lull herself back to sleep with her breathing. It must have worked, because when her mother knocked on her bedroom door, she had to pull herself up from warm slumbering depths.

'Mmmm?' she asked, not able to open her mouth. The painkillers had kicked in and her head was clearer. She felt fuzzy and shaky, and she knew that would last all day.

'Amanda?' said her mother. She opened the door and looked in. 'Sorry, love.'

Amanda looked at her mother, who was dressed in a floaty cotton dress with flowers on it, and a long cardigan which flapped around her knees. She was wearing lipstick so she must have been to church.

'What?' Amanda felt her mother ought to know not to disturb her on a morning like this.

'Sorry to wake you, darling. It's Isabelle on the phone.'

Amanda turned over. 'I'll call her back.'

Her mother shook her head. 'Love, it's urgent. Come on. Get up and talk to Izzy.'

Amanda levered herself out of bed without thinking. Her mind was too blurred for her to register what *urgent* could mean. She staggered downstairs and picked up the telephone on the hall table. Her mother pressed a hand to Amanda's shoulder. Amanda shook her off.

'Izzy?' Amanda complained. 'It's only half ten.'

She waited for Izzy to say something. After a couple of seconds, she heard a strange sound, which turned into a sob. 'Izzy?' Amanda asked. 'Izzy, what is it? What's happened?' Suddenly, she was wide awake. 'Isabelle! What?'

Izzy gulped a couple of times on the other end of the phone. 'Mrs Grey drove off the road last night. She's dead.'

Amanda could not compute this. She filed it away for later.

'What about Tamsin?' she asked.

'In hospital. I don't think she's badly hurt. I think she'll be OK.'

'Jesus.'

And then Amanda realised. She realised that Izzy knew it, and she knew it, and Suzii knew it. There was quite possibly nobody else in the world who knew the simple truth: that this was Amanda and Suzii's fault, that they had done it, and that they were going to have to live with the guilt for ever.

chapter forty

Amanda was enjoying herself. She was sitting too close to Roman, on the terrace of a smart bar, on the banks of a river. They were drinking champagne, although she was beginning to crave something stronger. And they were chatting in what Amanda thought was a surprisingly normal manner. It had been a while since she had considered herself normal.

'This woman,' Roman was saying. 'She completely wasted Susie's time. I mean, she's a nutter. Raving.'

'Why?'

'It's just a weird story that reminds you that there are some very unusual people out there.' He smiled at her, and Amanda simpered. 'I mean, Suze spends all her time shut away from the world, painting her pictures. She doesn't have a great social life here, in France, because she's not confident enough with the language. She'd be fine if she let herself go. She's quite happy, I think, with the way it is. But then someone like this kook shows up, crying about her supposed stalker. She's upset Susie, which she didn't need right now. I made the woman bloody cry, I can tell you.'

'Did you? You actually made her cry?'

'And I'd do it again.' He changed the subject. 'So, what are you going to do about your marriage, my dear?' He peered at her. She thought he was trying to read her mind. 'Don't take this the wrong way,' he said, 'but this morning you gave me the impression you were looking for excitement elsewhere.'

She laughed at how wrong he was. 'Jeez, Roman. That was a joke. I'm not that kind of a girl.' He raised his eyebrows. 'Seriously, I'm not. Don't you think I'd take more care of myself if I was out shagging? I honestly haven't been interested in that kind of thing for ever. Not even with Patrick.'

'*Especially* not with Patrick, by the sound of it.'

'Well, certainly not with anyone else either. And don't be mean about Patrick. He's not well, for one thing.'

'How not well?'

She drained her glass and held it out. She knew she must be very drunk indeed if she was sharing Patrick's medical secrets. 'Oh, I shouldn't have said anything,' she said, as casually as she could. 'It's like this great bloody thing we don't mention, Patrick and I. Banned from being thought about in the assumption and hope that if we ignore it it will go away.'

'You seem to have a few of those things.'

She scowled. 'I think Patrick genuinely never gives it a moment's thought.'

'"It" being?'

'Being nothing.'

Roman emptied the champagne bottle into Amanda's glass. 'Tell me.'

'Why?' She knew she shouldn't say any more. She knew it. There was no doubt about it: she should say nothing. Roman was not helping.

'Because I want to know.'

Amanda looked at him. He was not being fair, she knew that, but then, neither was she. She knew she was acting stupidly and dangerously, just by being here. They must have been missed by now, by Patrick and the children at least.

'And,' Roman added, 'because if someone's ill, ignoring it is the most fucking ridiculous way of dealing with it.'

'Now, *that*,' she told him, 'is the most sensible thing you've said all day.' She liked the way his T-shirt hung down from his shoulders. The outlines of his muscular torso showed through it. He was in good shape, which wasn't surprising considering how much exercise he did. For an instant, she thought of Dai.

'So?' he asked, leaning forward and staring wickedly into her eyes.

'Well, he just has these headaches,' she said, waving it away with a hand. 'And he's been going to the doctor about them. He tried to go without telling me, but I found an appointment card and assumed the worst. STDs, I mean. But luckily, no. He's got a consultant's appointment next week. I'm sure it's just a load of fuss over nothing. I mean, everyone gets bloody headaches, don't they? I know I do. But Patrick's are apparently worse than everyone else's. Partly, you know, because he's male. You guys always have flu when we have colds, don't you?'

'Hope it's nothing serious.'

'Shut up. We don't talk about it, do we?' She knocked back her drink. 'Come on. I'm leaving you miles behind, you lightweight.'

A waiter, wearing formal black and white, appeared next to them.

'Excuse me,' he said, politely. 'Will you be joining us for dinner this evening?'

Amanda's French was rusty, and she looked to Roman, who visibly pulled himself together.

'No thank you,' he said, in French. 'We are expected at home. But thank you. Could we have the bill, please?'

Amanda looked at her watch. 'Jesus fucking Christ!' she exclaimed, causing the people at the next table to turn round and stare. 'Quarter to eight! How in the name of Jesus did *that* happen?'

'Better get off,' Roman agreed. 'Have you got cash?'

Amanda reached for her pocket, before remembering that her dress didn't have them. 'Um. Not really, no. I didn't think about money.'

Roman looked at her, and she saw an element of panic in his

eyes. 'Then we're up shit creek,' he said quietly. 'Because I neglected to take my wallet to the bins with me.'

'Oh.'

'Sit here calmly. We can't do a runner because they know who I am. I haven't got my phone. Have you got a phone?' She shook her head. He thought for a moment. 'OK. There's a payphone in the lobby. I'm going to have to call Suze and ask her to bail us out. She might be able to pay over the phone, but I'd rather they didn't know about our cock-up, so I guess she's going to have to come down here with . . .' The waiter laid the bill on the table in front of them; an innocuous looking piece of paper tucked into a plastic clip. Roman unfolded the paper. 'Yes. With sixty-three euros and twelve centimes.'

'Oh.' Amanda's euphoria evaporated.

'And,' Roman continued, 'that is perhaps not the ideal outcome to this situation. I mean, we might not particularly have chosen to make Susie come right here, to see where we slipped away to and to pay for our champagne. It seems a little rude, when she's done an emergency dash to the hospital.' He paused. 'And we don't even know if Sam's all right. We are the scum of the earth, Amanda, you and me.'

Amanda felt nauseous. 'Susie can't come. I'll get Patrick over.'

'But we've got his car.'

'He can take Susie's. If she's back from the hospital.'

Roman thought about this. 'Not Susie's. Mine. The insurance covers anybody. But he's still going to have to tell whoever's around where he's going. And also he's going to see you sitting here with me, and all our empties.'

Amanda waved that concern away. 'Oh, Patrick doesn't get steamed up about things like that. But how am I supposed to call him when we've got no money?'

She was wretched. Five minutes earlier, she had been having a fabulous, glamorous, irresponsible time with a sexy man and a bottle of fine champagne. Now it all looked sordid and unpleasant. It said nothing good about her, or about Roman, or about either of their relationships. They should both be dumped for this, she realised. She knew she wouldn't be. Somehow, that fact was phenomenally depressing.

'He's got a pile of coins in the car,' she remembered. 'He keeps them for emergency phone calls, and road tolls.'

Roman raised his eyebrows and motioned with his head for her to fetch the money. He did not look happy.

chapter forty-one

I was too tired to force a smile. I poured a drink for everyone who was there, and felt furious about those who weren't. They had all known that there were drinks on the terrace at seven, just the same as there had been last night. Amanda was missing, with her children. And Roman was missing. Roman could be anywhere. I tried to tell myself that I didn't care. Roman came and went as he pleased. We had a laid-back relationship because we trusted each other. We liked it that way. That was the party line. I imagined myself asking for more. I pictured Roman running a mile.

'Here, Izzy,' I said, handing my friend a large vodka and tonic. Izzy took it with a grateful smile, and I noticed that her hand was shaking slightly. 'You've earned that,' I added. 'God knows.'

'You've earned more than this,' Izzy told me, and held her glass up. 'Cheers to you, Susie,' she said. 'Cheers to your Formula One driving.'

I nodded, then brushed her appreciation away. It already felt as if the race to the hospital had been inevitable, as if its outcome had been inevitable.

'Cheers to Sam,' I said, and we clinked glasses. 'Is he sleeping?'

'Like a baby. Much better than a baby. It's early for him, but he needs it.'

'Of course he does. He's got a lot of recovering to do.'

'I'll be checking on him all night, though. Susie, I know I said this already, but they said five more minutes could have been critical. The way you drove – it literally saved his life.'

'We should probably have called an ambulance. But it's so hard to direct anyone here, specially when you've got a foreign accent. I just didn't want them not to find us because I couldn't give the right directions.'

'I know. You did it. You were the ambulance.'

'Well, I'm unspeakably relieved he's OK. And if I feel like this, I can't imagine how you must be feeling.'

Izzy sipped her drink. 'Mmm. A strong one. Better every second.'

Tamsin came over. I smiled at her. We had bonded, during the hospital dash and, particularly, during the euphoric relief afterwards.

'No sign of Amanda?' she asked. 'I'd have thought she'd have the children back by now. What with their schedule and everything. Patrick says he has no idea where she's gone. She's not even insured for that car, apparently. Not to mention the fact that she has to be drunk.'

I shrugged. I didn't particularly care where Amanda was, and if she was drink driving, that was her responsibility. 'What can you do? It's their domestic situation, isn't it? Sorry, Patrick.' I realised suddenly that he was standing behind me. 'Sorry. I didn't see you. But really, what can we do? Do you want me to go out and look for them? Because I'd have no idea where to go. And what would I say if I found her?'

I looked curiously at Patrick. He was such a mild man. There had to be a kind of masochism on his part, in remaining married to Amanda. A part of him had to enjoy being sworn at and belittled. I wondered if he was embarrassed at having his eventful domestic life laid bare like this. He didn't look it. In fact, he was smiling. He was probably enjoying having Amanda out of the way. It gave him more leeway to leer at Tamsin.

'She'll be back,' he said. 'In her own good time. I'm actually quite pleased that she's taken the kids out. It's not like her to want to do that.'

'You mean, take them somewhere to play?' said Tamsin, with a smile. 'Maybe she's found a university summer school and enrolled them for advanced calculus.'

He nodded. 'It's a possibility.'

Amanda had guessed that I was going to tell Tamsin about the night of the ball. I was certain that she had done a runner. Had scooped her children into the car and driven off to the airport on an impulse. I looked at the sky. Clouds were building. I sensed an August storm coming, and I hoped Amanda and the children weren't going to get caught up in it, because the storms here could be vicious.

'Here.' I waved to the mosaic-topped table. 'Patrick. Tamsin. Drinks for you. I made them all quite strong because I thought Izzy needed it.'

Nobody had commented, yet, on Roman's absence. I felt that the gaping hole in my own life was exposed, yet none of them was noticing. Izzy knew about Natasha, and I was sure she was wondering about the superficial relationship we had. Izzy knew as well as I did that you couldn't call someone your soulmate if they didn't even know you'd had a baby.

'I don't know where Roman's got to,' I added, experimentally. 'Did anyone see him this afternoon?'

'Nope,' said Patrick. 'Definitely not here when I was looking for Amanda. I checked everywhere.'

'Even the attic?'

Patrick frowned. 'Attic? No. Didn't know there was anything up there.'

'It's Roman's little playhouse,' I found myself saying, scathingly, and I swallowed half my drink in one gulp. 'He's probably hidden away up there.'

'I don't blame him,' Tamsin said lightly. 'I know I've never had a boyfriend who would have hung around a gathering like this for long.'

'Mmm. True,' I agreed, and my mood lightened. Perhaps it was normal for a man to keep out of the way when his girlfriend's old schoolfriends were in the house. I remembered that I had left the phone off the hook impulsively, after I spoke to the police. I nipped into the study, and replaced it, then checked the time.

It was a quarter to eight, which was time to get the starters on the table. Luckily, it was a goat's cheese salad which didn't require any cooking. As I was dishing it onto plates for those who had bothered to turn up, I heard footsteps on the shingle path that bisected my front garden.

They were back. I stood in the door frame, and smiled at Jake and Freya. They looked shattered but at least they were smiling.

'Hello, you two,' I said. I was happy to see them. My evening was saved, after all: only Roman was missing, presumed upstairs. 'How are you doing?'

Freya frowned. 'Did you wonder where we were?' she demanded.

'Yes, of course. We've all been wondering where you were, but since your mum was with you, nobody worried.' I looked past them, to the road. 'Where is she?'

'Mum?' asked Jake. 'Mum's not with us.'

'Oh.' I thought about this. 'But you're OK?'

'We are now.' Freya looked upset. She looked as if she was about to cry. I put a hand on her shoulder, and ushered her into the house. 'Come and find your dad. Oh, God, look at you! What on earth have you been doing? You're filthy!' Their faces were clean, but the legs that poked thinly out from their shorts were encrusted with dirt.

'We had an adventure,' Jake assured me solemnly. 'Please may I have some water?'

'Water? Yes, of course. Look, go to the terrace and I'll bring it to you.'

'Thanks,' the children said in unison, and they were off. I saw them looking at each other, confused.

I poured two large glasses of water and put five ice cubes into each of them. I took the children's pasta – animal shapes, with tomato and basil sauce – out of the fridge and tipped it into a pan to warm up. I had already cooked it for Sam, and there was lots left over. Jake and Freya had, I thought, looked starving, so

I took two packets of crisps from my top cupboard and took them outside with me. I would normally put crisps into bowls, but I had a vague recollection that, if you were a child, crisps were better from the packet. That would stop the adults stealing them, too.

'. . . I mean, really for *hours*,' Jake was saying, emphatically. Patrick's jaw was slack and he looked guilty. Jake was pointing at the field next door. 'I can see why, now. It's because it joins on to the field above it, just right there, so we crossed over to the next field without realising it, so we were chugging all the way up that hill. We were so lost. We thought we'd never get out. It was really hot.'

'I'm sure it was.' Tamsin looked as if she wanted to laugh, but in a nice, incredulous way. 'So, hours later, what happens? You emerge where?'

Freya had her hand in Izzy's, but she let go to take her drink and crisps. 'Thank you, Susie,' she said politely. 'We came out on a tractor path, somewhere up there, but we couldn't see anything because of the maize. So we walked along it for *ages*, and I wanted to lie down and have a rest but Jake said better not, and then a man came in a tractor, and he was really, really surprised to see us. Jake talked to him because I was too scared. It was really hard to understand what he was saying.'

'Did he have any hair?' I interjected.

Freya smiled. 'No, he didn't have any hair at all.'

'That's Pierre. He has the farm over there. He's a nice guy. Did he help you?'

Jake took over. 'He knew you. As soon as he heard me trying to talk French he asked if we were staying with you. So I said yes, and he drove on a bit to where he could turn the tractor round, and we jumped up, which was pretty good fun, actually, and he took us back to his house. We aren't meant to go with strangers, but we couldn't do anything else because we were so tired and lost. His wife was surprised to see us too, and she rang you but it was engaged all the time. So she gave us water and she made us wash our hands and faces, and she gave us each a sandwich with ham in and we sat at her kitchen table for ages. It was quite hard to try to talk to her, but she was nice and she asked if we were on holiday and stuff like that.'

'We could see that she didn't know what to do with us,' Freya interjected. 'So in the end we said we'd come back here even though she wouldn't get through on the phone. Because we knew everybody would be here.'

'But she didn't want to let us wander off,' Jake said, 'so she said when we get back we had to get Susie to ring to say we were safe.'

'OK,' I said. 'I'll call her now.'

That should definitely have been a task for Roman. He would have charmed the hatchet-faced Bernadette. Instead, she was going to think I was irresponsible. I shook my head, wondering why everything that was going wrong was involving children.

The phone rang as I walked towards it. I snatched it up.

'Susie, it's Neil Barron,' he said quickly. I did not try to judge his tone, but hung up, waited a few seconds, and picked it up again. I knew he was redialling, so I punched the number in quickly.

There was something bothering me, too. I listened to the phone ringing up the hill, and at the same moment that Bernadette answered, I realised what it was.

'Oh, *bonjour, Bernadette*,' I said. '*C'est Susanna. Oui, merci beaucoup pour votre aide avec les enfants*.' I reassured the woman that they were fine, and pretended that everyone at the house had been looking for them and that this had somehow involved lots of phone calls which was why the line was engaged. I knew Bernadette didn't believe me. I knew that this very proper farmer's wife saw me as a strange and exotic weirdo who had no idea about the correct way to conduct one's life. I could hear her now, talking to her friends and tutting about what a good thing it was that Susie and Roman didn't have any children, because they clearly had no idea how to look after them, and did you know, they're not even married?

I thanked the woman again, and hung up. 'If the children are here on their own,' I asked the telephone, 'then where the fuck is Amanda?'

Patrick was wondering the same thing, and I bumped into him on his way indoors.

'Sorry,' he said. He looked depressed. 'Wondering where Amanda's got to.'

'Hang on a second,' I said, and sprinted upstairs. When I came back down, Patrick looked at me with a vague puzzlement.

'Oh, Patrick,' I said, and suddenly I could keep it up no longer. I took him by the hairy forearm and sat him down at the dining table. He was at the end of one of the long sides, and I took the short side at right angles to him. 'Patrick,' I said, 'I don't know where Amanda is, but Roman's gone too. I bet they're together.'

Patrick seemed to cheer up a little. 'Do you think? I'd like to think she was with a responsible adult.' He looked at me. 'You don't agree?' he added, uncertainly.

'No,' I said. 'If they're together, it's bad, not good. Roman is a wonderful man, but he can be as irresponsible as Amanda, just differently. They'd spark each other off, I can see it. Encourage each other. They're getting drunk somewhere together. I doubt they're actually . . .' I looked at the table and back into Patrick's eyes. 'I doubt they're being unfaithful to us. I don't think Roman would do that to me, and I'm sure it's not a trick in Amanda's repertoire.' Because Roman and I had never seriously discussed a permanent commitment, I had no idea whether he planned to stay with me in the long term or whether he liked me because I paid the bills. I was deeply insecure about every aspect of our relationship, and at that moment I could only imagine that he was unfaithful to me at every opportunity. Perhaps even with Amanda.

'Oh, gosh no,' said Patrick. 'No, that would certainly not cross Amanda's mind. She has her faults, but liking sex *too much* is certainly not one of them!' He half smiled. 'Sorry. So what ought we to do?'

I shrugged. 'I'll try Roman's mobile, but even if it's with him, it won't be switched on.' I tried. It wasn't. Neil Barron called back. I hung up on him before he got past the word 'It's'.

*   *   *

There was only one possible course of action, and that was to carry on without them. I could barely drag myself into the kitchen. I was sick of doing all this. My guests had been here for less than two days, and I was fed up. I had imagined myself a perfect hostess, tending to the needs of grateful friends, but in fact I was a slave. I was everything you didn't see at hotels, everything that children took for granted. For the second night in a row, I was going to present a three-course meal. I wished I had taken them out for pizza.

I bustled around the kitchen, imagining what Roman might be saying about me to Amanda, my old best friend. I knew he used me as a cashpoint. I knew our relationship suited both of us for different reasons. He kept me insulated from the world and from taking risks, and I funded his lifestyle and allowed him to do exactly what he pleased. It was a complex unspoken arrangement; and the trouble was, I really did love him and I wanted more. I thought that he had made it clear, over the years, that he didn't.

I had been too scared to be alone here. Now, suddenly, I was ready. I wanted more than Roman would ever give me. I was furious with him.

'Izzy?' I called. She appeared in the kitchen next to me. I pointed to the pot of salted vinegary water on the stove. 'When that boils, can you throw the langoustines in?' I said, grimly. 'They're washed and drained. Just chuck them in. I'm just going to do something upstairs.'

Izzy put her arm round my shoulders and pulled me close to her. For once, I relaxed.

'Are you packing his stuff?' she asked softly.

I nodded. She squeezed me. 'Do what feels right,' she said, 'but don't be too hasty.'

'How can it work,' I muttered into her shoulder, 'when he doesn't know about my baby? And when he won't let me have another? And when he won't talk about five years' time because he won't be tied down?'

'Do what you have to do,' she said.

Once I started packing, I almost enjoyed myself. I sacrificed two of my biggest cases, and used all of his backpacks. In went his pants. In went his T-shirts, his socks, his trousers and fleeces and shorts. Old stuff, painting clothes, designer items, favourite shirts. I threw it all in. It felt good. It was time for us both to move on. There was a lot to work out, a lot of explaining for me to do. I knew that I wasn't being fair on Roman. He wasn't evil. He was just Roman, and I'd always known what he was like. He had never pretended to want to marry me or to want us to have a family, or anything. He had always made it clear that he liked a life where he could play hard and, well, play hard. He loved his dangerous sports, and he loved his food and drink and relaxation. Nothing was going to curtail those pursuits. A baby would have forced him to grow up, and he wasn't ready for that.

We had never even hinted at the idea of growing old together. I had not, until now, given it much thought, but now that I did, I supposed that I had always felt that as long as I kept myself thin and fit, and as long as I kept earning, I would get to keep Roman. I knew that he would drift off when I was fat, or older, or poorer, or simply when he had a better offer. I had always quite liked that about him. I had enjoyed not being single, and I had enjoyed his company. He was fiercely attractive.

I had never opened up to him. It was not his fault that he wasn't psychic.

Still, he could go now. He was out with Amanda and I was humiliated.

I stopped my frenzied packing when I realised that the langoustines would be long cooked and that my guests, the considerate ones, were probably embarrassed. I paused. At that moment, there was a gentle knock on the bedroom door.

'Hello?' I said.

It was Izzy. I looked at her and she smiled back. 'OK?' she asked.

'Yes. Sorry.'

'I didn't cook the shellfish because if they only take five minutes, I thought it might be better to wait a while. Until we were ready.'

'Until I was ready.'

'It's not as if there's any hurry. We're still two people down.'

I zipped shut the backpack I was packing and dropped it from the bed to the floor, where it sat on top of three other bags. 'He can pack the rest of his stuff himself,' I told her. 'I'm going to try to be grown up about this. Amicable.' A thought occurred to me, and I looked at Izzy. 'What's everyone doing down there? How are they?'

'Oh, fine,' she said, sitting down on the bed. 'Patrick gazing at Tamsin. Kids embarrassed by him. God, Susie, I do envy you all this. This room is perfect.'

'Yeah, it's nice, for what that's worth. Luckily absolutely everything is in my name.' I wondered whether Amanda had crashed the car, drunk. I wondered whether Roman would have done anything to stop her.

'Izzy?' I said. 'I'd love to have a look on Roman's computer. To see if I've got any reason for being mad at him.' I screwed up my face. 'What do you think? Would it be terrible?'

Izzy raised her eyebrows. I was getting used to her new look. She looked nice, because her face was kind. I realised how few friends I actually had.

'Of course it wouldn't be terrible,' she said, carefully. 'I imagine that technically speaking it's your computer anyway. But what would you be looking for?'

I stood up. 'Emails. Websites. Come on. Upstairs is going to surprise you.'

I knew Roman wasn't there, but I still half expected to find him downloading music or checking the tide times. I switched the light on at the bottom of the stairs, and Izzy followed me up. The attic still surprised me. I hardly ever went up there because, although he never said so, I knew that Roman didn't like me there. I didn't like him in my studio, either, so I could hardly argue. He had painted the cheap floorboards white, and, to my annoyance, I noticed that the original beams, which held the roof up to its point, were now white too. The boards that insulated between tiles and beams were, naturally, white. Even though it was clouding over, light flooded in through the Velux and dormer windows that looked out in three directions. The room glared. Roman kept his attic scrupulously organised. I sighed when I saw his climbing harness and ropes on the floor next to the window. He had been abseiling to the terrace again. He was like a child.

I switched the computer on and looked at Izzy.

'Bloody hell,' she said, eyes wide. 'This is his? Sam would give anything for a playroom like this. Susie, your house is wonderful, but this is the best room in it. Why isn't your studio up here?'

I smiled. 'Because the light would be wrong.'

'The light's wonderful!'

'Not for me.' I stopped and thought about it. *The light would be wrong* had long been my excuse, but I wondered whether it was actually true. If I positioned myself correctly, I could harness the light, and it could be perfect. 'Actually, you're right,' I admitted. I felt sad. 'I'm very happy with my studio outside, but you're right. Roman took this attic over without asking twice. In fact he bagsied it the first time we looked at the house.'

I tried to imagine what I would do here without him. I would not be able to speak to the neighbours properly. I'd have to translate all the paperwork and take care of it. I would be lost. Then the beginnings of an idea started forming. I asked before I had time to think it through, because I didn't want the moment to pass.

'Izzy?' I said, casually, opening Roman's email and scanning down his in-box. 'Would Sam like this playroom? Would he like to go to French school? Would you and Sam like to move in with me?'

The phone started ringing. I ignored it. Someone downstairs would get it.

chapter forty-two

Patrick didn't know what was going on, so he put all his energies into Jake and Freya. They lapped up the attention. Freya kept remembering new moments from their adventure.

'One time I got on Jake's shoulders,' she said. 'And I made myself as tall as I could but I still couldn't see anything. Dad, I was so scared.'

'Poor Freya,' he said. He patted her on the shoulder, not really knowing what else to do. He paced around the dining room again, swamped by guilt. What did it say about them that not a single adult in the house had missed them? It was, of course, none of Tamsin's business. Nor Susie's, nor Isabelle's, and certainly nothing to do with that Roman bastard. It was Patrick's own fault; his and Amanda's. He was trying not to think about it too hard. Any blasted thing could have happened to them. Right now, they could have been lying unconscious in the field, and he would not be missing them. He would still be feeling vaguely pleased that Amanda had taken them out for pizza.

And he worked so damned hard, he spent so little 'quality time' with his children, that it was particularly remiss of him to have overlooked the fact that, when he was, for once, in charge of them during daylight hours, they were missing and scared, lost in a strange country. He was a shoddy father.

And, even worse, his wife was a dreadful mother. He was certainly going to have to confront her. He just wished she would come back now, so he could get it over with.

'How about a bath?' he suggested, as both children came to the end of their second large helpings of pasta.

He saw them looking at each other.

'A bath?' echoed Jake, frowning. 'Dad, it's a bit hot for a bath.'

He looked outside. It was a bit hot, Jake was right. It felt humid, too. Sticky. Not bath weather at all.

'Well, a shower then,' he said.

'Yeah,' Jake agreed. 'We reek. We need a shower.'

'I'm having the upstairs bathroom,' Freya said, leaping up.

'And I'm having some ice cream,' Jake told her, with a winner's smile.

The phone was ringing. Tamsin and Patrick looked at each other, waiting for Susie to answer it. Neither of them knew exactly where she was. It carried on ringing. Tamsin stood up and went to look for it.

'*Bonjour?*' Patrick heard her say, in one of the sitting rooms. 'No, it's her friend Tamsin . . . Oh. Hello, Roman. Mmm. No, not quite sure where Susie is, actually. I thought she was in the house but she didn't answer the phone. Patrick? Yes. Sure.'

Tamsin came back to the dining room, holding a cordless phone out to him. 'It's Roman,' she said, making a quizzical face. 'He says he needs to speak to you.'

'Oh, Christ Almighty,' Patrick said. 'Roman?' He didn't know what tone to adopt with Roman. He knew the man sneered at him. Roman was the kind of man he, Patrick, would never willingly spend any time with. He didn't have the faintest idea how to get any rapport going with this sort of man. Their lives could only possibly have overlapped via their wives.

'Yeah.' Roman's voice was lazy. 'Look, Patrick, we need your help. That OK? Could you come in my car? Keys are in the white bowl on the end of the kitchen shelf nearest the door. My car,

277

not Susie's. Yeah? Bring some cash if you would. Be doing us a big favour. Then, what you do, you turn left at the top of the street . . .'

Patrick had written the instructions down. He was not happy, but he had no choice about bailing out his wayward wife and the vile Roman. He followed his orders to the letter, driving slowly and nervously, knowing that he had drunk too much. Tamsin had offered to go with him, but something in him had shrunk away from that. It seemed perverse to turn up with this enchanting woman to collect his wife from her careless liaison with a smarmy Frenchman. That would have been tantamount to an admission that the marriage was a sham. Tamsin had made him a strong coffee and had offered to look after the children and make sure they went to bed, while he headed off to see exactly where Amanda had disappeared to.

The fact that it was a hotel was a nasty surprise. He parked outside, in the town square, and noticed that the sky had clouded right over. The air felt static, as if it were about to rain rather hard. He walked fast, knowing that already he was starting to sweat, into the lobby of the hotel. It was a chic little place; exactly the sort of venue to please Amanda. There was a woman sitting behind the reception desk who turned a bored gaze, assessed him, and smiled dutifully. She was blonde and improbably skinny, with heavy make-up on. He wasn't quite sure what to say to her.

'*Où est le bar ici?*' he tried.

The woman said nothing. She just pointed through the double doors at the far end of the foyer, and he walked slowly, not quite wanting to see either of them. Behind him, a telephone rang, and the woman answered it.

The bar was on a terrace next to a wide river. On the other side, willow branches dipped into the water, and a few wooden boats bobbed gently up and down. Patrick scanned the customers, feeling like a fool. He noticed the first drops of rain disturbing the surface of the river.

Amanda and Roman were at a table in the corner. When

278

Patrick looked at them, Amanda caught his eye for a fraction of a second, and looked away, pretending she hadn't seen him. She stared, instead, at the drink in front of her. It was something clear, in a tumbler. Something potent, no doubt. Roman, Patrick thought, genuinely hadn't seen him, and was watching Amanda drinking at the same time as searching for something in the pocket of his trousers. There was a dark blue bowl in front of them with three peanuts and a coating of salt left on the bottom.

'Hello,' Patrick said, in a fuzzy voice. He walked as purposefully as he could up to their table. 'Fancy meeting you two here.'

He ignored Roman and looked at his wife through narrowed eyes. She had to say the right thing now. She just had to. It could all still be all right, if she said the right thing. He implored her, silently.

'Patrick!' She was drunk, and effusive. 'Help is at hand! We are saved! Pull up a chair.' She waved her hand around vaguely. 'We'll get you a drink. Won't we, Roman?'

Patrick stared at Roman.

'Sure,' he slurred. He lifted a hand for the waiter, and looked into his own glass. He looked at Amanda, and waved his empty glass at the man as he approached.

'*Trois, s'il vous plaît*,' he called. The man nodded. Patrick wondered whether he was imagining the faintly disgusted look on the waiter's face.

'C'mon,' Amanda was saying. 'Come and sit down. Nice of you to bail us out. Drink before we go. We're just having one for the road.'

He barely recognised her. This woman was shouting. She was drunk, and she looked a mess. A strap of her dress had slipped down her arm and the top of her breast was exposed. Patrick suddenly felt brutal. The dress, he told himself viciously, did Amanda no favours. It was the kind of dress that would look marvellous on Tamsin or Susie. Amanda looked better when she dressed more conservatively. Her eye make-up was smeared on her cheek and her glass was imprinted with lipstick kisses. Patrick

279

surreptitiously checked Roman's face and collar. At least there was no lipstick on him.

'Stop looking at me like that!' Amanda barked. 'C'mon, sit down.'

Patrick could not control himself. After thirteen years, his meekness evaporated. He reached for his wallet.

'No,' he said, calmly but firmly. 'No, thank you, I won't sit down. Look at yourself, Amanda. You are a disgrace and I am ashamed of you. This is my fault, because I've let things get to this point, but they are going no further. This is where it *stops*.'

He took four crisp fifty euro notes and dropped them onto the table. He dropped Roman's car keys down, and picked up his own, which were next to Amanda's elbow. Then he turned and walked away. He was in awe of himself. Something was going to have to change, now.

It was raining hard by the time he found the hire car parked on the other side of the square. Amanda caught up with him as he was starting the engine.

'Patrick!' she said. With each drop of rain, she looked more of a wreck. Any façade of respectability was washed away. Passers-by were staring at her. He wound down his window.

'Patrick, don't be an arse,' she hissed. 'This was never meant to happen. We just got a bit carried away. It is a *holiday*. You've always begrudged me any fun.'

He considered the situation. 'Get in,' he said, because he didn't want her being driven back through the country lanes by that drunken moron. She climbed in next to him and smiled.

'So you forgive me?' she asked, in a silly, girlish voice.

'No, actually, I bloody don't,' he said. He couldn't manage an angry voice. This was as scary as he got. 'Sam nearly died. Our two were lost for the entire afternoon in a field of maize and were rescued by a passing farmer. I believe that Susie's re-evaluating her relationship with your *boyfriend* back there. And you have made our whole family a laughing stock.'

She was scowling straight ahead. The rain was coming down

faster, torrentially. The storm was crouching overhead, and Patrick hoped he would make it back before it burst. He hoped he could remember the way. He drove slowly, nervously, aware of his blood alcohol level.

'You're just no fun,' she said, grumpily. 'There's no blasted fun in my life, that's the bloody trouble. You can't blame me if I find it elsewhere.'

Patrick considered his response as he edged out of the town and tried to remember which turning he ought to take. He knew that whatever he said now was going to be crucial. He had to tell her the truth. There was really nothing left for either of them to lose.

Except that mothers always got custody, and if they split up, he would hardly ever see his kids.

He took the turning, and drove, slowly, up a hill. The trees on either side of the road made a canopy over him, and kept the worst of the rain off the windscreen. He put the headlights on. Then he pulled over, and parked on a dirt track that led up into the woods. He stopped the engine and gathered his courage. His heart was thumping and he hoped his wife couldn't see how scared he was.

'Amanda,' he said, hearing a quaver in his voice. 'Amanda. You are an alcoholic. It's destroying everything. You need to get help.'

She stared at him. For a moment, he thought he saw the real Amanda looking out, scared, from inside her eyes. Then hostility snapped back into place.

'I am not a fucking alcoholic,' she slurred. 'Speak for yourself, you old fart.'

'Then,' he said, 'if you won't take responsibility for yourself, I think we should separate. You can't get tarted up and run off to expensive bars with your friend's boyfriend, right under my nose, and expect everything to be all right. That is one humiliation too many, as far as I'm concerned. And I am out of here.'

He looked at her. She was shaking her head and smiling.

'What?' he demanded.

'You don't mean it, do you?' she said, laughing maliciously.

'What would you be, without me? A saddo single dad who never dared chat up a woman, is what. Living in some studio apartment, getting threatening letters from the CSA, lusting after women like Tamsin who wouldn't give you the time of day, and seeing your kids every other Sunday if you're lucky. Is that really what you want?'

He was icy. 'No! What I want is for you to go to rehab. Because if you don't I'm going to fight you every step of the way for custody, and I'll tell you what, the way you are at the moment, I'd get it.' He looked her in the eyes, amazed at how easy it was, now that he had started, to say it all.

'You fucking would not, you bullying prick.'

'I would. We both know you do the school run drunk. Every afternoon. Probably some mornings too – let's be honest. You know the other mothers gossip behind your back. All I have to do is tip the police off and they'd come and breathalyse you and that would be that.' He had no idea how much of this was true. He was desperate to get through to her. 'I don't want to break up the family,' he said. The rain was falling down the windows in a solid mass. He thought they should get back to the house. It was completely dark.

'Course you don't,' Amanda snarled. 'You are such a fucking wanker. I wish I was married to Roman instead of you. You're pathetic.'

Patrick started the engine up and pulled out, gingerly.

'Don't worry,' he said, mildly. He was furious inside. 'I hate you, too. In fact I wish I'd stayed with Melanie.' He looked at her. 'I was going to stay with her, you know. Rather than go out with you. But she dumped me.'

Amanda glared back. 'Well, I wasn't a virgin when we met. I'd had a two-year affair with a builder at school.'

Patrick smiled sadly. 'And you think that surprises me?'

chapter forty-three

Izzy and I went downstairs. I was feeling bad about the spying we had done on Roman. There was nothing incriminating in his email account, apart from a few brief communications with his ex-wife. My French was good enough to see that there was nothing untoward going on there. Relief was tempered with the knowledge that I shouldn't have done it. I felt he had got one over on me, somehow.

I glanced at Izzy. She looked contemplative. I hoped she was going to agree to my suggestion. I needed someone to do my accounts and run the business side of my life, but more than that, when Roman went, I was going to need a friend. I doubted I would stay in France for more than a couple of years, but with Izzy and Sam in the house, at least they wouldn't be lonely years.

Tamsin and Freya were still sitting at the dining table. Freya was in pink pyjamas, with wet hair, and she looked exhausted.

'Hey, you two,' Tamsin said. 'Patrick went off to rescue Roman and Amanda from somewhere. I didn't quite get to grips with the story but he took Roman's car.'

'Do you know where they were?' I asked. I didn't really care, not now.

'No. Not too far away, I don't think. Sorry. I'm sure they'll be back soon.'

'Mmm. I suppose I should get dinner ready. Starters on the table, at least. If everyone will be back soon. Or perhaps they won't be back soon after all. I don't know.'

'Well, Jake and I are going to bed,' said Freya.

I nodded at her. 'Good idea.' I remembered we shouldn't be talking about her mother in front of her, anyway. 'Sleep well. I'm sure you will after your adventure.'

'Night night.' She went up to Izzy and gave her a hug and a kiss. Izzy patted her back and kissed her cheek. I was jealous, but it didn't occur to Freya to kiss me, so I didn't embarrass us both by lunging. Jake appeared from the direction of the downstairs bathroom in a pair of short cotton pyjamas, wished us all a hurried good night, and followed his sister upstairs. We all let a reasonable amount of time go by, before Tamsin said what everyone was thinking.

'How in Christ's name did such a fucked-up marriage produce two such lovely children?'

I shook my head and widened my eyes. 'It shouldn't be possible.'

Izzy shrugged. 'I think that for all her faults, Amanda is a reasonably good mother, actually. Or she was for long enough to give them a decent grounding. Plus, they've got each other and they're quite a tight unit which must make it better. And actually, all that extra coaching and those ridiculous classes they go to probably stand them in good stead – gives them a social life and means they must only go home to sleep, really. I think they're great. I feel sad for Sam that he's destined to be an only. It's lovely to see that sibling bond.'

I looked at her. 'You never know.'

She returned my gaze. '*You* never know, either.'

I thought about it. 'No,' I said. 'It depends on a lot of things.'

The phone rang again. I asked Izzy to get it and to tell Neil or Sarah Barron that I wasn't speaking to them. She tried, capitulated, agreed to take a message, and nodded a couple of times before hanging up. Then she winced.

I looked at her.

'Tell you later,' she said. 'It's the last thing you need right now.'

We both turned our gazes to Tamsin. I stopped thinking about my bizarre clients, langoustines and new potatoes. The moment wasn't going to get any better than this.

Izzy gave a slight nod.

'What?' demanded Tamsin, staring from me to Izzy and back again. 'What are you two up to?'

I sighed. I was scared, and resigned. Izzy went into the kitchen. I sat down at the big dining table. It was pouring down, and nearly dark outside. I wondered whether many windows were open. They probably were. I stood up and closed all the ones I could see. Doing any more would be too distracting. I unplugged the phones, because I knew from experience that it was very possible for the telephone lines to be struck by lightning, and for any equipment that was plugged in to be destroyed.

I would not unplug Roman's bastard computer. It could fry.

I sat back down. The table had been made especially for the room, because we hadn't been able to find an antique one big enough and solid enough. The man who had made it had laughed and said we needed to have ten children to sit around it. Roman had said something sharp that I hadn't understood and the man had shrugged and retreated, his cheque safely in his pocket.

Izzy was back with a bottle of champagne and three glasses.

'This is not appropriate,' she said. 'But tonight was going to be champagne night, wasn't it, Susie? So we may as well drink it.'

I nodded. 'Yes.'

Tamsin was baffled. 'Why inappropriate?' she asked. 'OK, there's all this trouble with Amanda, but that doesn't mean we can't have a nice drink. I'm not going to let Amanda spoil my evening, and we deserve champagne anyway, after what Izzy's been through today. Let's toast Sam.'

I sighed. I wasn't scared any more. I wanted to get it over with. This was why I had asked them here.

'Tamsin,' I said. 'We have to tell you something. The reason Amanda's gone loopy is because she knew I was going to tell you and she didn't want me to. And Izzy thinks I shouldn't, but I'm going to anyway.'

Tamsin sighed and held up her glass. From the look on her face, I thought she had guessed, but then I told myself that was impossible.

'OK,' she said. 'Well, cheers, anyway.'

'Cheers,' we said.

'Tamsin,' I began. 'I need to tell you about the night of the ball.'

chapter forty-four

I shudder now to think of the way I tarted myself up that evening.
Amanda and I planned our outfits weeks in advance. Mine was a
shimmery blue dress that was two sizes too small, which must
have shown off my enormous arse in all its glory. It was strapless,
which could not have been flattering. My thighs spilled out from
underneath it, and my legs were held up by pointed blue stilettos.
I wore owlish eye make-up and some bright red lipstick, because
I thought it was sexy. No wonder every boy I met assumed I was
up for a shag. I must have looked like a street tart.

We started the evening at Amanda's house, because she lived
closer to the centre. We had a taxi booked for half past eight so
that we could totter in at nine, fashionably late.

Her bedroom was big and girlish, with a soft pink carpet, a
double bed which she occasionally shared with Dai if her parents
were away, and a huge white dressing table with a mirror which,
if correctly angled, could display myriad reflections stretching away
into the distance. She had a wardrobe full of ironed shirts, and
dresses, and little skirts. There was something extraordinarily innocent about Amanda's room, even when we were in it, in our tartiest
dresses, drinking shots of neat vodka and smoking out of the
window.

By the time the taxi arrived, we could hardly stagger downstairs. Even Amanda's vacant mother noticed the state we were in. She frowned as she stood at the door.

'You two look the worse for wear already,' she commented, pushing a strand of blonde hair behind her ear. 'And you haven't even got there yet. Do be careful.'

We burst out laughing. 'We'll be fine, Mummy,' Amanda said, going back and kissing her. 'Don't wait up.'

'You say that,' her mother complained, almost to herself, 'but you know I have to.'

At the ball, we found Izzy and Tamsin sitting on the sidelines, being, to be honest, a little bit boring. They had the wrong attitude. We could barely walk straight, and we started sizing up the talent at once. The willing talent made itself known by following us around the room in a small group, and this struck us as hysterically funny. The room was spinning, and I was not sure if I could keep drinking at this pace, but I needed to keep up with Amanda. For some reason it seemed important.

I danced. I remember throwing myself around the dance floor to the strains of the Shamen. I remember being caught by the arms of some boy I couldn't focus on. I remember blacking out for a few minutes and waking up on his lap, as floppy as a rag doll. He was pawing me, and I tried to take his hands away, but he kept putting them back, until I managed to stand up and lurch away to find Amanda.

The hours passed by in the sort of drunken haze that, as an adult, would make me scared and sick and terrified at my loss of control, but which as an invincible teenager just meant a good night out. Amanda and I drank ourselves through to the other side of drunkenness, until we almost felt sober again. Then we kept drinking.

And then we ended up at the bar slurring at Mrs Grey and ordering ourselves double vodkas.

'Suzanne,' Mrs Grey said, putting a hand firmly on my arm. 'No more alcohol.'

'But I'm eighteeeeeen!' I remembered telling her. 'I'm allowed.'

'You've had enough,' she said, looking at us as if she were trying not to laugh. 'You too, Amanda. You've had more than enough, both of you. Come on. Let's get you some pints of water to try to stave off your hangovers a little bit. You two are going to feel shocking in the morning.'

We nodded, and she procured us the largest glasses of water we had ever seen. Then there was a call from the other end of the room, and a moment later, Izzy appeared.

'Mrs Grey,' she said, tugging on her sleeve. 'Mrs Spencer wants you. Janie's ill in the toilets and they need your help.'

Mrs Grey sighed. 'Thanks, Isabelle,' she said. She turned back to us. 'Drink that water, you two,' and she got up and disappeared into the crowd of sweaty bodies.

Amanda and I looked at each other and grinned.

'Vodka, Izzy?' Amanda asked.

Izzy shook her head. 'Urgh, no way,' she said. 'I feel sick as it is and I don't want to throw up on . . . where is he? I've lost Thomas.'

'Four shots of vodka, please,' Amanda said to the barman. Mrs Grey's orange juice was on the counter next to me.

'And a new orange juice for Mrs Grey,' I said, innocently.

Amanda handed me two drinks. 'Here we go, then,' she said. 'A vodka each for us.' We clinked glasses and downed them, smiling as the poison entered our systems.

'And one for Mrs Grey,' I said, pouring my spare drink into the juice.

'Plus one for luck.' Amanda added hers to Mrs G's orange juice, and because we couldn't imagine that she wouldn't taste it, we poured her old juice in there too.

Izzy had started to turn away. She looked back at us.

'Hey,' she said. 'You're not actually going to give that to her, are you?'

Amanda and I looked at each other, and then at Izzy, who was nowhere close to as incapacitated and impervious to reason as we were.

'No,' we said, in exaggeratedly innocent voices.

'Why would we waste good vodka?' Amanda added.

'She'll notice,' Izzy said, walking away. 'She's not drunk. She'll taste it if you try to give her vodka.' And then she spotted Thomas, and she vanished.

*

Afterwards, Isabelle had no idea how she got through those weeks and months. She had been torn apart by an urge to confess which was countered by abject terror of the consequences. She had no idea whether she would be in legal trouble for failing to stop Amanda and Suzii pouring the vodka, but even if she wasn't, everybody would know. She could not bear the thought. She was bitterly disappointed in herself, but no matter how many times she decided to tell Tamsin, she said nothing.

Nobody at school spoke about anything else. Izzy stood in assembly staring at the ground as Miss Higgins broke the news to the school that Monday morning. She circumvented the groups of red-eyed girls, even though every group opened up to let her in, in deference to her status as Tamsin's best friend. 'How's Tamsin?' people would ask her, with a mixture of genuine concern and the thrill of tragedy. Rumours of spiked drinks swirled unstoppably.

On Monday afternoon, Izzy went home from school and shut herself in her bedroom with the telephone.

As she closed the door, she knew the moment had arrived. Tamsin was home from the hospital, and Izzy faced a stark choice. She could pick up the phone and call Tamsin, could try to say the right things in the face of unimaginable grief, and offer to go over and see her. If she did this, she knew she would tell her about Amanda and Suzii and the shots of vodka. Or she could sit on her bed for three hours, staring at the telephone, picking up the receiver from time to time and beginning to dial Tamsin's number, then hanging up. She could leave her best friend alone at the only moment when she really needed her. Isabelle saw her true colours that evening, and what she learned stayed with her for ever.

When her mother called her down for dinner, she called, 'Hang on!' That, she felt, was her last chance, her final opportunity. She looked at the phone again, and slowly she stood up, and she walked away from it. She was dirty with guilt and complicity.

She endured the funeral, and did her best to be supportive of her friend. But because she hadn't called her on that Monday night, both she and Tamsin knew that their friendship was over. Izzy, Suzii and Amanda stumbled through their last few months at school. They never spoke about what they had done. They barely spoke at all. They all did well in their exams, because studying was the only distraction they had. Then they parted.

chapter forty-five

I tried to look at Tamsin. I looked away. I forced myself to meet her eyes. She was watching me. I couldn't get any more words out.

'There was a moment.' I made myself say it. 'A moment when we handed her the drink. She was distracted. We thought she would taste it and tell us off. But she didn't. She just gulped it down. I'm . . .' I could not even say 'sorry'. It was a ridiculous word to use. People were sorry for spilling drinks in other people's laps. Sorry for letting a door go before the other person was through it. Sorry for standing on somebody's foot.

I pictured them again. Tamsin and her mother, trapped in the wreckage of a red Vauxhall Astra. Tamsin reaching for her mother's cold hand. Amanda and me pouring two shots of vodka into her juice.

I stared at the window. The rain was getting heavier by the minute. I could hear it slapping down onto the terrace; washing the dust away.

I looked back at Tamsin. Her face was expressionless.

'I'm sorry, too,' Izzy said. She looked shattered. 'I knew they were going to do it. They were too drunk to be responsible. I wasn't. I never imagined your mum would drink it. If I could go back . . .'

Still Tamsin said nothing.

'Amanda's desperate for you not to know,' I added. I needed Tamsin to say something. I knew she had to hate me. Now that I had told her, I wanted her to hate me. I had expected to feel cleansed in some way for unburdening myself. I thought that telling the truth was meant to make you feel better.

Nobody said anything. Izzy drank her champagne. I drank mine. Tamsin pushed hers away. I caught Izzy's eye. She shrugged slightly, a shrug that meant she had no idea what we should do or say next. I stood up to switch the light on. I thought about candles, because I knew the power was likely to go off if there was a storm, and I thought about closing the shutters, but I couldn't do anything.

We both looked at Tamsin. After a while, she stood up. She didn't look at either of us. She just walked to the door, opened it, and stepped out onto the terrace, into the storm.

Izzy and I looked at each other.

'Fuck,' I said. 'Sorry, Izzy.'

'Shall we go after her?' asked Izzy.

I looked through the window. Tamsin had already disappeared from view. It was almost pitch black outside.

Nobody should be out in a storm like that. I knew that Roman was out in it, somewhere, but he knew about storms, and he knew what to do. Tamsin was probably barely noticing the weather. I found my wellies in the utility room, picked up a torch, and set off into the driving rain.

She was sitting on the edge of the swimming pool. Her hair was plastered to her head and water was running down her face. Every few seconds she would wipe the drops from the end of her nose, but apart from that she seemed barely aware of her surroundings. Her feet were dangling in the water. She did not look up as I came close. The wind was blowing fiercely, but it was a hot, sodden wind.

Rain lashed my face. My hair hung down in rat's tails, and my dress clung tightly to my legs. I was instantly drenched. I started running. I suddenly wanted to get Tamsin's legs out of the pool before the lightning started.

I ran through the pool gate. Tamsin did not look at me. She glared ahead. I tried to read her expression, but it was too dark. I knew she was furious.

'Tamsin,' I shouted. The wind carried my voice away. 'I'm sorry,' I yelled.

She looked me in the face. I shivered at the pain in her dark eyes. She looked different as an adult. Part of it, prosaically, was because she no longer wore glasses. Her eyes seemed bigger. Mostly, though, the difference was in Tamsin. She was different, and damaged. She was not, at all, the Tamsin I had once known. I trembled as I waited for her to say something.

She looked as if she were about to speak, and then there was a flicker in her eyes, and she looked away.

'Take your legs out of the pool,' I shouted. 'There's going to be lightning and it feels like it's coming right this way.'

She shook her head.

'Tamsin!' I shouted. 'You're not safe!'

She was staring steadfastly away from me. I decided to say nothing for a while. I sat next to her and she didn't seem to want me to go away. She didn't seem to want to have anything to do with me either. Ten minutes passed. Fifteen, maybe. Twenty. No lightning.

Abruptly, she turned to me. Her face twisted as she looked at me, and I made myself keep eye contact.

'How could you?' she screamed. 'How could you have done that?'

I tried to think of an answer. 'I don't know,' I said quietly. 'I don't know how I could.'

'And how could you invite me here? After what you did? You were meant to be my friend.'

I could not answer.

There was a crash of thunder. I shuddered. I saw Tamsin cringe a bit, but she stayed resolutely where she was. Her gaze stayed, accusing, on my face and I had to keep staring back at her. The wind picked up, and small lumps of hail stung my face.

'Hail?' Tamsin shouted, suddenly. Her expression did not change. 'How is that possible?'

'It happens,' I yelled. 'I've never understood.'

She nodded. I tried my luck and reached into the pool, and tried to guide her legs out of the water. She resisted, then pulled her legs away from me, twisted her body around, and put her dripping feet on the stone tiles that surrounded the pool.

I pointed towards the house. 'We should go in.'

Tamsin stood up. She shook her head vehemently. 'Not in,' she shouted.

I wanted to get us to shelter. 'To my studio,' I yelled. To my relief, Tamsin nodded, and we ran together, through hailstones that were growing unfeasibly large, and up to the studio door. An enormous crash of electricity exploded directly over our heads. It was the loudest noise I had heard; it reverberated through my body like a bomb. The sky was bright purple, for a moment. The garden was lit up as if by daylight. I held my breath.

Everything went black again, and the rain poured down with renewed vigour. There was a creaking sound, and then a tearing crash, as a branch came off the oak tree. I opened the door of the studio, and pushed Tamsin inside.

It was instantly quieter. Rain fell on the roof above us, its noise muffled. I reached for the light switch, and was surprised that the electricity was working. The emergency candles that Roman had made me store here were on the window sill, where I could easily reach them if they were needed. The room was bare without the chaise longue, and I sat down on one of the cushions we had taken off it. Tamsin stood in front of me. I looked around the room. I often worked here at night, but this evening it seemed frightening. My easel was to one side, and there was a jumble of painting paraphernalia on the surfaces. A large jar of paintbrushes was on the opposite window sill. The rain was pounding down on the roof. I would still need to shout for Tamsin to hear me.

I thought Tamsin might sit down on another cushion, but she stayed in the centre of the room, where my easel usually stood, and she looked around. Everything seemed to be casting exaggerated shadows.

'Jesus, Susie,' she said, after a while. She had dripped a puddle onto the rug. She pushed her hair back and shook the water from her hand. 'All this crap. All these material goods. Your "lifestyle". It means nothing. It's all pretend, isn't it?'

'Mmm.' I looked at my lap and nodded. I knew she was right.

Tamsin looked at the ceiling, and then back at me, and suddenly we were seventeen and eighteen again. I worked hard to keep a grip on myself. My adult life had been an avoidance of this moment, until recently. She was shaking with what I supposed was rage. She had always been the strongest of us all.

'How could you invite me here?' she shouted suddenly. 'The three of you. Letting me chatter away last night, getting it all off my bloody chest. How could you? How dare you? The little conspiracy between you all. Don't tell Tamsin. But we should tell Tamsin. No we shouldn't. I don't know how you can live with yourselves.' She swallowed hard. 'I'm still trying to take it all in,' she continued, slowly and deliberately. 'And, actually, I cannot believe you did it. I can't believe that everything that's happened was because of *you*. You and Amanda and Isabelle.' She smiled a horrible smile. 'My three best friends. My best friends in all the world. You know, I wish I could say I worked it out. Everyone said Mum's drink had been spiked. I knew it had, because she would never have drunk alcohol in that situation. It just wasn't her, was it? And nobody was ever going to admit to anything, and there was no proof, so it was always going to be speculation.' She was staring at me, accusing and bewildered. 'And now that I look back – now that I know – yes, I can see it. You and Amanda and Izzy, but you and Amanda in particular, you couldn't say a word to me afterwards. I was on a different planet, but that particular betrayal, that disappointment, made it through the haze. The people I'd thought would be there for me no matter what, the people I wanted to lean on, were treating me like an embarrassing stranger. Fumbling for things to say. Practically crossing the street to avoid me. I was angry with Izzy, most of all, because she was supposed to be my best friend. But she knew what you and Amanda had done. She couldn't tell me. That explains it.' She looked at the wall. 'You three. You were the reason why I headed off. That was why I've been in Australia all this time and it's why I'm going back.'

I was looking at her face. She was biting her bottom lip. She closed her eyes briefly, and then opened them again.

I moved closer, and she didn't flinch.

'I'm so sorry,' I told her. She didn't respond. 'Sorry doesn't really cover it, does it? It was a stupid, drunken moment of idiocy. It is that one impulsive moment that changes everybody's lives for ever. I've longed to go back, every day. I've been back in my dreams. I've pictured it so often. That moment. Amanda and I, blind drunk. We don't put the vodka in Mrs Grey's drink. We knock it back ourselves, pass out, snog some boys, whatever, and it all just carries on being like a school ball is supposed to be. You and your mum get home safely, and the next day we have hangovers and on Monday we go to school and compare notes. That's it. That's the way it should have been. Or Izzy stops us. Or she drinks the vodka herself, or she tells your mum. Or you see us doing it, not Izzy, so you stop it.'

Tamsin inhaled deeply. 'I know, Susie,' she said, carefully. She was unreachable, unknowable. 'I do the same. Actually, I haven't, for a while. I stopped myself because no good can come of those thoughts. But I used to do it compulsively. I would create scenarios where I would say to Mum, before we leave home, "Mum, let's get a cab tonight. You won't want to drive. You'll be tired," and she says, "OK, good idea," and that's it. No crash, different life.' She shrugged. 'Where does that get you, though? And who's to say what would have happened then? Perhaps the cab would have crashed. Maybe that was her day to go. You can't know anything.'

I leaned my head back against the wall. 'I shouldn't have told you. I've needed to for ages. It's been overwhelming. Izzy thought I shouldn't have done it. She said it would only stir things up for you. Amanda was dead against it which is probably why she's off on a bender.'

297

'Roman?'

'Doesn't know. I don't think any of us has ever told anyone. My life fell apart when you went to Australia. I couldn't handle anything, and I had a baby, who died, and it was just . . .' I swallowed. 'But I knew that I'd tell you one day. I knew that I had to. You can't kill somebody's mother and then carry on with your life as if nothing ever happened.' I looked at her and then found I couldn't meet her eyes, so finally I looked away. I looked at her black clothes, at her wet hair slicked down by the rain. She inhaled deeply.

'Susie,' she said. 'I came over here because I knew I had to deal with it all, once and for all. Like I said last night. For years I'd known I ought to come back to Britain and lay Mum's ghost to rest. I thought I'd never understand exactly why it happened. I never imagined it would turn out to be your fault. But it's strange – it's as if on some level I did have some idea, because I was convinced there was a reason to come back. I just didn't know what it was. Nothing would have stopped me.' She shook her head, staring at the light. 'I do know that you're not the same person now as you were back then. I'm really, really sorry to hear about your baby. None of us are the same. It explains why Amanda is the way she is. I'm sorry that she's lost the side of her that Dai brought out. And part of me is thinking I should tell you not to worry about it, that it's fine and we're all grown up, it's water under the bridge, and my *stupid* mother should have noticed that what she was drinking tasted of bloody vodka.' She stopped, and drew a deep breath. 'Most people could drive home after two shots of spirits. Without driving off the road. She wasn't much over the limit. So perhaps the accident would have happened anyway.'

Suddenly Tamsin turned on me, her eyes flashing. 'But I can't do that. I can never forgive any of you. You ruined my life. I have a –' she made quote marks with her fingers in the air – '"good life" in Australia. I have a partner and a job. I see the sun. But I don't have a mother. I'm adrift. I'm always going to be adrift, without her. And . . .' She stopped, suddenly. Her face closed.

'There's no point. There's no reason to say any more. I need to get out of here.'

I opened my mouth, and closed it again, and the lights went out. I felt along the wall until I reached the window sill, and grabbed candles and matches, glad to have something to do. I was desolate.

I had never let myself imagine Tamsin's response. I supposed that I had secretly, selfishly hoped for some kind of forgiveness. I lit a candle, and looked for somewhere to put it. Blackout preparations had not extended to candlesticks, so I handed it to Tamsin and lit another for myself. The candlelight flickered over her face, and she looked ghostly and strange and beautiful. She looked like a choirgirl.

'I have to leave right now,' she said firmly. 'I can't stay here. Not with you three. The rain's easing off. Take me to a hotel.' She was right. The rain was stopping. The electricity had probably been cut off somewhere up the line, which meant that it would be back on before long. 'Come on, back to the house,' she added. 'You need to check everyone's OK. Izzy'll be in the dark. The children are probably awake, and if the others are back, they'll be running around like headless chickens. Drunk ones. I'll pack and you can drive me somewhere.'

'You really want to leave? Now?'

'Yes.' She turned. 'Come on. It's over.'

chapter forty-six

Patrick and Amanda ran through the rain to the house, keeping as far apart as they could. It was pitch dark and the house seemed not to be lit at all.

Amanda was trying to stay angry. She was trying to be furious with Patrick, because she wanted to believe that she was slighted, and he was wrong. If she was angry, everything could stay the way it had always been. She could not admit that he was right, that there was any truth at all in what he was saying, because if she did, then everything would have to end. She was crying, and letting the rain cover her face to disguise her tears. Amanda never cried.

She let Patrick reach the door first. He felt along the wall for it, opened it for her, and stood out in the rain to usher her in. She swept past without looking at him. She wanted to shake the water off herself, onto him, as if she were a dog.

Instead, she looked around nervously. There was a dim light coming from the direction of the dining room, so she walked towards it, unsure of herself and uncertain about everything. She edged into the dining room, and saw Isabelle, on her own, sitting at the dining table with an empty champagne glass, and two full ones, in front of her. A torch was standing upright on the table,

300

like a candle, lighting Izzy's face from below. She looked eery and ugly.

Izzy looked round and did a double take.

'Amanda?' she asked, as if genuinely unsure.

'What's wrong?' Amanda tried to snap, but it didn't work. She grabbed the torch from the table, and turned it on herself, in front of the mirror on the wall. Her face was dripping, and the rainwater had washed away everything. It had washed away her make-up, so she had huge slippery panda eyes. It had washed away her dignity. She was caught out, shown, she suddenly felt, in her true colours.

'Fuck,' she said, staring at the woman in the mirror. The lighting, she knew, did not help, but she was forced to acknowledge that it went deeper than that.

'That's not all,' said Izzy, and when Amanda turned the torch on Isabelle, she knew.

'She told her?'

Izzy nodded. Amanda froze. She wanted to ask what had happened, but there were no words. She looked at Izzy, pleading for it to be all right.

'Tamsin went outside,' Izzy told her. 'Susie followed. About twenty minutes ago.'

'In this?' She gestured at the storm.

'No, there's a little sunny spot in the garden.' Izzy looked at her. 'Of course in this.'

'Oh.' Amanda kept looking at Izzy, shining the light on her, trying to oblige her to answer unasked questions.

'She didn't really say anything,' Izzy said, relenting after a minute. 'Just that she was going outside. Put that torch back, Amanda.'

'Nothing?' Amanda felt dizzy and drunk, and very, very sick.

'What's nothing?' Patrick was standing behind her. Amanda wondered how long he had been there. Long enough, no doubt. 'Where's everyone? What's going on? Where's Tamsin?'

'Oh,' said Amanda. 'Nothing.'

She heard Patrick asking Izzy, but the blood was rushing in her

301

ears so loudly that she could only see their lips moving. She took a step back and leaned against the wall. She tried to take deep breaths. She didn't know what was happening.

When she forced her eyes open, she was lying on a sofa. Her feet were up on a cushion. She had definitely not been near a sofa a minute ago. She didn't remember moving. She shut them again, screwed them up, shook her head, and winced at the pain as her brain sloshed around. She opened her eyes; and she was still on the sofa. There was a lamp on in the corner. She was in one of the sitting rooms. The lamp was on, and that meant the electricity had come back. That was good.

She felt sickness rising in her stomach, and made an effort to keep it down. Then she noticed that they – somebody – had put a bucket next to the sofa, for her. She almost laughed. Not very glamorous. They could at least have provided a delicate bowl. A bucket was vulgar. Next to the bucket was a glass of water, and she gulped this down as quickly as she could. Then she threw up the contents of her stomach into the bucket. She had never been able to hold her water.

She found them in the dining room. Susie was back. Tamsin was still missing, and the lights were on.

Susie and Roman were sitting at the table, champagne glasses in front of them, talking in low voices. They didn't look up as she stood on the threshold, feeling unusually sheepish. She did not want to think about how she had reached the sofa; she was fairly sure she had not used her legs. Izzy and Patrick stood by the open window, leaning on the window sill, looking out at the terrace and the back garden, even though it was pitch black out there. Amanda stayed where she was, and eventually Patrick turned and saw her.

'Oh,' he said. 'How are you feeling?'

He didn't rush to her and hold her hand. He walked over slowly, but there was concern on his face. She almost crumbled; almost leant on him and cried. Almost, but not quite. She retained control. She wished she had checked the mirror. She did it now. Someone had cleaned the make-up off her face before they put her on the sofa.

'I'm fine,' she said, trying to be grumpy. 'Really.' She looked at him, hoping to be told what had happened, how long she had been out. She didn't want to admit her disadvantage by asking.

He didn't say anything.

'What time is it?' she asked, hoping to nudge him.

'Only half ten. It feels later. Don't you think?'

'I don't know.'

'Water?'

She remembered the bucket of sick. She had left it in the sitting room. She would go and get it in a minute. She shook her head.

Patrick suddenly reached for her hand. 'Amanda,' he said, urgently. 'We can make this work. Together. You and me. We can sort it all out.'

He was looking at her, expectantly. She let out a small, mirthless snort though her nose. 'You think?'

'Well, I'm willing to do whatever it takes.' She looked at him, and looked away, repulsed and scared. 'Really,' he assured her, squeezing her hand tightly. She let him, out of pity, and was surprised to find she was grasping him back. She remembered that she had been second to Melanie, all those years ago.

'We'll talk in the morning,' she said, pulling her hand away, and she walked over to Izzy and stood next to her, looking out of the window. 'Izzy,' she said.

'How are you feeling?'

'OK, under the circumstances.' She felt nauseous all over again as she forced herself to ask the question. 'What happened?' She paused. 'With Tamsin, I mean.'

Izzy carried on staring at the rain and the darkness. The storm had passed, but the rain was still pounding down. It was loud on the terrace. She spoke to the rain, not to Amanda.

'She's packing. I know we're all leaving tomorrow, but she wants to go sooner. I think Susie's taking her to Pau first thing in the morning. She wanted to go to a hotel right now, but I think Susie's persuaded her not to.'

'So you two really told her?' Amanda hung on to the window sill to keep herself steady. 'You actually told her the truth?'

'Susie did. Only Susie.'

'I can't believe she did that. Stupid cow.'

Izzy looked round at this. 'Susie needed to. She's been needing to do that for years. Not everybody is as good at denial as you are.'

'I'm not good at denial.'

Izzy laughed. 'Oh, Amanda.' She looked at her friend, genuinely amused. Amanda found that infuriating. 'Amanda, Crown Princess of Denial. What are you going to do? Are you going to let Patrick help you? Are you going to stop drinking?'

Amanda stiffened. 'Jesus, Izzy! This is none of your bloody business!' Then she crumpled a little. She hadn't seen Izzy for years and she might never see her again. If she was going to be honest with anyone, it might as well be with Izzy. She decided to try. 'I can sort of see that there's a problem,' she admitted, and it cost her a lot to get the words out. 'I can see that after today. But I think it's just the way I am.'

Izzy put a hand on her shoulder. 'It's not. You could be far, far better than this. You were, when we knew you. This isn't you, Amanda. This is you after years and years of guilt. I know, because I have a share of that guilt. You can change it all, but only if you want to. There are a lot of people out there to help. You wouldn't be on your own.'

Amanda was scared. She was scared even to be talking about it. 'You think I need to stop drinking completely?' Her voice was quiet. Izzy had to lean in to hear what she was saying. 'For ever? Because I don't want to do that. And whatever Patrick says, I'm *not* an alcoholic. A little drink is just what gets me through the day. Sometimes that gets out of hand.' Her face crumpled, and she made an effort and pulled herself together. 'You're right, though,' she said. 'It is guilt.'

'So try cutting down,' Izzy said gently. 'Try that, and see how it works. Try having, say, no more than two units a day. If you can do that, then you'd be fine, I'd say. Not that I'm an expert.'

'Hmmm.' Amanda touched Izzy's arm. 'And Tamsin? She didn't go mad? She didn't attack Susie, or anything? She didn't have a breakdown? Did she?'

Izzy reached up and pushed Amanda's hair behind her ears. 'No. She didn't. She wasn't even surprised, from what Susie said. Amanda, it's over. It happened years ago, and you need to forgive yourself. It wasn't just you. I could have stopped it. Tamsin could have been at the bar with us instead of sulking. Mrs Grey could have noticed the taste. She could have driven home safely anyway. She might have crashed if she'd been sober. It wasn't just you.'

Amanda smiled without joy. 'There's a bucket of vomit in the sitting room. Festering. Before I start forgiving myself, I need to dispose of it.'

Izzy shook her head. 'I'll sort it out. You get some sleep.'

Amanda nodded. 'Thanks,' she said, and smiled weakly. 'It feels like you're my mum.'

chapter forty-seven

I came in through the back door, with Tamsin. She wanted me to take her to a hotel, and I was trying to persuade her that she should stay here for the night, that I would take her anywhere she wanted in the morning.

Roman walked through the front door, dripping wet and carrying a torch, at the same time. We all saw Amanda. She lay, apparently unconscious, on the floor, with Patrick and Isabelle kneeling over her. Izzy was moving Amanda's limbs around, putting her into the recovery position. Patrick was wringing his hands.

'Maybe we should take her to hospital,' he said, looking dubiously at the rain through the open doors.

I looked at Roman. He stayed a few feet away from us all, looking on with consternation. He didn't come close. I knew he was panicking. Tamsin walked straight up to Amanda and pushed Patrick firmly out of the way.

'No,' she said, confidently. She had her fingers in Amanda's mouth, checking her airways. 'She's fine. We should put her somewhere quiet where she can sleep it off. Don't bother carrying her upstairs.' She looked at me, and I could see the unreadable hurt in her eyes. I wondered how long it would stay there. 'Good thing I've got a first aid certificate, this weekend. Can we stick her on the sofa? Put a sheet over her, some sort of receptacle next to her? She's had a hard day.' We all smiled at the euphemism. 'She'll be fine.'

Patrick knelt down and tried to lift his wife. He struggled for several minutes before Roman stepped forward.

'Come on,' he said gruffly. 'You take her under the arms. I'll carry her legs.'

When I saw Amanda being lugged around like a sack of potatoes, I had to look away. I shuddered at what my friend had become, and the way in which, in a day and a half in my house, she had shed all her dignity and pretence.

I shook my head, and poured another drink for myself, and for Izzy. Then I fetched a new bottle of champagne, popped the cork, wincing at how inappropriate the sound was, and poured glasses for Tamsin, Patrick and Roman. I sat at the table. Izzy stood at the window. She turned to me.

'What happened?' she asked, lightly.

'I think she's devastated.' I took a deep breath, and a sip of champagne. 'She wants to go to a hotel now. God knows where I'll find one that's open. Maybe I should have kept the secret. Now I feel that I've just handed all the extra suffering to the person who least needs it. Or deserves it.' I looked to Izzy, acknowledging that she had been right.

'I don't suppose we're going to be friends with her any more, are we?'

'Not a chance.'

We were silent for a moment. I remembered the phone call.

'What was the message, earlier?'

Izzy looked at me. 'Oh, something that could be positive. It looks as if your gamble paid off.'

'Which gamble? You mean the police?'

'Sarah Saunders rang to thank you. She's had them round. She says he's had them round too. I guess we can't know for sure, but they should be telling you pretty soon who's related to whom and in what way.'

I forced a smile. 'OK. That's good, I suppose. Jesus. I hope it's all OK.'

'Me too.'

'I thought it would feel more dramatic than this if we got the police involved.'

Izzy shook her head sadly. 'Real life, Susie. It isn't always this dramatic. Messy divorce. Lost marbles. I can identify with that all too well. It's the mundane stuff that gets you down.' She smiled. 'Luckily Martin never flipped like that, and nor did I, but I can imagine how possible it is.'

Patrick and Roman reappeared.

'Tamsin went upstairs,' Patrick announced, rather sadly. 'She said she was packing.'

I motioned Roman over to the table, and told him to sit down. I pushed his drink towards him. He shook his head.

'I've had enough,' he said, but then he picked the glass up anyway.

'Roman,' I said.

'Mmm?'

I took a deep breath. This was not going to be pretty, as Izzy had just said. 'It's over.'

He smiled, then frowned, and stared at me. 'What's over?'

'You know. Us.'

'You're not serious?' He looked hard into my eyes, and I willed the tears away. 'You are serious. Oh. Why?'

I fixed my eyes on a spot on the wall, beyond his head. Patrick and Izzy were talking. I didn't care if they were listening.

'Because I want more than you'll ever be able to give me,' I told him. 'Because there are big things I've never told you, and you've probably picked up on one of them by now. Because I'm still young enough to have children, but in ten years' time I won't be. Because I love you but I don't think you love me in the way I need you to.'

I looked at him. He looked baffled, so I carried on.

'Look at today. You buggered off with Amanda. You made me look stupid, and you – I suppose you made it obvious to the world that you couldn't really give a fuck about me. You're waiting for a better offer to come along, and if I got fat or poor or if I didn't bother with what I looked like, you'd be off. I'm just nice for the moment, and living in the moment is good, it's fine, but I need to find someone who can give me more than the moment.'

I looked at him again, expectantly. He was still frowning, so I said a bit more.

'And forget about me for a minute. You took Amanda out drinking. You let her drive when she was probably drunk, which is particularly crap under the circumstances. I mean, Roman, that's how Tamsin's mother *died*. And everyone but Amanda can see what a problem she has with alcohol. What she doesn't need is someone like you who'll legitimise her drinking and let her persuade herself that it's fine. She doesn't need to be sitting by the river drinking cocktails and having fun. That's the last thing she needs, and I wish you'd understood that.'

I stopped. I wasn't going to say anything else. Roman was looking at the table.

'You're right,' he said. It was a dagger. He looked up slowly. 'I mean, you're right about that. You're right about Amanda. I was a dick today, and I don't know why. I was just having a laugh, going for a drink with your mate. I didn't quite realise how bad she was until she got going on the martinis, and by then I was as into it as she was. Sorry. That was rubbish. Genuine crap.'

He reached out and stroked my forearm. I pulled away.

'But the other stuff. I'm trying to take it all in. Susie, *you* were the one who told me you didn't want children. Now, I would have been persuadable. Of course it suited me fine that you didn't want them. It made life simpler. It kept your work as the top priority and it gave us plenty of freedom. But when I said I didn't want babies, it was your lead I was following, Suze. Yours. If you had ever, in the past four years, even so much as hinted that you were changing your mind . . .' He smiled. 'It wouldn't have taken much to convince me. Because at the end of the day, I want what you want. I want what makes you happy. *And* . . .' He pulled on my sleeve until I looked at him, and I was bowled over, again, by what I supposed was love. 'And, Susie, more commitment is fine with me. It feels like absolutely the right thing to do, and it's felt a bit odd, a bit artificial, over the last year or so, that we're still hanging out together like we're twenty-five.' He smiled, grimly. 'And yet, this isn't quite the moment to propose, is it? Because you've just dumped me.'

'I've packed your clothes,' I said, in a small voice.

He sat back and folded his arms. 'So, what are these big things you haven't told me? What's the one I'm supposed to have guessed? Something to do with Amanda? Tamsin?'

I looked down. 'If I'm dumping you, I don't have to tell you. If I do tell you, you'll be the one kicking me out.'

He knocked back the drink he hadn't wanted. 'Try me.'

The phone rang. I waited for someone else to answer it. Izzy brought it over to me.

'It's for you,' she said. 'Your sister wants to know how the weekend's going.'